Mageborn:
The Final Redemption

By

Michael G. Manning

Cover by Donna Manning
Editing by Grace Bryan Butler
© 2014 by Michael G. Manning
All rights reserved.
ISBN: 978-1495279591

Printed in the United States of America.

For more information about the Mageborn series check out the author's Facebook page:

https://www.facebook.com/MagebornAuthor

You can also find interesting discussions and information at the Mageborn forums or the Mageborn Wiki:

http://www.illenielsdoom.com/

http://magebornwiki.com/index.php/Main_Page

Chapter 1

"The King is in a delicate situation," explained Rose. "There are rumors that Celior and Karenth have returned, and the church is feeling bold now that..." she let the words trail off, unfinished.

The Countess di'Cameron was irritated. Her friend Rose's continual reminders were unwelcome, and she was tired of the delicacy that the other woman continued to show whenever the topic of Mordecai's death came up. "Now that Mordecai is dead," said Penny, finishing the sentence for her. "Just say it, Rose. I'm tired of everyone tip-toeing around the tragedy."

Rose's eyes flashed with anger for a moment, but she suppressed the emotion. "It isn't easy for me either, Penny. None of us really know how to proceed under these circumstances."

"I don't care how *delicate* the situation is, I'll gut the first pompous fop that even hints that I should remarry!" barked Penny.

"No one has suggested that," replied Rose hastily, trying to placate her. "It's only been six months, no one would dare. I just want you to be aware that it *will* happen, probably within days of the anniversary of his death."

"Damned vultures!" spat Penny, not making any attempt to seem lady-like. "The very notion of a bunch of insipid lordlings sitting around, waiting for a full year to pass before they begin making attempts to steal his lands—makes me sick."

Lady Rose blanched a bit at the harsh words, though she completely understood the sentiment. "Your son will still inherit, but they will be clamoring to put someone with proper breeding and experience in charge of your estate."

"Because I'm a woman."

Rose nodded, "That—and the fact that you were born a commoner."

"I still don't care. I'll castrate the first one to suggest it," said Penny menacingly. Her hand drifted unconsciously to her sword as she spoke. Since Mordecai's death she had taken to wearing it constantly, along with the enchanted mail he had made for her.

"You should care!" said Rose emphatically. "If you stick your head in the ground and try to ignore this, you won't like the results. You have to plan ahead if you want to get the best out of this situation. You have children to consider."

"This has *nothing* to do with the children, and everything to do with greed," insisted Penny.

"That's where you're wrong," argued Rose. "James will be forced to act if you don't find your own solution after a year or so has passed." She was referring to James Lancaster, the King of Lothion.

"He wouldn't dare. Genevieve wouldn't let him," countered Penny.

Lady Rose took a deep breath. "The Queen understands the political situation just as well as he does, her personal feelings won't be a factor."

"He's the *King,* Rose. If he doesn't go along they can't force me to marry."

"The four churches are coming back into power now that Mordecai is gone. James' seat on the throne is already growing precarious. He can't afford to be stubborn now, or the Lords will rebel. Rather than make things worse by sheltering you, he will want to make use of you to strengthen his position," explained Rose.

"That's absolutely disgusting," declared Penny. The King had been Mordecai's uncle. She and Mort had been close friends with the entire royal family. "I can't believe he would try to use me that way."

Rose sighed, "You're looking at this backwards. It's an awkward situation for everyone. James loves you, but circumstances will force his hand. *You* should be thinking ahead, to find a way to help him and simultaneously put your children in a more advantageous position."

Penny closed her eyes and gritted her teeth, trying to hold back tears of rage and frustration. Once she had herself under control, she replied in a quiet voice, "We should talk about something else for a while."

Rose pursed her lips, sensing her friend's dangerous mood. She knew it would do little good to push Penny any further. "How are the twins doing today?" she asked. Talk of children was often the easiest way to shift their conversations to more comfortable topics.

Letting out the breath she had been unconsciously holding, Penny relaxed slightly. "Moira still seems to be handling it well. She cries now and then, but she has accepted the situation. Matthew—I'm not sure if he will ever understand. He still insists that his father is alive."

"It's natural to want to deny something so terrible," observed Rose, "but he will have to face the truth eventually."

"He won't listen to me," added Penny. "The last time I tried to explain it, he got belligerent and angry. I'm afraid if I keep insisting, it will only drive him farther from me. He won't say it, but I know he believes I somehow forced his father to leave."

"That's nonsense," declared Rose. "Even at his age he has enough sense to know that simply isn't true."

"I'm not so sure. The last thing he saw was me pushing Mordecai away, right before Dorian drew his sword to protect us. How is a child to understand that?" asked Penny.

"Perhaps it would help if Dorian talks to him," suggested Rose. "He might respond better to a man, and he knows that they were best friends."

"I think that would be a good idea. It certainly couldn't hurt," agreed Penny.

"He doesn't want to believe that Daddy is dead," said Moira unexpectedly from behind her mother. She had entered so quietly that neither of the two women had noticed her presence.

Penny turned and pulled her daughter close. "You shouldn't be sneaking up on your mother. How long have you been listening?"

Moira rubbed her cheek against Penny's shoulder, "Just since you said that Matthew thinks you made Daddy leave, but I know that isn't true. My other mommy told me what happened."

This was the first time she had mentioned anything about Moira Centyr. The ancient remnant of her mother had appeared during Mordecai's last battle and had protected them from the leader of the shiggreth. As far as Penny knew, the stone lady was unable to speak. She had remained mute during the entire event, until at the last she had returned to the earth, leaving no trace of her presence behind. "She spoke to you?" asked Penny, surprised. "Why didn't you tell me this before?"

"I did," answered Moira.

Penny started to argue the point with her, but as she cast her thoughts back to that day, she realized that it was entirely possible she hadn't been listening. She hadn't been at her best after... She caught herself there and pushed that thought aside, she had done enough crying for several lifetimes already. *Focus on your daughter*, she thought. "What did she tell you, sweetheart?"

"She said that she heard me calling her, that she would protect us," said Moira calmly.

Rose interrupted then, "I never heard her speak. How did she talk to you, Moira?"

Pointing to her temple, Moira answered, "In here, I could hear her voice in my head. I asked her to protect Daddy too, but she said she wasn't strong enough anymore; that Daddy told her to save us instead."

Tears started in Penny's eyes. She turned her head to look away, her throat too constricted to speak.

"What else did she say?" asked Rose, continuing the conversation while Penny struggled to regain her composure.

Moira paused for a moment, hesitating. She could sense her mother's sadness easily enough, and her magesight made it easy to see the tears Penny was hiding when she turned away. She thought for a second before answering carefully, "She said she loved me, and that she was glad I had such a good mommy to take care of me. She told me to be brave for Momma, especially if— something happened to Daddy."

"How did you know she was your mother?" said Penny, no longer trying to hide her tears. She and Mordecai had told Moira of her special past and how she had been given to them, but to her knowledge Moira had never seen the remnant of her actual mother before.

"I just did. She used to watch me sometimes, when I was little, but I couldn't hear her talk back then. You told me about her before, so I knew it was her," replied Moira, as if it were the most normal thing in the world.

Penny hugged her daughter tightly, unable to contain her emotions.

Moira returned the embrace, patting her mother's back with small hands. "I miss Daddy too, Momma."

Chapter 2

Grey light filtered through the opening to the cave as I slowly became aware of my surroundings. I was lying on stony ground, within a shallow niche in a hillside. It barely merited being called a cave, since it was more of a deep undercut.

How long I had lain there was a mystery to me. I seemed to be covered in a thick layer of leaves and assorted detritus. Sitting up, I brushed the loose debris from my shoulders and hair, and then I realized it wasn't leaves at all. The desiccated bodies of hundreds, no—thousands, of insects, had piled up around and over me.

"What the hell?" I said aloud, before reaching up to touch my jaw in surprise. When I had given myself over to fatigue and weariness, my mouth had been a ruin, utterly incapable of speech. Now it seemed to be perfectly fine. Rising from the mound of dead insects, I began hastily brushing myself off, while simultaneously checking to see if my other wounds had healed. They had.

I struggled to remember how I had come to be there. After my ill-fated battle with Thillmarius, Gareth Gaelyn, the dragon, had flown me to safety, for my family and friends wanted me dead. Or perhaps I was already dead? I shook my head in confusion. *I certainly don't feel dead,* I thought to myself.

The dragon had taken me to the southeastern foothills, at the edge of the Elentir Mountains, a distance many miles and at least five days travel (by mundane means) from Albamarl. The journey had taken Gareth less than a half day's flight, even burdened with my extra weight. After landing, he had sought to engage me in conversation, an odd behavior for the normally antisocial dragon, and I had been less than receptive.

The emotions I held after my last parting from my family were dark and soul-crushing. Logically I understood their fear and the excellent reasoning behind Dorian and Penny's decision to destroy me. If the circumstances were reversed I most certainly would have done the same. Still, logic and reason did nothing to ease the pain. My heart still held the image of Penny's face engraved within it, the look of revulsion in her eyes after my hand had touched her cheek. It had been etched, as if by acid, upon my soul.

Depression had overtaken me during the flight to the mountains, and once there I had rebuffed Gareth's attempts at communication. My body had still been broken and battered, resisting my attempts to heal it. In fact, I had been unable to use any power at all. The source of my aythar, the wellspring of my soul, had dried up, to be replaced by an infinitely dark void, an aching emptiness.

Filled with sorrow and weary beyond belief, I had sent the dragon away. In part I had done so out of a desire for solitude, and also for fear that, in my weakness he might take his aystrylin from me by force. I had stolen the small figurine from his ancestral home and if I were to lose it I would also lose my last and most powerful ally. Perhaps *ally* wasn't the best word choice though, for I had coerced Gareth Gaelyn into servitude with the threat of using his aystrylin to forcibly return his humanity. *Servant*—that was a better term for our relationship.

Tired, and growing weaker with each passing minute, I had wandered into the rocky hills, seeking a quiet place to rest. The cave, if it could be called that, had been the best place I could find, and I had crawled into it without hope of recovery. In reality, I had hoped to die. I didn't know the limits of the curse I had taken upon myself, but it seemed reasonable that if I grew weak enough, eventually I might expire from simple lack of energy.

Apparently, that thought had been naïve.

"I'm still here," I said, speaking aloud again. Interestingly, my depression seemed to have vanished along with my injuries. A strange feeling of calm had descended over my inner world, as if a veil had shadowed my painful feelings. Curious, I turned my thoughts deliberately to Penny and the children. I probed my last memories of them, searching for the ache of their rejection, in much the same manner that someone might probe the painful socket of a lost tooth with their tongue, even though they know it will be painful to touch.

I found nothing.

My heart had grown numb, or perhaps grey, as empty as the black void I saw within myself whenever I turned my magesight inward. My emotions had drained away along with my energy, leaving me an empty husk. *And yet I am alive and whole once more, with enough strength to move easily,* I thought silently. *Well, maybe not alive.*

It was at that point that I realized I also had no feelings of disgust, as I most certainly should have had. *I just woke up covered in dead roaches, centipedes, ants, and...* I kicked at the mound of dead things, shifting it with my foot to see what else it might contain. Along with the insects I discovered an assortment of mice, a snake, and largest of all, a dead fox. Most of the bodies had been perfectly preserved, as if they had dried out slowly without rotting or putrefaction. Only the fox seemed fresh, still warm to the touch.

"I must smell terrible," I observed, though there was no one to listen. Sniffing the air I could detect nothing rotten however, just the smell of dry dirt mixed with the fresh scent of the forest blowing toward the hills. *Touching me killed them, and did so in such a thorough manner that they didn't even rot. My body must have drawn the life from everything that came into contact with it, even the fox.*

Considering the fox, and its obviously recent demise, I figured it must have been what finally brought me to consciousness.

"Too bad for you," I said to the fox as I rubbed my now functional jaw. My internal numbness made it impossible to even enjoy my own sarcasm. After thinking for a few minutes I began walking west, traveling in the direction that would take me back to more populated areas. I had no real desire to do so, and I almost chose to head farther into the mountains, but I knew there were things I had to do. My normal motivations were completely absent, but no other course of action held any appeal to me either.

I considered calling the dragon to carry me, but I decided against it. I was in no hurry. Instead I took my time, walking carefully through the rocky terrain. The morning sunshine failed to warm me, as if it was reluctant to linger on my skin. It fell upon me and illuminated my surroundings, but it still left me cold.

Birdsong filled the air, cheerful as ever, but I felt no joy. The world had turned to ash; grey and flavorless. My sense of smell still seemed to operate, but my internal state rendered it meaningless. *This could get really boring,* I thought, but even that failed to bother me.

I traveled without stopping, without rest, walking onward through both dawn and dusk, heedless of whether it was day or night. My magesight made daylight irrelevant, and I never seemed to tire, so I kept moving. I was untouched by hunger or cold, and I wondered idly if I would ever need to eat; thus far the idea seemed unappealing.

Days passed and the land smoothed, becoming gentler while the trees grew more densely. Eventually I decided to try sleeping, but it proved to be a futile exercise. I lay in the darkness, hidden under leafy boughs that shaded me from even the moonlight, but sleep wouldn't come. My thoughts kept circling, turning over past events, and pondering the future. In the end, I rose and began walking again. Without the need for sleep or physical rest there was little difference in walking and lying still.

Over time, I became gradually aware of dim connections between my inner void and certain distant *others*. My best guess was that I had assumed Thillmarius' connections to the other shiggreth. The spell weaving that I had stolen from him probably acted as a sort of central fulcrum for the other undead he had created. I wondered idly whether it might enable me to control them, but I didn't bother testing the theory. It seemed pointless either way.

My first surprise came early one morning as I passed listlessly through the trees. My feet had brought me ever closer to Albamarl, though I had no real desire to see the city again. I simply had nothing better to do. My travel through the forest had brought me to the Myrtle River, the same river that would eventually pass by the capital. Following it simplified my journey, but it also brought me close to the various human villages that were built on its shores.

I had just skirted one small hamlet in the early predawn hours. Confident that there were no other humans within a distance of at least a mile or two, I had turned my thoughts inward, ignoring my surroundings while my body made its way, following the lightly wooded riverbank. It was a state similar to sleeping, but it brought no comfort or true rest. Instead, my thoughts merely circled, repeating past events and memories before my inner observer. Watching those memories, I felt nothing.

So absorbed was I, that I very nearly walked into a bear before I noticed its presence. A warning grunt brought my attention back to my surroundings where I found myself standing a scant two feet from a very large brown wall of fur, muscle, and teeth. Somehow my approach had startled the bear as well, for he jerked and rose to his hind legs at almost the same time.

That's a big animal, I noted mentally. Even fear seemed to have taken a vacation. Without stopping to consider that my magic was gone, I spoke, *"Shibal."* Then I had the familiar sensation of aythar moving and the massive creature slumped to the ground.

I felt slightly weaker as well.

It seems my magic isn't entirely gone after all, I thought. Using my magesight I tried to look inward once more, and as before, I saw the same black void that had replaced my center. It seemed different though, as if it contained an energy of its own. *The antithesis of aythar,* I decided. Perhaps I had accumulated the power from the animals that had died around me while I slept in the cave. There wasn't any way I could be sure.

"Yes there is," I said to myself then, and glancing down I appraised the bear slumbering before me. Reaching out I put my hand on its shoulder, and immediately I could feel its strength pouring into me. The great beast was a wellspring of aythar, and within its body I could sense the fire that represented the source of its vitality. Without conscious effort, my body drew at that source, pulling and absorbing everything there. The sensation I experienced during this was akin to being thrust into a fast moving river, a rushing cold sensation as the power flooded into me.

My emotions remained dead however, and I felt no pity as the majestic creature's inner fire dwindled and died under my hands. It was dead now, an empty lump of flesh, though I still retained a thin, dark connection with it. Even as I watched I could sense it beginning to draw life from other things around it. Plants, small insects, and things even tinier—everything in contact with the bear's corpse was dying, while a small dark core within the beast began to grow. It was becoming a monster, an undead beast similar to those that Harold and I fought years before, when we encountered Thillmarius within an underground cave.

Even numb as I was, I had no desire to follow in his evil footsteps. With a small effort of will I severed the link between myself and the dead bear. The darkness within it faltered and began to fade. Within moments it was nothing more than a corpse. Clearly any creatures that might be created by my *feeding* were connected to the spell-weaving that maintained me. Sever that link, and they withered away. I wondered about the other shiggreth that were linked to me.

I hadn't created them personally, but the links were still there. If they created others, were those linked to them, or to me? If I managed to destroy myself, would it end the entire miserable chain of cursed undead? Would humanity be safe then? I had too many questions, and even my best guesses were full of uncertainty.

Do I care? Do I want to die? I wondered, but even those questions were devoid of feeling. I pondered those thoughts as I continued traveling, but without my emotions I simply couldn't decide. Eventually I gave up and shifted my attention to exploring my ability to drain the energy from living things.

The bear had given me an incredible amount of strength, possibly more than I normally would have possessed if I had been alive again. The main drawback, as far as I could tell, was that it was limited. Once I used the power I had taken, it was gone. Unlike my natural aythar, it didn't renew itself with time. That wasn't too much of a limitation however, so long as I didn't mind killing things, and given my present state of mind, that didn't seem like a real problem.

I knew that soon enough I would be reaching Albamarl, and while I still couldn't find any real reason or purpose behind traveling there, I knew that if I was recognized, or if someone discovered my nature, I would be forced to fight those whom I had once loved and protected—or let them destroy me. None of those thoughts really worried me, though I was well aware that they should. Rather than leave things to chance I decided to experiment with my new power.

I killed numerous small animals, putting them to sleep first so that I could touch them. I tried simply willing myself *not* to draw the aythar from them, but that failed completely. My life-drain seemed to be an entirely involuntary thing, requiring only physical contact. After a while I stopped using animals; plants were much simpler to find and didn't require any spells to keep them from escaping. The small plants I used didn't have a lot of aythar to offer, but traveling through a forest there was an almost endless supply.

Eventually I learned the trick to not killing them. By creating a personal shield around myself, I could keep myself from inadvertently absorbing aythar. It was very similar to the shields I had used for years before my unfortunate transformation. As long as I kept it close against my skin, it was virtually undetectable to a non-mage, even if they touched me, and it made sure that no true physical contact occurred. I also discovered that I could alter its permeability with a certain amount of effort, which allowed me to drain energy more slowly. *It might make it possible to feed without always killing the victim,* I noted.

Technically I could do that now by limiting the duration of contact, but in practice it was hard to force myself to stop once I had actually touched something with my bare skin.

I thought about that and many other things as I walked on through the bright days and empty nights.

Chapter 3

Albamarl was much as I remembered it, and yet it still seemed different. The multitude of buildings faced in rose granite did nothing to warm me. The city felt just as dead as I was, much like everything else I had encountered. *I seem doomed to a cold empty existence,* I told myself silently, *and I can't even summon enough feeling to be depressed about it.*

As I wandered the city avenues in the late afternoon sun I thought of Thillmarius. He had seemed full of rage when we had fought. Where had his anger come from? Surely after years trapped in the body of a small boy he couldn't have still retained that much emotion? That was disregarding consideration of the thousands of years he had spent in some sort of bodiless limbo, yet he had been angry.

"I'm the last lore-warden of the She'Har and my people created the gods. No matter what your bestial kind achieves, you'll never be more than animals in our eyes!" Thillmarius had told me near the end. The bitter hatred in his voice couldn't have been faked. He had told me something else as well, which had turned out to be an uncanny prediction of my fate, *"Everyone gets a happy ending but you."*

"At least I survived," I responded aloud to the memory. It didn't feel like a victory, though. It felt like— *nothing.*

"You look lonely," said an unfamiliar woman's voice. "Why would a handsome young man like yerself be without a lady friend?"

The words should have startled me, but they didn't, I just hadn't expected anyone to speak to me. I had wandered into one of Albamarl's seedier districts, near the river docks. A glance at the woman and her overdone rouge told me quickly enough why she had called out to me. She was a prostitute.

"I'm married," I answered tonelessly, although the thought made me wonder. *Was I?* If I had truly died Penny would be considered a widow now, free to seek a new husband. I knew the thought should upset me, but like everything else it failed to stir my listless heart.

While I mulled those thoughts over the woman moved closer. She was near enough now that I'd have been uncomfortable if I were still capable of such a thing. Her breath was warm and I could see fine wrinkles around her eyes. She was probably a bit over thirty and a hard life had left its marks upon her. *How long before she can't continue this profession?* I wondered.

"You're a quiet one, love. Married doesn't mean much around here," she told me, leaning closer and putting her hand playfully on my chest. "Why don't you let me take you home and warm you up? You seem cold." She tilted her head as she spoke, looking at me through half-lidded eyes.

Her actions were meant to tempt me, of that I had no doubt, but of course they had no discernible effect. I focused my will tightly; making sure my shield would prevent me from inadvertently drawing her life-force away if she happened to brush my skin. "I'm not lonely," I answered bluntly. "You shouldn't touch me."

My words made her pause for a second and her eyes locked on mine. "I've seen eyes like that before, love, though never so sad as yours. Everyone's lonely, love. Why not let Sweet Myrtle ease your pain for a while?" She lifted her hand to my cheek. "So cold," she remarked, "let me warm you up. Surely a man like you can afford to sit by my fire for a while?"

I had forgotten my attire. Tattered and bedraggled as my garments were, they gave some indication of my former wealth. The material was too good and the tailoring had been exemplary, even though they had been traveling clothes. "Please…," I began, intending to finish with 'leave me alone', but I didn't get to finish. Rising on her toes, Myrtle put her lips to mine.

My shield protected her for a split second, until her tongue darted out to slip between my lips, and then something remarkable happened. Aythar unlike any I had experienced before, poured into me filling me with warmth; the world seemed to grow brighter around me. Her body jerked for a second as her life began flowing into me and her hands rose to push against my chest, an instinctive response to try and save herself from the empty void within me. My arms had already locked around her though, and I held the back of her head with my right hand.

An ecstatic rush of emotion flowed through me, coloring the world around me in brilliant hues that washed away the empty grey that had existed before. Passion, an emotion I hadn't felt since awakening, built within me, and impossibly I felt my heart begin to beat. My own tongue was moving now as I continued the kiss that Myrtle had begun. She began to sag in my arms, but I hadn't had enough, so I cradled her, lowering her slowly to the ground.

I wanted it all.

The taste of her lips, the softness of her flesh aroused parts of me that I had thought gone forever. In the pleasure of that moment, I considered undressing her so that I could explore the secrets of her body. I hadn't felt the joy of such intimacy since…

…Penny.

I released her suddenly, letting her sag senseless to the cold cobblestone road. My face twisted with pain as the enormity of what I had lost crashed over me. My breath came in short gasps as I struggled to contain the torrent of grief that threatened to overwhelm me. How had I forgotten this? *I've lost everything.*

I crouched there, stricken with a sadness too great to endure for an unknowable time, before eventually remembering the woman lying beside me. My initial fear was that she might be dead, but my senses quickly dispelled that notion. Her chest was moving as she breathed, her heart still beat, and within I could sense the flickering of her aythar. She would recover.

Staring at her face I saw her in a new light. Where before she had seemed unimportant, I now felt the urgency of her heartbeat, the precious struggle for life that continued even as I watched her body working to recover from the life-sapping kiss we had shared. *I almost killed her,* I thought remorsefully. *My existence can only bring death now; no good can come from it.* At that the images of my children came unbidden to my mind, assailing me with another barrage of sorrow as I remembered their smiles, their love, and their trust.

"My touch would kill them," I said aloud, as if I was speaking to the unconscious Myrtle lying before me.

"What's going on here?!"

The voice behind me was loud and masculine. My senses identified the speaker as a member of the city guard, one of Lord Hightower's men, before I rose and turned to face him. "This woman seems to have fainted, guardsman," I responded, using a tone of command that was almost instinctive to me now. "Give me a hand and perhaps we can find someone who knows her." I stared boldly into his face hoping he would respond to my authority without asking too many questions.

That proved to be a mistake. While I didn't recognize him, the guardsman's face showed astonishment and recognition as he saw my features. "Count Cameron?" he said hesitantly before stopping with a look of confusion. "Begging your pardon, Your Excellency, but..." he paused awkwardly.

"What?" I asked, letting my annoyance show. *Of all the rotten luck, encountering one of the guardsmen who would recognize me!*

"You are supposed to be dead, my lord. There was a huge funeral, mourners..." the guard stared at me before finishing, "... the King gave a speech."

"Listen, this really isn't the best time for this," I told him.

"They said the shiggreth...," the man stopped, and then his eyes flicked downward to stare at the unmoving prostitute. "She's dead isn't she?"

I could see the alarm growing in his eyes as he backed away, one hand scrabbling for something around his neck. Before I could say more, he brought out a whistle and began blowing on it, piercing my ears with its shrill cry, summoning aid. He was calling for the watch.

"Shibal," I said quickly, but the spell had no effect. I had forgotten that Walter and I had provided the city guard with protective necklaces years ago. People were staring at me now, looking out of windows and stepping out of doorways. I would be surrounded soon, and any nearby guardsmen would already be running in this direction.

"Son of a bitch," I muttered angrily, and then I spoke a few hasty words, summoning up a thick fog. I put a lot of force into it, and within moments the surrounding area was blanketed in a thick and impenetrable cloud.

People cried out in fear at the unnatural mist, while the guard continued blowing on his whistle.

Ignoring them all, I bent down to lift the unconscious woman, making certain my shield was in place before I touched her. She couldn't survive another of my life draining touches, nor was I sure my sanity would endure it either. Her aythar had filled me with something new, emotion. It had brought me to life again, though I could tell my heart beat was beginning to slow already.

She seemed light as I cradled her in my arms, carrying her through the fog. I had no idea where she lived or whether it was safe to simply leave here somewhere so I just kept walking, renewing the mists whenever they began to thin and using my magesight to avoid contact with the few people that ventured into the fog. An alarm had gone up, presumably that a shiggreth was loose in the city, though I wasn't sure.

What I did know was that nearly every door was locked, and most people had shuttered their windows as if a storm was brewing. My magesight revealed many people huddling in their homes, a lot of them praying to the shining gods, which mildly irritated me.

It also felt good to be irritated. The feelings and sensations that accompanied my emotions, *any* emotions, were so incredible as to make it difficult to remain properly irritated. Even my heartache was a welcome change to the endless grey I had lived with for the past few weeks.

"It feels good to be alive, even when sad and miserable," I noted. The thought was a new revelation to me. After enduring so much time without passion, motivation, desire, or any other sort of true feeling, I was learning now that even negative emotions were preferable to none at all. "Emotions are like flavors, sweet, salty, bitter... each has its place, and each is worth experiencing," I posited out loud.

I was brought out of my reverie by a groan from Myrtle, who I still carried in my arms. I watched her carefully, and felt sure that she would awaken soon. Putting her carefully down I moved away, far enough that her eyes wouldn't be able to find me in the fog, though I remained close enough to assist if she turned out to need more help.

Waiting, I watched as she gradually regained consciousness. Using a bit more of my stolen magic, I disguised myself as an old man before creating a wind to disperse the dense fog that cloaked the streets. In the distance I had already sensed armed parties of guardsmen beginning to walk the streets. I knew there might soon be Knights of Stone among them, if any were in the city. It was time for me to leave.

I began working my way out of the immediate area, all the while keeping my magesight trained on Myrtle. I had to be sure she made it home safely. I walked slowly, in keeping with my disguise, and I managed to leave the dockside district without being stopped more than once. The guardsmen asked a few simple questions before letting me continue on my way.

My inner eye however, remained on the wayward woman who was now resting in a small apartment. She had trudged there wearily after awakening where I had left her. I made a mental note of where she lived, though I couldn't say why I did so.

Once I had reassured myself that the woman would be alright, I turned my thoughts back to my family and thoughts of the past. They were painful memories, primarily because they represented things I could no longer have. My only solace was that they were safe. If nothing else, I had protected them, and one more threat had been removed. Thillmarius had been given his final rest and the shiggreth, while still dangerous, were under my control—maybe.

I hadn't tested the notion yet, but I was already certain I could find them through the links between them and the spell-weaving that now maintained my existence. Such links might enable me to command them, or put them to other uses. It was even possible I could destroy them without bothering to track them down. At the very least, if I managed to find a way to end my own cursed life and undo the spell-weaving that bound me, they should pass away as well.

I intended to test those theories before doing anything drastic though, and at the moment I wasn't entirely sure I wanted to escape the world anymore. My experience with Myrtle had given me something to savor, a bit of hope. Perhaps things didn't have to be as dark and bleak as I had imagined.

What if I just took a little, from lots of different people?

If I only needed power, plants and animals were enough, though humans seemed to be a much richer source. What I worried about was the loss of my humanity. The intensity of my emotions had already dulled a bit and I assumed they would continue to fade. How long before I would be completely dull and lifeless again? Once I had returned to that condition could I fully trust myself to follow the wishes of my more human self? What if I killed someone while trying to recharge my humanity?

Perhaps Penny would help me, I thought suddenly. With that thought came a rush of feelings, along with an unbidden fantasy... kissing her. My experience with Myrtle had been unexpected and overwhelming. What if I could control myself? The thought brought with it a powerful desire, a terrible craving. I knew then what would happen. My feelings would overpower my senses. My desire for my wife, more than anyone else, would be compounded and corrupted by my need for human aythar. *Touch her and there will be no stopping.*

I clenched my jaw in frustration. For her safety, as well as my children's, I would have to stay away from all of them. *As long as I exist—as long as there are shiggreth, they will never be safe.* There could be only one outcome, and it wouldn't be a happy one, at least not for me. The only good news was that my friends and family already thought of me as dead, so at least they wouldn't suffer any additional trauma at my passing.

There were still several obstacles in my path however. First and foremost being Mal'goroth himself, the dark god had to be dealt with before I could allow myself to rest. Millicenth and Doron also needed a permanent resolution of some sort; otherwise I'd be leaving my friends and family at their mercy.

They were created to serve mankind, not threaten it, I thought to myself. Memories began surfacing as I followed that observation to its source. No longer bound by my fear of the past I searched for the information I knew had to be locked within. Thillmarius had said that his people created their gods, but that was only the beginning. *We followed their example and created our own—but when?*

That question brought an image forth in my mind, a woman's face, one I recognized, Moira Centyr. I had never seen her human face in life, but one of my ancestors had. *She was beautiful,* I noted, comparing her mentally to my daughter. The resemblance couldn't be denied. *The gods couldn't have been created without her family's special gift.*

I began following a chain of ideas and thoughts, ideas that had led to many conversations between Moira Centyr and the man she had loved centuries before, the ancestor I had been named after.

Chapter 4

The Countess di'Cameron sat in her study, staring out the window that illuminated the small writing desk. She was in Albamarl, staying at the Illeniel house. The Thornbears had planned a visit to see Rose's parents, the Hightowers, and Dorian's mother, Elise Thornbear. Lady Thornbear had taken up residence in the capital recently, to remain near her close friend, the Queen.

Rather than stay in Cameron alone, Penny had chosen to make the trip with them, offering the use of her house while in the capital. In reality however, she simply hadn't wanted to be alone. Rose had a house of her own in Albamarl, but she had chosen to stay with Penny anyway, on the pretext that Gram preferred to enjoy time with Moira and Matthew.

All of them understood the truth however; no one wanted Penelope spending much time alone.

They had made the trip using the World Road, which had been operating steadily for nearly a year now. They could have had one of the Prathions transport them directly, but Penny had preferred to make the trip using the road, possibly for nostalgic reasons. The majority of their travel had consisted of a half day's ride from Washbrook to Lancaster, where one of the entrances to the World Road was located, followed by a short ride from there to the capital itself.

A noise from downstairs told her that Rose and Dorian had probably returned. Peter arrived at the door of the study a minute later to confirm her suspicion. "The Thornbears have returned, my lady, along with a guest, Lord Stephen, son of Earl Balistair," he informed her.

"What?" snapped Penny, "I specifically told *that woman* I didn't want any visitors." By 'that woman' she was referring to Rose.

Peter merely pursed his lips, there was no good reply to her statement, nor was one desired.

"Tell them I will be down in a few minutes, I wasn't prepared to receive a guest," she added in a flat tone. In truth though, her attire was perfectly acceptable and she had no reason to delay. She simply needed a moment to collect her thoughts and control her irritation.

When she finally appeared downstairs over fifteen minutes had passed, a delay that most would consider rude without good cause, especially when the guest was a nobleman. Penny didn't care. She found them sitting in the front parlor, sipping tea and eating the dry, thin cakes that were popular as snacks in Albamarl.

Dorian and Rose sat together on the divan, across from Lord Balistair. Despite his occasional awkwardness in the past, Dorian looked entirely comfortable meeting with a fellow peer; he and Rose had both been raised and trained for such occasions. In contrast, while Penny's rank in the peerage was technically greater, she had been born a commoner. She still had to expend conscious effort to appear relaxed in such company.

Everyone stood upon seeing her. Dorian was the first to speak, "Your Excellency, please forgive the unexpected visitation. May I present Lord Stephen Balistair? He came here at my insistence." He added those words to account for their breach of protocol; ordinarily another noble would send a card requesting an introduction before appearing unannounced.

Penny wondered how Rose had managed to maneuver her husband into such a situation. She had no doubt regarding the true source of this unexpected guest. Her eyes appraised the young lord standing before her. Lord Stephen was lean and muscular with tanned features that spoke of extended periods of time in the training yard. He wore a sword, and the calluses on his hands told her he had spent many hours practicing with it. His bearing was military and his height was respectable, slightly above average though a bit under six feet, if Penny had been forced to guess. *Almost as tall as Dorian, though definitely shorter than Mordecai,* she thought to herself before wincing at the pain that observation brought.

She stared into his blue eyes as she replied, "If what Dorian says is true, I cannot hold it against you. You are welcome in my home, Lord Stephen. Please sit." She made a point of not offering her hand to him in greeting. *Let him fawn over someone else.* Penny could almost feel Rose clenching her teeth at the brusqueness of her response.

Stephen Balistair stood awkwardly for a moment before he realized that Penny had no intention of following the ordinary rules of introduction. "It is a great pleasure to meet you, Countess," he said, recovering his composure. "I have long been an admirer of your late-husband, if you'll forgive me for mentioning it."

Penelope moved past him to take a comfortable chair that would put her farther from where the young nobleman had been sitting than any other seat in the room. "My husband had many admirers and even more enemies, you did not need to present yourself here to tell me that," she said, rebuffing him.

Stephen's face flinched slightly at her cold reply, though he kept his expression respectful. Luckily, Rose came to his rescue, "Actually, we encountered Lord Stephen at my father's house. He had come to relay news of recent disturbances near the docks. After hearing what he had to say, Dorian asked if he would be kind enough to recount his news to you personally."

Penny glanced at her friend's face, trying to spot her duplicity. As always, Rose's face was unreadable.

Looking back at Lord Stephen, she noticed a glint of gold on his left hand. *He's married,* she realized with an inward sigh of relief. She had felt certain this was part of some plan to begin socializing her with the eligible bachelors of the kingdom. Now she merely felt embarrassed to have been so impolite.

"I may have been too harsh. Please overlook my remarks, Lord Stephen. I have not been myself of late," Penny said, gesturing again for the others to take their seats.

"Given your circumstances recently, I think I can understand something of what you've been through, Countess," responded Lord Stephen.

Penny's embarrassment evaporated immediately. "I sincerely doubt that," she answered, struggling to contain a more bitter response.

Dorian's mouth opened momentarily, as if he wanted to say something on Stephen's behalf, but a quick nod from Rose cut him off. When he began again a second later it was definitely on a different course, "Stephen has some news that may relate to what happened to Mordecai last year."

Those words drove out Penny's subtle wonderings at Rose's motivation instantly. If they had come from any other source she might have reacted more skeptically, but Dorian's pain at Mordecai's loss was nearly a great as her own. "Please explain, Lord Stephen, and be quick to the point. You have my full attention," she commanded.

Lord Stephen sat a bit straighter and launched into a quick explanation, "Late this afternoon an alarm was raised in the dockside district. One of the city watch discovered a man leaning over a dead woman near an alleyway. When he approached the man, the stranger straightened and pretended to request assistance."

"What do you mean, pretended?" she asked impatiently.

"The guard knew him on sight having learned his appearance while working at the palace a few years back. He identified the man as the late-Count di'Cameron. Because of this, he was able to recognize his danger before the creature could get within arm's reach of him. He retreated and used his whistle to summon aid," explained Stephen.

Penny's knuckles were white where her hands gripped the arms of her chair, and she struggled to retain her composure. "Were they able to restrain the creature, or did they d—destroy it?" she asked, unable to prevent her voice from cracking slightly.

It was a foolish question. Standard procedures called for immediate cremation of any shiggreth found, regardless of the situation. Stephen's face reflected a deep sympathy as he went on, "No, it summoned a fog and while search parties were organized quickly, it escaped nonetheless."

"And the woman?" she managed.

"Her body had disappeared as well, probably for the reasons that…," Stephan began.

Penny cut him off, "the reasons one would expect when dealing with shiggreth. Did anyone identify her or report someone missing afterward?"

"Not thus far," he replied.

"Do you have any further news?" she questioned.

"No, Countess, and I apologize for being the one to bring you such a painful reminder of…"

She dismissed his apology with a wave of her hand, "My feelings are not your concern. I neither want nor need anyone's sympathy, no matter how well intentioned. Now if you will excuse me I'd like to be alone. I'm *sure* you understand," she said cutting him off in a bitter voice. She stood and started to leave the room, pausing only at the doorway, "If you do receive any more information, please do not hesitate to inform me."

She made it up the stairs and nearly to her bedroom before her exterior calm began to crack, first with a tremble in her breathing, followed soon after by a hot tear on her cheek. She wanted only to be alone, but Rose had followed quickly on her heels. The other woman opened the door and entered the bedroom immediately after her, without waiting for an invitation. They had been friends for many years.

"You were rather hard on Lord Stephen," Rose observed.

Penny used a handkerchief to dab at her eyes before turning to answer her intrusive friend, "Perhaps you will make my apologies for me. I don't seem to be fit for proper society these days, Rose."

"I do understand that, Penny. You know I do," responded Rose, "but there are others out there who can appreciate your loss as well, if you'll take the time to listen to them."

"What do you mean?" asked Penny.

"It was pure coincidence that Lord Stephen brought the news, but the reason Dorian and I asked him to come and repeat it for you directly, is that I thought perhaps you would benefit from hearing his personal story as well. He has suffered in a similar way to what you have," said Rose.

Penny's eyes narrowed, "I should have expected you had a secondary motive. Nothing is ever simple with you is it?"

"He lost his wife a few years ago, when several shiggreth slipped into Malvern. He had to order her cremation personally. The two of you have quite a bit in common....," Rose explained, but her words were cut short by a stinging slap.

Penny's hand burned from striking her friend. The action had come so quickly it surprised her, and she had barely managed to reign herself in in time to keep the speed and force of the blow from reaching potentially dangerous levels. Even so, a trickle of blood ran from the corner of Rose's lip where a nail had torn her skin, and her face was already reddening.

"Never Rose! Never again! Do you understand me!? I have had it with these games! If you are truly my friend, then act like it! Stop trying to maneuver me!" yelled Penelope. The rage inside her burned hotter than she could ever remember feeling before.

Despite the pain, Rose's face remained calm. Blood dripped from her chin as she replied, "I have never been anything but your friend, Penelope. Through fire and blood, childbirth and death, I have always supported you. One of these days perhaps you'll pull your head out of your ass and realize that sometimes there are things more important than *your loss*—things like your children, your people, and possibly even the friends you are too blind to appreciate!"

Anger and shame warred within Penny in equal portions, making it impossible to think. "Please leave," she said at last, uttering the only words she could manage.

Moving briskly, Lady Rose stepped out before slamming the door behind her. After she had gone, only the image of her angry blue eyes remained to haunt Penny's mind.

She spent the next hour struggling with the emotions that seemed to undercut every rational thought she attempted. The idea of Mordecai wandering the city as a shiggreth haunted her. How much did it remember? No one knew exactly how much of the victim's memories remained. Over the years they had discovered that most didn't even remember their names, having become nearly mindless creatures of pure hunger, but on a few occasions they had encountered a few that retained the ability to speak and obviously some of their memories. Those were the worst, for they sometimes fooled their former loved ones into trusting them.

Stephen had mentioned a sudden mist, presumably summoned by the shiggreth. In the past only Timothy, the leader of the shiggreth, had possessed any magical capacity, beyond the usual life-draining abilities of his kind. If the undead one that had resulted from Mordecai's death retained some or all of his powers—the consequences were unthinkable.

Penny's emotions finally settled, drifting down from anger and confusion to a more tolerable melancholy depression. She also felt embarrassed for her behavior with Rose. While she still felt her anger had been valid, her reaction had been unforgivable. *I owe her an apology,* she thought, grimacing.

She went to look for her, but she could find no sign of the Thornbears. Their room was empty, and they were nowhere to be found.

Peter confirmed her suspicion as soon as she went downstairs, "Sir Dorian and Lady Rose departed roughly a quarter of an hour ago, Your Excellency. Sir Dorian told me to inform you that they had decided to stay at Lady Rose's city house for the rest of their stay in the capital." The chamberlain's eyes revealed nothing of his inner thoughts on the matter.

"What about the guard detail?" she asked.

"He took two of the men at arms, the rest Sir Dorian left to guard you, along with Sir Cyhan and Sir Egan, Your Excellency," answered Peter promptly.

"Very well, find Sir Cyhan and send him to my room," she ordered.

Peter's eyebrow twitched for a moment. "Yes, my lady."

She stopped him, "I'll thank you to keep your thoughts to yourself Peter, unless you would prefer another job." Penny had had enough of other people's opinions and judgments.

Her chamberlain bowed crisply, "As you wish, Countess."

She didn't bother acknowledging his response; she was already heading upstairs toward the bedroom. Once she had shut the door behind her she began peeling off layers of clothing, shedding her dress. As sometimes happened, her irritation had left her feeling confined and restrained, and tight clothing only made it worse.

She had the dress off before Cyhan's knock on her door.

"You may enter," she said promptly, while giving herself one last check in the mirror.

The large knight entered the room quietly, shutting the door behind him before standing attentively a few feet within the room. "You sent for me Countess?" he asked, ignoring the obvious meaning of her attire.

"I need to work off some energy," she told him.

"Here?" he said incredulously.

"Where else?"

"The room is too small, and while that might provide excellent practice in close quarters fighting, it will undoubtedly result in significant damage to the furnishings," he replied flatly, demonstrating the point by unsheathing his sword and swinging it in a slow arc.

Penny thought for a moment but came up blank. "There is no practice yard here, and it would be unseemly for me to practice in the street."

"The kitchen then," suggested Cyhan, "It is slightly larger, and most of the furnishings and equipment there are significantly more durable."

It will also have the added benefit of putting Peter's uncharitable suspicion to rest, she thought, still annoyed by the memory of his expression.

"Very well," she nodded, moving to the door, her chainmail rustling audibly now that its sounds were no longer dampened by the dress she had worn over it.

"Are you still wearing your armor under your dresses," the large warrior questioned as he followed her.

"I only remove it to sleep, and sometimes not even then," she replied without looking back.

"Your safety is our responsibility," he returned.

"Safety is an illusion," said Penny, "but this armor was made for me by my husband, and it's the closest thing to safety I have left now. I will not trust my family's protection to anyone else." She stopped for a moment before asking, "Does that offend your pride?"

Cyhan was slow to answer, and when he did it was with more words than she had heard him offer in quite some time. "It might bother some, but any true bodyguard would be glad. Your safety should be their primary concern."

"I did not ask 'any bodyguard', I asked you," Penny reiterated.

"I cannot judge you for doing exactly as I would do myself."

Chapter 5

I had been wandering the city for almost two days since my encounter with Myrtle. In the past I might have sought shelter somewhere, but in my present condition shelter wasn't really a necessity. Rain, heat, cold, none of those things bothered me anymore. I never got tired or fatigued, so I simply walked. Avoiding the city guard was a simple task that hardly distracted me from my real task, which was entirely internal.

I followed the threads of memory that I had found, regarding the creation of the shining gods. Each recollection led to others, and it was merely a matter of time to piece them together into a logical whole. The information I discovered, lurking in the shadows of my mind, was at times shocking. It was also sad. At long last I learned the story behind my daughter's parents, my ancestor Mordecai Illeniel and his lover, Moira Centyr.

While I examined these things, I learned secrets that made my confrontations with the shining gods seem laughable. It was no wonder they had sought to eliminate the Illeniel family. Their creator had left the keys to their undoing indelibly recorded in my ancestral memories.

I still had no easy answer for how to deal with Mal'goroth, though if the things I had learned about the human gods held true for the dark gods of the She'Har there might be one person that held the key to their defeat.

I had a larger problem, though. My feelings, my emotions, had faded. The grey emptiness that had been my existence for the past few months had returned. The only feeling still remaining to me was a dull longing, a craving—to recover the passion I had so recently discovered. I only knew of one way to do that.

Increasingly my mind returned to the same thought, Myrtle.

I still remembered where her home was located, and I often found myself wandering in that direction. I was drawn to the memory of her vitality, her emotions—her life. I wanted more of it.

Initially I chided myself for such desires. I knew they were foolish. I knew it was wrong. My transformation into a life-sucking monster had made me ashamed, but as my emotions faded, so did my shame. My guilt passed away, leaving me amoral and empty, possessed only of an unsatisfied craving.

She probably wouldn't be missed, I rationalized. *If I were to do something like that, it would probably be best to stick to undesirables, the people no one would care about.* The thought was entirely logical, and yet I knew I would have found it repugnant—if I had been capable of such a feeling. *Maybe if I stick to criminals, I could be an undead vigilante.*

That might sit better with my moral and emotional self, once I had taken what I needed. Not that I cared particularly; even guilt was better than the endless grey death of my current existence. An image of myself, cast as a tragic hero suffering eternally while being forced to prey upon the very people I sought to protect, played through my mind. At that moment it seemed preferable, almost artistic, compared to the empty void that resided where my heart used to be. What would Mother think of me then?

Somehow I doubted she would see much difference in who I decided to prey upon. I would still be a monster.

The debate went on within me for hours, until sometime around midnight I found myself standing outside Myrtle's home. My feet had taken me there without conscious effort, while my mind pretended to be concerned with the deeper moral issues of taking a life to temporarily restore my humanity. *What about using a criminal?* I reminded myself.

It doesn't really matter. You're here, take what you need. The only thing of importance is that no one will miss her. She's just a whore. My hand opened the door even as my mind made the small effort needed to unlatch it from the inside.

And Lady Thornbear was 'just a whore'?

"Just shut up," I said aloud and then I stepped into the darkened interior of Myrtle's small home.

I had already examined it closely with my magesight of course, but my physical vision confirmed what I had learned earlier. She was alone, sleeping on a small cot in the corner. There was a small hearth, but it held no fire. Wood was probably an expense she couldn't afford. The weather was currently relatively mild anyway.

I stepped through the cluttered room carefully, making as little noise as possible. Once I stood looking down upon her I hesitated. Should I begin in a rush? Or proceed slowly? I had no idea what would be better—perhaps slowly, to savor the moment.

Reaching down I drew the thin blanket that covered her aside, exposing her eminently female figure, clad only in a light nightgown. Even sleeping, she looked fatigued. *Maybe I'm doing her a favor.* Unable to wait any longer, I let my fingers lightly brush her bare knee, while removing the shield that would protect her from their dangerous effect.

I shivered as a delicious sensation of warmth and energy traveled up my arm, giving me goose bumps. Myrtle stirred slightly, one hand pulling at her blanket, as if she had felt a chill. *I suppose she did,* I observed.

She pulled the blanket upward, but my hand was still beneath it, so I ignored her movement. Instead I moved along her thigh, the aythar growing more powerful, the closer I got to her heart. Her eyes opened then, and even in the dim light she recognized me, as fear caused her heart to jump within her. She opened her mouth, presumably to scream, but I moved too quickly for her. With my right hand I caught her head, and kneeling, I covered her mouth with my own, to stifle her cries.

Her aythar was a torrent, flooding into me like a golden river of light and joy. My victim struggled for less than a second, her body twitching and then sagging as she fell into unconsciousness. My heart was beating now, and my own body felt as though it were on fire, burning with waves of pleasure and energy. For a moment my thoughts drifted toward Penny, but I clamped down upon them quickly. Sadness and regret could come later.

A new sense of urgency, fear of my reawakening morality, caused me to feed more quickly. Throwing back the blanket, I kept my mouth upon hers while my hands held her now limp body against mine. I could hear Myrtle's heartbeat faltering, growing erratic, but the aythar continued to roar into me. I wanted it all.

"Momma?" said a small voice from the doorway. "Is one of your friends here?"

Shock, fear, shame, and disgust ran through me, warring for first place in my debased heart. Releasing Myrtle's body, I let her fall back into her tiny cot. Terror kept me from turning to face the small child standing behind me. *I was killing her mother—right in front of her. What sort of animal am I?*

"I'm sorry child, I didn't realize anyone else was here," I replied while simultaneously replacing the shield around myself, the one that would protect her from my dark influence.

The girl's eyes narrowed slightly as I turned to face her. Going on appearance, I'd have judged her age at seven or eight years, but a hard life had left its imprint on her. Suspicion hovered around her eyes and I was pretty sure that her use of the word 'friends' had been just as much of a fiction to her as it was when her mother first used it as an explanation.

I could see that she had already taken note of her mother's unconsciousness when she spoke again, "Who are you?" She was edging slowly to one side with just a hint of nervousness now. My senses told me that a knife lay under a thin blanket on the floor in the direction she was heading.

I held up my hands in a gesture indicating I meant no harm. "Forgive me, I'm not one of your mother's friends, but I'm here to help."

"Are you a physician?" she asked, her mouth struggling with the last word. She continued edging toward the hidden knife.

I seized on the idea she had handed me. "I am a physician, but not the usual sort," I agreed.

"Momma says the physicians charge too much, and most of the time they don't help nobody, leastwise not if you're poor," she replied, showing her first hint of a child's normal guilelessness as she repeated her mother's wisdom.

My heart was breaking inside as I watched the girl's bravery in the face of such a frightening situation. Her life had already taught her to deal with the unusual. "I'm not going to charge anything. Your mother is very ill, and I don't think I can help her—but you can."

That got her interest. The girl's eyes brightened, and she stopped edging toward the knife. "How?"

"Is that a tea kettle you left by the door?" I asked. I could sense the heat and steam rising from it. Apparently the child had gone to boil water, possibly over a charitable neighbor's fire.

She nodded.

"Go ahead and make some tea for you and your mother. She'll want some when she awakens," I instructed.

The tea was merely a distraction of course. I needed a moment to think and study the results of my assault on Myrtle. This time I had drained her to within moments of her death, and I wasn't sure she had enough aythar left to recover. While her daughter made tea, I focused my senses upon her—seeking her center, the wellspring from which her aythar emerged.

It was dangerously weak. It still struggled to supply her with energy, but her body was like a dry lakebed now, so empty that whatever new aythar appeared was instantly soaked up. The flame that represented her spirit was flickering, about to go out for good.

Her daughter, by comparison, was ablaze with aythar, like a small bonfire next to her mother's candle-flame.

"What's your name?" I asked as she placed a rough cup beside her mother's cot.

"Megan."

"Megan, your mother is very weak right now, and she needs a special kind of warmth that people make inside themselves. I think you can help her if you can give her some of yours," I explained. "Does that make sense?"

"A little," she responded quietly.

"This warmth is called *aythar*. I want you to pay attention, and I'll try to teach you some words that will help you give her some of yours," I told her.

"Why don't you do it?" she asked, with the embarrassing directness that children often have.

I flinched inwardly. Such a thing might be possible, but I hesitated to dare it for fear of making a mistake and killing her. "I wish I could but if I try it might make things worse. It's better if it comes from someone close to her, someone she loves," I said, twisting the truth a bit. "Do you understand?"

She nodded again.

Over the next hour I taught her the phrases in Lycian that would help her to pass some of her aythar to her mother. Despite her youthful vitality, Megan's *emittance*, her ability to channel aythar, was very limited, just as it was for most humans. She managed to keep her mother alive though, and that was the most important thing. Given a day or two Myrtle should recover, assuming she wasn't assaulted by another shiggreth.

By me, I thought bleakly. *What will happen in a few days, when my emotions finally disappear again? When I'm nothing more than an amoral emptiness, looking for something to fill the void?*

I would kill her—or, if not her, some other poor soul, unlucky enough to catch my attention.

My only sure way of preventing such a thing was to destroy myself before it could happen. *Or steal enough aythar from people to keep yourself from getting to that point,* I added mentally. Such a thing would be risky. Any lapse of self-control could lead to a tragedy. Sooner or later I'd make a mistake and either take too much, or wait too long before feeding.

I pushed those dark thoughts aside and decided to focus on the present. Reaching into one of my pouches, I brought out a handful of assorted coins. It was a pitiful gesture to make, leaving money for them as if I was trying to buy forgiveness, but I knew it was important. Even if it did nothing to assuage my guilt they needed money to live. Myrtle wouldn't be in any shape to provide for herself and her daughter for at least a few days.

I removed the gold coins, replacing them in my pouch. Such valuable currency would only get the child robbed, or beaten as a thief. Even the silver would be a danger for her, but perhaps her mother could use it once she had recovered. What they really needed was a protector. No amount of money would help them in the long run, not without a patron or employer.

In my current condition I wasn't fit to take such a role, but I had an idea that might help.

I left the coins on the cot next to Myrtle. She and Megan were both asleep now, the child having finally exhausted herself. As I stepped out into the night air I could tell that it was now closer to dawn than midnight, not that it mattered to me.

My next goal was to find paper and ink. I had a letter to send. Fortunately I had an easy place to obtain such things; after all, I owned a house in the city. I let my feet find the way for me.

It was time to go home.

Chapter 6

Less than a half an hour later and I found myself standing in the street outside the house I had inherited from the father I had never met. Now that my eyes could look upon it I wondered why I had waited so long to come here. Since Marc had moved out, it had been unoccupied, except for my family's occasional visits to the capital.

Assuming that my family was safely ensconced at home in Cameron there was little reason I shouldn't avail myself of its shelter and resources.

My family.

That was the trouble. If they happened to be within or if they arrived while I was inside... nothing good could come of that. "I'll just get what I need and leave," I said aloud, trying to reassure myself.

What about Lyralliantha?

That thought reminded me that I had more problems than just saving the woman I had nearly killed. I still had a dark god and Illeniel's Promise to deal with. Technically, I also had one or two of the shining gods to worry about, but with my current knowledge they fell into the 'asset' category now, rather than the detriment category. *So many things would have been easier if I had overcome my fear of the secrets of the past sooner,* I chided myself.

Illeniel's Promise might be difficult. In order to satisfy my ancestor's pledge, I needed to free the last living She'Har from the stasis enchantment he had used to protect her from the scourge that destroyed her people.

Thanks to the knowledge granted by the loshti, the ancestor fruit of the Illeniel grove, otherwise known as Illeniel's Doom, I knew the key phrase that would release the stasis enchantment. What I wasn't entirely sure about was how to remove the spell-weaving that Thillmarius had placed around it to prevent anyone other than him from freeing her.

Mal'goroth was the biggest problem. I had no easy solution for him. He was bigger, stronger, more powerful than me, and had nothing to lose. In the past relative power hadn't been quite as important. An archmage becomes the power he seeks to wield, which meant there were often ways to circumvent such disadvantages so long as I didn't lose myself in the process. Against Celior I had borrowed the strength of the earth itself to imprison him, and against Thillmarius I had fused myself with his identity in order to steal the spell-weaving that sustained him.

Since my struggle with Thillmarius I had been unable to exercise my abilities as an archmage. I could still hear the voice of the earth, faintly, but I couldn't seem to reach it. Most of the smaller voices I could no longer hear at all. It was as if a shadowy veil had fallen, isolating me, preventing me from touching the universe around me more directly. I still retained my abilities as a wizard, but I no longer produced my own aythar, I had to steal it from other living things.

All of this meant that my options for dealing with Mal'goroth were limited. While I had dealt with two other gods without my abilities as an archmage I didn't think those methods would work here. I had no way to construct a vessel strong enough to contain Mal'goroth, which is how I had captured Karenth, and I certainly couldn't hope to fool him with a bluff, as I had with Doron.

With the knowledge of the loshti, which I was still trying to assimilate, I had the potential to access an incredible amount of power. I could thank my ancestral namesake and Moira Centyr for much of that mixed blessing, but it still wasn't enough. Mal'goroth had devoured his fellow dark gods, and possibly Millicenth as well, absorbing their strength and making him more powerful than even the strength of all four of the shining gods combined.

The best hope lay in Lyralliantha herself. While the vast knowledge I held contained countless gems it was woefully silent on the matter of how to control the dark gods of the She'Har. I simply couldn't believe that such a sophisticated and powerful race would create something that dangerous without a means of controlling it.

That brought me back to the house in front of me. Inside I could find both the materials to write and send my letter, and the last remnant of the ancient race that might doom or save us. My first step was simply going inside.

My magesight was unable to sense anything within the building; a multitude of enchantments prevented that sort of prying, which meant I couldn't tell if anyone was currently inside. I was forced to more mundane methods. Following an alley that led between my house and my still partially demolished neighbor's house I went to the coach house that stood in the lane behind. It was a separate, and smaller building that I had purchased and repurposed years ago.

Tyndal, my father, had apparently had little need for coaches, but my frequent trips to the capital had made it clear that we needed easy access to transportation other than our feet. We didn't actually own a coach, or keep horses there. We didn't stay in the city enough for that. Instead we usually borrowed a coach and horses from Lord Hightower, since Rose and Dorian almost always came to the capital with us. On the rare occasion that we came without them we'd simply borrow one from the king.

A quick look inside showed me that the building was empty, a good indicator that no one was in the house at present. It was still possible that they were in the city and had gone out, but if that were the case I only had to worry about encountering servants. I was much less fearful of that eventuality than I was of coming face to face with Penny or one of my children.

Now that I could reasonably expect that they weren't at home I went back to the front of the main house but there I encountered an unexpected obstacle, though in retrospect I should have considered the possibility. The door wouldn't open for me. Shields, no shields—it didn't matter. It stubbornly refused to acknowledge my identity, and I already knew better than to try forcing it. Years ago I had tried that and the house had responded by trying to turn me into an extremely well done piece of meat.

Staring at my hand helplessly I had a second idea. There was more than one way to enter the house. Returning to the coach house I went inside; it was normally unlocked when we weren't using it, not that a lock would have stopped me.

I withdrew my enchanting stylus from one of my pouches and rapidly sketched a circular diagram on the ground. My memory was still as clear as ever, and I knew the destination key for every one of the teleportation circles within my house. They were all within a single room/hall on the second floor, an area set aside for just such things.

Within a few minutes I had a workable circle. I had constructed the runes using simple scratches in the soft earth, so I had to be careful not to smudge the lines as I stepped into it. I would only need to use it once, so permanence wasn't a concern.

A few words and the expenditure of a small amount of my stolen aythar was all that was needed and I found myself inside the hall of circles.

I hardly expected what I found there.

Standing in the doorway that led to the rest of the house was a man in full plate armor, heavily enchanted and armed with one of the 'sun-swords' I had created, in short, one of the Knights of Stone.

A lifetime of harrowing situations had honed my reflexes—I responded instantly by gaping at him stupidly. My first thought was, *Why are the Knights of Stone guarding my home?* My second thought was perhaps more appropriate, *Oh, shit!*

Sir Egan, whom I recognized from the designs on his breastplate (despite my stupor), reacted much more quickly; his sword was in his hand with a silent speed that struck terror in my heart. The sharp end of it was already pointed in my direction, and I knew he meant business.

I erected a shield with a thought and a word at the last possible moment, but it barely slowed the man who had once sworn himself to my service. The enchanted steel cut through the barrier as if it were almost non-existent and continued onward to remove my right arm and the lower part of my right leg before whipping back upward. Time seemed to slow almost to a stop as I watched my arm fall away. There was no blood, at least nothing recognizable as such. My long dead flesh held only a thick dark liquid that was probably just a remnant of my vital fluids.

The backstroke probably would have completely bisected my torso, if it hadn't been for the fact that the loss of part of my right leg had already sent me falling backward. Instead, the tip of the greatsword cut a deep slash through my chest, cleaving ribs and sternum apart as if they were made of clay rather than bone.

Throughout the violent process, I felt remarkably little pain, nor did I suffer the shock that such an injury would have caused me if I had been properly alive. Unfortunately Sir Egan was well acquainted with fighting shiggreth. He was far from done. Before I had finished collapsing he had already taken a step back, straightening his stance and pointing his blade firmly in my direction. I knew exactly what was coming next.

I managed another hasty shield, but even as I did, I knew it was pointless. The flames were produced and focused by a rune channel I had wrought in the blade itself. The only defense I had that could deflect them was the enchanted set of shield stones that still lay in one of my pouches. The fire burned its way through my shield and began devouring my flesh.

I screamed then, for the flames brought a pain with them that simple cuts had lacked. That would likely have been the end of me, but for a simple distraction. Penny arrived.

The flames stopped as Sir Egan held up one hand to warn her away, "Please step back, my lady. It still has his magic."

My body was a ruin of charred and burned flesh. I had curled instinctively into a ball, protecting my face and belly, but everything else was a horror. The fire had taken only a few seconds to do that much, a few more and I would be reduced to ash.

"Is that him?"

I heard her voice and turned my head to face her, opening my eyes to see her once again, although my magesight had already shown her to me. Our eyes locked for a moment and the revulsion that passed across her features nearly undid me.

"Yes, my lady, I recognized him immediately," answered Sir Egan.

Her face hardened, and I sensed the children running down the hallway. They would be there in just seconds. "That's not my husband. He died fighting to protect us. Get rid of that abomination before they see it. I won't have it dishonoring his memory!" She stepped back to keep Moira from reaching the doorway while Sir Egan turned his attention back toward me.

I wondered what would happen if my body were completely incinerated, but even as I considered the question I realized I already knew the answer. My ancestor had done the same thing to Thillmarius once, sending his cursed spirit to wander the void. The same would happen to me. The spell-weaving wrapped around my soul would never let me fully die, but without a body…

"Penny," I began, wondering if I could somehow convince her, and I saw a shiver run down her spine as I said her name. Whether I might have persuaded her or not, I never got the chance to find out. Glancing downward I realized I was still lying upon the teleportation circle I had arrived on.

Sir Egan's hands tightened around the hilt of his sword as he unleashed the flames again, but they failed to reach me. With a word I was gone.

Chapter 7

Every teleportation circle has two keys that have to be specified when the circle is inscribed. One key that identifies the circle itself, and another that identifies the circle that is its destination. The impromptu circle I had created in the carriage house had been set to take me to a circle inside my home in Albamarl, but that circle had been keyed for Cameron Castle, which turned out to be fortunate. I arrived inside the circle building in the castle yard. While I had had guards posted on the building for years, they normally stayed outside, and today was no exception.

I lay there, a wretched mass of burned flesh. Absent the flames, I had virtually no pain, but I knew I must look terrible. My newly separated arm and lower leg lay underneath me, so I rolled over and pulled them out. A visual inspection revealed that other than the brute fact of their excision from my body, they were generally in better condition than the rest of me.

I could tell that my flesh was already repairing itself, regenerating. *That would've been a handy trick so many times when I was alive,* I thought to myself. As an experiment, I held the end of my severed arm against the stump it had once been attached to. The flesh began knitting itself together almost immediately. I wondered what would happen if I lost the arm—would I grow a new one? There were too many unknowns for me to judge. I pushed the thought aside and used my power more actively, sealing the skin around the edges to help hold it in place better. I repeated the process with my leg.

The healing process, if that was the proper term for repairing dead flesh, seemed to take a long time and I worried that someone might wander in and discover me. Since the only people that could activate the circles were wizards, like Elaine or Walter, that meant I'd be in serious jeopardy. As Sir Egan had just taught me, even a Knight of Stone was a terrible risk for me.

After a couple of hours I was able to stand and move normally. The regeneration process required less energy than I'd expected. My aythar no longer restored itself naturally and I felt slightly weaker once the healing was finished but I still retained a considerable amount of power.

During my trip through the wilderness I had collected a considerable store of aythar from various plants and animals, the human aythar I had gotten from Myrtle, despite its special qualities, was a drop in the bucket beside that. *Is there a limit to how much I can collect or retain?*

That was when I had my final epiphany. *Not really, you're just like the gods, an immortal parasite feeding and growing fat on the aythar of living beings.* That was probably why Moira and my ancestral namesake hadn't used living people for their experiments. It was likely also the reason the She'Har hadn't used this particular spell-weave on themselves. *Well, until Thillmarius used it on himself in desperation,* I amended mentally.

I made a conscious effort of will to stop feeling sorry for myself. Things needed doing and being in Castle Cameron wasn't really the worst place. For one thing I knew the place intimately, and I could easily replace my ruined clothes here. Now that I knew Penny was in Albamarl, it was an easy guess that my children and probably Rose and Dorian were there with her. I just had to avoid the Prathions while I moved about. It would also be easy to send my letter here, since as far as I knew Lady Thornbear still lived nearby in Lancaster.

The Prathions would be the biggest problem. While I could probably create an illusion to disguise my appearance from normal folk, their wizardly senses would immediately detect such a ruse. If I possessed their skill with illusion, or invisibility in particular, I could circumvent them—but I didn't.

Walter, and his two adult children, Elaine and George, all possessed the family gifts. Only his wife, Rebecca was a non-mage. Officially they lived in Arundel, a barony that owed fealty to me, but in practice all three of them spent significant amounts of time in Castle Cameron. Well, they had back when I was alive. It was anyone's guess now. With my death they might have had fewer reasons to stay close at hand.

Either way, I needed to find some method of fooling them soon. If I intended to spend much time in Albamarl or other civilized areas I was bound to run into them. If my recent appearances had created too much alarm, they might soon be tasked with tracking me down. While I had never feared facing any of them in terms of relative power, my ability to hide was nowhere near sufficient to evade them. A direct confrontation would only lead to their deaths, or if I surrendered, my failure to accomplish my goals.

"C'mon, think Mordecai!" I chided myself, "You're supposed to be the most brilliant enchanter since the days of yore. Find a solution." Thankfully my horrifying transformation hadn't impaired my sense of humility.

It was an accurate assessment of my options however. Since I no longer seemed to be able to interact with the voices of the earth and wind, my wizardly ability was all that was left to me, and as time had shown, enchanting was my best skill. It wasn't particularly useful in hiding me from other wizards, though. A solid enchantment might block magesight, or even hide an empty area from it, but I had never succeeded in using it to create true invisibility, not the sort the Prathions seemed to create anyway.

I don't need invisibility. I simply need to keep them from seeing the void.

Any well-constructed enchantment could block magesight. I could enchant my clothes... once I had obtained new ones, of course. I immediately discarded that notion, enchanted clothing would be suspicious. It might help to hide my nature, but it wouldn't cover my entire body, and it certainly wouldn't hide my identity. I was the only highly proficient enchanter in the world. Walter and his children were only occasional dabblers. Anything as unusual as enchanted clothing would be immediately obvious.

Unless...

"If a lie cannot follow rules one or two, it should be so preposterous or unbelievable that no one will doubt it." That was the third rule of lying, and I could still hear Marc's voice in my mind as he had reminded me of it years ago.

"He would have loved this," I told myself, feeling again the twinge of pain that came whenever I remembered my lost friend. I needed to reach my workshop.

Rising I made a quick inventory of my possessions. My clothing was practically non-existent now. I still had my boots, though they had seen better days. The belt, that had until a half an hour ago held my magical pouches, was now ruined. The flames had burned away the half of it that wrapped around my back. Fortunately, the part in the front, where my pouches were, had been shielded by my body when I had curled up on the ground.

I collected my pouches and the burnt remains of my clothing. It wouldn't do to leave evidence here of my arrival. Naked now, except for my boots, I moved to the door that led outside and used my magic to create an illusion, disguising myself as one of my guardsmen. I just had to hope I didn't run into the very man I was impersonating—or any of the Prathions.

My next obstacle was getting out unobserved. It would be highly suspicious if I tried to exit the supposedly empty building, no matter what disguise I was using. The best option would be not to be seen exiting. To that end, I used a simple bit of magic to create a loud noise outside the building, making it emanate from around the corner. The sound I chose was that of a man being struck and then slamming into a wall, something I had heard many times before. *Which says volumes about the quality of my life experiences,* I noted.

As expected, the guard outside heard the noise and quickly ran to investigate. I monitored his movements with my magesight, and as soon as he went around the corner I opened the door to step out, closing it behind me. I waited his post, knowing he'd be back within seconds, once he saw there was nothing where the sound came from.

I recognized the man immediately as he returned; it was Jerod, one of our more experienced guards. He had been on the list of candidates for elevation to the Knights of Stone. If I hadn't died unexpectedly, he would have probably been knighted by now. As it was, it was unlikely there would ever be any more. "What the hell are you doing off your post soldier!" I shouted at him as soon as he spotted me. His face registered alarm when he realized who I was.

He snapped to attention as he responded briskly, "Investigating a sudden noise, Captain!"

The illusory disguise I had chosen made me look like Carl Draper, the captain of my castle guard and the most senior non-knight. I had picked him because no one else would bother him with questions, unless I ran into the man

I was impersonating. I might have chosen one of my knights, but my illusion had limits and trying to pretend I was wearing full plate armor would have been problematic, one random moment of contact would have given me away.

I spent the next minute or two giving Jerod hell. I should have felt bad about it, but it was the most engaging conversation I'd had with another human being in quite some time. The biggest challenge was not grinning at him while I dressed him down verbally.

Once I felt he'd had enough I left, giving him one final warning not to let me catch him off his post again. After that I headed directly for my first destination, my workshop. As I went, I scanned the castle environs carefully, watching for any sign of Walter, Elaine, or George. I had yet to detect any of them, and my hopes rose. If they were absent I'd have a much easier time moving about.

Lady Luck decided to be kind for a change, and I encountered no one on my way to my workshop. *It's about time. She's been nothing but a bitch to me lately. Dead, exiled, even burned—if I didn't have bad luck I'd have none at all,* I observed silently. I did spot Gavin Traylor, the smith I had hired, but that was to be expected since my workshop was very close to the smithy. He was busily hammering away at his latest project, so if he noticed my passing it was only peripherally.

Having reached my shop, I made sure no one was observing me before I entered. It might spark some curiosity if the guard captain was seen entering my workshop without a plausible excuse. I put my hand on the door handle and pushed. It stubbornly refused to budge.

"Sonofabitch!" I cursed under my breath. I had forgotten the door enchantment. To deter the curious, particularly some of the village youths, I had enchanted the door to only open at the touch of certain people. Much like the door in Albamarl, this one no longer recognized me. *And this is why you should have set it up with a password instead, idiot!*

Of course, no one expects to die and return as an undead life-drinking monster. I could probably be forgiven for not anticipating that eventuality. Reaching into one of the pouches I was still awkwardly carrying I pulled out my enchanting stylus. Using it as a simple rune channel I created a thin line of power with it, cutting the door from its hinges. I hadn't bothered to set up serious protections for the rest of the door or the walls, the lock enchantment had simply been a deterrent.

I tried to make the damage as unobtrusive as possible. I would have to put the door back in place once I was finished, and I didn't want anyone to know I'd been inside, at least not in the immediate future. The door fell outward as I cut the final hinge, so I caught it with one hand and held it in place until I had stepped inside, pulling it back into position behind me. A few quick words and I created a temporary spell to hold it in place until I was ready to leave.

Once again I lamented the loss of my abilities as an archmage. While they were dangerous to use, in the past I might have simply used them to move through the wall without damaging it or the door. *No helping that now,* I thought, turning my mind back to the task at hand.

Rummaging through the odds and ends on my worktable, I was caught by the memories of my many projects. "So much of this will go to waste," I said to myself, "No one will have a clue what these things were made for." I spotted a heavy leather belt and used it to replace the one that had held my magical pouches. Then I began adding things to them.

My hand came to rest on a set of rune-inscribed diamond cubes, each of them measuring two inches on a side. While the material they were made of was of incalculable value, it had been easy for me to obtain. I had asked, and the earth had supplied—much like the iron I had used to construct the Iron Heart Chamber. I had used diamond because while the cubes didn't store power when at rest, when in use they would have to handle enormous quantities of aythar. Iron might have been adequate for the task, but I wasn't sure.

When in doubt, make it better than you think it needs to be. Royce had taught me that, and while it was sometimes a pain in the ass, it had always served me well. Of course I wasn't sure this project was really usable. I had designed the cubes with the God-Stone in mind, as a possible method for using its enormous power, but then put them aside as impractical. The Iron-Heart Chamber had been a more reliable trap, and the World Road, a more productive use of the God-Stone's power.

I still have access to the God-Stone if I wanted to use it, and a short detour here would make the same possible with the Iron Heart Chamber. I glanced down at one of my pouches, the one I never opened. Making an impulsive decision, I picked up the twenty-seven diamond cubes and placed them in a different pouch. I didn't have a lot to lose anymore and the meaning of 'risk' was changed entirely when you were already dead.

Straightening up, I belted on my pouches. *If I had a mirror I'd look hilarious. Buck naked and wearing nothing but a belt and some ratty boots.* Naked wasn't the problem though; I could cover that with an illusion. What I needed was something that would hide my nature from magesight, something that wouldn't arouse suspicion.

Walking across the room I opened a large footlocker that had lain undisturbed for a number of years. "Never thought I'd see a use for this," I observed. Within the chest lay a suit of full plate armor, similar in design to the armor worn by the Knights of Stone—my armor. It was enchanted and sized to fit my frame.

I had created it to please Dorian, who insisted that, as a feudal lord I should have my own armor. He nagged until I had made it, mostly just to shut him up. After that he had never found an occasion that I really needed to wear it. At most formal events noblemen wore fine clothes and fabric which, while uncomfortable suited me far better.

As a wizard I had avoided the armor because it blocked the easy flow of aythar. Being encased in enchanted plate restricted the range of my magesight significantly and made even the simplest of magics difficult. It was roughly analogous to hiding inside a dark closet and looking through a keyhole. I had made a number of modifications to this suit to accommodate my abilities, the most notable being the ability to make my helm permeable to aythar when desired. That would allow my magesight to operate at a level close to normal, but it would also make my true nature visible to any nearby wizard. The gauntlets also had been created with built-in rune channels, and the matching sword that I wore with it was also made to channel power.

In most cases, my personal shields were far more effective for protection and they afforded me more freedom of movement, along with not restricting my abilities. When I did need something more substantial I had my enchanted shield stones. In almost every instance, the armor was more of a hindrance than a help—until today.

Wearing this, I should be able to avoid raising suspicion should I encounter one of the Prathions. Their skill with illusions and invisibility made them somewhat more perceptive when it came to detecting shiggreth. While it had taken me some effort to learn to spot the 'empty places', the voids, that a shiggreth created, Walter had noticed them immediately. His children had been no different. With this on, I'd simply appear to be one of the Knights of Stone. As long as I didn't come into close contact, I should be able to pass unnoticed by them.

One remaining problem was that the armor was blazoned with the Cameron arms, declaring my identity to anyone who saw it. A small illusion would hide that however, so long as I didn't get close enough to another wizard for it to be noticed.

Putting armor over naked skin was normally a big no-no, but thankfully, the arming gambeson was packed in the same chest. A large quilted garment, it was meant to be worn over a knight's small clothes, to protect skin and body from the abrasions and pinches that full armor inevitably caused. It felt odd wearing it without trousers or an under-tunic, but I could remedy that once I got to my personal wardrobe.

Once I had the armor in place, a task that took close to half an hour, I spoke the command word that would make the helm transparent to magesight. Examining the area within and without the castle I noted at least three of the Knights of Stone in the vicinity. None of them had their helms on, so I was able to identify them easily, Sir William, Sir Thomas, and Sir Edward.

Sir William appeared to be heading through the gate and into Washbrook, so I chose him to impersonate. He had the additional advantage of being a known prankster, so any unusual behavior on my part could be chalked up to some unfathomable joke. I created two illusions, the first within my armor to make my face appear to be his. That would be needed only if someone asked me to remove the helm, something I'd have to refuse to do if either Walter or his children were in the vicinity.

The second illusion, which was much more awkward to create, was a disguise to change the external appearance of my armor. I disguised the Cameron arms and made them appear to be William's. Such an illusion would have been easy normally, but making it while wearing enchanted plate was difficult. If you've ever tried to thread a needle while wearing heavy leather gloves, you'll have an idea of how frustrating delicate magic is under those conditions.

Once I was finished, I added the sword belt and since I had been forced to remove the belt of pouches while armoring, I put it back around my waist. All told, I felt significantly less graceful and after I made my helm opaque to magesight, I also felt half blind. I could still sense things with my magesight, mostly through the various openings in the plate as well as the eye-slits, but it limited my range to distances of less than fifty feet or so.

"I feel like an idiot wearing this," I complained to no one in particular.

I left the workshop the same way I had entered, using a crudely crafted spell to hold the damaged hinges in place. The armor made even simple things difficult. My best estimate was that the magic would last a few weeks at best before it failed, and the door fell open again. *Then they'll wonder who broke in and pillaged through my things.*

From that point, I strode boldly across the courtyard, until I had reached the main door to the keep. The doorman, a fellow I recognized but couldn't name, held it wide for me. I nodded toward him as I passed, but I wasn't sure how well the gesture worked given my accoutrements.

Most of the people I met inside moved aside quickly when they saw me coming, hopefully out of deference. It was either that or they were worried my ridiculously bad fashion sense might infect them through sheer proximity. In my mind's eye I looked like some absurd metal clad ape. I also noted many of them giving my head a second look, no doubt wondering about the helm. No one wears a full-face helm indoors, or outdoors either really. The Knights of Stone usually put them on only when required to do so.

I made for the stairs as quickly as I could. The fewer people who saw me, the smaller the chance that I might be uncovered. I failed to realize the flaw in my previous thinking until I got to the upper floor where the door to my home was located. Officially it was the door to our apartment, but in reality the portal enchantment on it led to a secluded home deep in the mountains.

The outer door in the hallway had two guards standing beside it, even though Penny and the children were in the capital. That door was normal enough. My goal was past that, the inner door leading from the foyer. It was the enchanted one. If the wrong person put their hand on it the doorway led into a perfectly normal apartment, a decoy. Only when I put my hand to it, or those I had specified, would it lead to our hidden home.

That was the problem.

Identity enchantments no longer recognized me as Mordecai Illeniel. I had learned that lesson twice now, and this door would be no different. Since this door led to a place that wasn't actually *here,* there was no way for me to bypass it. I would have to physically travel to where my home was located, a journey of nearly a day if I was flying and practically impossible on foot. There was no teleportation circle in my hidden home. I had avoided putting one there to avoid the danger of someone being able to teleport there if they learned its key, so consequently I couldn't make a circle to go there myself either.

Well shit.

I kept walking along the corridor, not pausing as I passed the two guards. They had stiffened when they saw my approach, and they visibly relaxed when I entered the stairwell at the other end of the corridor. Let them think I was merely checking up on them.

I went down one floor before leaving the stairs again. Sir Harold was headed up, and my magesight had barely given me enough warning to avoid him. He would surely have far too many difficult questions for me to risk meeting him.

The floor I was on now held guest rooms and some of the quarters for more senior staff, such as my chamberlain, Peter Tucker. It also held my mother, Miriam's apartment. My senses confirmed her presence and I was torn by a sudden desire to see her, but I knew it was a bad idea. *You can't go home anymore, not even there.*

Instead I headed for Peter's room. He was close to my size and his room wasn't far down the hall. Since Penny was in the capital I imagined that he had probably traveled with her. It would be unlikely that anyone would stumble upon me in his living quarters. My diminished magesight was still good enough to confirm that it was empty before I tried to enter. The door was locked but a small bit of magic would be enough to open it—or so I thought. Five attempts later and I was forced to remove my gauntlets, as well as make my helm permeable to aythar, before I could manage the delicate trick of getting the pins to align so the plug could turn.

Once inside I breathed a bit easier, though I still returned my helm to its more opaque state. While exposed I still hadn't detected any of the Prathions, but one of them could show up at any time.

I wasted no time stealing a pair of trousers and an under-tunic. Peter had enough clothes that I hoped that he wouldn't miss them. There might be trouble for the other staff if he thought they were stealing. I was tempted by a pair of shoes inside his wardrobe, but I knew those would be noticed for certain. My own boots were in a sad state.

Walking across half of Lothion had done them a serious disservice.

Peter's room also had a particular convenience I had sought in Albamarl, a writing desk. A few sheets of expensive paper were tucked away in a drawer and a tightly stoppered bottle of ink sat next to a metal nib pen. I was a bit surprised at the investment. Most people, well, most scriveners anyway, still used quills. Metal pens were relatively new and still quite expensive, few beyond the rich bothered to invest in them.

He always did put a lot of effort into his calligraphy, much like the rest of his job. For a man that had wanted to kill me when I first hired him, Peter had turned into one of the most reliable and trustworthy servants any nobleman could have. *Funny how things had turned out,* I noted.

Dipping pen in ink, I began a short letter:

Elise,

I am writing to you now from very unusual circumstances. You may or may not recognize this handwriting, but I am sure from the content you will soon realize my identity, so I won't bother trying to hide it. I was your son's closest friend, and you entrusted me with some of your most personal secrets a year and a half ago.

While I understand that you can no longer trust me, given my 'condition', I nevertheless have a favor to ask of you.

I recently encountered a woman, a stranger, plying the trade you once did when you met Gram. Through no fault of her own she was injured; assaulted might be a better word. The guilt for this crime is entirely my own, nor can I be certain that I will not do worse in the future. My only hope to repay her for the harm I have done is to recommend her to your care. Given your past you were the only one I could think of that might understand her plight well enough to empathize.

Her name is Myrtle and she has a daughter named Megan. I will enclose the address below so that you can find them. Thank you in advance for whatever aid you are able to provide them. They deserve whatever recompense you are willing to give them on my behalf.

I know you will have many questions as you read this but I do not have the time to anticipate them, nor do I think it would be profitable for me to answer them all. I am not the man I once was. My mind remains intact, but I can no longer trust myself entirely. Likewise, I would advise you not to either.

If you care for Penny's sanity, please do not disclose this missive to her. It would only increase her anguish to discover that I have, in some part, survived my transformation. The important facts have not changed. I am essentially dead. I am dangerous to everyone I come in contact with and I cannot with any surety claim that I will not become worse in the future.

I intend to do my best to remedy this situation, and I know you will understand that there is only one way to do that.

~A former friend.

I didn't bother putting my name on it, for some reason it didn't seem right. As I had alluded in the letter, it was better if my death was considered final. No need to add the shame of the present to my name or my family.

Folding the paper I wrote her name on the outside, Lady Elise Thornbear. Before my untimely demise she had still been living in Lancaster. My next stop would be to slip it under her door there. I had thought to mail it when I was in Albamarl, but now I figured it would be faster to take a circle and deliver it myself. *But first I have business down below,* I thought.

Chapter 8

I made it to the ground floor and had passed the kitchens on my way to the entrance leading to the cellars, when I felt the arrival of a mage. Although my magesight was effectively limited wizards often give off flashes of aythar if they aren't shielded. Walter had often told me that I gave him the impression of a walking bonfire whenever I completely released my shields.

A short burst of energy signaled the use of one of the teleportation circles, and the *feel* of it made me think of George. I sensed several more flashes before they disappeared abruptly, probably when he remembered to put his shield back in place. *Sloppy George, you should know better than that.* I had taught him, as well as his sister, to keep their shields up constantly, even when teleporting—perhaps especially then.

He had probably grown lax in my absence. While he had always been an able student, he had never impressed me with his diligence.

I managed to get to the cellar door and down the stairs before he entered the main hall itself. After that I relaxed and began moving at a normal pace. Our relative positions within the castle put us at an absolute distance of around forty yards from one another. Close enough that I was sure he would be conscious of my presence even without concentrating. The enchanted plate that the Knights of Stone wore was not exactly inconspicuous to magesight, it positively glowed.

As long as I was far enough away that he didn't notice the illusion I had placed over the arms, I figured I would be alright. I continued onward and downward. It would probably seem suspicious if I stopped for no apparent reason. My paranoia reached new heights as I considered where George's mental focus might be. If he was paying attention, he might wonder why one of the Knights of Stone was down in the cellars—and heading deeper. He might also wonder why I had my helmet on. Then again he might simply be engrossed in a conversation with someone and not looking suspiciously at everything going on around him.

Deep breaths, he might leave soon if you're lucky. Good advice, except I didn't need to breathe anymore. That had become a superficial activity. Quite often I only remembered to breathe these days when I tried to talk. It's hard to speak without a lungful of air.

I reached the entrance to the Iron Heart Chamber, and by now the distance between us was great enough that I had no hope of knowing if George was still in the castle or whether he had gone somewhere else. I waited several minutes before finally taking the risk of making my helm permeable to magesight. Hopefully, if he was still in the vicinity he was far enough away that he might not notice a distinctly shiggreth-like empty place on top of a suit of armor.

Lady Luck smiled on me, and I found no trace of him within my range. *'Bout damn time she should throw me a bit of kindness.* I withheld any further complaints. She might turn on me again at any time.

I stared at the door in front of me. There were several options available to me at that point. I could take the key that would allow me to draw power directly from the Iron Heart Chamber without doing anything else, which was the safest option. I could take the key and draw some of the power from the containment now, a slightly riskier option since I might be discovered the longer I stayed there. Then there was my third option, the riskiest of all.

My time searching through the convoluted labyrinth of memories had yielded a number of important secrets. One of which might make all the difference now. I needed friends, or if not friends at least servants.

I opened the door.

Nothing happened.

"Well that was anti-climactic," I said aloud as I entered. This time I had an audience.

Karenth the Just lay sprawled on his back in the center of the room, staring blankly at the ceiling. He didn't bother to respond, and my magesight indicated that his strength was negligible. There was barely enough left for him to maintain a visible form.

"Get up," I commanded.

His eyes focused on me then, "Or what? You've taken everything already."

"Or I'll do something dire," I responded.

Karenth snorted, "I'm immortal. You can't kill me. I don't experience much in the way of pain. You've already done the worst, locking me in here."

"I could unmake you," I threatened.

"I gave up hope for that long before you were born," he replied dryly. "Why are you dressed like that?"

"I'm hoping to start a new fashion trend."

The melancholy god laughed, "Then there's no hope for your kind."

I grimaced, "I think I liked you better when you were a megalomaniacal, wizard-hating, misanthrope." Then I knelt beside him before lowering my head to floor level, so I could whisper four soft words in his ear. Long forgotten words, the keywords Moira Centyr had given to my ancestor, the day Karenth was created.

His eyes widened in shock, "How?"

"Get up!" I commanded again. This time there was no sarcastic reply. The Shining God rose from the floor to stand before me.

"Yes, my lord."

"Do you have enough strength to travel?" I asked.

"I began gaining strength the moment you opened the door, my lord. If you allow me to leave, the prayers of my followers will gradually restore me," he answered without deception.

"You were hoping to delay our conversation long enough to gain the strength to escape?"

"No, my lord, I hoped to gain enough strength to kill you, unlikely as it may seem," said the now docile god.

For some reason, that remark set me to laughing; it was probably my first real laughter since defeating Thillmarius. When I had finished, I noticed Karenth staring at me curiously.

"That was not a joke, my lord," he stated seriously.

I nodded, "I just find it humorous that for once our goals are completely aligned. You'd like to kill me, and I'd like nothing more than to be dead—really dead." That seemed to confuse Karenth even more, so I removed my helm.

His face registered surprise once his senses were able to see what I had become, and then a smile curled his lip. "You have become like me," he noted.

That insight jarred me mentally. I hadn't directly compared the two, but in most functional senses, the spell-weave binding me acted in the same way as the enchantment that had bound Karenth. The main difference being that I was originally a live human being, while Karenth had been created as a sentient magical construct by the magic of the Centyr family.

"How long was it before you began to hate humanity?" I asked suddenly.

His eyes narrowed as he stared back at me. The enchantment compelled him to complete honesty as well as obedience now that I had given him the key words. "Not long. I was born a slave to the will of your predecessors. I cannot remember a time when I didn't hate humankind."

"Looking at things from a human perspective, it looks like you had a pretty sweet deal," I commented.

"It was an arrangement we created for ourselves, once our masters were gone," rebutted Karenth. "Should we give thanks to the sheep once the shepherd has vanished?"

I was still puzzled. According to the memories I had found, the creatures now known as the Shining Gods had been relatively well treated. Aside from occasional tasks, their burdens hadn't been overtly cruel. "I don't understand your bitterness. What did you want that your masters didn't give you?"

"Death—or never to have been made at all."

I stared at him. After a moment I finally questioned, "Why?"

My new servant looked at me with pity, "Do you like what you have become? You are a dead thing. There is no true life in you, no feeling, no passion—not even joy or sorrow, yet you cannot die either. There is no end, no hope. You will persist as you are for eternity, a mockery of life. Your only pleasure will be fleeting, stolen from the chattel you once protected." Karenth paused to let his words sink in fully before repeating his question, "Do you like what you have become?"

Well, when you put it like that. I still refused to accept that I might sink to the level that Karenth and his fellow magical constructs had. There was still one major difference between us: I was human, at least originally. He had been created as an artificial sentience. The essence of his argument was correct though, I didn't like what had happened to me, and I could also feel sympathy for his plight.

"I don't agree with your actions in the past but I can understand your pain. When this is done, I will unmake you," I told him.

Karenth laughed. "Your ancestor said the same. He died before he could keep his promise. I have even less hope for you."

"I cannot die," I reminded him.

"There is that," agreed Karenth, "but Mal'goroth may be your undoing nonetheless. Your intentions mean less than nothing to me. If you do not unmake me, if I am left master-less, I will use my freedom and spend eternity making your people suffer."

I glared at him, but there was little I could do to threaten him. He was already under my control. "Take this letter and leave it under the door of Lady Elise Thornbear. Make sure she finds it. Once that is done, I want you to gather information for me in the capital."

"As you will, my lord," he replied with a subservient bow. "What sort of information do you seek?"

"Listen to the councils of the King. I want to know the state of affairs in Lothion. See if you can discover anything regarding Mal'goroth as well. I would like to know what he's been doing while I was away," I answered succinctly.

"If I go near that one you will no longer have a servant," he informed me.

"He cannot destroy you," I reminded.

"He can devour whatever power I have accumulated and imprison what is left of me. My usefulness will then be at an end."

"Avoid contact," I told him. "I will return to Albamarl within a day or two. Find me and report what news you have then."

"Very well, I will take my leave, my lord." Karenth bowed and started toward the door. Before he passed through it, he put his hand against the wall. "What will you do with…," he left the question unfinished.

"The power I extracted from you?" I said, clarifying his question.

"Yes."

I sighed, "I'll probably take a link with me so that I can draw upon it as I need."

"That seems inefficient," he noted.

"What do you mean?"

"You are an immortal locus now. There is no limit to what you can contain," he explained.

That was news to me. I was already holding a considerable amount of aythar from the animals and plants I had killed, not to mention my encounters with Myrtle, but I hadn't given much thought to figuring out whether there was a limit. "I hadn't really considered it in that light," I admitted.

"You will have to learn to stop thinking like a human. It limits you."

"I appreciate the sage advice," I said sarcastically. "Now get going."

Once he was gone I went back outside the chamber and found the key rune for the enchantment that had imprisoned Karenth. The key rune was a link, an enchanted crystal that would allow me to draw and use the power stored within the Iron Heart Chamber. I had originally planned to simply keep it, using the power only as needed, but now I wondered if I should try doing what Karenth had hinted at. *I could try to absorb the power, holding it within myself.*

For a normal mage, drawing and attempting to contain that much power was suicide. Just a tenth of it was certain death. Even for someone as powerful as I had been, anything beyond a few percent of that total would inevitably cause permanent burnout. Karenth and his ilk had been created as purely magical beings, little more than an obedient mind and the ability to store and utilize aythar. Now that I was trapped as an undead monster, I was essentially the same, with the exception of still having a physical body.

Could I contain that much? Could I control it?

Only one way to find out.

I put my hand against the key rune and began to pull inward.

Chapter 9

"You're too tense," said Rose, using her most soothing tone.

"Who could relax with someone hovering over them all the time telling them that they're tense?" responded Dorian with a bit too much emphasis.

Rose bit back an angry response and instead removed her hands from his shoulders. She rarely lost her temper, but that action was enough to communicate her feelings.

Dorian caught her hand before she could move away, "I'm sorry. You're right."

"You aren't the only one under a lot of stress," she reminded him.

"I know," he agreed. "I just don't like the turn things have taken since Mort died."

"Which things? The resurgence of the four churches, or the Council of Lords putting pressure on the King?" she asked.

"Both, but especially the new 'miracles' that the churches are claiming. We know for a fact that Celior is still sealed away in that magic gem of Mort's, and Karenth is in the Iron Heart Chamber. So how can they be appearing and giving commands to their followers?" he said, restating some of the news they had heard.

Rose nodded, "You already know my theory."

"That one of the other gods has stepped in to impersonate them?"

"Mm hmm," she replied.

He studied her face carefully. Dorian had been blessed to marry one of the most intelligent women in the kingdom—one of the most intelligent *people*, man or woman. He had learned to trust her insights over the years. "There's still something missing though; the motive doesn't make sense. If one of the other gods wanted to expand their power they should be using their own name, to sway believers."

"That depends on the agency behind this, and their ultimate goal. Stealing followers would be the best way to increase relative power, for one of the Shining Gods, but according to what Penny and Mort told us last year, Mal'goroth is on an entirely different level of power now. He might not care, and according to what we learned in the past, he cannot gain power directly from human worshippers, not without sacrifices," she explained.

Dorian rubbed at his neck, trying to ease the tension in it. "So you think it's Mal'goroth?"

She shook her head negatively, "We can't make that assumption. I was merely giving one possibility. We don't have enough information to guess at all the possible motivations the other gods might have. Perhaps Millicenth or Doron is trying to create civil unrest without drawing blame on their own followers?"

"To what end?"

"Civil war. A change in our governance might allow them to restore their former place within Albamarl and within our kingdom," she posited.

Dorian sighed, "And no matter which of them is doing it, and for whatever reason, it's creating a lot of difficulties for James amongst the nobility."

"Which is the other side of the coin," noted Rose. "One of the lords could be behind it, hoping to usurp the throne with backing from the churches."

"Only Tremont has enough power to claim it, and he has no way to heal the sick or fake a divine revelation," countered Dorian.

"You are too honest, Dearest. You have no way of imagining the deceptions some men are capable of," she answered while leaning in to kiss her husband's cheek.

Dorian chuckled, "Or some women, eh?"

She nipped his ear lightly, "Be glad I'm on your side."

He grew more serious. "I am. Since losing Marc, and then Mort—I don't know what I'd do without...," he began.

"Shhh," she abjured him. "Let's not start down that road. It only leads to dark thoughts and things are gloomy enough these days. I spoke to Father and his men have been put on alert. Some of my personal contacts have reported strange movements in the city."

"Are you referring to Mordecai?" Dorian asked.

"No," she said, waving her hand to indicate that she meant something entirely different. "Unusual groups of people, usually men, congregating at odd hours."

"A precursor to riots?"

"The city watch reported them first, and they don't seem like mobs. The groups are too small, ten and twenty at a time. My contacts within the city have indicated that most of the men in these groups appear to be strangers rather than citizens," she said, elaborating.

"Has there been an excessive influx of people at the gates?" suggested Dorian.

"That's the first thing Father suspected, but it's difficult to tell. If someone is sneaking a large number of men into the city, they've done it so carefully that no one has noticed it yet," she replied.

Dorian Thornbear's jaw clenched for a moment, "I really wish James had listened to me now."

"He rejected your proposal?"

He nodded. "I don't understand his reasoning."

Rose smiled, "He's making a show of strength."

"It won't matter if he's dead! How does refusing my offer of protection show strength?" argued Dorian.

Lady Rose ignored his question entirely. She went to the sideboard instead where she poured two cups of wine, the second cup she mixed with a portion of water from a pitcher. She handed the first to her husband, sipping from the watered cup herself. "You're getting upset again. Drink that. It will help loosen you up before dinner, otherwise you're liable to get indigestion again," she told him.

Her husband glared at her for a moment before accepting the cup. "You still haven't answered my question."

"Since Mordecai's death his position has gotten weaker and with the new resurgence of miracles and appearances, the church is gaining power, not just among the commoners, but also among the nobility. You, and the Knights of Stone, are seen as representatives of Mordecai, since he founded your order. Consequently you are presumed to be enemies of the gods. Your presence guarding the King would antagonize the pro-church nobles and stir more trouble with the populace. It would also signify that the King believes his own men are no longer sufficient to keep him safe," she explained. Taking a long draught from her cup she then finished, "Not accepting your offer avoids those problems and conveys a sense of confidence and strength."

Dorian considered her words. As usual she made sense, not that it changed his opinion. "Why didn't you give me your argument before I went to see James this morning?"

"Would you have altered your plans?"

He laughed, "Not a bit. What would you have counseled him?"

It was Rose's turn to laugh then, "I would have tried to convince him likewise. I fear that the present dangers outweigh the political exigencies."

"You would have made an excellent queen," Dorian told his wife. He said it as a joke, but he meant it as a serious compliment. "Your mind understands both the politics as well as the practice of ruling."

"I would be a terrible queen. I overanalyze everything; it would take me forever to make decisions. I'm also a failure when it comes to trusting the judgments of others," she said, resisting his suggestion.

He stared at her thoughtfully for a moment before taking a risk, "Is that what happened with Penny?"

The temperature in the room seemed to drop several degrees as she focused her eyes squarely upon him. "In what sense?"

"Your failure to trust the judgment of others," he stated bluntly. He refused to back away from the point, but he did take a large swallow of his wine to help brace him in case he had gone too far.

"I wasn't trying to force her into anything. I just want her to start thinking now, while she has time to anticipate the future. If she keeps her head in the sand, she'll be caught off-guard when they start putting pressure on her!" she shot back. She seemed to lose her normal calm whenever the subject came up.

Dorian finished his cup. "She isn't an informant or an associate, nor is she an ally, she's your friend. It isn't your job to correct her thinking."

Rose's eyes lit with fire now, "What sort of friend would I be if I let her make a terrible mistake?"

"People make mistakes. It's part of living," Dorian said evenly. "You gave her your advice already. Now all you can do is offer your support. Continuing to press your argument on her will only make you into an additional problem for her. It's time to lock ranks and stand by your friend, even if you disagree with her choices."

"And if her choices bring her to even greater tragedy?"

"You face it with her."

Rose scowled. "She has a family. We have a family. If she gets stubborn and brings herself to ruin, what of us? Do I drag my own family into a calamity by supporting a friend that could have avoided the problem by making sensible choices?"

Dorian rose and walked to stare out the window, gazing at the colors painted by the sunset. "You're overthinking it. Sure, sometimes we make mistakes and one thing can lead to another and before you know it the whole *world* can fall into ruin. Most of the time though, you stick up for your friends, and when trouble comes it decides maybe it should back off, because you and your friends are too strong to take on when you're all together. People aren't chess pieces, and there aren't any perfect moves. You stick by your friends, and if one of you gets a bloody nose, well—maybe you all get a bloody nose, and maybe those that did it learn not to mess with you. Most of the time nothing terrible happens at all, and everyone just goes on with their lives."

Lady Rose stared at his back. *Sometimes I think he's the stupidest, most stubborn man I've ever met, and then he says something like that.* Stepping forward she put her arms around his waist, hugging him from behind. "I should apologize to Penny, shouldn't I?" she admitted.

"You would have figured that out sooner or later," he said quietly.

She pressed her cheek into his back, feeling the firmness between his shoulder blades. "Maybe. She is my closest friend. You are a wise man Dorian. I could learn a thing or two about such things from you."

Their discussion of friendship had sent Dorian's mind into the past. "I'm probably not the best person to lecture anyone on that subject," he stated darkly.

"Why would you say something like that?" she murmured from behind him. She immediately regretted the question though, for she knew where his thoughts were headed now.

"Because all my friends are dead," he answered softly.

She squeezed him harder. "Let's both just shut up now. Neither of us is very bright sometimes, talking about such things right before dinner."

He stood still and after a moment he turned, to embrace her fully. Neither spoke, they had had enough of conversation. They held each other for a long time and shared their sorrow in silence. As usual he did not cry, and she pretended not to notice the wet drops falling on her shoulders. By the time the bell rang announcing dinner, they both had dry eyes.

Chapter 10

I left Castle Cameron and the town of Washbrook on foot. I considered taking a horse, since I meant to return to Albamarl, and the idea of using one of my teleportation circles there had lost its appeal. My experience at the working end of a Sun-Sword had taught me more caution and I didn't want to risk another confrontation. With the armor I had on, the enchanted flames would be less of a danger to me. The greater risk was that I might hurt one of my former friends.

I had a better mount in mind anyway.

Once I was several miles from the nearest farmer's cot, I brought out the small figurine that was linked with Gareth Gaelyn, his *aystrylin*. Holding it in my hand, I sent my thoughts into it, *I need your wings. Come to me.*

I couldn't be sure of how distant he was, but I knew he could cover most distances within Lothion in less than a day. Even flying from its most remote border to the opposing side would take less than two days. The dragon was fast.

My own flying method, using my enchanted stones, was potentially even faster but I wanted to talk to Gareth anyway.

While I waited I spent the afternoon experimenting with my new condition. I had drawn on the power stored within the Iron Heart Chamber. I had started slowly, unsure of myself despite what Karenth had said. When I reached the point at which I knew I should have been at my normal limit, I became exceedingly nervous. The caution I had developed during my years as a wizard was difficult to abandon. When nothing untoward happened to me, I drew more power. It had taken me hours, drawing it first in small portions but then later in huge gulps as I grew more confident.

I now held virtually all of Karenth's former strength within me.

The biggest disappointment had been the lack of feeling. I had hoped that perhaps since the aythar had originally come from human worshippers it would restore my emotions, which were again beginning to fade. Apparently the aythar needed to come directly from the source for that to happen. Acquiring it second hand seemed to strip it of whatever quality it was that produced the passion, the vitality, of a living human being.

In short, I would still need to feed directly from people to maintain my moral and emotional state.

I removed one of my gauntlets to look at my hand again. Physically it still appeared to be normal, but to my magesight it was like looking at the sun. I no longer looked like the shiggreth. Rather than an empty void, my magical appearance was more similar to that of a being made of pure liquid sunlight. I wore the armor now to make it easier to hide my presence. Without it, shielding myself enough to avoid detection would be much more difficult.

What would happen if I took the power from the God-Stone as well? I wondered. Following that line of reasoning, I could do the same with Millicenth and Doron as well, if I could find them. Would the strength of all four be enough to face Mal'goroth on even terms? I mentally considered the vision Penny and I had both witnessed when the gods had physically crossed over into the world. I had gained a clear understanding of their relative strengths at that time, and they had been dwarfed by Mal'goroth. I couldn't even make a reasonable guess, but I had a lot of doubt. *I can't afford to risk everything in a head to head confrontation. Dead, immortal, whatever I am, I need to stack the deck in my favor.* A lot of people were still depending on me, whether they realized it or not. I could probably survive just about anything now, but the people relying on me needed more than that, they needed me to win.

A shadow fell over me, followed by a rush of wind as the dragon descended to land in front of me. Gareth Gaelyn stared for a long minute before he spoke, "What have you done now?"

"I had a conversation with one of the Shining Gods. I made him an offer he couldn't refuse," I said cryptically.

"And he climbed into that suit of armor with you?" The dragon's facial expressions were limited, but if he'd been using a human face, one eyebrow would have most likely been lifted.

I grinned, "Not a chance. The only thing in here is me. I sent what was left of him on an errand."

"I cannot decide whether your fortunes are rising or falling," retorted the dragon. "You keep bad company."

"Gods and dragons?"

"The latter does not cancel out your association with the former," replied Gareth.

Who would have imagined a dragon that enjoyed a bit of banter? I thought. "Enough," I said, abandoning the topic. "I need transportation—and advice."

"Tell me where you wish to go, and I will take you. My advice is to return my aystrylin when we arrive," he answered immediately.

I glared at him, "I'm not ready to forgo your services yet." Then I climbed up his bent foreleg and situated myself at the base of his neck, slightly forward of his shoulders and massive wings.

"Your power is such at this point, that I would think friends would be more valuable to you than servants," observed the dragon that had once been human. Without waiting for instruction he launched himself into the air, using powerful wing-strokes to gain altitude. He immediately began heading south, although I hadn't given him a destination yet.

Now that we were airborne, the rushing wind made it difficult to be heard so I sent my thoughts directly to the dragon. *Am I meant to believe that you wish to be friends?* I asked with a sarcastic mental inflection.

That would be unlikely, he returned. *I meant your current tactics in general. Your predominant actions of late have been to compel obedience, first with me, now with the gods. Meanwhile, you have forsaken your friends and family.*

I didn't like the judgmental turn of his observations. *I didn't forsake them, they forsook me. I am still working to protect them.*

Semantics, Gareth disagreed. *You never gave them a chance to make an informed choice.*

They made the same choice I would have, I thought back bitterly. *I'm dead. I'm a monster.*

I'm not so sure about that, speculated the dragon.

Which part, me being dead, or me being a monster?

The dead part, there is no doubt you've become a monster, he responded dryly.

Then it hardly matters whether I'm alive or not.

I don't know, said the dragon, *being a monster isn't so bad. I think I would miss being alive more.*

***

This is good. Set down here for a bit, I commanded.

We had been flying for a couple of hours, making our way back toward Albamarl, when I had spotted an isolated cottage. My emotions were still functioning, albeit at a much lower level than when I had been alive, but I didn't want to let them drop below the point I considered safe. I had decided to feed before I was too far gone again.

"Why are we here?" asked Gareth aloud. Apparently he preferred the use of his voice when the wind was no longer a problem.

"I need to feed," I replied bluntly.

"You already have as much aythar crammed inside you as one of the gods. Are you so greedy that you must take even the tiny amount these people have?" he asked me.

I made my helm permeable to aythar, so that my magesight could function normally. As Gareth's words had alluded, there were several people in the nearby home, five, to be precise. Given their relative ages and genders, it appeared to be two parents and their three children.

"It isn't really the quantity that matters to me," I told him, and then I proceeded to explain what I had discovered about my condition and its relation to human aythar. He seemed to accept what I told him calmly enough.

"You have definitely become a monster," stated the dragon.

"Your amazing clarity and succinct analysis never cease to amaze me," I replied drolly.

Gareth snorted, "I could care less whether you value my opinions, just don't touch the children."

"What?"

"I wasn't whispering," said the dragon calmly.

Every time I thought I had a solid understanding of the draconic archmage, he surprised me. "Was that a threat?"

"Do what you wish with the adults, but if you wish to retain my assistance, don't touch the younglings," he reiterated.

Now that I thought about it, he had also insisted I leave my son behind when I had first awoken from my transformation. Did the dragon have a soft spot for children? I pulled out the small figurine in my pouch. "I still have your aystrylin. Have you considered the consequences of arguing with me?"

"I have my limits. Some things cost more than the threat of my aystrylin will buy you," said the dragon, rebuking me.

"I thought you cared nothing for human beings," I stated, but the sentence was phrased more as a question.

He turned his scaly head away. "Go. Feed. Just remember the consequences of your choices." His body language made it clear that our conversation was over.

I shook my head and began making my way toward the house. *I never intended to harm any children, but his sudden protectiveness is interesting,* I thought to myself. Reaching into one of my pouches, I brought out the diamond cubes. *Might as well test these now, on something small.*

It took me several minutes to set them up, moving from position to position around the building, but once I had everything in place, it worked flawlessly. The amount of power required to activate the cubes was fairly large, even for an area as small as that occupied by the small cottage, but I was able to reclaim the power once I was finished with the enchantment.

As planned, it rendered everyone within helpless, while I was still able to move freely. I drew heavily on the man, but not quite as much as I had done with Myrtle. Hopefully his family would be able to cope without him for a few days while he recovered his strength. Stopping was difficult, but since I began with a clear plan and the conviction that I wouldn't kill, it was easier than the last time.

When I had finished, I deactivated the cubes and carefully packed them away again. Using the dimensions of the cubic volume I had tested it on, along with a rough estimate of the amount of aythar I had used to activate the enchantment, I was able to do some crude mental mathematics, comparing the reality to my previous calculations. *It's going to take something close to a full*

Celior to use them at the fullest area I designed them to cover, I concluded. A Celior was what I had named my unit of measurement for aythar. It represented the amount of aythar I had started with when the God-Stone had first been created. It was also close to the same amount of aythar I had drawn from the Iron Heart Chamber.

My thoughts were interrupted when I reached the clearing where I had left the dragon.

"What the hell was that!?" he asked in a tone that almost reeked of panic, if a dragon's voice were capable of conveying such an emotion.

I lifted one eyebrow and gave him my most nonchalant expression, "Just a little test—something I created a few years ago." I realized too late that he wouldn't be able to see my face inside the helm I had on.

"For what purpose?" He seemed thoroughly unsettled. "Surely that wasn't what it appeared to be?" He stopped short of naming the enchantment.

I decided it couldn't hurt to be honest for a change. "I originally created it with the intention of using it to capture one of the Shining Gods if one came calling, but I abandoned the idea later as impractical."

"Impractical? It shouldn't even be possible! It's insane…," he spluttered.

It was amusing to see one of the most powerful creatures in Lothion, not to mention the only dragon in the world, get so flustered. I didn't make much of an effort to hide my humor. "Yes, impractical. The problem was that it would take the power of a god to fully activate it. I also worried that if anything went wrong the feedback might free Celior as well as whichever one of his siblings I was keeping under lock and key."

"You're a fool Mordecai Illeniel! Did you not stop to consider the other consequences?" the dragon roared at me. He had finally lost his calm.

"Which ones?"

His eyes seemed to glow. "When Moira Centyr defeated Balinthor, the energy released destroyed Garulon, creating an inland sea! What would happen if such a thing were to occur again? What if it involved the power of two gods? Your foolishness could destroy the world!" The area the dragon was referring to was indeed now appropriately named the 'Gulf of Garulon'. It was a fact I was already well acquainted with.

"It wouldn't be the first time," I retorted dryly, thinking of my first transformation into an earthen giant, "but that is precisely why I never used it."

"That's hardly comforting."

"I'm dead," I told him. "I'm not well suited to comforting people anymore." Having just fed, my emotions were more sensitive than before, and the words brought a painful sting. After a brief pause I added, "Still think I need friends?"

"After what I just witnessed, I think you need to be murdered in your sleep, if such a thing is possible. The world will never be safe so long as you are in it," he announced.

The seriousness of his words struck a humorous chord within me, bringing a laugh to my lips. It was a direct contrast to the darkness that lay over me. "I couldn't agree with you more, Gareth, and as soon as I've removed Mal'goroth and restored Lyralliantha, I would consider it an honor if you would find a way to release me."

I had already climbed into my customary riding position, and the rushing wind as we took off almost kept me from hearing his next words, spoken as softly as they were.

"You need friends now more than ever."

Chapter 11

My return to Albamarl was greeted with a noticeable lack of fanfare. Likely because no one knew I had returned. They'd probably have done their best to provide a huge reception if they'd known. *A very warm reception indeed,* I told myself silently. *Perhaps I'm becoming cynical. I don't think this 'living death' thing really suits me.*

I still wore the armor to help shield me from magesight. An illusion gave me the appearance of a middle-aged farmer, but anyone that brushed up against me would quickly realize something was wrong. Without the armor, I'd have been visible to any wizard within miles, a blazing beacon of aythar.

As it stood, I would most definitely attract Walter's attention if I came within range of his normal magesight, or within range of his children, but at least I didn't glow like the sun. I wasn't particularly concerned about being captured, not anymore, but a confrontation might lead to injuring one of my former friends.

I really should have run away with the circus, I observed, *this wizarding thing hasn't worked out well for me.*

I had left the dragon several miles from the city before venturing in on foot. He seemed glad enough to be quit of me for a while. Not that I could blame him. Witnessing my latest magical innovation had apparently made him very uncomfortable. Before we parted I made sure he knew to remain within the area.

In less than an hour of entering the city, a stranger found me walking along one of the larger streets. He matched my pace, and soon enough we were walking side by side. His face was unfamiliar; regardless my magesight had already identified him.

"Would you like to find a quiet place to discuss matters?" the now diminished god asked me.

I glanced over at Karenth. He was disguised as an old man, wearing clothes that would seem appropriate on a dock worker. His grey beard and weathered skin spoke of countless days spent under the harsh sun. I couldn't help but admire the quality of his illusion. "Do you think we would be less likely to be overheard?" I said, responding to his question with one of my own.

"Probably not."

"Then let's talk while we walk. The weather is beautiful, and I have nowhere better to be. What have you discovered?"

"The peaceful calm you see around you is but a thin veneer overlaying a city close to erupting in violence," he informed me without preamble.

"And the main actors?"

"There are several; the four churches have become re-energized. Their more devout followers have been filtering into the city in small groups. Others seem to be doing the same, though their allegiances are harder to identify," he began.

"Any guesses?"

"The Shaddoth Krys, or those owing allegiance to the Duke of Tremont, or both," replied the former god.

Shaddoth Krys was a term meaning 'shadow-blade' in Lycian. It was also the name of Mal'goroth's secret organization of assassins and more devout followers. If they were involved, their god might not be far behind. "Where did you find your information?"

"Primarily from listening to conversations between Hightower and the King," answered Karenth. "They seem well informed, but I doubt the King realizes the extent of the danger, especially from the churches."

I frowned, "What's got them so stirred up now?"

Karenth smiled, "Celior and Karenth's auspicious return, along with your death. Doron and Millicenth's followers also seem to be experiencing a resurgence of miracles and divine appearances."

I patted the pouch containing the God-Stone and my link to the Iron Heart Chamber. "Celior is still safely contained, and I've not given you permission to make public appearances since releasing you. How is this possible? Charlatan priests?"

"Possibly, but I suspect it is worse than that," he replied. "I can feel Mal'goroth's presence hanging over the city like a dark pall. He may be subverting my followers along with devotees of the other churches."

"Is he able to gain power from their prayers?"

Karenth chuckled, "No. In fact I've noticed an increase in the aythar I'm receiving now, probably as a result of the increased activity."

"That makes no sense. Why would he help you?"

"If it is him, he may not care. My power is vastly diminished now. It would take decades, if not longer, to restore what you took from me. Nor would he be worried about my siblings. His strength is far beyond ours now." Karenth paused for a moment, searching for words before continuing, "Have you ever seen a cat, once it has caught a mouse or bird? I think this may be something similar."

As usual, it seemed the only news was bad news. "Do you know where my family is currently?"

"You did not instruct me to observe them," he answered with some reticence.

In fact I had forgotten to give him that command, but I was familiar with his intellect. "Answer the question."

"I do not know, but they left your house after the lunch hour. I cannot say when they will return, though I suspect that it is only a short outing," he admitted.

"In future try to anticipate my needs better, even if I don't give you explicit instructions," I ordered.

Karenth looked down. "I can only act as you command."

His reply irritated me. "Don't give me that!" I snarled. "I know exactly how intelligent you are, and I expect you to exercise that intellect on my behalf. Have I made myself clear?"

"Yes, my lord," he acquiesced.

I watched him carefully for a moment, thinking. "Don't think to obey my words and disobey my intentions," I told him. "Your fate is tied to mine now and things could be much worse for you than they are already."

He answered me with a blank stare.

Leaning in closely I whispered, "I have your maker's memories. I know exactly how that enchantment that holds you together works, and if I don't think you're living up to your potential, I might decide to alter it. The possibilities are much more varied than hoping I will unmake you, or betting on an eternity as you are, if I fail. You could spend *eons* broken and worthy only of pity."

The fallen god's eyebrow twitched for a moment. "Do you think your people would admire you for such cruelty?"

"I haven't forgotten the people who died when you attacked my home," I snarled back.

Karenth smirked. "Point taken. I would also add that you seem to be adapting to immortality very quickly."

His words struck me like a hammer, but I refused to give him the satisfaction of seeing me hesitate. "Go. I'll meet you here tomorrow to find out what else you've learned. Bring writing implements, I may need to send another letter." So saying, I turned my back on him and walked away.

⁂

This time when I teleported into my house I was expecting trouble. My main concern, that my family might be home, was already covered. My second concern, that Sir Egan or one of the other knights might be waiting for me, wasn't really an issue any longer.

The attack came even sooner than the last time, before I even had a chance to get my bearings. The enchanted blade struck my left shoulder, heading in a downward direction. If I hadn't been wearing the armor, it would have removed both my head and right arm. Because I was wearing armor, I instead bore the brunt of the attack as a powerful downward shock on my shoulder, threatening to drive me from my feet.

I managed to stay upright but immediately found my right leg swept from beneath me as my armored opponent moved with blinding speed. His sword altered course, shifting as he spun with his leg sweep, changing from a second swing to a directed thrust. It came in with lightning precision, tearing through the chainmail at my armpit, one of the few places not covered in actual plate. It sank smoothly in, ripping through bone, muscle and organs, until the point emerged on the opposite side.

Son of a bitch! He's fast, I thought, as my mind struggled to keep up with current events. My opponent had attacked with inhuman speed, and within a split second altered his strategy to account for my plate armor. If I had been human, or even another Knight of Stone, I would have already been dead. *Thankfully, I'm no longer human,* I noted with a sense of irony. It was probably the first time I had ever been grateful for the fact.

My own speed and reflexes were much greater now, not that I had much skill in using them. I managed to grab the defender's wrist, locking his arm, and the sword it held, safely in place. A blade through my chest wasn't really much of a problem for me. Having my armor removed and my body cut into sections; *that* would have been a problem. I grinned inside my helm as I finally realized which of my knights was working so efficiently to destroy me.

"Cyhan!" I greeted him, even as I held his arm still. My own strength was now greater than his, and for a split second I entertained the notion that I might have a chance to explain my situation to him.

I hadn't factored in the man's uncanny tenacity, or his ability to react near instantly to changing battle conditions. He said a word while gripping the sword tightly, not in an effort to remove it from my chest, but to keep it in place as the Sun-Sword's fire erupted within me.

The world exploded for a moment as the flames raged through the inside of my armor, shooting outward from the joints and even filling my helm. Chaos and pain assailed me before I finally found my balance. The fire was channeled through an enchantment, so I wasn't able to absorb or control it, but that scarcely mattered. I was power incarnate now. My ravaged flesh healed more quickly than the fire could burn, and where the two contested, light spilled from my wounds like liquid gold.

I laughed madly, a feeling of near insanity creeping over me as I realized my initial fear had been pointless. Cyhan never relented in his attack, and I admired his determination. The realization that his best effort was having little to no effect had to be unsettling, yet he never stopped or tried to escape. Even a man as conditioned to battle as he was, had to be experiencing fear now.

Rising I kept his sword hand firmly in my grip while I used my other hand to lift him bodily, until he was nearly above my head. It was a shame I had to kill him. My face was locked in a rictus grin inside my helm, and despite the thought, I was filled with an exhilarating sense of power. I would crush him.

With a casual pull I jerked his arm free from the sword, and I felt one of the bones in his forearm snap at the sudden violence. Then I lifted him completely, preparing to drive him headfirst into the stone wall. His armor could protect him from almost anything, but I knew I had the strength to break it. I had the power to do almost anything. He was battering at me now, struggling to tear himself free, but even with his earth-bond his blows were futile. With his feet off the ground, he had no leverage, and my own power had blossomed around me, anchoring me in place.

I surged forward, my power driving me like some terrible juggernaut. It was time to end it.

No!

The voice was a mental scream, emerging from somewhere deep within. It sounded like my own, but I knew it wasn't me. It came from the dark core that resided at my center. The timing caused me to hesitate at the last instant, robbing my charge of some of its power. Even so, Cyhan was driven into the wall with incredible force, and the point of impact was at his shoulder instead of his head. One of his pauldrons cracked, and the wall itself collapsed. I released his now limp body and stared down at it.

He was probably dead, and for a moment I couldn't have cared less.

I have to check! This isn't the sort of man I am, dead or not.

My inner-self was getting to be rather irritating, but I had to agree. My behavior was not normal. I had never been so ruthless, so uncaring. I made my helm permeable to aythar, improving my magesight so that I could see him properly with all of my senses. His heart was beating, though he was unconscious, probably a concussion, definitely a broken collar bone, broken forearm, dislocated hip, and a variety of bruises…

"Or in Cyhan's terminology, 'Tuesday'," I noted dryly. The comment surprised me and I began to chuckle. It was too bad my friend wasn't conscious to appreciate the humor. It was one of the few jokes he might have connected with.

Although the jest was thoroughly inappropriate and probably showed a lack of empathy, it was much more in keeping with my normal demeanor. *Maybe I haven't gone completely mad yet.*

"Sorry about the injuries old friend," I said aloud. "Nothing personal." Then I picked my way through the rubble and out of the room. I had a lot to accomplish, and I wasn't entirely certain how I would manage everything.

My magesight, now unimpeded by the helm, had already told me that the house was empty, except for the unconscious body of my friend. *There's a relief. Maybe I can avoid killing or maiming anymore people from my former life.*

Rather than waste time, I headed directly for my goal, the chamber below the house, where Lyralliantha lay. She was the key to both of my problems, fulfilling Illeniel's Promise and putting a stop to Mal'goroth. As the last remaining She'Har, I hoped she would have the knowledge necessary to bring Mal'goroth to heel. My extensive memories had confirmed that the Dark Gods had been created, in a very similar fashion to the Shining Gods, but I still could not find the knowledge that would show me how to control them.

Even if I did, it might be impossible for me to use it. While the Shining Gods were created using a special enchantment, the Dark Gods had been constructed around a type of spell-weaving, one very similar to the one that now kept me alive. No human had ever been able to use their magic, although it had been the inspiration for the human art of enchanting.

I needed Lyralliantha to stop Mal'goroth. I could only hope that she wasn't too bitter about how long it had taken her lover's descendants to get around to fulfilling the promise.

Descending the final set of stairs to the stone door, I suffered a moment of panic as I wondered what I would do if the door were shut. I had been able to open it before only because of my family identity and my ability as an archmage. I no longer met either of those requirements.

I hadn't closed the door, so it should still be open, unless it automatically closed after some set period of time. If it had closed, I would have to use my power to rip the very foundations of my house apart to get inside.

My magesight still saw only the illusion of solid stone as I approached, but once my physical eyes were able to see it, I breathed a sigh of relief. The doorway yawned wide before me, just as I had left it.

I entered without pausing, and I felt better once I knew I was within the illusion. The chamber would cloak my presence much better than the armor I wore. Nothing had changed inside the circular room. Lyralliantha still lay in the stone sarcophagus at its center—waiting.

I felt a palpable tension rising around me as I drew closer to look inside. The sensation was new, something I hadn't encountered during my first visit, as though the air had been charged with static electricity.

Lyralliantha still looked as lovely as she had the last time I had been there. Silver hair and smooth skin that were somehow still accented by the white gown she wore. My goal was less than an arm's length away now, with only one obstacle barring me from accomplishing my purpose—Thillmarius' spell-weaving.

On my first visit I had uttered the command phrase that should have released her from the stasis enchantment but the She'Har lorewarden's magic had prevented it from working. I had to remove that before I could undo my many times removed great grandfather's enchantment.

I leaned in, focusing my senses more precisely, trying to study the alien magic that overlay the human enchantment. Despite the knowledge that the loshti had granted me, the structure of the She'Har symbols twisted and connected in ways that defied human logic. I could interpret their meaning individually, but understanding their whole, their context, was beyond me.

"And *that's* why he invented enchanting, because only one of the tree people could possibly understand that tangled crap!" I muttered testily. The feeling of tension in the air increased noticeably as I moved closer. Something pulsed inside me.

Standing still, I turned my senses inward, trying to understand the interplay between the magic inside me, and the magic around Lyralliantha Illeniel. It made no sense at first, until I recognized the convergence in the patterns that composed the two spell-weavings. The one wrapped around my grandfather's enchantment was complementary to the one that anchored my spirit to the realm of the living. *They were both created by the same evil bastard after all,* I noted.

The memory of my ancestor's battle with Thillmarius told me that the two had been created at very nearly the same time, possibly even simultaneously. Thillmarius had locked her stasis to prevent anyone else from freeing her, and at the same time protected himself from the vengeance of her husband. *Fat lot of good it did him, though. He wound up burned to ash.* Remembering that made me smile; my own battle with Thillmarius had ended in a much less satisfactory manner, even if it had been more permanent.

No amount of examination would allow me to understand what I was seeing however, so I decided to experiment by climbing up onto the sarcophagus, attempting to bring the two spell-weavings closer together.

My efforts were rewarded with a surge of energy, and I felt the spell-weaving that was wrapped around the wellspring of my life begin to move. At the same time, the one that encased Lyralliantha began to come loose—they were moving together. A sudden fear gripped me, and I leapt away before the two pieces of magic could come into contact.

When they come together they'll cancel each other. Lyralliantha will no longer be trapped, and my spirit will be free of his curse. I took a moment to consider the ramifications. My soul would be set free, and find itself in a dead body. As an archmage, it might have been possible to restore my body to its former state, but not if I was already adrift and sinking into the void. All of that completely ignored the fact that currently I no longer seemed to possess my abilities as an archmage.

There was also the problem of all the aythar I now contained. Once the spell-weaving that anchored and contained me was gone, that energy would be released. My normal self couldn't possibly control it, and the fact that I would be in the middle of dying would only add to the confusion. *I'll blow Albamarl off the map. Historians would have to rename the region, 'The Sea of Lothion'.* For some reason that thought brought another strange giggle to my lips. I was definitely becoming slightly unhinged.

I spent the next quarter of an hour considering the possibilities before making up my mind. Drawing out the link I had brought from the Iron Heart Chamber I began channeling power into it. Before I could do anything risky, I'd have to reduce my aythar to a level that was close to my normal living level.

The process took several hours. I attempted to rush it at first, but the iron link began to glow red hot as I steadily overloaded its capacity to transfer power. To avoid an inadvertent explosion, I had to slow down. It seemed ironic that I was forced to surrender the power so soon after taking it, not to mention being a serious test of my patience.

Though I worried that Penny or the others would return before I finished, the house was still empty when I had finished my preparations. *Apparently not all my luck is bad.*

I stood at the edge of the sarcophagus now, having serious doubts about my proposed plan of action. *This will be the end of me, and Mal'goroth will still be free. You can't even be sure she'll have a way to deal with him. What if you're wrong?* Then again, maybe I was tired of trying to solve every problem myself. "Someone else will have to save the world next time. I'm retiring," I announced to the empty room.

I climbed up and levered myself into position above the She'Har woman. I would have to lower myself into the sarcophagus with her to make sure the two spell-weavings came into contact. The image of my body lying next to that of the beautiful Lyrallianatha sprang into my mind. *What if Penny finds me like that? It isn't going to look good. Perhaps I should have written a note?*

"It would have been nice to have spent my last day thinking intelligent thoughts, but clearly that was never going to happen," I told myself. Then I lowered myself into the stone box.

The reaction was immediate, and I felt the spell-weavings begin to unwind, melding and dissolving as they merged. My body grew heavy, while my spirit felt a contradictory sensation of incredible lightness, a shadow had been lifted. My vision grew dim as I looked down at Lyrallianatha and realized that the stasis enchantment was still intact. It took a supreme effort of will to make my dead lips form the words, "Your husband waits for your return... and your forgiveness."

The stasis enchantment vanished, and my body dropped a few inches, settling awkwardly over hers, once the magic that preserved her no longer held me up. I worried I might smother her but the power to move my limbs was no longer mine. My body was dead, wooden, and I was drifting.

The dark shadow that had surrounded me for so long was gone. The veil had lifted, and the voices of wind and earth were louder than ever, welcoming me like old friends. Louder still though, was the song of death, a dissonant hum that no longer seemed foreign. It tugged at me, drawing me away in a new direction. The void beckoned and I had no strength to resist.

Maybe I'll get to see Marc, I thought idly.

Chaos erupted around me then, a turbulence that disturbed everything, like the ocean on a stormy day. I found myself tossed about, and the darkness that had settled over me was now punctuated by light and occasional bits of color. Vibrant blue eyes seemed to stare at me and I felt another force struggling to change the direction my spirit was taking.

I should've known dying wouldn't be easy.

The battle seemed to take forever, and I had little control over it. Something strong had me in its grip and was determined not to release me. Eventually I began to sense things around me, things from the physical world. The voice of the earth returned and above me I could see a woman gazing at me with eyes of electric blue—eyes like my own. Her hands trailed sparkling lines of magic in a variety of blues and golds, She'Har spell-weaving.

Her magic was pushing me downward, trapping and enfolding me—forcing me into a cold lifeless place. My body lay beneath me, a sterile horror of grey skin and dead flesh. *No!* I cried, but there was no one to hear my plea.

The lines of magic tightened, creating a feeling of pressure as I was compressed into that dark place. The voice of the earth faded as the veil descended over me, cutting me off from the world I had once loved. I was alone in the darkness. My last thought echoed in my mind, *Why?* From someplace far removed, I heard my mouth utter the words, though it was no longer me controlling it, "Why have you done this?"

At least someone agrees with me, I thought to myself.

Chapter 12

My eyes opened, revealing me in a situation many men would have found envious. I was in the stone sarcophagus, wrapped in the arms of an amazingly beautiful woman. Not that I could feel much of her softer features, while she was in a thin gown, my own body was still encased in steel. I knew her name, Lyralliantha, and while the memories I had inherited regarding her were affectionate, my personal feelings were significantly different now.

"Why have you done this?" I asked, unable to find any better words to express my dismay.

She stretched and rose from the stone box, moving gracefully. She answered me in her own language, though I understood her, "I will ask the questions. How long have I been asleep?"

I had been violated, snared, and reinstated within my dead body. Rather than a peaceful death I had been resurrected, this time through no will of my own. I was still a monster and I hated her for it. "This is the thanks I get? Someone finally frees you after all this time, and the first thing you do is deny them a proper death and ply them with questions? Necromancy is forbidden." The spell-weaving she had used on me, like the one Thillmarius created, and like the ones that created their Dark Gods, had been strictly banned by the She'Har long ago.

She said a few sharp words, and a strange feeling ran through me. Then she asked again, "How long have I been asleep."

"Approximately two thousand years, give or take a few decades. I don't have an exact count," I said as truthfully as I knew how. I had no other choice. *Sonofabitch!* I cursed silently as I realized she had bound me to obedience. My situation was similar to Karenth's.

"Where is my *Kianthi*?" she said, continuing her interrogation. The word she used referred to something that could most closely be translated as spouse, or in her case, husband. She was looking for her mate.

Memories raced through my mind, whether I wanted them or not. Opening my mouth I answered, "Across the sea, beyond the area now called the Gulf of Garulon. He has taken root in a place that is now an island, without a name, lost to the knowledge of men." I pointed to the west to indicate the direction. Having satisfied the compulsion I relaxed for a moment and then added, "Are you always a bitch when you wake up, or is it just because you're two thousand years old?"

Her lips twitched into a smile, "You are angry with me?"

My eyes narrowed, "Damn right, I'm pissed!"

"Then why did you awaken me, and why did you reek of Thillmarius' magic?" she responded calmly.

That was a long story, but I did my best to summarize without leaving out any important details. Her geas gave me no choice to do otherwise. I explained the current events as best I could, covering my struggle with the Shining Gods, the return of Thillmarius, and his eventual defeat, when I had stolen the spell-weaving from him that kept his spirit anchored in the world of the living.

As I talked I was forced on several occasions to stop and give descriptions of some things that had happened over the past thousand years or so of history, in particular the war with Balinthor and the destruction that had created the Gulf of Garulon. Lyralliantha was patient throughout my lecture, stopping me at times to ask pertinent questions or get extra details when she needed them. She never asked me to repeat anything, and it was quickly apparent that her sharp mind retained everything she heard. In her eyes I could see her thoughts moving, and I suspected she had insights into some of the events I related that were unknown to me.

"After examining you, I realized that the only way to remove Thillmarius' spell-weaving so that I could release you from the stasis enchantment was to sacrifice myself before completing my other goals, but I felt you were the only hope for stopping Mal'goroth," I said, finishing my summary.

"And yet you are angry with me for recreating the magic that keeps you from passing over," she observed. "Your goals and emotions are not entirely in agreement with each other."

I sighed, "The hope of ending my unfortunate condition was a relief to me. I'm ready to lay my burden down. I have little left to contribute to my family, aside from pain."

"Your family?"

The expression on her face bespoke a combination of humor and sadness. I knew she hadn't forgotten my recent summary, so her question made little sense. "Considering the geas you've already put upon me, I am beginning to suspect you have little sympathy with my situation."

A silent shiver ran through her body, and her face contorted in sudden pain. After a few seconds whatever had caused her discomfort passed and she relaxed, unclenching her fists. "I have more sympathy for your people than you realize, and having heard your tale I understand that I owe Mordecai Illeniel and his family a considerable debt."

Although her body language was odd, it was her words that concerned me more, "What do you mean *his* family?"

Her body stiffened for a moment before she answered, "You told me you were unable to enter this dwelling through the normal doorway, because of its magical protections. You were able to do so before your change, yet now it no longer recognizes you. Have you considered the implications of that?"

I watched her carefully. She appeared to be experiencing some sort of cramps. "I assumed that my transformation had made me unrecognizable to the identity enchantments," I replied. After a second I added, "Are you alright?"

"Not really," she answered, "but this is to be expected. I will need to return to stasis soon. Will you be able to recreate the enchantment?"

"If required, of course I can. What's wrong with you? We still need your help with Mal'goroth, or at least your knowledge. I won't restore the enchantment until you at least tell me how to control him," I insisted.

"You are arrogant, but you will do exactly as I command," she shot back with a spark of anger in her eye. "You will receive the knowledge you desire only after my orders are completed and I am reunited with my Kianthi. Only then will we help you to stop Mal'goroth."

As she spoke, I noticed something strange about her feet, her toenails seemed too long, or perhaps it was the toes themselves. She closed her eyes, and her fingers moved in delicate circles, forming something from her magic that had the appearance of a small green bird. When she had finished it flew around her twice before darting away in the direction of the open door to the chamber. Once it was gone she began climbing back into the stone sarcophagus.

"What was that?"

"Just a bit of magic to tell my Kianthi where I am, one way or another we will be reunited," she said simply. She arranged herself comfortably in the same position she had been when I first found her.

Her husband, my most distant ancestor and the first human wizard to bear the name Illeniel, couldn't possibly travel. Thanks to her earlier command, I had seen his fate. Sometime after he had placed her in the original stasis, he had transformed himself into one of her race and soon after that he had found an isolated place to take root. He was a tree now, assuming nothing had happened to him in the two thousand years since.

"Trees can't move," I told her.

"Then you must take me to him," she stated, "Otherwise he will send the *Kriteck* to find me."

The word brought forth another set of recollections. The Kriteck were the guardians, soldiers, and warriors of the She'Har. Unlike their normal children, born of the mother-trees, the Kriteck were created as needed by the father-trees. They were unable to take root or reproduce themselves and their lifespans were limited to a period of only two or three months. "But only a father-tree could… Oh!" I answered in my most intelligent fashion.

My ancestor *was* a father-tree now, even though he had originally been human.

"After you have restored the stasis enchantment, you will use your best judgment to get me to where he has taken root. Do not let the Kriteck have me unless you have spoken with him. Once you have, you will treat his words like my own. Obey him utterly. You will make this your first priority, taking precedence over your other plans. You will not remove the stasis from me again until I am near him. Once he and I are reunited you will be free from my service." Her words felt like a straightjacket settling around me, and I knew I could not disobey them. Reaching out, her hand produced another tiny object, a small green stone. As far as I could tell it had been made purely from magic alone.

She continued, "This will destroy the spell-weaving that binds Mordecai Illeniel to this world. It will also unmake you, giving you the death you desire. You may use it only after my first commands have been fulfilled. You may not share it or reveal its existence to anyone else until those commands have been satisfied, nor may you find any other means to circumvent the spirit of my orders. Do you understand?"

I wanted to scream at her, *No, I don't understand a damn thing,* but unfortunately her true question had been whether I understood her orders. "Yes, I understand," the words issued from me without my volition. After my answer my voice was my own again, so I spoke quickly before she could command me to remake the stasis enchantment.

"Wait, I still don't understand what's wrong with you. Why do you need to be in stasis, and why did you say 'his family' earlier?"

She smiled sadly at me. "Look at the memories— from when he put me here. You already know why I must stay in stasis. As for your other question, perhaps it would be kinder if I don't answer, since you haven't realized it yourself."

"Realized what?!" I almost shouted, "Just tell me!"

"You are not Mordecai Illeniel," she answered. "You are a simulacrum, a remnant. That is why his magics don't recognize you. That is why you don't have some of his special abilities. You are a magical echo, created by Thillmarius' spell, and the memories Mordecai left within the body you now animate. Mordecai Illeniel is dead."

I stared at her in shock.

"That is why you have no emotions of your own, only those you receive from fresh human aythar. This is one of the main reasons that particular type of magic was banned by my people," she added. "It is also why we never used it on a living person."

The truth of her words was undeniable, even though I wanted with all my heart to deny them. Being dead was bad enough, being nothing more than a magical construct, a shadow of a dead man—the truth was too cruel. "Then I am—then Mordecai is…," I couldn't fathom how to finish my question in an intelligible manner.

Somehow she understood me anyway, "Mordecai's soul is caged within you, inside the spell-weaving I created to keep you from fading. As I said before, once you use *that*…" she pointed at the green stone she had given me, "…his soul will be free to pass on, and you will cease to exist."

I wanted to cry, or scream, surely I was going mad. Instead I asked numbly, "How do I use it?"

"When the time comes, you, or whoever you appoint to the task, need only to destroy it. It can be easily crushed," she said.

"Sounds just like…"

She smiled, "Yes, I borrowed the method from your story. I quite liked his idea for linking enchantments using glass beads. Your Mordecai was an interesting man."

A sudden thought occurred to me. "Can he hear us? Is he aware—in there?" I pointed at my chest.

"No one really knows. At the very least he should have been aware of the world briefly when you destroyed Thillmarius' spell-weaving, but once I rebound him—I don't know. He is dormant now."

I nodded, "I think maybe…"

She didn't let me finish. "I've waited too long already. Put me back in stasis and obey my commands."

"But…"

"No more talking. Obey me—now," she commanded.

My mouth closed and I did as she bade me. Even my mind gave itself over, focusing entirely on the complex task of restoring the stasis enchantment.

Chapter 13

I wasn't able to regain any autonomy until the enchantment was complete. My mind stubbornly refused to turn aside from the task. It was an odd sensation, and when at last I had my freedom back, I felt sorry for Karenth for a moment. I hadn't treated him any better.

And apparently I'm no more human than he is, despite my delusions.

Straightening from my work, I surveyed the heavy stone sarcophagus. It wouldn't be simple to move. It had to weigh hundreds of pounds by itself, not to mention the slight additional weight added to it by Lyralliantha.

I silently cursed her impatience. If I had been given a moment's free thought, I could have devised several better arrangements, any one of which might have made it much easier to move her. *Why had she been so rushed anyway?*

Lyra had told me the answer lay in my memories, so I took a minute to search them, following the thread she had given me—the last few minutes before she had been put into stasis, over two thousand years ago.

The answer, once I understood it, was so simple I was surprised I hadn't realized sooner. The odd appearance of her feet should have clued me in immediately. She was preparing to set down roots.

The She'Har had an interesting life cycle. Those like Lyralliantha, who took humanoid form, were actually immature. Although they were intelligent, animate, capable of magic, etc..., they were in reality children. They were born in pods that were grown by the mother-trees, although they did require pollen from the father-trees to produce their living children.

Once they had emerged from their pods, whole and seemingly adult (at least to human standards), they could spend decades or even centuries before transitioning to their adult tree form. These children were sustained by another type of fruit produced by the mother-trees, called *calmuth*. Calmuth was the only nutrition the children of the She'Har required, although my memories showed me clearly that they had enjoyed many human foods as well.

The mother-trees could only produce enough calmuth to feed a certain number of these children, and when they could no longer eat calmuth it triggered a change in their bodies. She'Har young that stopped eating fruit from the mother-trees would take root, becoming new trees and fortuitously, producing more fruit to feed the other children.

Lyralliantha had been the last of her kind. Although my ancestor had protected her from the fate that destroyed her people, he could not produce the calmuth that she needed to remain as she was. After a period of only a few weeks, she had begun the change.

He had placed her in magical stasis, protecting her from the remnants of what had destroyed her race, while simultaneously halting her transformation. Later, after his battle with Thillmarius he had discovered that without his enemy he had no way to free his lover. After years of struggling to find a way, he had at last surrendered his burden to his son, charging him with finding a way to free her. His last act as a human had been to transform himself into one of the She'Har and wait to take root in the place he had prepared for them.

Their story had been tragic, and the sons of Illeniel had failed to fulfill their father's promise. Lyralliantha's hurry made sense now. She had been afraid of taking root here, hundreds of miles from her Kianthi—from the only hope of restoring her people.

Reaching into one of my pockets, I touched the small figurine that would allow me to call the dragon. *Come as soon as you can. I will meet you near my house in Albamarl. Don't worry about avoiding observation.*

With that taken care of, I uttered a word and used my magic to lift the stone sarcophagus, levitating it in front of me. I had been inside the house for over five hours now, and I knew it couldn't be long before someone found me.

Ascending the stone steps I made it to the ground floor of my house, and my magesight found Cyhan nearby in the hall that led to the kitchen. *The stubborn bastard woke up and dragged his mangled body down two flights of stairs hoping to warn someone.*

A pang of guilt ran through me as I considered the damage I had done to my former friend, or Mordecai's former friend. *I'm never going to be able to keep the distinction clear in my mind.* In the end I decided not to bother, for my purposes I might as well be Mordecai. I still intended to achieve his goals, protect his family, save humanity, etc…

"Stupid never dies," I said to myself, repeating one of his favorite phrases. "Mordecai might die, but his 'stupid' lives on." That set me to quietly chuckling. I had finally properly understood my identity. *I'm his 'stupid', living on to accomplish his foolish plans.* I laughed louder at that thought, stopping only when I heard a painful gasp coming from Cyhan.

The taciturn warrior was still inching his way along, trying to reach the door. I lowered Lyralliantha to the floor and walked over to kneel beside him. "You are a bigger fool than even Mordecai," I told him fondly. Removing my gauntlet and making my helm transparent to aythar, I reached out toward him, intending to remove his necklace and render him unconscious. Healing him would be simpler and less painful if he were deeply asleep.

My family chose that moment to arrive, and I sensed Penny enter first as the front door to my house swung open. She was holding Irene in her arms, and Lily was close behind her with Collin in tow. The twins and Sir Egan entered immediately after them, and I felt my daughter's attention focus upon me the instant she passed the threshold.

"Momma, someone's in the house, in the hall with Sir Cyhan," announced my daughter without hesitation. "He's hurt bad, Momma. I think he's dying."

They were still out of sight in the foyer, around the corner from the hallway I was in, but with my senses I could see them clearly. Penny passed Irene to Lily immediately and directed them with her hands to go back outside. She had her sword out, and I could feel the enchanted chainmail I had made for her under her outer garments.

I had to admire her efficiency in responding to an unknown threat, with one exception, she stepped forward to investigate for herself. Sir Egan caught her by the elbow, pointing toward the door where Lily and the children waited outside. He followed that gesture with another, indicating his eyes and then sweeping his hand outward.

Clenching her jaw Penny nodded in agreement. It made far more sense for her to protect her children and let her bodyguard reconnoiter. *She's stubborn as ever, but at least she shows some sense where the children are involved,* I thought, agreeing with her decision.

I still had no idea what to do when Sir Egan turned the corner and saw us. I'm sure it was a confusing sight, Cyhan on the floor with me kneeling over him and a large stone coffin on the ground beside us. Even worse, my brain chose that moment to wake up and remind me that I no longer had the immense power I had entered with earlier. In fact, after the enchanting and my short trip carrying Lyralliantha, I had even less aythar to spare than the more 'human' amount I had had just an hour ago.

Unlike me, Sir Egan knew exactly what to do. "Stand and step away from Sir Cyhan! Declare yourself!" he shouted. He had his Sun-Sword out, and it was pointed menacingly in my direction.

I wondered idly what would happen if he tried the same thing Cyhan had, ramming his sword through one of the joints in my armor. I had a pretty good guess, considering my current condition. *He'd burn me to ash.* As often happened when I was caught red-handed in the midst of a crime, my first thought was of Marcus. *What would he do?*

Facing him calmly, I took an artificially rigid stance. Using a silent spell I altered my voice to imitate the deep gravelly tones that the house golem, Magnus used. "My creator named me Brexus," I said, borrowing the Lycian term for 'payment'. *Obviously I have some unresolved mental issues,* I told myself as I realized what name I had chosen.

"What have you done to Sir Cyhan?"

"He attempted to prevent my entry, when I would not desist, he attacked. I have rendered him incapable of further attacks," I responded matter-of-factly.

"By what right would you enter this house and assault its lawful guardians?" he asked, following up his first question.

I had to admit, Sir Egan knew how to play the role of outraged knight. Dorian must have been giving them lessons. "Your rights and boundaries do not concern me. I answer solely to my master."

"Then name him, so we can take up our grievance with him, after you have been safely locked away," replied Sir Egan.

His words are so proper it's almost cute, I thought, reminded of some of the old romances I had once read in

Lancaster's library. "My master's name is Mordecai Illeniel, and my instructions do not allow for such delays. Please move aside," I answered in monotone.

"Drop your sword, and remove your helm," insisted Egan.

My helm was still open to aythar, which made magic much easier, although I had already replaced my gauntlet. Even so, I thought I could manage enough control to immobilize him without doing any permanent damage. I raised my hand to face him, palm outward.

"Don't fight him Egan. Run. You cannot stop him." The voice was Cyhan's. He was painfully gasping his warning from behind me. "Get the Countess and the children clear!"

I didn't bother waiting to see what he decided, with a word I wrapped the knight's body in invisible bands of force, pinning his arms and weapon against his side. I had learned from the past not to let them move freely. If I had encased him in a larger shield to imprison him, he might have used his enchanted blade to cut his way free. I had also learned from my previous two encounters not to give one of my knights even a second to act. They were inhumanly fast.

As if to reinforce that point, I found myself sailing backward to strike the wall. Penny had darted back in, even as I was binding her guard. She had struck me barehanded under the chin of my helm. Before I could recover she caught my leg in her arms and proceeded to do her best to imitate a whirlwind. I outweighed her by quite a bit, but she overcame that by swinging me in circles with herself as the fulcrum. My head began striking hard objects with incredible regularity.

"It's not going to work girl, it's one of the gods!" shouted Cyhan, trying to warn her off. "You have to run!" He was doing his best to drag himself over to the still bound Egan, probably to try and free him.

Yes please, listen to the man. Retreat, so someone can save me! I thought, which wasn't easy considering the constant battering. If I had still been living, I would have been unconscious or hopelessly nauseated already—if not badly injured. *"Lyet bierek!"* I shouted in desperation.

It was one of my oldest and most basic spells, the flashbang. Given my chaotic circumstances I wasn't able to focus on a single point as well as I normally could, so I simply put as much force into as I could manage. The resulting flash of light was accompanied by an explosive boom so loud I wondered if perhaps I hadn't made a mistake and destroyed my own home. I found myself on the ground, and my magesight showed me Penny reeling, blind and deaf a few feet away.

My advantage, slight as it was, wouldn't last for long, so I used another spell to bind her and Cyhan in the same fashion as Sir Egan.

"STOP!" someone shouted, and suddenly I could no longer move. I was surrounded by a powerful field of aythar. The spell being used was crude, the method was similar to burying someone in sand, unlike the tightly focused bands I had used on Penny and the others, but the end result was the same. Moira Illeniel had entered the fray.

My daughter glowed brilliantly in my magesight for she didn't know how to shield herself. *Why hasn't Walter taught her yet?* I wondered. Her power was shocking in its intensity, and I began to realize perhaps, what Walter had been trying to tell me once when he had tried to describe my own appearance to his magesight. She made the Prathions look dull and even Elaine was probably only half as bright as Moira's power seemed to be.

I was amazed and proud of her at the same time. I was also a bit worried. Given my weakened condition she was quite a bit stronger than I was at the moment, and she had numbers on her side. My only advantages were skill and experience, but while I was hampered by the fact that I didn't want to hurt her, she had no such hindrance. The look on her face also had me concerned; I had never seen my daughter with such a fierce expression.

"Don't you dare hurt my mother!" she yelled.

While I couldn't agree more with her sentiment, I couldn't imagine what I could possibly say to convince her to let me go—plus the power she had wrapped me in blocked everything but sight. As I struggled, I could see my son move past her to claim his mother's sword from the ground. He held it up in front of him and took a stand in front of his sister.

The image of the two of them, bravely facing an unknown foe and hoping to protect their mother, was enough to break my heart. Never had I thought to see my own children staring me down with such intense resolve, but I couldn't afford to weaken.

"Thylen pleitus," I muttered, focusing my will and sending tiny blades of force outward, destroying the field that held me with a minimum of effort. Moira was incredibly strong, but she no longer wore the amulet to protect her mind. No wizard did; it restricted our magesight too much, but unlike more experienced wizards, she hadn't learned to shield herself yet. *"Shibal,"* I said quickly, focusing my power directly on her open mind.

The spell was meant to put her harmlessly to sleep, but I hadn't reckoned with my daughter's strength of will. She staggered, eyes drooping, but she didn't fall. Instead I saw her aythar flare as her determination hardened. Her back straightened, and fury cloaked her in an expanding sphere of power. It was similar to a traditional shield, but far more aggressive in nature. Sharp blades of pure force grew from it and began to whirl around her as they expanded.

What in the hell is that? I was awed by her untrained potential even as the blades began tearing at the walls around her, destroying stonework and slamming into my armor. Unfortunately her lack of skill showed as one of the blades clipped her brother, slicing deeply into his side and sending him into one wall. There was blood everywhere.

Time seemed to stop, as I watched him collapse, hemorrhaging badly. Unable to penetrate her shield, I did the only thing I knew and lifting my sword I used it to channel a blast of wind, battering her back toward the door. Before she could recover I made it to his side and brought my sword to bear on his throat.

"Don't move, or I'll kill the boy!" I shouted, stopping her in her tracks even as she prepared to attack me again.

All eyes were on me then, those of the bound warriors, and most especially those of Penny and Moira. I could see Moira's thoughts racing as she tried to figure out a solution that would save her brother, but I didn't give her the time. Fumbling with my pouch, I brought out my enchanted shield stones, and with a word I sent them out to surround me, Sir Egan, and my dying son.

Removing my gauntlets, I quickly brought out the link to the Iron Heart Chamber and created a makeshift link between it and my shield stones. Creating such a link without prior preparation was risky, but my knowledge and practice over the years were enough to manage the task. Moira was already battering my enchanted shield, and without the additional power it wouldn't last against her rough blows. Once the link was finished, I breathed a sigh of relief; nothing short of a god could interrupt me now.

I brought my attention to bear upon Matthew now. His wound was serious, and my senses told me that he would die within minutes if I didn't heal him. The main problem was my extremely low level of aythar. If I touched him now I'd probably inadvertently drain his life away even as I was fixing his body. The link to the Iron

Heart Chamber was now effectively tied up, but I had another source close at hand—Sir Egan.

Egan's eyes were desperate as he helplessly watched me remove his gauntlet, exposing his bare hand. "I want you to draw upon the earth. It will help offset what I take from you," I told him, but I didn't wait to find out if he understood. Clasping his hand in mine I began to draw heavily upon his aythar.

The fire of fresh human life raged within me as I drew upon him, sending a powerful cascade of emotions into me, and mixed in with it was an ancient power, the deeper strength of the earth. I pulled at him until I feared for his life, filling myself with as much as I thought he could spare before releasing his hand. It wasn't easy letting go, but I had something more important waiting for me.

My son's wound wasn't complicated and healing skin and muscle had always been easy for me. Today was different, though. I had to tightly control the flow of aythar to avoid draining his life even while I sealed blood vessels and fused tissues back together. That extra complication, combined with the awkwardness of the armor I wore made my task far more difficult. It also didn't help that Moira seemed to think I was killing her brother.

The enchanted shield vibrated with her frantic attacks, but I didn't dare look up from Matthew until I had finished closing his wound. I was careful to make sure that all the vessels were properly rejoined and that the skin and other tissues were lined up. A sloppy job would leave him with scars that could hinder his freedom of movement for life.

When I finally finished and looked up, I was shocked at Moira's face. Her skin was red and her eyes swollen from desperate tears. At some point she had freed Cyhan and her mother. Penny had a hand on Moira's shoulder, as if to calm her, but the intense look in her eye made me flinch inwardly.

"You can't hide in your shell forever," she said in a dry voice that sent chills down my spine, "Eventually you'll have to come out, and when you do, I'll take you apart."

Moira looked away for a moment, "The dragon's coming."

"We can't let it take him away," answered Penny.

It was clear that they hadn't been able to see exactly what I had been doing, and they had assumed the worst. I stared at both of them, trying to decide the best method for negotiating a peaceful resolution. Gareth was getting closer, but escaping my shield and reaching the dragon would be problematic. As I watched, Moira's eyes became glazed as if she was focusing on something far away. Faintly I could hear her voice, reaching into a place I could no longer touch.

Mother, help me. I need you.

She was calling for Moira Centyr.

The stone floor beneath their feet began to flow as if it were made of liquid stone, boiling upward to form the body of the Stone Lady, Moira Centyr—my adopted daughter's mother. With my magesight I could see her aythar wavering. She had almost nothing left to spare, and even the cost of manifesting now might be too much for her, but she had come anyway, responding to her daughter's call.

I replaced my gauntlets and picked up my son's unconscious form. I needed a bargaining chip. With my wife and daughter both standing against me, I had no hope of escaping. Gareth couldn't get inside, and I was far too weak to force my way out. "The boy is still alive," I announced in my deep artificial voice.

"What do you want...," said Penny quickly, before adding, "...and who are you?" Her features were written with her unspoken fear. She already suspected my identity. Too late I realized I had forgotten to replace the illusion hiding the Cameron arms that decorated my breastplate.

Since I was covered from head to toe in enchanted armor, she had no way of seeing my features as I replied, "I am Brexus, created to serve Mordecai Illeniel. I seek only to remove the body of the She'Har woman in accordance with his commands."

It was immediately obvious that my wife didn't like anything I had just said. She frowned angrily, "My husband is dead. How can you claim to be taking his orders? Why are you wearing his armor?"

"He created me before his death, to ensure his wishes were carried out if he should die too soon," I improvised. The helm helped. Penny knew me too well, if she had been able to see my face, my lie would have been easily caught. *Of course, if I didn't have the helm on she'd also be able to see my identity with her own eyes.*

Penny's eyes narrowed, "That doesn't explain why you are wearing his armor."

"I am the armor."

"You removed the gauntlet a moment ago," she countered.

I sighed inwardly. *Why is she always so damned observant?* "There is a rudimentary clay body within, but the primary enchantments that I consist of are built into the armor itself."

Cyhan spoke then, "Whatever is inside the suit, it cannot be human flesh. It survived the flame of the Sun-Sword after I thrust it within."

"Take off the helm," ordered my stubborn spouse.

"I cannot," I stated flatly. "The boy needs assistance. Let me take the She'Har woman, and I will trouble you no more."

"Give me my son, and I'll let you leave," she replied. "You may take no one else."

"Lyralliantha is not your concern," I argued. Wing beats announced Gareth's arrival in the street outside.

"And *my* son is none of yours!" Penny bit back sharply. "The people of this house are *my* responsibility, and I'll turn none of them over to—to whatever you are! If Mordecai really did create you, then you can rest assured, he would not want you harming his children."

Obviously, I thought to myself. *If only she'd just get out of the way and let me get on with it.* After a long moment's hesitation I decided to accept her terms. "Very well, let me leave, and I will give you the boy once I reach the dragon."

During our conversation I had been able to faintly sense a hidden conversation occurring between my daughter and the remnant of her original mother, but I had no way of knowing what they had discussed.

"You'll give me my son before you set foot over that threshold," returned Penny.

I nodded, "I will trust you at your word, Countess."

I glanced at my daughter as I prepared to take down the enchanted shield; she had been strangely quiet since summoning her namesake. She was gazing at me now with a mournful visage, as though she had been struck by some tragedy. *Perhaps she just fully realized that her misstep nearly cost her brother his life.* In the confusion of our short battle I wasn't sure if she had noticed or whether she thought I had somehow been the one to wound him.

I pushed those thoughts aside and took down my shield. As I did, I kept the link to the Iron Heart Chamber in my hand, drawing steadily on it to replenish my power. I couldn't be sure my family might not change their minds about letting me escape.

I handed Matthew to Penny as I reached the doorway. Her nearness took my breath away, or it would have, if I had still needed to breathe. The urge to touch her hand as

I passed our son over was nearly irresistible, but she was careful to avoid any contact, a fact that only made my longing worse. For the first time since my transformation, I was grateful that my eyes were no longer capable of tears.

She allowed me through the door, and I walked toward the dragon that waited in the street, once again leaving my family behind me. Stepping up to Gareth's massive foreleg I started to climb up, but a presence made me turn. Moira Centyr stood close behind me.

I know what you are. I tried to help her understand, her voice said in my mind.

Looking past her I could see my daughter's face half buried in her mother's side, fresh tears stained her cheeks. *That was cruel and unnecessary,* I admonished the Stone Lady. As I communicated with her, I could see her body crumbling, her aythar was exhausted. She was about to expire at last.

A sudden idea inspired me. *Gareth, I'm going to do something stupid. If my family tries to stop me, I want you to growl and look menacing. Don't hurt them, just make sure they don't try to interfere,* I told the dragon.

Removing my gauntlets, I paused for a moment before casting a shield around the crumbling form of Moira Centyr. While Penny wasn't able to see what was happening, my daughter gasped, and I worried she might try to intervene. I brought my enchanted shield stones out again and recreated my shield, this time around myself and the Stone Lady.

What are you doing? Holding me will gain you nothing, my time is done, Moira Centyr's mental voice informed me.

Don't distract me, I replied in the same fashion, *I need your help, so I'm afraid I can't let you pass on just yet.* I relinked the Iron Heart Chamber to the enchanted shield around us before taking out my silver stylus. Using it, I began circling the Stone Lady, inscribing precise runes into the air around her, creating an intricate linked pattern.

It was an enchantment, but creating it without a solid substrate was an incredibly difficult task. I had to maintain a careful image of the whole, even as I worked to expand and complete the remaining portion. If my concentration were to waver at any point, the whole structure would collapse before its completion.

Moira Centyr's thoughts were desperate now. *Please, no! You can't do this to me. I have tried to aid you at every turn. Why do you betray me thus?!*

I ignored everything and continued my work. It wasn't until I heard my daughter's voice that I nearly stumbled and lost my place. "Don't! You're hurting her!" she cried from beyond the outer shield. Still, she made no attempt to interfere. Either she knew that the shield was beyond her power, or she had resigned herself to accept whatever I was doing. I had to wonder how much her mother's remnant had told her.

Seconds passed into minutes while I worked, losing track of time. I had narrowed my focus until the only things that existed for me were the runes I was inscribing and the memory I had plucked from the distant past. The memory of Moira Centyr and the first Mordecai's secret project, the enchantment he had created to save them from the dark forces looming over their world—the enchantment that had created the Shining Gods.

This is wrong! She cried again in my mind.

Tell that to the woman who originally created you, I retorted.

She did not fix me in this world for all eternity. She knew what they had done before was a mistake.

I quite honestly, do not give a damn. You will assist me until my goals are complete, and then I will release you, if you so desire. The enchantment was complete now, and it contracted, crushing inward to bind the magical sentience that was all that remained of Moira Centyr. Without pause, I uttered the words that I had built into the enchantment, binding her to my will.

Her head bowed in defeat as I removed the inner shield that had kept her in place while I worked. *I am your slave. I had not thought you capable of such evil. I misjudged you,* she informed me mentally.

I know the feeling, I responded. *I don't have the luxury of being nice anymore, but one way or another I WILL stop Mal'goroth.*

Examining the immediate area, it appeared that my audience had decided not to interfere. My daughter was watching me with wide eyes, holding her mother's hand. Penny's face was inscrutable, and Sir Egan had recovered enough to stand beside her. Since things were still calm I took down my enchanted shield for a second time. No one moved.

Climb up on the dragon, I commanded, demonstrating for my new servant. Moira Centyr followed reluctantly. *Keep your silence too, I don't want you talking to anyone else just yet, most specifically my daughter.*

Gareth gathered his legs under him to leap once more into the sky, and I turned my head away. Watching my family was too painful, and my daughter's eyes were both sad and accusing. She projected her thoughts to me for the first time in her young life.

Why are you taking my mother away? The touch of her gentle mind made my heart ache.

I closed my eyes and focused my magesight on the sky, refusing to answer. It was too much for me. The dragon leapt into the air, and the wind thundered with the sound of his powerful wing strokes.

Father?

My resolve broke when I heard that word. *She isn't your mother. She's an echo, a ghost, the same as I am.*

She told me that, but both of you are wrong. Mothers and fathers are not born of blood. You are my father as much as the man that you were made from—as much as they are my mothers. She sent me the mental image of herself, holding Penny's hand, followed by the image of the Stone Lady.

Then do as I say, as he would have said, 'Take care of your mother and your brothers and sister.' I told her. My heart was heavy, and I was grateful that Gareth's flight had almost taken us beyond the range of my ability to communicate.

Faintly, I heard her last thought, *I love you.*

The dead cannot cry, but tears are the least of the pains one can feel.

Chapter 14

Elise Thornbear stood quietly in the street in the dockside district of Albamarl. She wore an old grey wool dress, patched and worn with age. It was unremarkable, other than for its cleanliness. She had had it freshly laundered before borrowing it from one of her servants. In her hand she carried a small basket.

Her hair was caught up in a tight bun, and without jewelry or any other adornments, she could have been almost anyone—anyone other than a noblewoman. Since returning to live in Albamarl, she had re-visited many parts of the city, for nostalgic reasons mostly, but she had never found a reason to go to the dockside area. Even during her youth, working as one of the 'Ladies of the Evening', she had never had reason to frequent it. The few women who plied the world's oldest profession here were not church sanctioned.

His condition aside, it's hard to believe Mordecai would be attacking prostitutes in this part of town, she considered silently. *There are better places in town to find willing women, or whores—or prey, if that's what we are to him now.*

The door in front of her was unpainted, grey and weathered by sun and rain. It was typical of the houses in the area. She knocked softly on it and waited patiently until one of the occupants came to the answer it.

"Who's there?" a small voice asked through the old wood.

Elise had anticipated this situation. She knew that the woman she was looking for would be highly suspicious of anyone unexpected. Strangers didn't knock on doors in this part of town unless they were trying to collect money. It was one of the reasons she had dressed as plainly as possible.

"I'm looking for a Mister Cobb. I was told he lived close to here, but I'm not familiar with the area," she answered, giving the name of the neighbor whom she had just spoken with while looking for Myrtle's house.

There was a brief pause before the child's voice responded, "He doesn't live here. He's next door."

"Oh thank you!" Elise said gratefully. "I do appreciate your help. Do you think you could point it out to me? I'd rather not have to knock on any more strangers' doors."

Megan hesitated, but the woman outside seemed harmless enough, at least by her voice. After a moment, she opened the door enough to point at the house on the right hand of theirs. "He lives over there," she said cautiously. "He isn't in trouble is he? He's a nice man." In fact, he frequently allowed Megan to use his hearth to heat water for herself and her mother, since they couldn't afford wood.

"What? Oh no! Hardly that, dear, I came to bring him some food and medicine. One of his friends asked me to come round. He's taken sick, and of course no one can afford what the physicians charge," Elise lied easily. "I'm a midwife, but I also collect herbs, and these days I tend more to the sick than I do young mothers."

"Oh," said the young girl with a look of consternation. Thoughts were tumbling about in her mind, but it was unclear whether her unspoken thoughts or her caution would choose her next words.

Elise didn't wait to find out. "Thank you for your help, Miss. Can I offer you some bread? I have more than Mr. Cobb needs, and it was kind of you to help me." She pulled at the cloth covering her basket to reveal a large round loaf.

That simple act overcame Megan's suspicion. "We could sure use it, ma'am. Momma's been very sick lately, and we haven't had much." She left unspoken the hope that perhaps the kindly woman might be able to do more.

Lady Thornbear's brow creased in an expression of worry, "Would you like me to take a look at her? Perhaps I could help."

"We don't have anything to pay you," answered Megan, but her eyes were hopeful.

Elise studied the small girl for a second. "I won't ask you to, but perhaps someday if I need help you could return the favor."

"That seems fair," answered Megan seriously. She stepped back to let the older woman into the home she shared with her mother.

The interior of the small house was dimly lit, but after she had examined, it Elise decided that too much illumination might only make the dismal nature of their home more apparent. A woman, Myrtle presumably, lay upon a small bed along one wall. There were few furnishings and the small rickety table and cold hearth did little to relieve the emptiness.

Megan's mother seemed to be fast asleep, but when Elise checked her forehead she found it to be far too warm. Laying her head against the woman's chest, she listened to her heartbeat. She didn't like what she heard. *She's fevered, and her heart is beating too quickly.*

"How long has she been like this?"

"Several days…"

Elise frowned, "Has she been able to eat or drink much?"

"I've given her water, but she doesn't drink much. We ran out of bread yesterday, and Nikko took our money," answered the girl.

"Nikko?"

"Momma pays him to keep the watch from bothering us," replied the girl.

I sincerely doubt he has anything to do with the watch, thought Elise, but she merely nodded in response. "Can you fetch some hot water for me? I see you have a kettle there."

After a short time the girl returned with a steaming kettle. Opening her bag, Elise removed a small sachet and set it into the water to steep. "This should help her fever, and if she drinks enough it will steady her heart as well," she told the girl. "Your mother needs more fluid inside her. Come here. Listen to her chest," she added, motioning for Megan to listen to her mother's heartbeat.

"It sounds sort of fluttery," observed the girl.

Elise nodded. "When you don't have enough water in you, your blood shrinks, and your heart tries to make up for it by beating faster. It can be very dangerous. Look at her skin." She pinched the flesh on the top of Myrtle's hand. "See how it stands up? That's another sign. Sometimes people get sick and can't get better simply because they don't drink enough to last until they get over it."

Once the tea was ready, Megan attempted to wake her mother up. It took several minutes of shaking, cajoling and constant nagging, but eventually Myrtle roused herself enough to take a small sip. Her eyes were glazed, and it was obvious that she was mildly delirious. She failed to even notice the stranger in her home before she closed her eyes again.

"That won't do," said Lady Thornbear, pursing her lips.

"Shouldn't we let her rest?" asked Megan. "She did drink a little."

"Not nearly enough," explained Elise. "She'll die if you let her keep resting. What do you think are acceptable methods to wake someone up when they're like this?"

The girl thought hard for a moment, "Loud noises?"

Elise nodded, "That's a start, but you've already tried that. If that doesn't work you could try slapping or cold water."

"You aren't going to slap her are you?!" said Megan, alarmed.

Lady Thornbear smiled, "No, but when the choices are between dying and putting the patient through something uncomfortable, sometimes you have to choose the crueler option. Luckily I have something here that will probably work more easily than resorting to such crude methods." Reaching into her basket she removed a small glass vial.

"What's that?"

"Chemists call it 'sal ammoniac', but you've probably heard it called 'smelling salts'," replied Elise as she unstopped the vial and waved it under Myrtle's nose. The unconscious woman inhaled sharply, and her eyes flew wide as she turned her head, seeking to escape the sharp smell of ammonia.

"Who're you?" asked Myrtle as her eyes focused.

"Drink this," ordered Lady Thornbear, ignoring the question.

Myrtle shook her head, refusing the cup. "Did Nikko send you? Why are you here?"

Sighing inwardly Elise glanced at Megan, willing the girl to silence as she lied, "Yes, of course, Nikko sent me to make sure you recover. Now drink this, or I'll be forced to have him come see you personally."

That seemed to work. Myrtle took a long swallow before pushing the cup away again, but Elise wasn't done yet. Shaking the other woman she spoke again, "Finish the cup, dear, or I'll be forced to harsher measures."

Myrtle's eyes opened and this time she finished the small cup before closing them again. Elise let her rest this time.

"Will that be enough to make her better?" asked Megan.

Lady Thornbear smiled kindly, "Oh heavens no, she'll need much more, but she can't take it all in at once. We'll let her sleep a while and then wake her up again in an hour."

"Will you stay that long?"

"I'll have to see to Mr. Cobb first and take care of a few other things, but I'll be back after that," she told the girl.

After leaving the poor dwelling she did indeed visit Mr. Cobb. Her true purpose was to bribe him, making certain he wouldn't reveal her lie to the girl if asked. She also inquired regarding the whereabouts of Nikko, claiming she had some business with him as well.

Mr. Cobb was helpful enough, especially once he had seen the color of her coin, though he did seem concerned whether she meant harm to Megan and her mother. Nikko turned out to be a well-known figure in the local area and Mr. Cobb didn't mind sharing that information at all.

It was several hours before Lady Thornbear returned to Myrtle's tiny home, but she had accomplished her goals. Megan seemed glad to see her and let her in immediately. "I wasn't sure if you would really come back," admitted the child.

Elise patted her gently on the head. The girl seemed intelligent despite her youth, probably a result of learning to survive at an early age. "My business took a little longer than I anticipated. Did your mother drink the rest of the tea?"

The kettle was nearly empty. Megan had roused her mother hourly to drink more, using the smelling salts when necessary. Myrtle's fever had improved as well. Lady Thornbear had the girl fetch more hot water and prepared another batch of tea.

Once that was taken care of, and they had given Myrtle another cup she began asking more direct questions. "Did your mother have any unusual visitors before she became sick?"

The girl was reluctant to answer the question, possibly for fear of revealing her mother's occupation, but over a period of an hour, she eventually relayed the entire story, describing their strange visitor from several nights past. Without realizing it, she had gradually come to trust the older woman, though she would have been hard pressed to know exactly why.

Elise Thornbear stayed several hours more before finally packing her things to leave. She had learned everything she wanted to know, though the answers had left her with more questions. She stroked Megan's hair again before she left. "I'll be back tomorrow morning to check on your mother," she said reassuringly.

She returned the next day with a carriage and several of her gentler servants. With a bit of discussion, she convinced Megan and her mother to return with her to her home in the city. The girl was nervous, but Elise gave her little opportunity to refuse. Lady Thornbear was extremely persuasive when she wanted to be.

Myrtle would be given a job among Lady Thornbear's staff once she recovered, and Elise had high hopes for Megan. The girl seemed unusually bright.

Nikko died of an unknown stomach ailment the next day.

Chapter 15

We flew to the west, following the Myrtle River as it made its way to the coast. Since we had started in late afternoon we soon found ourselves flying at night but the moon was up, and Gareth seemed to have little problem seeing in the dark. The weather was clear and the moon bathed the world below us in a fascinating array of white and dark areas. The river itself appeared black, but in the distance it would glow where the moonlight was reflected toward us.

If I had been a poet, I might have been tempted to craft a verse to honor the occasion, but as it was, I just settled for being suitably awed.

Moira Centyr had been silent since we had left Albamarl behind. I still thought of her by that name, even though she wasn't truly the original person. It was much easier than anything else, for she had never been given her own name. *Not like me, since I managed to name myself 'Brexus' a few hours ago,* I thought quietly. *I guess the name is appropriate though, for I will indeed pay a number of debts before this is all over.* I started to add, 'or die trying', but I realized a more fitting phrase might be, 'or I can try dying.'

Our flight took us over the town of Turlington, which nestled itself at the edge of the Wyvern Marsh, where the river fanned out into a wide delta that fed a huge swampy region. The marsh itself had been named that because the original founder of Turlington had thought the multitudes of crocodiles that made the region home were rather dragon-like. He might have rethought his opinion if he had seen my current mount. The difference between

Gareth Gaelyn and the reptiles that made the marsh home was fairly striking.

For that matter, it was probably a good thing that we were flying over at night. The inhabitants might have panicked if they had seen the colossal form of the dragon flying over.

That thought set me to chuckling at the mental image of the town's citizens running for cover, and Moira shifted in front of me when she felt my laughter. Still, she kept her silence.

"Are you ever going to speak to me again?" I said from my perch behind her. I was forced to shout to make myself heard over the rushing noise of the wind.

You have not given me permission to speak, came her rather terse reply in my mind.

I winced inwardly as I recalled my last words to her. While I had not really intended for her to never speak again, my command had carried the force of the enchantment's binding behind it. She had quite literally been unable to communicate without my permission. "I completely forgot about that," I responded. "You are free to communicate or act in any other way, except if you think it will be in opposition to my wishes, and currently my only wish is that you remain with me."

I understand.

She didn't bother adding anything else, which gave me the impression she probably hadn't forgiven me for my actions earlier. *That's fine; I can handle the silent treatment. In fact, I prefer it,* I thought, though I didn't broadcast it to her. During my years of marriage I had often wished Penny would resort to the silent treatment, but that had not been her way.

Gareth was slowly losing altitude, gliding ever lower until we were skimming just a few hundred feet over the top of the cypress trees that predominated in that part of the marsh. I directed my thoughts toward him, *Why are we descending?*

We near the coast, he answered, not bothering to add any further explanation.

While neither Moira nor I really needed rest or sleep anymore, I realized that was probably not true of our still living transportation. *That makes sense,* I replied. *We can rest there before continuing on in the morning.*

Where do you intend to travel from there? He asked.

It was a perfectly reasonable question, since I hadn't bothered to share my intended destination with him yet. *We keep going west, over the ocean.*

There's nothing but water and more water once you get past the odd coastal island, he replied with a mental tone of curiosity. Gareth landed on a large but relatively solid stretch of sandy beach. The region where the marsh met the ocean was mostly shallow salt water, thick with reeds and other saltwater plants, but the dragon's eyes had found us one of the few areas with good solid ground.

"There's an island," I said, using my voice now that the noise of his wings had abated.

"I didn't see one," Gareth returned, as though his vision alone could see the entirety of the wide seas. Then again, I had to admit, the dragon's eyes were at least as good as an eagle's. If he had flown above the coastline in the past, he might have been able to see for many miles on a clear day.

I smiled, though the expression was wasted in my helm, "It's a bit farther than your eyes can see from here."

"How much farther?" he asked suspiciously.

I gave the question some thought before answering, "I'm not certain, but roughly the distance we've flown today."

"We covered more than half the breadth of Lothion today. There is nothing that far out, other than the empty deeps," Gareth told me, stating it as a matter of fact.

Moira chose that point to chime in, "Gareth speaks the truth."

"The golem is correct," responded the dragon, before adding silently, *You have not told me why you insisted on bringing that creature along.*

His aside startled me. It had never occurred to me that he didn't know who she was. After all, the two of them had been friends before the war with Balinthor, over a thousand years ago. They had been the only two living archmages at the time. Of course, she looked a bit different now, with a body made of earth and stone.

Before I could explain, he spoke again, "How do you know my name?"

I remember the days before the war with Balinthor, she answered, broadcasting her thoughts to both of us now. *My creator lived and worked beside you then, before you became a dragon.*

"A strange turn of phrase, to say 'creator', if you were one of the Targoth Cherek you were not one of mine. Did Moira Centyr create your bond after my—transformation?" The phrase he used, 'Targoth Cherek' was the old term for a warrior given the earth bond by an archmage.

Moira didn't respond immediately, and she sent me a private thought, tinged with reluctance, *Perhaps it would be best to leave my origin a secret. It would only bring him pain.*

I have kept many things to myself, but it would be unfair to hide this from him, I told her. Opening my mouth, I spoke aloud, "Moira created her as a sort of copy of her personality and memories before she fought Balinthor." I kept the reason to myself. I doubted even the dragon knew that my daughter wasn't actually my own child.

The dragon's eyes grew wide with astonishment. "I thought that was forbidden to your family."

It was, said the Stone Lady, casting her face downward, *but she chose to do so anyway. There were none remaining that had the right to gainsay her decision at that point.*

What the dragon was referring to was the special gift of the Centyr line of wizards, the ability to create sentient minds from nothing but magic itself. Much like the Prathion talent for invisibility, her family had been able to craft intelligent spells, for the purpose of making temporary servants, or helpers. Their creations had taken many forms, sometimes being nothing more than tiny birdlike messengers, and sometimes being complex entities used to imbue mechanical servants with intelligence.

The one rule the Centyr wizards had always kept, was never making a true doppelganger, or clone of themselves. It was regarded as cruel and inhumane, and given my own status as something similar; I had to agree with their reasoning.

I watched the two of them with interest, two beings who had existed for over a thousand years now. Two witnesses and participants in one of the greatest tragedies humankind had ever experienced; two who knew each other but had not spoken since the day Gareth had transformed and slain both the enemy and the people he had meant to protect. For such a long awaited meeting, they were surprisingly subdued. Neither said anything for a long while.

After what felt like hours, though it was probably only a couple of minutes, the dragon spoke again, "So you remember..." He let the words trail off, unable to finish his sentence, though we all knew there could be only one event he was referring to.

I am not truly Moira Centyr, but I have those memories. I remember it all, just as if I had been there myself, she answered him.

The air itself seemed to hum with barely suppressed tension. The emotions coming from Gareth were so powerful that even his tightly controlled mind with its strangely reptilian nature, could not hide them. His inner pain throbbed, and my own heart seemed to resonate in time with it. It reminded me of the day I had become what I was now, the day I had been separated from my family and everyone that I knew and loved.

"Perhaps it would be better if I left you until morning. I need to hunt and…" began the dragon, turning away.

Moira stepped forward in a rush, placing her hand on his massive foreleg before he could take flight again. *Wait. You must know this. She forgave you before she died. So did the others, even Mordecai, though he was angry at first. They understood your mistake, and they felt the same desperation. They—we… we all made our own mistakes.*

Her use of the name, 'Mordecai' confused me for a moment, until I realized she was referring to my ancestor, the man she had loved.

"Mistakes? I didn't make a *mistake!* I murdered my own people. Ripping and burning, I destroyed everything I cared about," spat the dragon in a bitter tone.

Your mind was not your own, after the transformation…

"It was *this* mind. The one you see before you now. I did not change again. In my rage I killed everything that moved, and when nothing moved I waited. I waited and hunted for *days*, catching the survivors as they emerged from hiding!" he said, shouting down her attempt at consoling him.

Moira was not swayed by his fury however. *You were a new creature, maddened by your new body and senses, driven by instincts you had never experienced. You adapted and eventually you learned to control yourself, or we would not be able to converse now.*

"You did not kill your…" he started, but she cut him off.

I destroyed a nation, and all the innocents that still hid within it. I helped create the Shining Gods, and I bear the guilt for everything they have done since we left them orphaned and unmastered. GET OVER IT. If I can forgive you, if I can forgive myself, then you can do so as well. You've had a thousand years and more to grieve. Her mental voice was taut with emotion, and at points rose to the psychic equivalent of a shout.

Listening to the two of them, I had to wonder at her resolve. I had once slaughtered most of the healthy male population of Gododdin, when they had invaded Lothion, and I had yet to completely forgive myself. After that I had been responsible for the deaths of a number of innocents as I attempted to protect *my* friends and family. Peter and Lily Tucker always came to mind first when I considered that. While Moira's argument carried a lot of force, I had never fully forgiven myself. I had merely learned to live with the guilt.

I opened my mouth to add my own thoughts, "I've suffered from my own mistakes as well, but I think perhaps…"

"Stay out of this!" growled the dragon immediately, cutting me off. His words were echoed by Moira's mental sentiment.

The two of them stared at one another silently for a minute before I realized they were conversing privately, leaving me out of the conversation. It was an unpleasant sensation, and it was a relief when Moira finally asked me, *Since we have stopped traveling for the night, I would like some time alone with Gareth, to sort out our past. May I take my leave of you until tomorrow?*

The question surprised me, but I acquiesced readily enough. "Certainly, just make sure you both return with the dawn."

The dragon dipped his head in acknowledgement and lowered his body so that the Stone Lady could climb back on. Within moments they were gone, and I was left alone on the sand, surrounded by the natural beauty of the salt marsh behind me and the glory of the sun setting over the ocean before me. I couldn't help but wonder what they would talk about.

It was useless to speculate, so instead I enjoyed the grand display of pinks and oranges in the clouds behind me, while the sea itself became infused with pastels reflected by the foamy wave tops. Without the need to sleep, the night would be tedious. Even the usual camping chores, a fire, a meal, etc…, were unnecessary. *Once I've finished this business, I will be unnecessary as well.*

Such melancholy thoughts were my frequent companions these days. With a sigh I drew out my link to the Iron Heart Chamber and began the long process of drawing out its power. It would be needed in the days ahead, of that I was sure.

Chapter 16

My traveling companions returned in the wee hours of the morning, before the sun had made its appearance. Perhaps 'companions' was too generous a term; menials or thralls might be better words, since I had given them little choice in their circumstances. *I'm in a cheerful mood this morning,* I noted sarcastically.

I noticed one major difference after their arrival. The Stone Lady was no longer stone.

When I first detected the dragon at the edge of my magesight, I identified both of them without trouble, primarily because of their distinctive aythar. While Gareth Gaelyn was large and imposing physically, his powerful aythar shone like a beacon. Moira Centyr's was much more subdued, in large part because she no longer produced aythar as a living creature would. She had only what remained from her creator, a supply that had been steadily dwindling over the centuries, until my enchantment had altered the basic nature of her existence.

It wasn't until they drew closer that her drastic physical change was apparent to me. She was flesh and blood now. Her artificial spirit, with its limited aythar caged by my enchantment, was still the same; no wizard would mistake her for a normal human, but she now resided within a body made of living flesh. Dark hair, almost black, framed a pale face with light grey eyes and pale pink lips. Her new form was beautiful in an almost casual fashion, none of her features were striking, but their combination was pleasant to the eye.

I hid my surprise, "Much better, you looked like shit yesterday."

Her brows lifted in amusement, "The man whom you resemble was much nicer. Your comments don't suit you. You'd have a much better time of it if you quit trying so hard to set yourself apart as an asshole."

"I'm glad to see that our time apart has renewed your interest in banter," I said, inspecting her discreetly. She was garbed in little more than a plain woolen shift. "I would also remind you that you didn't know Mordecai very well. He was not nearly so kind as you like to think."

The dragon was laughing inwardly. It wasn't something that could be seen, but I could feel his mirth, and it irritated me.

"You definitely got his stubbornness in full measure," she commented. "Aren't you curious about my change?"

Rather than validate her remark, I answered honestly, "In fact, I am."

Gareth chose that point to join in. "After our conversation last night, I offered to alter her body for her. It was—a small gift."

I suspected that he had meant to say 'repayment', but had changed his mind at the last moment. From what I knew of the ancient archmage, he did not believe that he would ever be able to atone for his crimes. It was also one of the very few times I had known him to use his abilities as an archmage. He had transformed his own body once or twice in the past, but doing so for someone else was an egg of a different color.

From my own experience, it involved an extreme level of intimacy, for accomplishing it would require the same sort of entanglement that was used during the most advanced types of healing. Simple healing required only wizardry, but major restorations required a sort of intuitive, innate self-knowledge. That sort of knowledge couldn't be acquired externally. Gareth would have been forced to *become* her to some degree, before he could then transform her body to the human form she remembered.

The most remarkable part, to my mind, was that in the past Gareth had made a point of showcasing his defiant independence. He had made me believe it was a fundamental part of his draconic nature, yet the type of joining Moira's transformation necessitated completely belied that idea. Either the dragon had been lying to me all along, or he felt an enormous debt to this shadow of a woman he had once known.

It also told me that he was still fully in command of his abilities both as a wizard and an archmage, no matter how many centuries he had been living as a dragon.

All of this passed through my mind in a matter of seconds, while my conscious mind struggled to find a fitting reply. "This is going to ruin your reputation if it becomes public knowledge," I said at last.

Moira Centyr burst into raucous laughter at that point. Not the delicate, feminine, partly suppressed laughter that women sometimes use, but the more honest sort, full of snorts and unladylike whoops. It had been more than a year since I had heard a woman's laugh, and it startled me how much I missed the sound.

"We need to speak privately," I told the dragon before addressing Moira, "For the next five minutes you can no longer hear, nor will you use any other means to eavesdrop on this conversation." Her expression became irritated as my command took effect, robbing her of her auditory capacity.

Ignoring her expression, I nodded at Gareth and began walking away, indicating that he should follow. "That was rather heavy handed," he informed me.

"Ask me if I care," I replied, "I don't have time to worry about my social capital. I'm not even a real *person* and I have a lot to accomplish."

The dragon's eyes narrowed, "Then give me your commands, *Master*, so that we can keep this conversation short." His tone was laced with sarcasm.

"The enchantment I used to keep her from disappearing is the same one that was used to create the Shining Gods. If nothing is done about it, she will be forced to persist forever, something I am sure she does not want, especially considering how well *they* did with their immortality," I explained. Leaning close to the dragon's head, I whispered the words that were the key to Moira's enchantment. "Did you hear me clearly?" I asked afterward.

"Yes."

"Those words will enable you to release her when this is over," I explained.

"Why do you share this with me?" he asked.

"Because I trust you will do the right thing, even if I cannot," I stated plainly. It was clear enough to me now, especially since he had transformed her—that Gareth Gaelyn cared deeply for the well-being of Moira Centyr's shade. That made him the perfect candidate to entrust with this knowledge.

"You are undying, it is unlikely that you will not be present to do whatever is necessary for her yourself," he argued mildly.

"I don't particularly like my condition, and even putting that aside, the *real* Mordecai is still in here," I said, tapping my chest for emphasis. "The spell-weaving that keeps me here also keeps his soul trapped within. If he is to be allowed to truly rest in peace I have to find a way to put an end to this." Because of Lyralliantha's command I was unable to tell him of her gift, but it was hardly necessary to make my point. "Rather than take chances, I think it's important to make sure that someone else knows how to unmake her, someone she can trust."

Gareth stepped around my words to ask a pointed question, "Are you someone she can trust?"

I smiled at him, though I knew he couldn't see my face behind the steel helm, "Neither of you can trust me. I have other priorities that I will put before yours. I would damn both of you to accomplish my goals without blinking an eye."

"Sharing this information does not help you," he observed.

"This is merely a kindness of convenience. Don't read more into it than that," I answered, before turning back to walk toward where we had left our temporarily deaf companion. Her hearing returned soon after, though I suspected her mood would take longer to recover.

"About this island you say is across the ocean...," began Gareth.

"You sound skeptical," I interrupted.

The dragon paused for a moment, issuing an almost inaudible rumbling. Was he growling? "In my day the world was fairly well mapped, and that part of the ocean was known to be empty," he said at last.

"In your day the Gulf of Garulon didn't exist either," I reminded him.

A hiss escaped him. "I lived there. You hardly need point that out."

"I'm telling you there's an island there, a large one. You could fit all of the Lancaster estate and most of mine as well on it," I stated firmly. "It has been there since long before the war with Balinthor or the creation of the Gulf."

Moira intervened at that point, "I think what Gareth is trying to get at is that there was a lively shipping trade back then, between Lothion, Gododdin, and Garulon. While most of the mariners stayed within coastal waters, some did venture farther on missions of exploration, including a few wizards. Nothing as substantial as the place you describe was ever found."

"It wasn't meant to be found. The man who created it wanted to be certain of that," I informed her.

She scowled at me, "Perhaps it would help if you revealed your source of information. Obviously you have discovered something, but we can't assess its reliability without knowing more." The set of her jaw hinted at controlled irritation, hiding just below the surface.

As so often was the case lately, I was tempted to react violently. *That's not normal, I wasn't like this before.* I struggled with my anger, waiting until I had a firmer grip on my words before replying, "I have a lot of information now, but I will not share its source, other than to tell you it was a family secret." *A family I am not truly a part of.* "What I can tell you is that my ancestor, the man who created the Elentir Mountains, also created this island. And for reasons very similar to your own when you hid your daughter, he made sure it would never be discovered accidentally."

"If it isn't there, we may have to swim back," observed Gareth. "After flying a full day out I don't know if I'll have the strength to make it back to shore."

I took my gauntlet off to let him gauge the power I had taken from the Iron Heart Chamber. "If necessary, I can get us back."

Noting the immense power I was radiating, Gareth made a different observation, "You don't need us at all. Why do you insist on dragging us along then?"

"You are the last living archmage, dragon or not," I said. "There are things there you should see. I may not be able to defeat Mal'goroth. I may not be able to fulfill Illeniel's promise. If I can't do both, the world is forfeit. You are the best hope of success if I fail. *That* is why I'm dragging you along."

"Those are things to share with a friend, an ally, not a slave," he remarked.

"I don't have those luxuries anymore. I'm gambling that you will prefer to pick up where I left off if I cannot complete these things."

A deep rumble came from the dragon. "You assume too much regarding my intentions."

I don't think so. Not after what happened last night with Moira Centyr. I kept my thoughts to myself, though. "Let's get going. We've talked enough," I told them.

Gareth snapped his teeth together with a loud crack, an action that I assumed meant he was angry, but before he could respond Moira held up her hand. "Arguing won't do us any good. We may as well see what this hidden island of his has in store for us," she said in a calming tone.

"If it is there," grumbled the dragon.

"As hard as it may be to believe, he hasn't shown himself to be a fool yet. Do you really doubt him, or do you just like bickering?" she asked pointedly.

Gareth gave her a hard stare before bending his foreleg for us to climb up. Muttering under his breath I could hear, "He's still an asshole." Considering the volume of a dragon's mutter, I had to assume he meant for me to hear him. I ignored the slight and took my place on his neck, a bit in front of his powerful shoulders.

It was an accurate assessment of my disposition these days, I admitted inwardly.

If Moira replied to him, it was silently and without including me.

*
**

We had been flying for an hour with the sun at our backs and the endless water stretched out for what seemed forever in every direction. The silence, except for the tireless beating of Gareth's wings, had become comfortable, and my thoughts had been drifting. Considering the past, my mistakes, my family, I wondered where I had gone wrong. *Correction, where 'he' went wrong.*

I was surprised when Moira's thoughts broke into my reverie, *There are some things you should know.*

I raised a mental eyebrow but didn't bother to formalize my question.

As you already know, the Centyr family was long known for their ability to create magical sentience. While you are not the result of a deliberate spell such as I might have woven, the nature of your condition is very similar.

I smiled inside my armor. *I'm not a gambling man, but I'd be willing to bet you're about to give me bad news.*

She glanced backward, and I could see the seriousness of her expression. I couldn't help but admire the improvement in her now human face. It conveyed her emotions much better than the stone and earth had.

The Centyr wizards had centuries to practice their craft, experimenting with our special gift, learning how to create stable personalities, she began.

Does this have something to do with the reason you didn't use live humans when you created the Shining Gods? I asked.

Yes.

I had already spent considerable time combing through the memories of my ancestor. Primarily the parts regarding the way he devised his enchantment, but also some of his conversation with the original Moira Centyr. *The primary reason was because of the cruelty involved in trapping a human soul. You would essentially be killing a living person and caging their soul. Isn't that what you told my ancestor?*

Now it was her turn to be surprised, and the emotion was easily read in her reply, *How would you know that?*

I told you, my sources are private, I answered calmly. *In any case, I already know what's happened to the real Mordecai. There isn't much I can do about it now, but when the time comes I plan to release him if I can find a way.* Because of Lyralliantha's order I couldn't relay the fact that I already had a method available to do so, but I had considered telling her once I was free of my compulsion.

There is more to it than that. Minds created from magic tend to be highly unstable. Even among the Centyr, it was a mark of great skill to create one that remained stable for more than a few years. Very few of us could manage one that showed true resilience.

That didn't sound encouraging. *What exactly do you mean by 'resilience'?* I asked.

Long lasting mental stability, the best of us could create complex minds that would remain stable indefinitely, similar to a living person's, she clarified.

Then why in the hell would you use them when you created the Shining Gods?

She sighed mentally, *I was one of the best. It was thought that they would remain stable for as long as they were needed, perhaps even forever.*

Well, you royally screwed that one up then, I admonished her. *I'm glad I'm not your handiwork, although you still seem to be holding up well.*

I was perhaps her best work, and I have spent much of the past millennium sleeping, until Mordecai arrived anyway. I do not think you will fare as well, she informed me bluntly.

So I'm likely to go insane. Where have I heard that before? I asked sarcastically. Much of my early career as a wizard, Mordecai's career anyway, had been spent fretting over the voices that everyone thought indicated incipient insanity.

She shook her head. *This is no joke. Given your unusual origin I cannot guess how long it will take, but you already show signs.*

Signs?

Irrational anger, violence, behavior not in keeping with your original's personality, she explained.

From what I can recall, he frequently became irritated when he was under stress. I don't think I've been that different, I countered.

Did he ever try to kill a friend? Cyhan's wounds did not seem minor.

That was in the heat of combat, I retorted, *he was out to kill me.*

Yet you were in no danger from him.

I could feel myself growing steadily angrier at the conversation. *He killed innocents.* I was referring to the 'real' Mordecai.

Only by accident, she rebuked me, *or when it was unavoidable.*

I fought to control myself. *What do you suggest, 'Oh Sage'?* I asked bitterly. *You must have some wisdom to guide me.*

Unfortunately, I do not. You must work quickly.

I growled in frustration. Even as an immortal the universe seemed keen on denying me the time I needed. *On the bright side, insanity can't be worse than what I've been living with so far,* I thought, but I kept that one to myself.

Chapter 17

Elise Thornbear stepped carefully from the carriage while one of the footmen hovered nearby, watching to see if she might need a hand while she descended the short steps. She nodded gratefully toward him, but despite her middling years she needed no assistance, she was still quite hale.

She had come to see Genevieve, the Queen of Lothion and her closest friend. In fact, that had been her main reason for moving to Albamarl. With her husband gone and her son busy with his new family, she had found much more to keep herself occupied moving in the rarified atmosphere that surrounded the royal court.

While she had kept the news of Mordecai's secret letter quiet, at least in regard to Penny, she felt that James should be aware of it. It would make an excellent topic of discussion with Ginny in any case.

As she crossed the courtyard she noticed a sturdy fellow, mostly bald, with a sallow complexion. He was entering his own carriage and while she was certain he must have seen her arrive; he took care not to look in her direction—probably with good reason, for she recognized him.

Addicus Shreve, she thought, naming him internally. *Why is he here?* Her heart sped up as she considered the implications. Pausing, she moved to address the head groomsman, "Excuse me young man, who is that gentleman leaving just now?"

The man was startled but answered readily enough, "Alan Shenwick, milady, a logistics consultant hired by Lord Hightower."

"I see," she said mildly, though the man's words had alarmed her. "How long has he been coming to the palace?"

The groom looked uncomfortable, "It really isn't my business to consider these things, milady."

Elise gave him a charitable smile, "I understand you aren't encouraged to gossip, but I'm to meet with Ginny today and I think she might remember the fellow you just pointed out. Surely you could speculate a bit for me?"

"Ginny, milady?"

She gave him a slightly sterner expression. "The Queen, Genevieve," she said to clarify.

"Oh!" he replied, eyes darting to the side anxiously. "Begging your pardon, the man has been coming for several weeks, though I'm told today was the last day of his commission, so he probably won't be back."

"Thank you," she answered graciously, before turning away. She struggled to keep her steps modest and evenly measured as she began making her way from the courtyard. Her deepest impulse was to scream and run, but she knew panic would help no one.

She stopped as soon as she had entered the main palace and a glance got her the attention of the chief chamberlain, a man named Adam. He came over quickly enough, bowing his head subserviently. As the chief among the palace staff he was a man of considerable power and influence, indeed, these days even many noble visitors hesitated to trouble him without good cause. Otherwise, the wait for an audience with the king could take considerably longer than it might if he were more favorably inclined.

Of course, he knew Lady Thornbear quite well since she visited almost daily. "Do you need something, milady?" he asked submissively.

"You are most observant," she said, complimenting him. "I will be seeing the Queen shortly, but I'd like you to relay a message to His Majesty, as well as his daughter if she is here today."

"What message, milady?"

"It is private, so if you'll provide me with pen and ink...," she said, letting her sentence trail away.

In no time at all he had brought a sheet of parchment and one of the newer steel tipped pens. She wasted no time drafting two identical notes, one for James and one for Ariadne. Folding them she passed them to Adam's waiting hand. "I trust you will not read them or allow them into any other hands but theirs," she said sternly.

"Of course, milady," he returned solemnly.

"Very good," she acknowledged. "Now if you will excuse me, I must be seeing the Queen now."

"Would you like an escort?" Adam asked promptly.

She smiled, "I know the way, and an escort would merely delay me. I'm sure the guards know me well enough by now."

She was, of course, correct. No one troubled her on her way to the private part of the palace reserved for the royal family and their closest friends and retainers. Most considered her the 'de facto' lady-in-waiting for the Queen, though she did not actually hold that position. A variety of men-at-arms bowed respectfully as she passed, but none questioned her. She reached Ginny within less than five minutes, walking at her fastest pace to cover the distance. The palace was quite large after all.

Genevieve smiled when she saw Lady Thornbear enter the room. Gesturing to a tea tray that had just been brought in, she greeted her friend, "Elly! You should try one of these scones. The cook says he's found a new recipe and I hear..."

Her words cut off abruptly as Elise dashed across the room to bat her hand aside, knocking the pastry she had held to the floor.

Shocked she started to exclaim, "What in the world has…"

Elise shushed her with a sharp look, holding one finger to her lips. "Are we alone?" Her eyes moved sideways to indicate the sides of the room, an unspoken reminder of the hidden guards that kept a watch over the royal family in virtually all areas of the palace.

Genevieve pursed her lips and then rose gracefully from her seat. She walked toward the door, looking back to make sure Elise was following her. They passed through two more rooms before greeting two guards as they entered the most private area of the royal living quarters. Once they were inside and the door was closed she questioned her friend, "Alright, Elise, what's got you so worked up?"

Lady Thornbear wasted no time. "As I left my carriage today I spotted a man I recognized, someone I knew from long ago, before I met Gram. I questioned the groomsman, and he told me that he'd been working in the palace for the past few weeks."

The Queen frowned, "Someone from the place where they had you working or…"

Elise shook her head negatively. "No, someone from the church itself, one of my teachers," she clarified before adding the final nail, "their master poisoner."

Genevieve's eyes opened wide. "They aren't even supposed to be in the city, how would they get such a person in here?"

"I don't know Ginny. The man has never been widely known. Only his students ever met him within the church itself, otherwise I wouldn't even have known who he was. Frankly, I'm surprised they haven't tried something like this before, unless they were worried about further retribution," said Elise. "But then, Mordecai is gone now, and there's a lot of growing support for the four churches with these new miracles."

"Enough," said the Queen. "What do you think he might have done? We have tasters, and the kitchen staff are carefully watched."

"I don't know. There are a dozen different things they might try. Poisoning you and James are only the most obvious, and there are poisons that take days or even weeks to show their effects; tasters won't guarantee your safety," answered Elise. "The first thing we need to do is make certain that James and your children know. None of you can eat or drink anything that has already been prepared for you, nor can you eat anything that is expected to reach your plates. That means dining with friends or getting your meals in some other unexpected manner. Your routine sources are the ones that are most vulnerable."

Genevieve responded, "I've already had my morning tea and that wasn't my first scone for the day."

"They may have been safe. We don't know when, where or even who they plan to poison," said Elise. "You might want to empty your stomach anyway." She gestured toward her own throat with a single finger.

The Queen grimaced but nodded. "I'll be back in a minute." She went to find a chamber pot.

While Genevieve was occupied Elise kept herself busy by borrowing the use of the writing desk. She penned another short missive before taking it to the guard outside the door. "Please have this carried to Sir Dorian Thornbear, my son. As of yesterday, he was staying at Lady Rose Hightower's house...," she finished by giving him the address, even though she had written it on the outside of her note.

"Forgive me, milady," said the guard, after patiently letting her finish, "I am not allowed to leave my post under any circumstances. There is a bell pull to summon one of the servants for other purposes..."

"I don't have time to wait. Find the chamberlain; tell him the queen wants this sent by runner immediately. *Not* the regular mail, she wants a runner sent *now,*" she used a tone indicated she would brook no delays.

Giving his fellow guardsman a look, the fellow took the note and promptly left.

Lady Thornbear turned to the second guard, "What's your name?"

"Jonathan Greenly, milady," he answered promptly.

She nodded, "Do not report your fellow guard for leaving his post, do you understand? I know how you people operate. If he gets in trouble for obeying the Queen's order I'll see you whipped and your commander can be damned. Have I made myself clear?"

The man swallowed visibly, "Yes, milady."

She gave him a gracious smile and closed the door. When Genevieve returned from her purge Elise spent a few minutes explaining the notes, both to Ariadne and James as well as her newest note to Dorian.

The Queen took in the information quickly. "My daughter is going over some of the royal accounts this morning, so she'll probably be with the chief factor and the head accountant. James won't get your message for at least an hour though; he's meeting with Tremont and some of the other lords this morning. Your note will most likely be held at the door until he finishes with them," Genevieve informed her.

Elise worried but she knew that would have to be good enough. *If his meeting lasts too long, we'll just have to make a scene, but that can wait until Dorian gets here,* she thought to herself.

James was gritting his teeth again. It was a habit that Ginny had frequently cautioned him about, warning that he would damage his teeth over time, but since he had taken the throne he found it difficult to stop. Today he did it because he was meeting with the more powerful lords of Lothion, men whose lands and power made them important, and while each of them owed their allegiance to the king, any one of them could be a source of serious problems if they decided to rebel, especially if the others didn't unite behind their sovereign.

His eyes narrowed as he came to the double doors that protected the small conference chamber. Four men stood guard there as usual, but their livery was that of Hightower rather than the royal design. "Who are these men?" he asked Mathias, the guard captain who was escorting him.

"Many of the guardsmen are down with the flux this morning, Your Majesty. Possibly something they ate last night. Lord Hightower sent a large contingent of his men to manage palace security until things get back to normal," replied Mathias promptly.

James stopped, "How many are ill?"

"Almost three in four, Your Majesty, everyone who ate at the barracks mess last night. I've recalled those that were on leave. Luckily I usually eat with my family, or I'd be down with it too."

"How about the other staff?" asked James.

"They seem to be fine. I have men looking into it, but at the moment it seems to have only been the barracks food that was affected. Those eating at the common tables haven't had any sickness."

The King resumed walking, "Do you have enough men to guarantee the palace security?"

Mathias nodded, "For now, Your Majesty. Lord Hightower's men have allowed me to cover the essentials, though I imagine the city guard may be shorthanded now."

"Let us hope the city doesn't come under attack then," said the King wryly.

One of the guards held the door as they entered, announcing James' entrance loudly to the men gathered within. The room held a moderately sized table with eight chairs. Behind four of them stood some of the most powerful lords in the realm, waiting for their monarch to take his seat before they themselves could take their places: Lord Andrew Tremont, Duke of Tremont; Lord John Airedale, Count and landowner of massive tracts of forests in the east; Lord Martin Balistair, Earl of Balistair and owner of some of the most productive farming regions in the nation; Lord Brad Cantley, Duke of Cantley and master of almost half of the kingdom's shipping trade; and Lord Lyle Surrey, Baron of Surrey and many other coastal estates.

Three seats had no one standing behind them, those of Count Malvern and Lord Hightower, as well as the seat belonging to the Duke of Lancaster. Count Malvern had been unable to make the journey to the capital because of age and declining health. As for the Lancaster seat, while Roland had recently been given the title of Duke, he had requested a pardon to be absent from this meeting. He was still ill at ease with his new responsibilities, a matter that probably worried his father.

James hadn't expected Lord Hightower to be missing. Turning his head he spoke to Mathias, "Where is Hightower?"

"I'm afraid he is also ill today, Your Majesty," responded the captain.

The eighth seat (actually the *first* seat, according to protocol) belonged to the King himself. James sat carefully while Mathias held his chair. Once he had taken his place, he motioned to the other men in the room, "You may be seated." Mathias stood behind and slightly to the right of the King, his job being to safeguard James' well-being.

"I'd like to thank everyone for their trouble coming today, especially those of you who had to travel," began James. He didn't bother using the royal 'we' for this occasion. The yearly meeting of the High Council, attended by all the noblemen of Lothion would begin in another week, but this meeting was reserved for those with the most influence. It had started centuries before as a way of ensuring that the greater powers of the kingdom agreed upon major matters in preparation for the more general gathering. Despite the layers of tradition that had settled upon it, this meeting was still far more informal.

Andrew, Duke of Tremont, interrupted, "I cannot help but notice your son's absence. Malvern is understandable, but Lancaster is not so far, especially when you consider the new World Road your pet wizard built."

To speak out of turn, without invitation, was a major breech of etiquette, eliciting a gasp from the other men in the room. Mathias tensed at the insult, but James held up his hand, "You overstep yourself Tremont. Do not think your position shields you from the responsibilities of protocol."

Andrew Tremont stood, sliding his chair back. It was an even greater insult to rise without permission, but it didn't seem to worry the man. "I think we've all had just about enough of your protocol, *James,*" he replied, sneering as he referred to the King by his first name. While the two men had been friends once, in their youth, it was beyond the pale now for him to take such liberties.

James Lancaster's eyes took in the table with a glance. John Airedale seemed visibly affronted at Tremont's behavior, but the other notables seemed different—nervous rather than shocked. That alone told him that Tremont's behavior was anything but reckless, the man was planning something.

James stood. "What's your game, Andrew? You wouldn't stick your neck out like this unless you thought you had something to gain, so why don't you go ahead and get it out in the open."

Andrew Tremont laughed, "No game, old friend. You've had a good run, but your time is done. Your wizard is gone, and the gods are angry with you for your blasphemy. It's as simple as that; the people need a ruler who will respect the gods."

"And I'll bet you think you're the man for the job," said James. "We'll see whether your opinion changes after you've been in prison a while." The last thing he needed at this point was to be forced to jail the most prominent of his nobles, but Tremont had left him no choice. "Captain, have him taken away."

"Yes, Your Majesty," said Mathias before signaling the hidden watchers to send in the guardsmen.

Andrew Tremont merely laughed, a smile on his lips. The doors opened as the guardsmen on duty entered, but rather than putting hands on him, they raised crossbows, pointing them at James Lancaster.

Chairs clattered as the men seated at the table abandoned their chairs, moving to the sides of the room— out of the line of fire. Captain Mathias stepped in front of his king, sword drawn. Lord Airedale had stepped back, but seemed visibly confused, shifting his gaze repeatedly between the crossbowmen and his monarch.

The air was taut with tension while Tremont smiled triumphantly at James Lancaster. John Airedale was the first to break the silence. "What are you doing Andrew?" he said, addressing Duke Tremont. "Have you lost your mind?!"

James answered him in even tones, "It's pretty clear what's happening, John. Tremont is planning to take the throne of Lothion. The first step is regicide."

Andrew Tremont laughed. "It appears you have a choice to make John."

Earl Balistair spoke then, "You told me Airedale was with us."

The Duke of Tremont glared at him angrily, "He will be. I knew John would vacillate, so I felt it would be better to present our proposal as a brute fact, rather than a vague possibility. It's amazing how people's opinions will firm up under pressure."

"How very like you, Andrew. You lied to each of them didn't you? Telling each in turn that the others had already agreed to your plan; do you think they'll be happy with such a treacherous king?" said James loudly. He could sense some hesitation in the other lords, and he knew the longer he kept them talking, the more likely they would be to lose their nerve. "You need not side with him gentlemen. I will pardon your treason now if you abandon his conspiracy."

"It's rather too late for that, James," replied Andrew Tremont, gesturing to the men with crossbows he ordered, "Shoot him."

No one moved. The guardsmen holding the weapons looked visibly shaken. "No one said we'd have to kill the King," announced one of them nervously.

Andrew swore and took one of his guardsmen's swords from him. "I'll do it myself then, since no one else has the balls." Facing Mathias he ordered, "Out of the way!"

The captain of the royal guard refused to step aside. "One step closer and I'll gut you like the pig you are Tremont!" he shouted back.

The Duke of Tremont looked at his bowmen, "Kill him."

His men had no problems shooting non-royalty; four bolts appeared in the captain's chest. He collapsed with a wheezing sigh, unable even to cry out, his lungs having been pierced. He died quickly.

John Airedale's eyes were on James, and the former Duke of Lancaster could see desperation in them. In that moment James wondered if his own eyes looked like that. *He wants to live, and he knows if he sides with me they'll kill him.* Looking back at the man James silently tried to forgive him, before reaching down to reclaim the guard captain's sword.

The guardsmen's weapons were empty, for they had all fired on the captain, and Andrew Tremont knew better than to let the King arm himself. Both Tremont and Lancaster had trained with swords since their youth, but he doubted his own ability to overcome his old rival in a one on one confrontation. Leaping forward he stabbed the King of Lothion as he tried to pry the sword from his dead bodyguard's hand.

The long blade passed through James' midsection, missing his lungs and heart though it tore through his liver and stomach. With a surge of adrenaline he made it to his feet, sword in hand, even as his shirt turned red from a wash of blood. "You were always afraid to face me weren't you Andrew?" he said, spitting the words at the Duke of Tremont. "You are a coward even to the end."

"This is your end old friend, not mine," said Andrew Tremont with a sad smile before adding, "It isn't Ginny's end either. I'll be paying her a visit soon."

James' eyes went wide, "You bastard! She won't have you."

"I won't give her much choice, and the people will accept the transition better if the old queen marries the new king," gloated Andrew.

James Lancaster took a step forward, trying to reach his murderer, but Tremont danced back nimbly. The other man knew it was only a matter of time now, better to let blood loss and fatigue do its work.

The next minute was a grotesque mockery as James tried to reach his opponent, bleeding and turning paler by the second as he lost blood. He gripped Mathias' sword in his right hand, while holding his belly wound with the left, vainly trying to keep his intestines from pushing outward as he moved. John Airedale stood to one side, silent even as tears streaked his cheeks.

Eventually James could no longer maintain his posture and grabbed a chair, trying to remain on his feet. Andrew stepped forward then, thrusting through the cushioned seat-back to pierce the King's chest once again. Falling backward in a futile attempt to escape the steel that had already wounded him, James collapsed on the floor.

Leaning over him, Andrew looked down with a pitiful expression. "How the mighty have fallen," he announced dramatically.

The King's eyes were glazed now, but he still managed to speak, "Spare my children, Andrew, please..."

Tremont smiled, "Your children are dead, and I'll be fucking your wife before your blood finishes cooling."

"I'll see you in..."

Andrew silenced his monarch with another thrust of cold steel, driving through the base of James' throat. "Fools should be dead and not heard."

Wiping the blade off with James' cloak, Andrew looked up at Count Airedale. "Have you made up your mind yet, John?"

John Airedale's voice warbled as he answered weakly, "The King is dead. Long live the King."

The Duke of Tremont grinned insanely. "I like the sound of that. Now, I wonder what our good Queen Genevieve is doing this morning."

Chapter 18

"If Your Highness would give me some more time, I'm certain we can sort out any discrepancies in the ledgers," said Willard, rubbing absently at his bald pate. It was a nervous habit he had developed in the years after losing his hair, though some teased him that he'd lost his hair because of his constant fussing with his head.

Ariadne gave him a severe look, "I understand that you'd prefer to have anyone else look at these books, rather than someone who might actually add up the columns, but that is exactly why I'm here."

The older man paled, "I hope you don't think I've committed any indiscretions, Your Highness. I have served as the royal purser under three kings now, and I've never stolen from the kingdom!" He ran his hand across his bare head again.

Ariadne sighed. King Edward had been no fool, and she really had no reason to doubt the royal purser's honesty. If he had been a thief, he would have been caught long ago, but she still believed it served a good purpose to keep those in charge of the gold honest. "I understand your worries, Willard. Rest assured that if all I find are minor mistakes or honest errors, there will be no problem, but my father has tasked me with reviewing your records. I will not come back next week. The whole point of this exercise is to check the books when no one is expecting it. Are we clear on this point?"

Willard let the air out of his chest with a defeated sigh, "Yes, Your Highness."

"Now, if you'll fetch the factor's ledgers as well, I can see if..." she paused, for a runner had appeared in the doorway, although the guard wouldn't yet let him pass. "Do you have something for me?" she asked, interrupting the man's explanation to her men.

He bowed deeply, "Yes, Your Highness, a note from Lady Thornbear. She seemed to feel it was quite urgent."

She stood and crossed over to him, holding out her hand, "Let me see." Her guards let him pass the folded sheet of paper to her. Opening it she scanned the brief message written there:

Act normally, but do not eat or drink anything until we have spoken. Please see me as soon as possible. I will be with your mother.
~Elise Thornbear

Puzzled she folded the paper and slipped it into a small purse she kept at her belt. "You'll be relieved to know that I have to leave for a bit Willard," she informed him, "but I will return as soon as I can."

"Should I put the ledgers away for now, Your Highness?" asked the purser.

She smiled at him. "I hope to be back in an hour or two. Don't pack them up until after lunch if I don't make it back before then." She turned to the messenger, "Thank you for the message, you may return to your duties now."

The man waited until she and her bodyguards had started down the hallway. It would have been improper to walk ahead of the princess, even if he might have taken a faster pace. Instead he followed quietly a few feet behind them. As they went she heard a commotion ahead, from the direction of the stairs. It sounded distinctly like fighting.

The two men with her tensed, drawing their swords and moving to put themselves in front of her when the door to the stairs crashed open, and the body of a newly killed soldier fell through. He wore the King's livery.

From the noise it sounded as if quite a battle was unfolding on the stairs.

Ariadne Lancaster was stunned, and she stood staring dumbly at the bleeding form lying on the stone floor some twenty feet ahead. No one else had yet emerged, but from the sound of things, the fighting was fierce. Luckily her guards reacted more quickly. One of them did the unthinkable; grabbing her arm he began hustling her in the other direction. His companion followed close behind. "What are you doing?" she asked once her mouth caught up with her observations.

"Your pardon, Highness, but whatever is happening, we need to get you safely clear of the area," answered the man who had her by the arm. The other man was looking for an alternative route from the corridor, but the only thing close at hand was a small storage room. Thrusting the door open, the two of them rushed her within, shutting the door behind them.

The messenger was still standing in the hall when armed men started boiling out of the stairwell. Some of them were wounded, but most seemed unharmed. All of them wore Hightower's colors. They rushed past the unarmed man without a word.

Inside the small room, Ariadne was feeling a bit claustrophobic. Dim light entered only from a large gap under the door, making it difficult to see. It was a small supply closet, barely five feet by five. The walls were lined with shelves holding parchment and vellum, binding materials and ink. "If there's something happening out there, shouldn't you be helping?" she asked her guards.

The one that had spoken earlier grimaced, "I understand, Highness, and I feel a coward hiding in here, but our first priority is your safety." A piercing scream from the offices she had just left reached their ears.

"She isn't here! A messenger came, and she left a minute ago."

Ariadne recognized Willard's voice. It was followed by a heavy sound, as if someone had struck something hard—or perhaps the sound of a body hitting the floor.

"They're going to find us," she cautioned her guards. "There aren't any other ways up from this part of the keep." The accountant's offices were situated outside the royal treasury, and for obvious reasons, there was only one corridor leading in or out of that part of the palace.

The guard that had been silent finally spoke, "Well we aren't just going to walk out and hand you over to them." In his nervousness he forgot to include the proper form of address.

"From the sound of it, there are over a dozen men out there. This room will be one of the first places they check when they start searching. Even if you kill several of them, you will still die. Let me show myself. They will take me prisoner, and you may live," she urged her guardians.

"Our duty is to protect you from anyone and everything; whether they wish to kill you or just take you prisoner makes no difference," replied the less talkative of the two men.

"What are your names?" she asked them, embarrassed that she hadn't bothered to learn them before.

"Alan," said the first guard. "Alan Wright, and this is Evan Brown." He gestured at the other guard, who bobbed his head as if they were meeting her for the first time.

"Why do you ask, Your Highness?" questioned Evan.

"If people are going to give their lives for me, then I think I damn well ought to know their names," she said in a fierce whisper.

The noise outside indicated that the invaders were returning from the office. "You there, have you seen Princess Ariadne?!" She guessed they must be questioning the messenger who had been in the hallway.

"Yes, sir, I have," the man returned in a shaky voice. Alan and Evan both tensed, for the man was standing not far from the door they hid behind.

"Where?"

"She was in that office, when I came to bring her a message. She left after that. She was in a terrible hurry," replied the messenger.

"Where did she go?"

"Up the stairs, sir, that's the only way out of here!"

A thump resounded through the door, followed by a cry of pain from the messenger. "We just came down those stairs, you lying cretin! If you just delivered the message, we would have seen her!"

"Please, sir! I came five or ten minutes ago. I swear! She went ahead of me! I was just dawdling here. I knew they'd put me to work again as soon as I got back!" pleaded the messenger.

There was a brief pause, "You men, get your asses up the stairs double quick! Find her before she finds help! You three stay with me. We need to search this area, in case this idiot is lying to us."

The sound of boots signaled the hurried pursuit of most of the armed men, but as soon as they had gone, Ariadne heard the one in the hall speak again. "If I find her down here, I'll kill you for lying," he growled at the messenger.

"No, sir! I'm too lazy to lie," answered the man pitifully. Another thump and a howl rewarded him for his words.

Ariadne glanced at her protectors. Their swords were out, and their faces were grim. They knew there weren't many places to search, and their hiding place would probably be the first to be examined. She put her hand on the door handle and nodded at Alan and Evan.

"Even if you're truthful and lazy I..." began the invader but he was interrupted by a crash from behind him.

The princess flung the door wide with a bang while her two men at arms rushed out. The messenger lay on the floor less than ten feet away with four men standing around him. Two of them were wounded immediately as Alan and Evan leapt forward with their swords, hacking at the necks of those closest to them. Blood was everywhere, and the corridor was a chaotic mess of struggling bodies within seconds.

Despite their surprise, the fight soon became a deadly standoff as Ariadne watched her protectors trading blows with the men wearing Hightower's colors. The combatants seemed evenly matched, and the invaders fought cautiously, defending themselves rather than aggressively pressing their attacks.

They only need to buy time. We'll be outnumbered if their companions return, noted Ariadne grimly. That observation disturbed her deeply, for it meant that not only was she still trapped, but it also implied that the men felt they controlled the palace itself. They weren't worried the palace guard might rescue her.

She needed to tip the balance in their favor, for time wasn't on their side, but the only weapon she had was a steel bodkin hidden in her dress, a gift from Rose Hightower years before. She drew the blade out and held it in front of her. The weapon seemed small and inadequate in her hand when compared to the bulky men in leather cuirasses. Each of them bore a longsword that dwarfed her small blade, and she probably weighed less than half what the smallest of them did.

Searching frantically for something she could use to help her guardsmen, she almost failed to see the messenger's next action. Both sides had ignored him once the fight began, but he still lay sprawled on the floor a short distance behind the invaders. He had been badly beaten, but he rose on his hands and knees, crawling toward the feet of his assailants.

Ariadne almost called to him before she realized what he meant to do, and then she closed her mouth quickly. Moments later one of the men backed into him, tripping over the messenger to fall awkwardly on the stone floor. Before he could regain his feet, the messenger wrapped his arms around him, ignoring the armored man's kicks and punches as he struggled to free himself.

The fight was over quickly after that. Alan and Evan were easily able to overcome the remaining invader, before finishing off the one that the messenger was grappling with.

A ghastly silence came over them then, as they stared at the carnage around them. Her two protectors were gruesome to behold, and the messenger had a frightening collection of bruises and scrapes, one eye was rapidly swelling shut.

"What now, Princess?" asked Evan.

She stared at the three of them. In the space of a few short minutes Ariadne had seen more violence than she had since the attack on Lancaster years past. Her brain was numb and her inner observer took note. *You're going into shock.*

"We need to get upstairs first. We're trapped here with only one way in or out. Obviously there are more of them, and they seem to feel comfortable that the palace is largely under their control," said a calm voice. It took a moment before she realized it was her own. "That indicates that my father has somehow been isolated and is unable to rally the defenders."

"There may not be many defenders, Your Highness," said Alan. "Most of the palace garrison were sick this morning. Hightower's men were here to take up the slack."

"Do you think Hightower is trying to stage a coup?" asked Evan.

Ariadne interrupted, "Enough speculation, we need more information before we can make assumptions. Take off your tabards."

"Beggin' you pardon, Princess, but why?" queried Alan.

"There are probably too many to fight through. I want you to put on their tabards. If necessary you can 'escort' me past them," she explained.

Evan was aghast, "They're covered in blood! Are we supposed to pass as corpses?"

"Take a look at yourself," suggested Ariadne. "You've got as much blood on you as they do. Who is to say they didn't win this fight?" She looked over at the messenger, "You too. Change your colors. Put some armor on as well. That fellow looks about your size," she pointed at one of the dead men.

The messenger was visibly frightened. "But, Highness, I—I'm no warrior!"

"What's your name?"

"Harper—Gerold Harper, Your Highness," he answered.

She smiled at him, "Well, Gerold Harper, you've shown as much courage today as some men do in a lifetime. For now, you are my soldier, until the danger is past. Arm yourself and stand with me." As she spoke she could almost see her father's commanding figure, proud and tall. *He definitely would have said that,* she thought.

Changing tabards was quick and easy, but getting Gerold into unfamiliar armor took longer than Ariadne was comfortable with. Time dragged on, and with each passing second she feared one of the previous set of enemies would return. When at last they were ready, she was fairly chomping at the bit. "Let's go," she commanded, and without waiting she started toward the stairs.

The three men looked at each other silently behind her back, unspoken words passing between their eyes. "Just like her father," said Alan, voicing the thought on all their minds. They hurried to catch up.

Alan and Evan positioned themselves on either side of her, while she urged Gerold to take the lead. "Take my arms," she said, looking at her two guards. "If we encounter more of them, our story is that you've taken me prisoner."

They nodded and held her arms, though it made them uncomfortable to take such liberties. Neither of them remembered having done the same only minutes before. Adrenaline had done the thinking for them at the time.

On the stairs they found five dead men, two wearing the King's colors and three in Hightower's. Ariadne was still struggling to understand what was happening, but she strongly suspected that the men wearing Lord Hightower's livery were anything but 'his men'.

They stopped at the first landing. The door there lead to the ground floor of the palace. "Are you sure we should exit here, Your Highness?" Alan asked her.

"If we go higher, we could be trapped," she told him.

"There aren't really a lot of easy ways in or out here either," he countered, "the main gate and the two side gates are probably guarded by the enemy if they've come this far."

She nodded, "We need to discover who controls the gates. That will tell us much about the state of the palace interior, and provide our only route to escape if it should prove necessary."

"Shouldn't we try to get to the King?" asked Evan anxiously. "The meeting chamber is two floors above us."

Ariadne flinched inwardly at the thought. If the palace were under enemy control, she and her three companions might be the only ones capable of rescuing her father, while on the other hand if her father still retained some control reaching him might be the safest place she could find. *Either he's secure and trying to regain the palace, or he's been captured, in which case that's the last place I should go.* There were too many uncertainties.

"We don't know enough, but I doubt anyone would go this far without making sure they had the necessary resources to complete the job. To do otherwise is to sign your own death warrant. Therefore we'll operate on the assumption that our best hope is to escape. We'll know a lot more after we open this door," she said firmly.

Gerold opened the door while her two 'captors' led her out into the long hall that was one of the most heavily trafficked on that side of the palace. It led to the inner gardens at one end and the formal throne room at the other. In between it met numerous cross corridors that led to servants' areas, the kitchens, the laundry, and a miscellany of other rooms that kept the palace functioning. The barracks connected to the palace on the opposite side of the palace complex.

"Which way?" asked Alan quietly once they emerged. The hall was empty at the moment, but it probably wouldn't be for long.

"Head toward the center, we can turn there and make for the kitchens. We might be able to get outside to the small garden," she suggested. The small garden was the common name for the vegetable garden that the palace cook maintained. Unlike the decorative inner courtyard gardens, it actually connected to the outer ward, the area between the palace proper and the protective walls. It seemed like the most probable means for reaching the outer walls without attracting a lot of notice. The usual path around the throne room and through the great hall was almost certainly guarded.

They reached the wide common door to the kitchens easily, but once they entered they found a sea of staring eyes and silent fear. The cook, his assistants, the scullery boys, and most of the palace staff were gathered in the center of the huge room. There were two other doors leading into the kitchen, besides the one they had just used, and each was guarded by a pair of sullen faced men in Hightower's livery.

The two guards at the door they had just passed through looked at them with interest. "You found her? Why'd you bring her up then? His Lordship said to kill her straight away," questioned one of them.

A variety of things passed through Ariadne's mind in an instant. The revelation that they meant to kill, rather than capture her, indicated that someone wanted to rid the kingdom of Lancaster heirs. That meant they would also be trying to kill her parents, and Roland. *If they haven't already.*

Alan and Evan had gone utterly still, eyes on her as they tried to figure out whether she meant to keep up the fiction of her capture or try to run for it. The kitchen staff and other servants were also staring at her, unsure of what her presence portended.

Ariadne pulled her arms loose from Alan's grasp, jerked the long knife from Evan's belt and drove it through the thick leather of the enemy guard's chest with both hands. Surprised, the man staggered back, too shocked even to cry out as he slumped to the floor, dying. Alan and Evan were quick to respond, and drawing their swords they dispatched the second guard before the man realized they were his foes.

That left four invaders, two at each of the other doors. They were drawing their weapons now, shouting for the staff to stay still while they advanced toward the princess and her three guardians from two directions.

They had taken no more than a couple of steps when her voice rose above the confusion, "They're here to kill the King! Take up arms and drive them out!

No one moved. Frozen by fear, the kitchen staff and maids watched as the swordsmen closed on their princess and her three protectors. Gerold was visibly ill at ease with his weapon, and being outnumbered, it was likely that Evan and Alan would be overwhelmed quickly. Making matters worse, two more of the enemy appeared in the doorway behind them. It was now six to four.

"Careful boys, the bitch has teeth!" shouted one of the invaders, pointing at the man Ariadne had stabbed.

Desperate, Ariadne leapt sideways toward one of the stoves, before the circle could close in. Snatching a boiling pot from it, she ignored the sudden pain in her hands as she flung the contents at one of their foes. The boiling broth hit him solidly in the face. Blind and screaming he fell back.

Her attack seemed to galvanize the castle staff into action. Coming out of their paralysis, the cooks and maids began snatching up pots and pans, skewers and knives. The kitchen had no shortage of potentially deadly implements. Several grabbed soup pots and flung them at the warriors in Hightower's colors.

Their enemies were surprised and surrounded before they could adjust for the sudden change. The brawl that followed was rapid and ugly as they were struck by thrown pots and long skewers from one side, and Alan and Evan's swords when they turned their backs on them. Amazingly, neither Ariadne nor her guardians were injured, although one of the scullery boys received a bad burn to one of his arms when some thrown soup struck him by accident.

The servants were energized by their violent success, and Ariadne seized the moment. "Pick up their swords. Take their armor if you can wear it. Skewers and knives, use whatever you can find to arm yourselves! They won't take us without a fight," she said grimly.

They quickly did as she said, but one man voiced their uncertainty, "I'll gladly fight for you, Princess, but do you think we can win?" Everyone paused, waiting to hear her reply.

Ariadne Lancaster straightened up, instinctively making the most of her five foot three inch stature. She was a small woman, barely more than a girl, and her dress was ripped and bloodied. "It doesn't matter if I can win or not. The question is whether they can convince me that I should give up," she said in a quiet voice, barely loud enough to be heard.

It was a trick she had learned from watching her father address his men, whether they were powerful lords or simple servants. The room grew quiet as everyone tried to hear her, and she had their full attention now.

More loudly she repeated herself, "I'll say it again. It doesn't matter if we can win. The only thing that is important is whether they can convince us to give up. It doesn't matter if they have more swords, or men! Can they invade our home and trample us under? Is it our place to be obedient to the will of an aggressor simply because we don't *think* we can win?"

The room was deathly still now, and they had all unconsciously moved back a few feet, creating a clear space around her. Turning she looked each of them in the eye, one by one, letting them see her conviction.

"I say it *is not!*" she shouted, answering it for them. "I don't give a *damn*, whether they have more men or swords. I will fight. I will make them fight for every inch, and if I am beaten—I will spit in their eyes!"

A shout went up from the castle staff as they brandished rolling pins and iron pans above their heads.

"It doesn't matter if we can win! They *cannot* make us surrender!" she shouted, finishing her speech.

Chapter 19

The dragon was veering off to the right again, ever so slightly, sending us more northward.

You're changing course again, I told him mentally to avoid the complication of all the wind noise. *You need to head due west from here.*

I am heading due west, he argued.

No you aren't. The magic is interfering with your mind again.

I would sense something if there were magic nearby, and dragon minds are highly resistant to the types of magic that affect human minds, he informed me.

I sighed inwardly. *There are no 'dragon minds', you are the only one. Regardless, this magic isn't of human creation. We need to shield your mind with an enchantment, simple spells won't work.*

How do you intend to create an enchantment up here? I cannot simply stop. I am far too large to hover, he responded with a sarcastic note to his thoughts.

Then maybe you need to go on a diet! I shot back angrily. Once again I found my anger seemed to appear for very little reason, despite the fact that my overall level of emotion had been slowly dropping for the past two days.

Moira's amusement came across lightly. *I doubt a skinny dragon could carry both of us.*

Fly close to the water, I told him, ignoring her joke. *I will make a place where we can land and take care of the necessary enchantment.*

How?

Just fly low and slow, I instructed him.

A few minutes later we were skimming just a few feet above the surface, although our speed was still considerable. I removed my gauntlets and gave him one final instruction, *flare your wings as if you were landing.*

The wing beats stopped as he complied, and we dropped toward the surface of the water. Uttering a short phrase in Lycian, I used a bit of magic to make the waves stop. The ocean surface was as hard as stone now for a distance of some twenty yards in every direction. It was similar to what I had unknowingly done years ago when I first discovered my magic. *Correction, when he first discovered magic,* I thought. Keeping up with the distinction was tiring.

Once we were down, I brought out two sets of stones, the ones for my flying device as well as the ones that would create an enchanted shield. "You'll need to take a smaller form to fit inside this," I told Gareth.

"A human form?" he asked, skeptically.

"You can use that lizard-man crossover of yours if that makes you more comfortable," I explained. "The main thing is that you can't be much larger than we are." I gestured to Moira and myself.

Moira frowned, "Lizard-man?"

"You'll see," I answered.

In the span of less than half a minute, Gareth had shrunk and reformed into the same half-human, half reptile shape he had used when I had first met him. The ease and speed with which he shifted from one form to the other was nothing short of amazing.

"You certainly don't waste time," I said, somewhat admiringly.

He replied with an unsettling smile full of sharp teeth, "The family gift."

I hadn't given it much thought. "I thought it was an archmage talent."

Moira stepped in, "It is for us, but the Gaelyn wizards were all capable of full transformations, whether they were archmages or not."

I reviewed some of my ancestors' memories of Gareth and they agreed with what she had said. Having near limitless knowledge was a flawed gift in many ways. I often had to know what I wanted to know before I could remember it. It resulted in a number of blind spots.

"You were a genius even among the Gaelyn family," I muttered without thinking.

"I find your odd comments very disconcerting," replied Gareth. "At one moment you seem ignorant, and at another you seem to know things that shouldn't be possible."

Moira nodded her head, "It would help if you explained where your information comes from."

"Too bad."

She wasn't enthused by my response. I ignored the glare she gave me and uttered the words that would cause the stones to form my mostly transparent airship. The stone disc flew apart into its twenty eight separate pieces, six formed a hexagon above, and six formed an identical hexagon beneath. That was the 'top' and 'bottom' of my flying device, and they were separated by six feet to enable most people to stand upright within it. Twelve pieces formed a dodecagon midway between them, much larger than the hexagons, giving the overall airship a disc-like shape that, had it been more visible, would have looked something like a jeweler's diamond cut, if both sides looked like the top. The four remaining pieces helped round out the top and bottom, giving my device a more aerodynamic shape.

Gareth didn't look impressed, but I suspected his semi-reptilian face wasn't capable of such subtle expressions. At least that's how I chose to interpret his nonchalance as he stepped aboard. For Moira's part, she looked wistful, almost sad.

"Something wrong with it?" I asked her.

She shook her head as she entered. "No, not at all, it just reminds me of the past. The world that was lost when we fought Balinthor. It gives me hope that perhaps mankind can rise again. Perhaps we can rebuild the wonders of the past."

Her words touched something within me, but the only reaction that reached me was a spark of bitterness. "You mean 'they'," I corrected her. "You and I are not part of humankind."

"You're right of course, but I have had a lot of time to dwell on my existence. I like to think that our actions are more important than the truth of our origins. We can have meaning, even if we are ultimately fictitious," she stated with a certain conviction.

I filed that away under things to think about as I activated my second set of stones. These were my enchanted shield stones. While the flying airship created a sort of force-field around us, it wasn't meant to be protective. My shield stones on the other hand, could be set to protect us from almost any type of external force. More particularly, it should prevent the She'Har spellweave from affecting Gareth and Moira's minds. It would protect mine as well, but with my armor on, it wasn't really necessary.

Once I had finished, we were encased in a sort of double walled shield, the outer one provided the aerodynamic shape, while the inner would keep our minds free from external magic. Using my magic, I shaped the air around us and lifted us into the sky, propelling us forward with the wind.

The experience should have been as exhilarating as it had been the first time I had done it, ferrying Roland to see Marc, but it wasn't. My emotions had become much duller over the past two days, and consequently I felt only a faint thrill. Based upon what I knew, I figured I had only a couple more days before my emotional level became what I considered dangerously 'numb'.

And considering how much power I'm holding now, that wouldn't be wise.

I flew us close to the surface, staying only about twenty feet above the rolling ocean, following the proper course now. There was a sensation of almost intangible pressure against my shield stones, and while I couldn't yet see anything; that pressure told me we were getting closer to our goal.

"I really can't tell any difference in the direction you're taking," offered Gareth. "I was heading due west before."

Since he wasn't connected to my shield, he couldn't feel the magic it was keeping at bay. "Just wait," I told him. "It won't be much longer."

"Until what?"

That was when we finally passed through the illusion that had shielded the island from both our eyes and minds. Where only a moment before there had been nothing but endless waves in every direction, we now faced a truly enormous island. It was thirty miles across, judging from our current perspective, and the central region rose with several snowcapped peaks. The island was formed around those few mountains, with sweeping and deeply forested lowland reaching out to surround them. It was easily the size of the Lancaster and Cameron estates combined, with Arundel's thrown in for good measure.

"What the hell!?" shouted Gareth in alarm. Moira's reaction was more subdued, but I could tell she was surprised as well. "Where did that come from?"

"It was there all along," I supplied blandly. "Well, for the last two thousand years in any case."

"It's huge! I should have been able to see something that size from fifty miles away."

"Their magic was concealing it."

"Their magic?" Moira had chosen that moment to speak up.

"The She'Har."

She kept her calm demeanor. "I was taught to believe that they were all gone."

"Well, yes, and no. As you have seen already, one of them lay in stasis within my family's home. Her mate, the last remaining father-tree, dwells here," I said, beginning my explanation.

"So there's only one—besides her," said Gareth hoping to clarify.

I nodded.

"Then how in the world did he manage to cloak that entire island and hundreds of miles of ocean around it? Never mind the fact that I'm not even certain an enchantment could accomplish such a thing..."

It could, I started to say, but that was another topic. "It was done with a massive spellweaving. That's the term used to refer to the She'Har magic, which is similar in many ways to our enchanting, except for its rather more spontaneous attributes. Most spellweavings can be created as rapidly as you or I might cast a simple spell, but their nature is much more immutable..."

"We learned about that as children," interrupted Gareth. "They used to tell us about it in our history lessons. I just never expected to ever encounter them."

"You're about to encounter a lot more than illusions once we land," I informed them both. "The entire island is most likely guarded by the Kriteck, and they've had a couple thousand years to fine tune their defenses."

"The 'Kriteck'?" questioned Moira.

"Think of them as the guardians and soldiers of the She'Har, but they're a bit more complicated than that. The father-tree can create them in any form nec...," I began.

Gareth interrupted again, "You just told us there was only one here."

I nodded, suppressing my irritation. "That's right. The Kriteck aren't considered in the same way that the She'Har and their children are. They're temporary and sterile. They only survive two to three months, and they possess only as much intelligence as the father-tree endows them with. Some of them are less intelligent than your average dog, while others may be as smart as you and I. It all depends on what the father-tree has in mind when it creates them."

"How many of these—things, could there be?" said Moira.

I shrugged, "I have no way of knowing. A lot, a few, it depends in part on their size and complexity. He could produce legions of tiny ones, a few very large ones, and anything you can imagine in between. The main limitation is how many he can *grow* in a given time span, because they all expire within a few months. The bigger the father-tree, the more he can produce."

"Why would it produce small ones?" asked Gareth. "Wouldn't they be too small to fight effectively?"

I grimaced. "Two thousand years ago humanity was nearly wiped out by very small ones. They were so small you almost couldn't see them without a magnifying glass. A soldier can't fight what he can't find."

"How would something that small hurt someone?"

"It's a long story, one we really don't have time for today. The important thing to realize is that the Kriteck could be anywhere and almost any size. The larger ones can use magic, and there could be a lot of them, so diplomacy is paramount," I explained.

Gareth grinned, showing a mouth full of uncomfortably sharp teeth, "So don't start any pissing matches. Don't worry."

Moira seemed puzzled. "There's one thing that bothers me. If this 'father-tree' you keep talking about is that powerful, why didn't it finish the war with humanity? Why are we still here?"

Her words brought a lot of uncomfortable memories to the surface, things that were best left unsaid, at least for now. "This one is the one that saved us from the She'Har."

"You've left a lot out of your story. Why did he help us, when he should have been our enemy? Surely he has a name? You haven't mentioned it yet, but with as much information as you seem to have, you must know it."

Her questions were probing areas I didn't really want to discuss. *A name?* I thought to myself, *the only one that would mean anything to you is Illeniel, and I certainly don't feel like explaining that right now.* "If you need a name you could think of him as 'Tennick'," I suggested.

"That's a rather human surname," she observed. "I used to know several Tennicks. Why not just call him 'Smith' if you're going to make things up just to satisfy my curiosity."

Plainly she thought I was lying. "Whatever you prefer," I said noncommittally, "but his name is Tennick."

We were almost to the shore, a thin strip of beach overshadowed by a looming jungle of trees and vines, when we got our first sign that the island was inhabited. Lines of power shot forth from three locations to grapple with our airship. Our forward progress slowed dramatically, and I didn't bother fighting their efforts. We weren't here to start a war, quite the opposite.

"Is that them?"

That was Gareth, tension written in his posture. I nodded, "The Kriteck—yes, they won't let us near the tree until we've gotten permission." They were drawing us in now, and I had given up any pretense of controlling our movement. Our craft came slowly down to land on the beach. A delegation emerged from the trees to meet us.

The creatures that came forward to greet us looked like something from a lunatic's worst nightmare. Two of them had the appearance of something like a praying mantis, if praying mantises were seven feet tall. Their bodies were covered in a black chitin looking substance, layers of hard armor, which if you were to examine closely you would discover that it had more in common with wood than chitin. Another slunk forward on four legs looking much like a massive cat covered in dark spikes rather than fur, it was at least twice the size of a tiger.

A rough but vaguely human-like voice issued from one of the mantis-like forms, but the language was nearly unintelligible.

"What was that?" said Gareth. "I couldn't understand."

"I think it said 'purpose'," suggested Moira.

The words had brought more memories to the fore. "It was our language, but the dialect is very old," I explained. "They asked us to state our purpose." Addressing the Kriteck I responded, but not with the same tongue. While I could understand the old human dialect, I wasn't sure I could replicate it properly. It was similar to my own language but had a very different system of pronunciation. Instead I used the language of the She'Har, "We have come to see the father."

"That is not possible."

"I have come to present information about the father's kianthi," I explained.

"Present your information to us," they responded.

I thought hard for a minute, staring at them. Tennick had become a lot more like the She'Har than I had anticipated, and his Kriteck reflected that. With a few words I disassembled our shield and our airship, then I recreated the enchanted shield, but this time I left myself outside of it. It now protected Gareth and Moira.

"What are you doing?" asked Gareth.

Don't leave the shield, I told them both silently, *if you do, they will be able to use you against me. Normal shields won't keep their spellweavings out.*

You aren't going to fight them are you? asked Moira with some concern.

I hope not. If I do I will lose, in which case Gareth must destroy the island before they breach the shield around you, I explained.

What? How? Why? Gareth seemed alarmed.

I gave him my most charming wink. *The island was created by an archmage, and it can be destroyed in the same fashion.* I looked down, indicating the earth beneath us. *If they try to take us by force, you must make sure the father-tree doesn't survive.*

I'm not sure if that's possible for me, Gareth relayed uncertainly.

I had already wasted too much time. Returning my attention to the Kriteck I addressed them, "You must take me to the father. She sent me here to assist with reuniting her with her kianthi."

"She is not here," said one of the mantis-like creatures.

"You will not approach the father," added another. "You must give us your information."

"I will give you nothing until I have spoken with the father," I answered adamantly.

What are you saying? asked Moira silently; neither she nor Gareth could understand the ancient tongue.

I'm negotiating. Don't distract me, I replied.

Apparently I was the only one that felt that way, though. "We will take the information," came the voice of the tiger-like Kriteck, while simultaneously its magic sprang forth. Spellweavings struck me from three sides, attempting to reach what passed for my mind.

The armor protected me from most of it, but it wasn't meant to be an absolute protection, not like the shield I had placed around my two companions. The She'Har magics were tenacious, and they writhed and wove, seeking the openings in my suit; like living things they were worming their way inward.

I bore the might of a god, but my power would be useless once their spells reached me. Similarly, my magic would be all but useless against my opponents directly; something human wizards had once had to learn the hard way. Kneeling, I thrust my hands into the ground, channeling my power crudely but effectively. I didn't bother attacking *them* with my magic; I simply removed the ground from beneath them.

It was a tactic my original-self had once used against Cyhan. The three Kriteck disappeared, falling and then being swallowed as I buried them with the sand that flowed back over the holes I had created. I acted with such speed and force I hoped the sand would crush them, but their bodies were far too resilient for such an easy victory. I drew my sword and held it horizontally in front of me, waiting for them to unearth themselves.

I didn't have to wait long. Within seconds their power made itself felt, thrusting the sand apart and downward as they began to rise from their ineffective tombs.

Sweeping my sword in a sideways arc the line of power I channeled down the runed blade of my sword and neatly bisected each of them as they appeared one by one, cutting through their armored bodies with ease.

"You should have thought about your defense more. Overconfidence is a killer," I told their bodies somewhat smugly.

Gareth gave me an odd look. "You said you would lose."

"Try not to sound so hopeful," I returned. "This isn't a victory though, there will be more and they'll be more cautious. If they fight smart I can't win."

More were approaching already. I could sense them moving, large and small, through the dense forest. They made no attempt to hide themselves as they closed upon us.

"Let me speak to the father!" I shouted in their language. "There is no need for conflict. I am here to help, but if you try to force my hand, I will destroy this island!" I wasn't sure I could follow through on my threat. With as much power as I currently held it might be technically possible, but their spellweavings might be able to control or absorb such a crude attack. Realistically, Gareth's ability as an archmage was the best hope for that type of retribution, but I doubted he would be allowed the time it would take him.

More importantly, that wasn't my mission.

They were around us now, fifty yards out and remaining still. Large and small, in forms that flew, climbed, and crawled, they waited. The smallest of them had very little aura, but the larger ones glowed with power in my magesight. They were poised to wipe us out of existence.

A tense minute passed before one of them spoke, "The father has awoken. He would speak with you."

"That is all I could wish for," I answered. "My companions will be unharmed until I return." I said it as a declaration, but there was certainly a question in my mind.

"The father wishes to see them as well."

That was unexpected. Considering their current level of paranoia I hadn't thought they would allow all three of us that close to the tree. Then again, the decision had obviously come from Tennick, and he must be curious.

I gave the formal bow expected in such situations, a sort of half bow with a sweeping flourish, but it was wasted on the Kriteck. They were not created for courtesy or diplomacy, they were created for protection and their minds were not overly cluttered with etiquette. Why bother, when they would only live a few months?

They led us on a narrow path through the largely untamed wilderness. It was evident that if we had not been with them they would have moved much more rapidly. Indeed, if we hadn't been worried about creating an incident it would have been much faster for us to fly, either with my machine or via dragon-back. Neither Gareth nor Moira suggested such a thing, though. We walked and we didn't speak unnecessarily.

We passed a multitude of island life, small mammals and birds mostly, but a few island deer as well. None of them showed the slightest sign of fear at our passing. Large predators were noticeably absent and it was clear that humans were a novelty here. The fauna here had never been hunted.

Our journey took hours and I had no idea how much further we still had to go. My magesight's range was limited and my normal vision was completely occluded by the jungle canopy. I knew I should be looking for a massive tree, but until we got within a mile or so of it I would have no way of knowing it was close. It was nearly dark when we finally reached it.

"What is that?" asked Gareth quietly.

He hadn't specified what the source of his question was, but I imagined it must be our destination. "This armor impedes my senses somewhat, but you're probably talking about Tennick. How far away are we?" I responded.

"About a mile and a half," said Gareth, "If that's really him. It's huge."

Fifteen minutes later I was able to confirm his observation, "That's him." The tree in question was some sixty feet in diameter at the base and it rose up over four hundred feet in height. "He's done well for two thousand years."

"Done well? Do they get bigger than this?" asked Gareth incredulously.

I shrugged, "They can. The most rapid growth occurs in the first few hundred years. After that they slow down, but they never really stop growing. They have quite a bit of control over the process though, so it varies a lot."

"I don't understand. You talk as though you know them intimately," observed my companion.

I wasn't sure how to respond to that. Beyond the human memories I had inherited, the loshti also contained an incalculable record of the Illeniel She'Har going back over stretches of time that boggled human reason. "I know more than I should," I said and left it at that, but in my mind's eye I saw visions of the past, cities grown from thousands of such trees harmoniously linked together.

"What are those things rising up around it?" questioned Moira. "You said there was only one tree."

"Most likely they are offshoots. The father-tree can expand in a vegetative manner, sending up new parts of itself from the roots. Their cities were grown in a similar manner," I told her. "In this case I can't be sure but given the arrangements they might be specialized Kriteck."

"How so?"

"They create the smaller ones from fruiting bodies that grow from the main tree, but if something exceptionally large is necessary he could grow them like that, as large offshoots," I said, trying to explain.

Gareth spoke then, "Why would he make them that large?"

"I don't know," I replied, but inwardly I worried. The Kriteck were produced for two primary purposes only, defense and war.

Chapter 20

A loud knock sounded from the door, a heavy masculine rapping. The Queen's guard was usually more considerate before announcing visitors, and the King himself didn't bother knocking, which left only a few possibilities. The person at the door wasn't her guard and was therefore most likely to be a close friend or family member.

Genevieve glanced at Elise, the same thoughts passing unspoken between them. She nodded and Elise crossed to the door.

Opening it, she started speaking immediately, "Thank goodness you're here, Dorian. We've been..." Her words stopped short. Andrew, the Duke of Tremont, stood in the doorway. An odd smile graced his features. Behind him a large number of guardsmen in Hightower's livery filled the antechamber. The Queen's doormen were not in sight.

"You seem surprised," said Andrew his eyes bright with barely suppressed glee, or perhaps insanity would have been a better term.

No, thought Elise, *that's bloodlust, or blood and lust.* Her eyes darted over him, noting the stains on his clothing as well as his ruddy complexion. *He's drunk, but not from wine.* Her mind processed that information before reaching a looming abyss—the unthinkable had occurred. *No!* She stared at him in shock before bowing meekly, "Your Grace, your visit is most unexpected."

"Of course it is, bitch. Now get out of my way," he answered disdainfully, pushing her aside. His men began entering behind him. "Four should be sufficient," he commanded quietly. "Close the door. The rest can guard the hall."

Genevieve had not stirred from her seat. "Have you no knee for your Queen, Andrew?"

He laughed, "You were never *my* Queen, Ginny, but that is about to change. The time for genuflection is at an end." Glancing at Lady Thornbear, he spoke commandingly, "Take a seat, whore. Over there." He pointed at a chair to one side of the room.

Before Elise could move, Genevieve spoke up. "Not there, come sit beside me Elly." She indicated the chair closest to her.

Tremont looked amused, but he made no move to dispute the change in seating. "You always were a stubborn one, Ginny."

Genevieve looked at him with barely suppressed anger, "You were never this mad, Andrew. What have you done? Why are you here?"

"Why, I've come to discuss our wedding. Why else would I be here, Dearest?" he replied. Stepping forward, he took a seat across the table from the two women. But for the strange guardsmen in the room, they might have been about to have tea.

Genevieve Lancaster's eye twitched ever so slightly, but she gave no other sign of distress. Still, Elise could see the strain of the emotions playing under the surface of her friend's calm demeanor.

"You might recall that we are both already married," said Genevieve.

Andrew smiled, "Wrong on both counts."

The Queen's hand was shaking now, so she hid it in her lap, clutching her dress to keep it still. Desperate she looked at her friend, "Elly, would you be a dear and fetch some wine?" Looking back at her husband's murderer, she asked, "Would you care for a glass?"

Tremont licked his lips. "It's a bit early in the day, but I must admit I am a bit parched."

"Where were we?" said the Queen.

"I was just about to offer my condolences on the passing of your husband," said the duke smugly. "I also thought I might explain your current options to you," he added.

Genevieve froze for a second, and then her eyes went to the wall where a decorative dagger was displayed.

"Don't even think about that, Ginny," said Andrew soothingly.

"You killed him, didn't you?" she said bitterly. Her shoulders sagged slightly as the words left her lips.

"This isn't my blood," said the Duke of Tremont, lifting the front of his shirt. Elise placed three glasses of wine on the table.

"Presumptuous bitch!" he snarled at Lady Thornbear. Snatching up the glass she had placed before herself, he threw the contents in her face. "How dare you think to drink in the presence of your betters?"

Neither woman moved as an uncertain tension filled the room. At last the Queen spoke, "Please sit down, Elise. Andrew, I would thank you to be more considerate of Lady Thornbear." Lifting her wine, she drank half the glass in a long swallow.

"My apologies," said Andrew. "It's just that I am not used to sharing wine with whores. I shall try to be more tolerant." He lifted his glass to his lips before pausing. His eyes were on the two women, but neither so much as glanced at the other. He took the glass away and instead offered it to Elise. "In fact, take my glass, Lady Thornbear. My behavior was rude."

Elise's expression did little to disguise her hatred. "You are most kind, but I have lost my taste for wine."

"Drink it," he responded evenly, one hand moving to his sword. "Or would you rather I make your Queen drink instead?"

"You think I poisoned your wine?" said Lady Thornbear with a raised eyebrow. Reaching out she took the glass from his hand. She took a large drink before setting it on the table. "Perhaps that will satisfy your worries."

Andrew's expression changed to rage, and his hand swept and struck Elise with a heavy backhanded motion. She fell to the floor, stunned. "Try not to look so wounded. My men will take care of your concerns shortly," said Tremont venomously. Turning, he addressed Genevieve, "Let's get down to brass tacks, shall we?"

"You'll hang for this, bastard," replied Genevieve Lancaster. "But before that, why don't you lay out the details of your crimes for me." Her face showed a new resolve.

"Watch your tone, Ginny, else I may change my mind," warned Tremont.

She glared daggers at him, "Very well, what are these *options* you were rambling about?"

He smiled. "You can take a coward's death and face immediate execution, or you can be more rational and marry me. It would go a long way to ensuring stability during the transitional period."

"You think you can be king?"

"Someone must be," he countered.

"I have children," she answered.

Andrew's face assumed a mocking expression of false pity. "There has been a terrible fire in Lancaster. I am very sorry for your loss."

Genevieve's eyes started with tears, but her voice remained cold, "What of my daughter?"

"I have yet to decide, but if you spurn me, she will make an even better choice for Queen. She is still young enough to provide me with heirs after all," he said thoughtfully.

He will kill one of us regardless, thought Genevieve, *if he hasn't killed her already.* "Very well," she said, "Execute me. I prefer that to any alternative that includes taking to your bed." Disgust was written in her features. *My death might spare her life.*

He laughed, "Oh, I was afraid you might say that. Did you think I would be noble about your death? It won't be an easy one. I'll have my fill of you before I slit your lovely throat, Ginny. Then I'll feed your remains to the pigs, along with your husband's. After that we'll see what Ariadne thinks of *her* options."

Genevieve sighed before reaching out to take a glass from the table. Her hand passed over her own to grasp the one that Elise had offered to Tremont. She drained it in a single draught.

Elise gasped and started to rise, "No!"

Andrew Tremont was startled. "So it *was* poisoned! You nearly had me, bitch." He sneered at Lady Thornbear. Looking at Genevieve he added, "Don't think that will stop me. I'll have my pleasure of you before you die, and your daughter after that." On his feet now, he started to approach her.

"The poison is a potent one, and easily passed through the skin. I would encourage you to do just that," said Elise coldly, stopping him in his tracks.

Andrew growled in frustration, but he didn't move. Then he barked an order to his men, "You! You do it."

None of his men moved, fear and uncertainty in their faces.

As soon he looked away, the Queen lunged toward him, her hands scrabbling at his belt, seeking to draw his dagger. He struggled with her for a second before pummeling her to the floor with his gloved hand. A solid kick to the stomach made certain she didn't get back up.

Elise drew a slim bodkin from beneath her dress as she surged toward her friend's assailant. She nearly reached him before one of his men clubbed her shoulder with a heavy truncheon. Something popped as she fell, sending waves of pain radiating through her. Her right arm was numb, and the dagger fell from her grasp. Snatching it up with her left she threw it at Andrew.

Her aim was poor and it missed, slicing the Duke of Tremont's left cheek as it passed. The world went black as something struck her skull, and she shuddered painfully as more blows struck her body where she lay on the floor.

"Don't kill her, yet. I want to see whether she really is poisoned." That was Andrew's voice, though it sounded as if he was speaking in a cave. Elise's vision began to return but it was blurry and disjointed. Someone lay sprawled nearby. She assumed it was Genevieve.

"Watch them," said the Duke of Tremont. "I'll be back shortly. Once the palace is secure we can lock them up."

After he had gone, the two women lay in silence. Elise couldn't be sure, but she thought there were still guards in the room, watching them. Not that it mattered; she could barely breathe, much less move. Some of her ribs had cracked, making it impossible to draw more than short desperate gasps of air, and her right arm was still numb. As her vision cleared, she found herself staring into Genevieve's eyes. The other woman had crawled closer, though she was clearly badly hurt as well.

"You shouldn't have drunk the wine, Ginny," said Elise between gasps.

The Queen of Lothion's reply was slow and pained, "I knew. It was better than living if what he said was true."

Elise Thornbear's vision grew blurry again as tears filled her eyes. "You were always braver than I was."

"Not true," answered Genevieve Lancaster sadly, "You drank it first. If I have to die, it could be worse. I don't want to be without them—or you, my best friend." Her hand snaked out, to close around Elise's.

Except the poison won't kill me, Ginny, thought Elise woefully. *My body is inured to it. You'll die without me.* She didn't say that however, clutching her friend's hand instead. "We'll be together 'til the end."

"We'll see them again," said Genevieve. "Gram and James will be waiting for us."

"I'm sure of it," answered Elise. Her breath was coming easier now, though the poison was making her nauseous. She would be sick for days, even without the injuries she had taken.

"And the children," said the dying queen with a catch in her throat.

"No!" argued Elise. "I know a liar when I hear one, Ginny. That man was lying. They're fine. He was tormenting you with lies."

"Is that true?" asked Genevieve drowsily. She had taken in much more of the wine and the poison was having its effect, causing her eyes to glaze.

"I swear it," said Elise with conviction. She had always been a good liar. "And when Dorian gets here, they'll pay in blood."

"Dorian was always a good boy."

"Mordecai too," said Elise.

Genevieve rolled her head a little, "My nephew is gone already."

"No," said Elise. "He isn't gone far enough, not for this lot. If Dorian doesn't kill them all, Mort will make them wish they were dead."

"Tell James I love him," said Genevieve, delirium was setting in.

Elise Thornbear felt her throat close as her emotions overwhelmed her. Finally she choked out, "We'll tell him together."

"You're right. I think I can see them…" Genevieve's voice tapered off. She did not speak again.

Chapter 21

Dorian sighed, his collar itched and the midday sun wasn't improving matters. His mother's note had been a welcome distraction. Rose had been planning to visit Penny, a reconciliation visit, and her anxiety over the matter had made her a real pleasure to be around. Her tension had transmitted itself to both Gram and their daughter Carissa, with the result being a confusing chaos.

The strange message from his mother had been almost a relief, arriving just in time to help extricate him from an awkward conversation. *It still seems odd, though. Mother has never asked me to come to the palace on such short notice before.*

The only part that really bothered him was that he had to change into his best clothes. His normal attire was rather more 'functional', and the rest of the time he wore armor. While his more formal clothes were slightly more comfortable than armor, they were just as hot, and he never felt quite as at ease in them.

Rose had already begun loading the children in the carriage when the messenger arrived, so he chivalrously offered to walk to the palace instead. Despite the heat and the extra time, he felt he had definitely gotten the better end of the bargain.

The Grandmaster of the Knights of Stone had just turned the last corner, and now he could see the palace looming ahead, several blocks away. The road he was on ended at the front gate, but something about it bothered him. *The gate is closed. Why is the gate closed?* He increased his pace without consciously thinking about it.

The guardsmen who were normally posted outside by the street were conspicuously absent. Dorian's eyes searched the top of the palace wall, but he failed to see the sentries who should be patrolling. That didn't mean much though; they might have just passed out of view. The gate bothered him anyway. *The gate is never closed, only the portcullises,* he thought, and it was true—except in time of war. In fact, the gate was so rarely closed that it merited special attention once yearly, to make still it was still in good working order.

He was within twenty yards now, so he decided to call out, "Ho, the gate!" He slowed his steps as well. A long minute passed, and Dorian repeated his call several times before a face appeared in one of the arrow slits immediately above the entrance.

"What do you want, making all that racket!?" said the guardsman.

The man's tone set Dorian's teeth on edge. If he had been wearing a hat he might have thrown it to the ground in anger, not that he was prone to such gestures. "I am here to see the Queen! Why is this gate closed?" he shouted back.

The stranger grinned, "The palace is closed today. Come back some other time."

"I will not come back! I was just summoned," said Dorian, hedging around the truth slightly. "Do you know who I am?!"

"A pompous prick?" answered the gatekeeper with a snicker. Dorian could hear several other men in the gatehouse begin to laugh as well.

"My name is Dorian Thornbear, and if you don't let me inside immediately there will be hell to pay," he informed the men within.

The man at the window started to reply when someone tugged on his sleeve. He leaned back and low whispers could be heard. When he reappeared, his expression had changed, "Do you mean *the* Dorian Thornbear, as in, *Sir* Dorian Thornbear?"

"Yes!" Dorian answered in exasperation.

"I don't believe you," replied the stranger smugly.

Dorian's eyes seemed to bulge outward, "Do you honestly think I would lie about that?" It had been well over a decade since someone had called him a liar.

"Well, anyone could *say* they was Dorian Thornbear, but you don't even look like him," answered the guard seriously.

Dorian stared at the man for a long moment, flabbergasted. "What am I supposed to look like?" he asked finally.

"For one thing you should be bigger."

"Everyone looks smaller when you're looking down on them from twenty feet up!" shouted Dorian. He had already lost his patience. He was now trying to decide whether to find it or do something questionable. This was the royal palace after all, and it didn't do to assault the King's residence, even if the gatekeeper was an ass.

"Look. They say Dorian Thornbear once threw a rider *and* his horse over his shoulder, so he'd have to be bigger than you," said the man.

Dorian took a deep breath, "I'd like to speak to your commander or anyone else, for that matter."

The fellow above seemed offended. "No need to get touchy. If you're really Dorian Thornbear, where is your armor? They say Sir Dorian always wears shining plate, and that he carries an enchanted greatsword that can cut through anything."

"I don't normally appear before Their Majesties accoutered for war!" Dorian was thinking hard now. Something terrible had happened. He had decided to keep up the blustering façade but inwardly he was certain that the man at the gate was most definitely *not* one of the King's men, and that led to all sorts of bad conclusions.

"Fair enough."

"Does that mean you believe me now?" asked Dorian. *If I had two of these daggers I could scale the wall easily,* he pondered silently, thinking of the assault of Doron's god-ridden warriors on Cameron Castle. Unfortunately he only had his longsword and one dagger, and while both were enchanted, it would be difficult to use the sword for climbing.

"Yeah, sure."

"Are you going to open the gate then?"

"One moment."

The man vanished, and Dorian wondered what would be next. *Probably crossbowmen,* he thought, *that would be the obvious thing, and here I am without my armor.* He was considering making a dash along the street. If he was going to try and scale the wall, it would be easier to do so somewhere where there weren't people waiting inside to shoot him. He was visibly surprised when the massive wooden gates began to open. The outer portcullis began rising as well.

The inner portcullis hadn't moved, though.

"Come on in, your Lordship," came the gatekeeper's voice.

It was a classic strategy for a castle under siege. The outer portcullis would be raised to allow some of the enemy into the entrance of the bailey, while the inner portcullis stayed down. Once they were between the two, the outer portcullis was dropped, and those trapped inside found themselves in a very bad place. The ceiling of the entryway had many 'murder-holes', openings that would allow the defenders to drop boiling pitch, molten lead, or in some cases to simply shoot their opponents.

Dorian decided it was a compliment that they felt the need to treat him as one might deal with an army. "I'll have to decline your courteous invitation," he announced.

"Suit yourself," said the man above.

It was about then that Dorian heard the sound of boots. It was a sound he was quite familiar with, the noise of a large company on the march. Looking behind, he saw a large group of soldiers approaching along the street following the same course he had. There were at least eighty of them, if not more. His eyes narrowed as he saw they wore Lord Hightower's colors, but his hope was short-lived. Years of experience with soldiers, and more specifically with Lord Hightower, had taught him what disciplined armsmen looked like, and these were anything but.

These were mercenaries, and the fact that they were hiding behind his father-in-law's livery sent a chill down his spine. *I can't let those men enter the palace,* he realized, and then he heard the sound of fighting from within the palace itself.

It all began to fall into place then. Someone was attempting a coup, they already had men within the palace, and they controlled the gate. The men approaching were their reinforcements. *All is not lost, or they wouldn't still be fighting. At least until those men get in there.* Dorian suddenly wished the gate was closed. *They'll be opening the inner portcullis once I'm dead.*

He was wrong on that count, for the inner portcullis now began to rise, opening the way for the oncoming soldiers. *I guess they don't think I'm that dangerous after all,* he noted.

The new arrivals were still some fifty yards away, and Dorian knew he had little time. Glancing around he spotted only one thing that might be useful, a large wagon parked across the lane, directly opposite the palace gate. Moving quickly to it, he dragged the empty vehicle to the palace entrance, parking it halfway in front of the entrance before turning it over to rest on its side.

The fighting within the gatehouse seemed to have intensified and his tormentor was no longer available to question him about his actions. The wagon now blocked nearly half of the ten yard wide entrance, leaving Dorian with only a fifteen or sixteen foot opening to guard. Dorian drew his sword. It seemed small in his hand as he examined the large contingent approaching him. *I need something bigger, otherwise this will take forever.*

The man commanding the disguised soldiers called out as he got closer, "You there! What do you think you're doing?"

Dorian faced the underside of the wagon, inspecting one of the heavy iron axles. It consisted primarily of a six foot rod that spanned the distance between two of the wheels. "I'm planning the defense of the palace. What does it look like!?" he shouted over his shoulder.

"Don't be foolish. Get that rubbish out of the way," ordered the mercenary captain.

Bracing himself, Dorian took two rapid swings with his sword, putting his entire body into them. Even with an enchanted sword, it wasn't easy cutting through an iron rod that was an inch in diameter; if it had been any thicker he might have reconsidered. The two wagon wheels fell away, and with a few more casual swings Dorian freed the axle from the hardware that secured it beneath the wagon frame. He sheathed his sword and hefted the iron rod, testing its weight. "I'll be with you in a moment," he told the impatient captain.

The rod weighed something less than twenty pounds, which would have made it far too heavy to use as a weapon for any length of time—for most people. It suited Dorian and his current needs almost perfectly. He gave his full attention to the mercenary captain now, who had just begun to give orders to his men.

"You should think carefully about this," he told the man.

The captain backed up, edging away from the iron staff. "If you don't drop that ridiculous weapon and stand aside I'll have you cut down," answered the scruffy officer.

The leader of the Knights of Stone measured the captain with his eyes before deciding to ignore the man. Raising his voice he spoke to the soldiers directly, "My name is Dorian Thornbear! Some of you may have heard of me, or not, it really doesn't matter. Today your master, whoever he may be, has sent you on an ill-considered mission. Inside the palace is a battle, and you have been sent to help consolidate some lordling's unlawful scheme to dethrone our King. You should turn back now if you wish to survive to see the morrow."

The soldiers responded with a mixture of laughter and whispers, although some of them looked vaguely uneasy. Their captain spoke again, "I think most of us have heard of Dorian Thornbear, not that it will do you any good. Where are your men, Lord Thornbear? Do you regret leaving them at home? Why don't you surrender?"

The unarmored knight looked at him sadly. "I do regret their absence, since without them I cannot offer you any quarter or mercy."

"Kill this lunatic," said the captain.

The words had barely left his lips before Dorian leapt forward, whipping his iron staff across in a powerful swing that struck the captain's helm before continuing on to break the arm of the soldier next to him. The mercenary officer collapsed, dead from the shock of the blow, while his aide screamed and fell back.

The soldiers already had their weapons out, and they tried to close on the lone warrior, but Dorian moved too quickly for that. His iron weapon was a blur of deadly momentum as he charged forward, sweeping men aside like broken dolls. Armor was no help against the crushing blows, and the weight of his weapon made it impossible to stop once it was in motion. One man tried to block his strike with a shield, only to have his forearm shattered by the force of Dorian's attack. Men cried out in pain, arms and legs mangled. Only those whose skulls were broken remained silent.

Break their morale first, thought the veteran knight, *then force them to come to me.* His forward charge had left the gap undefended, and some of the soldiers had shifted to bypass him. He retreated, taking those from behind, clearing the entrance once more. The battle paused as the now leaderless mercenaries stared at him from ten feet away. Nearly twenty men were down in various states of injury, six of those were dead, and the rest had broken bones. Almost a quarter of the enemy soldiers were no longer able to fight, and the rest seemed uncertain. No one wanted to approach the palace gate.

"Lose your taste for the fight yet, boys?!" shouted Dorian, taunting them. "Come closer and I'll give you more!" The mercenaries drew back at his ferocity, and Dorian stepped forward to bring the heel of his staff down upon the chest of one of his wounded opponents. An audible crack was heard as the man's ribs broke, and his moans changed into a sickening gurgling. "I told you, no quarter," said Dorian sadly.

A crossbow bolt flew by without warning, passing so quickly that Dorian was only aware of it from the feeling of air as it narrowly missed his nose. *I knew it was too good to last,* he thought ruefully. His eyes spotted several crossbowmen in the back readying their weapons, one of them having obviously just fired.

"Now you've done it," he announced loudly and charged forward.

The men standing before him fell over themselves as they scrambled to move out of his path, leaving the bowmen defenseless. Dorian's staff crushed the skull of the one that had fired and swept the weapon from another's hand as it passed. He glared at the others before walking back to his position at the gate. "I'll kill the next man who fires a quarrel at me!"

Dorian's shoulders itched from the weight of their eyes as he walked back. Several men pointed their crossbows at him, but none of them fired. They had lost their nerve, thoroughly intimidated by the seemingly unstoppable warrior. The only thing holding them together now was the safety of numbers.

"As I said a moment ago, since I'm alone, I don't have the luxury of offering you mercy or allowing you to surrender, but my duty is to guard this gate. That means if you choose to run, I can't give chase," declared the stalwart knight. "That's the only advice I can give you."

The mercenary troop had lost its will to fight and without their leader they were uncertain what to do. They retreated fifty feet while their squadron leaders spoke with each other, trying to decide the best course of action. Dorian smiled as he watched them arguing.

"Dorian is that you?"

It was a woman's voice, coming from the direction of the palace wall. Looking up he spotted Ariadne standing atop it. "Your Highness!" he shouted when he saw her. "Are you alright?"

She gazed at him curiously, "I'm the one guarded by a stone wall while you fight in the street and you ask if I'm alright? We control the gatehouse now. Get inside so we can close the portcullis!" A crossbow bolt nearly found its mark while she talked, forcing her to duck behind a merlon.

The Knight of Stone whirled back to the mercenaries, furious. "What did I tell you?!" Taking his staff in hand like a javelin, he drew his arm back and launched it toward the man who had fired the shot. The heavy metal rod struck the unfortunate fellow squarely in the chest, breaking his sternum. The crossbowman collapsed as

Dorian turned his back on them and walked through the palace gate. The outer portcullis descended behind him.

The princess met him inside the gatehouse, motioning him in through one of the inner doors. "In here," she told him, "It isn't safe in the courtyard." Her dress was torn and bloodied in several places, and she carried a heavy carving knife in one hand. A large group of men and women were with her inside the building.

"It isn't safe outside either," remarked Dorian as he ran his eyes over her motley assortment of servants and cooks. Most of them carried various implements from the kitchen; rolling pins, heavy pans, and assorted cutlery. Some of them had weapons that had probably been looted from the enemy, and a laundress carried a heavy wooden rod normally used to clean clothing; it might have seemed a laughable weapon, except for the bloodstains now adorning the wood. "When I saw you atop the wall I hoped you were in control of the palace. Why are you in the gatehouse?"

"The palace is swarming with soldiers, most of them in Hightower's livery," she informed him. "This seemed to be our only path to escape."

"Where are the men who were holding the gate against me?" asked Dorian.

Alan broke in, "Upstairs, in the room over the entrance, we left them where they died." He ducked his head as he saw Ariadne's annoyed glance. "Forgive me, Princess. I spoke out of turn."

Dorian led them up to double check the condition of the enemy. There were six of them in the small room, and they were very dead, stabbed and bludgeoned by an odd assortment of weapons. He spotted the man who had been taunting him from above the gate. "Shame he had to die," he observed aloud.

"Did you know him," asked the princess.

He shook his head, "No. He just reminded me of Mordecai, an excellent sense of sarcasm."

She gave him an odd look.

He shrugged, "I've been a fighter most of my life. After a while you learn to separate the violence from everything else, otherwise you go mad. He was my enemy, but he was probably also an interesting fellow to share a mug of ale with."

Evan interrupted then, he had been looking out one of the arrow slits, "Beggin' your pardon, Highness, but there's still a crowd of soldiers outside."

Dorian frowned. "I think I had them cowed but they've had some time to regroup now. They'll probably give us some trouble if we try to take you out by the main gate, Princess."

Ariadne looked worried, "There's also the matter of my mother and father."

And my mother, Dorian added mentally. "Do you know if they are still alive?"

"I have no way of knowing, but I fear the worst. I would probably be dead myself if it weren't for a message your lady mother sent to me. I was heading to meet her and Mother when we were nearly captured," she replied.

"She must have discovered something when she came to visit your mother this morning," supposed Dorian. "How did they take the palace?"

"Most of the palace guard took ill. Hightower's men came to replace them until they could recover. It appears that they were put in place for the express purpose of murdering my father," Ariadne informed him.

"They aren't Hightower's men," Dorian told her immediately. "These men are barely soldiers. The discipline of those I encountered in the street is deplorable. I suspect most of them are mercenaries, or the disguised servants of a degenerate lord."

"I never believed they were Lord Hightower's," she said, easing Dorian's fear. Lord Hightower was his father-in-law after all, so he was understandably worried. "The real question is who is behind this?"

"I wish I knew."

Ariadne looked thoughtful, after a second she spoke again, "I need your advice, Sir Dorian. How do you think we should we proceed from here?"

"At this point your first priority should be finding safe haven and it doesn't look like there are many options. I would suggest you aim to reach the Illeniel house. Penny is there, and once inside the enchantments should keep you safe. Hightower's residence may not be reliable by comparison." *In fact, my father-in-law might be dead at this point,* worried Dorian, but he didn't verbalize that sentiment. After a second he continued, "I may be able to get you safely past the mercenaries outside."

The princess seemed suspicious, "And what would you do after that?"

Dorian moved away and began stripping the armor from one of the dead soldiers. "My duty, Princess, to King and Country."

"Please be more specific."

Dorian thought the largest man's armor might be big enough to fit him, although it wasn't easy undressing a corpse. He glanced up at the princess. No matter what their circumstances she still remained Marc's younger sister in the back of his mind. "After I get you clear, I will return. Your mother and father are still here somewhere. I cannot abandon them if they may still be alive. If possible I will rescue them. There is also the matter of my own mother."

He rejected the idea of trying to wear the dead man's gambeson, its smell was prohibitive. Instead he decided to simply wear the chainmail over his finer clothes. They were thick enough that they should provide adequate padding, but he imagined Rose would be displeased with the result later. A simple round shield and plain metal helm completed his arming.

"Gather your folk and get ready to follow me out. Give me a ten second lead, and by the time your people reach them, they should be in disarray. You should also switch clothes with one of the...," Dorian began, planning their escape, but Ariadne interrupted.

"No," she said.

The heavyset knight was confused, "What?"

Ariadne repeated herself, "I said 'no'. I have no intention of leaving you to face this alone."

"That's foolish," returned Dorian. "You may be the only remaining heir, for we have no way of knowing how Roland fares."

"I agreed with you," she replied, "but your arrival has changed matters. We have a chance of salvaging something now, more so if you have people to help you."

Dorian looked at the motley collection of servants before returning his eyes to hers and lowering his voice, "How much help do you think this lot will be?"

"They fought their way free from inside the palace with me," she said defiantly. "They may not look like much, but there is fight in them."

"I can't condone this idea."

The princess gave him a cool glare, "Too bad. You will submit yourself to my command, Sir Dorian, and I command you to help me rescue my mother and father. Besides, if you do find one of them, or your own lady mother, you will need assistance. What if they're wounded? Can you fight and carry someone?"

"That's irrelevant," said Dorian. "My sworn duty is to the *King*, not you. I will see you to safety before doing anything else."

"They might both be dead."

"In that case, your brother will be elevated to sovereign," responded Dorian.

"Most usurpers take care to eliminate all descendants. There is a strong possibility that I am the only remaining heir," argued Ariadne. "If that is the case, then *I* am your sovereign."

Dorian groaned. Ariadne was giving him a headache. "You argue that your entire family may be slain, making you the next Queen, and my liege—so that you can order me to help you save them? Surely you see the contradiction in that." He studied the men and women who had fought to escape with their princess. Some of them were wounded and only three appeared to be actual guardsmen, but all of them held a certain look in their eyes. They had not lost their spirit.

How did she rally them like this? wondered Dorian. "How many of you are willing to follow our suicidal princess back into the palace to rescue the King?" he asked them.

A chorus of 'ayes' and other affirmative noises answered him as they raised their odd collection of weapons and implements. One of the guardsmen answered clearly, "Where she goes, we go."

"What's your name?" asked the Knight of Stone, focusing on the soldier who had spoken.

"Alan Wright, Your Lordship."

The guard next to him spoke up, "The same is true for me, Your Lordship." The third guard, who seemed subtly uncomfortable in his armor, nodded as well.

Dorian bowed before Ariadne. "Very well, Your Highness, if these good folk have decided to throw their lot in with yours I have no choice. I cannot force you to leave, nor can I keep you from following me, therefore I will make the best of it." Turning to her followers he began issuing commands, "Those of you still able, strip the bodies. If there's anything you can use, take it. Those of you who are wounded will remain here. Put on the enemy tabards and bar the doors when we leave. You will have the most important job. Hold the gatehouse until we return, it's probably our only hope for getting out of here alive. Those who are still capable of fighting will stay with the princess and me."

Ariadne looked hopeful, "Do you have a plan?"

"Honestly, I do not," said Dorian, grimacing. "The fact that you and your crew managed to escape and take the gatehouse tells me that the enemy didn't expect any armed resistance. Sometimes surprise is a more potent weapon than superior numbers. They must be aware of you by now, but I doubt they expect your group of surly servants to turn around and invade the palace."

She raised an eyebrow, "Surly servants?"

Dorian shrugged, "I kept bad company as a child and poor attempts at humor were a frequent offense." *Marcus and Mort would have laughed at my inept joke, but probably only from pity.* His absent friends were never far from his mind.

"They'll wish we was a lot less surly before we're done!" announced one of the scullery boys.

"Grab those spears," said Dorian. "They'll be a lot more effective in untrained hands than what most of you are carrying."

Chapter 22

We stood before the central trunk of the father-tree. Seeing its massive size up close with our normal vision made it seem all the more impressive. Tennick was *huge*. In terms of size, human kind had not seen anything like it in over two thousand years. *And this is what I'm going to bring back to the world?* I thought, questioning my motives again. Not that I had any choice in the matter at this point. Lyralliantha's commands would not be ignored.

"How do you speak to them?" asked Gareth. He and Moira stood beside me while a ring of Kriteck surrounded us, watchful that we did nothing harmful to the father-tree. "Can it communicate telepathically?"

"Yes," I said nodding, "When it's awake it can. But only the tree can initiate the exchange."

"I don't understand."

"You have to think like a tree, a really old tree. They don't actually sleep, their minds just move at a vastly slower pace than ours. They operate on an entirely different timescale than we do. When I say *awake,* I'm actually referring to special moments when the She'Har accelerate their thoughts. During times of emergency or stress they will speed up to more human-like speeds—mentally that is," I explained.

"So what do we do?" said Moira.

"We wait," I told her.

The loshti remains within my line despite a hundred generations. Your memories are clear, yet you are not my son.

The mental voice came with a powerful presence that swept over us. In some ways it was like the aura possessed by the gods, or myself now that I was heavy with power, yet there were subtle differences. As the father-tree's attention focused on us, I felt a sense of depth and complexity that was absent from my previous experiences. Tennick's mind swept over us, examining and studying. I had the feeling that he knew more about us within those first few seconds than even we were aware of.

Your son is dead. I am a poor copy, but still I am left to fulfill his will, I responded.

State your purposes, the presence demanded.

You have already seen within me. You know them, I replied.

I do. State them, so that I may know what 'you' know of them, said the last tree of the Illeniels.

I sighed inwardly, *the restoration of the She'Har and the preservation of your children.*

Our children, the mind of the first archmage informed me. Images flashed through my mind, of Matthew and Moira, little Conall, and tiny Irene, before I had been separated from them.

My first impulse was to deny that they were *my* children, since both Lyralliantha and Moira had made it clear to me that I was not the original Mordecai, but even as the thought started I realized that in every way that mattered, they were my children as well. *Yes, our children,* I agreed silently.

The Kriteck are very agitated. They expected the arrival of my Kianthi. It will be difficult to restrain them.

That puzzled me. *Do they not follow your will?*

In general, yes, but I created many of these with complex intellects, in preparation for the coming trials. Though their lives are short, they are stubborn and willful.

What trials? I asked.

You have seen the beginnings. The god-seeds have returned to this world, and Mal'goroth has upset the balance. There will be a reckoning. The struggle that is building will test existence itself.

'God-seeds' was an unusual word in the She'Har language. It might be more correct to translate it as 'spirit-servants', but it had no direct cognate in the human tongue. Tennick was referring to entities that we called the Dark Gods. *What will you do?* I questioned.

Ultimately, I am the cause for this disruption. Lyralliantha will help me to atone for my mistakes, but the burden of my sins will fall upon your shoulders. Your people will decide the fate of this world.

I didn't like the sound of that, but it was what I had expected. *What must I do?*

Lyra was wrong to bind you, just as you were wrong to bind those with you. The two beside you will be pivotal in the coming storm. Rely on their strength, trust them. Slavery will lead only to destruction. The Kriteck will accompany you. Lyra must be returned.

I felt a shift in the earth as if something had moved. Shifting my attention, my magesight revealed that four massive growths surrounding the father-tree had broken away. The newborn Kriteck unfolded, stretching massive wing-like appendages as they began to move. Their bark-like skin was covered with small vines, but as they moved I could see that they were shaped like a grotesque parody of Gareth's dragon form, except they were each easily twice his size. Their heads were much smaller in comparison to their bodies, and there was no visible mouth, just a multitude of eyes.

They lowered their bodies to the earth, and the forest around us came alive with movement. The Kriteck were climbing onto their massive flying brethren. I was amazed at their numbers, as well as their variety. Tennick had created them in many forms, small and large.

Bring my Kianthi to me, he commanded.
And then? I asked.
Then we go to war.

Chapter 23

"Keep that shield up, Your Highness," admonished Dorian. He had made Ariadne take one of the wooden round shields from the gatehouse. She couldn't wear any of the armor but he hoped it would offer her some protection.

She grunted, "It gets heavy, keeping it up all the time."

"Then put your dagger away and use both hands," replied Dorian. "I'm more worried about you catching a stray arrow than whether you can stab someone." They were inside the front entry hall now. The resistance so far had been minimal. Four guards had been stationed inside the doors but Dorian had killed them before Evan and Alan had even crossed the threshold behind him.

"Where are we going?" asked Gerold. It was the first time he had spoken since they met Dorian at the gatehouse and there was a nervous warble in his voice.

"The royal living suite," announced Ariadne. "Mother and Lady Thornbear were there when they sent me that message."

"Begging your pardon, Highness, but shouldn't we find the King first?" queried Alan.

The princess' face blanched for a moment, "I think we'll have a higher chance of success reaching my mother."

Dorian put a hand on Alan's shoulder and leaned close to his ear, "The King is most probably dead. They would have made sure of him first. The Queen *might* be alive."

Alan winced, "Forgive my presumptuousness, Your Highness."

Ariadne straightened her back and lifted her chin, "Never fear to speak to me openly, Alan, regardless of our current or future stations. Any that follow me today, fighting for my sake and for the sake of Lothion shall be held high in my regard." She raised her voice, making certain that those around her could hear, "I will never forget the bravery and loyalty of those who fight beside me today. You have inspired me with your courage and honor, whether you be man or maid. I will forever hold those with me now as dear to my heart as my own family."

The crowd around them gave a subdued cheer, raising spears, swords, cleavers, and one odd rolling pin over their heads. More than one eye was moist at hearing her sentiment.

"Let's get moving then," said Dorian, heading to the left into a side hall that would take them to the nearest staircase. The royal suite was two floors above them.

The first major resistance met them outside the stairs. A score of soldiers had been posted there to control access to the upper levels. Dorian could only assume that a similar number had been stationed at the other three sets of stairs in other parts of the palace. It didn't matter anyway, they had been spotted, and their only course at that point, was forward.

"Follow me, lads! For the Princess!" shouted Dorian to those behind him, and then he started forward. He walked at first, using long strides and a quick step. It gave those following a chance to find their courage as they followed his lead. He quickened his steps and was soon moving at a jog as their charge developed a steady, lethal momentum. At the end he leapt forward, dashing into the enemy to break their formation before his disorderly allies reached them.

He was met with spears and pole arms, but he swept them aside almost negligently, moving like a dancer despite the heavy chain he wore. The men facing him might have been standing still in comparison with his speed as he slipped through their weapons and began to bring his terrible sword to bear. The first two men were dead before he had passed between them, and then he moved sideways, slicing and killing those that held the spears, for they were the greatest threat to his friends.

Blood and confusion followed, and cries of pain echoed in the hall as men lost life and limb, mostly at Dorian Thornbear's hand. His speed and power, combined with a lifetime of practice and training, made the fight more of a slaughter than a contest, and the chaotic crew of weapon bearing palace servants that followed him made it a gory massacre as they fell upon the wounded he left behind him.

The fight was over almost as soon as it had begun, and Ariadne was grateful that their losses were few. One of the scullery boys had been stabbed through the thigh and another was dead. None of the enemy had survived.

"Not bad," said Dorian, looking at Evan. "Remember to keep the shield up, you keep letting it drop like that, and someone's going to take advantage." Turning to Alan he continued, "Your form was excellent, but you need to keep the elbow of your sword arm tucked in closer to your body. You'll have more power in your swing that way." He glanced at Gerold last, shaking his head a bit. Ariadne hadn't mentioned that he was actually a messenger, rather than a guardsman. "You need a lot of practice. For now though, just try to keep the shield in front of you. It does you no good at all if you keep it behind you while you lead with the sword."

Alan and Evan ducked their heads as Gerold answered, "Thank you, Your Lordship."

They made their way up two flights of stairs before emerging on the third floor. Several more of the palace servants were there, and they quickly joined the princess' band of defiant heroes. Traveling through the halls, they maintained the initiative, finding and killing several more pairs of enemy soldiers. The rebels died before they understood quite what was happening. Even Dorian couldn't help but feel a sense of hope at the ease with which they made their way to the royal suite.

His hopes were dashed when they found the Queen.

Four men were stationed within the room where her body lay. Dorian and Ariadne's band of liberators showed them no mercy. Evan and Alan killed the two closest to the door, while Dorian charged the ones stooping to rifle the Queen's still form. His mother lay beside her.

The looters were dead before they could stand.

Kicking the corpses out of the way he knelt beside Genevieve Lancaster. Before his hand could reach the Queen, his mother's eyes told him that her friend was dead.

"Mother!" cried Ariadne, shaking Genevieve, hoping beyond hope that her mother might be merely unconscious. "Mother, please wake up—please!"

Dorian turned away and tried to help Elise ease her way up from the floor.

Elise gasped at the pain, "Careful Dorian, I think my shoulder is dislocated, and my ribs are definitely cracked." Her words came in short bursts, for she could only take small, quick breaths.

Ariadne had gone silent, her face buried in her mother's chest. A laundress and one of the cooks assisted Elise while Dorian went back to the princess.

"I'm sorry," he told her gently.

Her head came up suddenly, a cold look in her eyes. "Don't be. This was not your fault." She stood, brushing away his attempt to assist her. "Lady Thornbear, what of my father, do you know whether he is alive?" she asked in a firm tone.

Elise shook her head negatively, "They told us he was dead."

"Ariadne…," began Dorian.

The princess raised her hand to forestall Dorian's words of concern, "Not now, Dorian. My grieving can wait for now."

"He also claimed there was a fire in Lancaster," continued Elise, "but I think he lied. He also said that you had been captured, Your Highness."

Ariadne's eyes wavered for a second—bright with moisture, but then they steadied, gazing into the distance. "I see," she said tonelessly.

"We need to leave, Princess," Dorian told her. "It isn't safe for us to remain here."

"We need to find Tremont and the other noblemen who gathered here today. They had a meeting with my father. The traitors will be among them," she answered, ignoring his statement.

He frowned, "What are you thinking of doing?"

"Justice must be served," she declared solemnly.

"This is no court, Ariadne, this is war. High justice is in the hands of the King's judges. What you are thinking of is plain vengeance," he warned her. By 'high' justice Dorian was referring to the power of execution.

Ariadne Lancaster's eyes focused on him then, "Except for treason, Sir Dorian. The King retains the right of high justice in matters of treason."

"But you are not…"

"My family is slain," she interrupted. "To the best of our knowledge, I am the last scion of Lancaster. *I* am your monarch, Sir Dorian," her words were cased in steel. "We will proceed to the meeting chamber where my father met with his council today. We may yet find them there." As she spoke, her face grew smooth, losing its natural expressiveness, even as her posture took on a sterner form. Her pronouncement had wrought a change in her, as though her subconscious came to accept the fact as she spoke.

She hasn't been crowned, and considering the present events, she might never be, but I've seen a woman become a queen today, thought Dorian with a bit of sadness. Whatever the outcome, the young girl he had always known as Marc's younger sister would never be the same. Her change of tone had resonated with the other people in the room, and they were now on their knees.

"The King is dead. Long live the Queen," pronounced one of the cooks softly.

The veteran knight studied the faces of those around him. He alone remained standing. Gazing seriously into Ariadne's hard eyes he made his choice and fell to one knee. "I have served Lothion all my life. I served your father in good faith, and I will continue to serve the crown. You have my pledge of fealty...," he paused there for a moment before continuing, "...Your Majesty."

She looked calmly down upon him. "I accept your fealty, Sir Dorian. Please continue to use 'Highness', for I have not yet been crowned, and if my brother lives he will take precedence. For now, I will carry the burden of your sovereign, until Roland's fate is known."

Dorian stood at her signal, and he might have imagined it, but he thought he saw a flicker of emotion pass over her. *She is strong, but this day will test her limits—if we survive.* "I still advise you to escape, Princess. The palace is no longer safe."

She disagreed, "I must see my father first, and if possible those who were to meet with him today."

They made it back to the stairs and the second floor without meeting any resistance, a fact that bothered Dorian. He couldn't help but feel that their situation must inevitably get worse. It was just a matter of 'when'.

The hall leading to the small meeting chamber was empty, though they could hear voices through the door.

"Your opinion counts for nothing, Airedale! You'd best keep your thoughts to yourself if you plan to keep your head on your shoulders."

The voice seemed familiar but Dorian couldn't put a name to it.

"That's Earl Balistair," said Ariadne beside him. "Open the door, Dorian, we've found the viper's nest."

"We don't know how many men are inside," he cautioned.

She looked unconcerned. "It's a small chamber. It couldn't hold enough men to be a threat to you."

It isn't 'me' I'm worried about, thought Dorian. Pushing his worries aside he thrust the door open and entered with a rush, surprising the men inside.

The room turned out to be lightly occupied; only four men were within, and all of them were lords of the realm. Martin Balistair whirled to face the open door with shock registering on his face. The man he had been haranguing, Count Airedale, sat on the floor beside the bodies of two men, one of whom was surely James Lancaster. Two others sat at the table that occupied the center of the room, Duke Cantley and Baron Surrey. None of them looked happy, but Airedale's face took on an expression of hope when he recognized Dorian. No one moved.

Dorian's sword was in his hand as he moved purposefullly toward the King's body. "Stand aside," he commanded them, pointing at the back wall. "Over there if you please."

Duke Cantley was the first to find his spine, "On whose authority do you give such commands, Sir Dorian?"

"Mine," declared Ariadne as she entered the room. Alan, Evan, and Gerold had entered ahead of her and were maintaining their positions around her defensively. The rest of her band gathered in the doorway or kept watch on the hall.

Cantley and Balistair both blanched when they saw her appear, while Baron Surrey remained studiously silent. Only Count Airedale seemed glad of her arrival. "Thank the gods you're alive, Princess," he said with tears in his eyes. "Tremont said they'd killed you."

Dorian motioned for them to move again, and this time Brad Cantley moved, taking his place against the wall while the knight knelt to examine James Lancaster's corpse. It took little time to confirm the fact of his death, and Dorian looked at Ariadne with sad eyes to confirm her fears. "I'm sorry, Your Highness," he said.

She nodded and looked back at the lords standing along the wall. "Which of you were present when he died?" she asked.

None of them answered for a moment, until finally Airedale spoke, "We all were here, Your Highness. Tremont…"

"Silence!" she ordered. "I will ask the questions. Who slew my father?"

Cantley answered promptly, "Andrew Tremont, Your Highness."

"How did he die?"

"The Duke ran him through as he sought to pick up a sword to defend himself," answered Cantley again. "We didn't expect…," he started to continue, but she cut him off.

"One more word, Cantley, and I'll have you put to the sword. Disobey me again at your peril," she growled. "Do you understand me?"

He bowed quickly, "Yes, Highness."

"Which of you tried to defend your King?"

Surrey finally found his voice, "It happened so quickly. Tremont had replaced the guards. There was nothing we could do!"

She nodded at Dorian, and he could see cold murder in her eyes. Stepping forward, he slammed the hilt of his sword into Baron Surrey's stomach, using enough force to drive the wind from the older man's lungs.

"I will ask again: Which of you fought to defend your King?" she repeated.

They remained silent.

"Then I pronounce you all guilty of treason," she said bluntly.

"All of us?!" gasped Airedale.

Cantley was more forceful, shouting, "You cannot judge me! You have no authority, nor do you have any proof of such a preposterous charg…" His words cut off suddenly as Dorian treated him much the same as he had Baron Surrey.

She addressed John Airedale then, "Count Airedale, you alone seem surprised. Do you have something to say in your defense?"

His head was down as he replied, "No, Your Highness. I have no defense except to say that I knew nothing of what they had planned. I was a coward and failed to act in James' defense."

"Do you honestly think you can lock us up?" said Cantley from the floor. "Tremont has an army. He controls the capital now!"

Ariadne held up a hand to forestall Dorian before he silenced the errant lord. "You bring up a good point, Lord Cantley. You will not be imprisoned. The punishment for treason is death."

"But we haven't had a trial!" cried Martin Balistair.

She looked straight through him, "That *was* your trial, Lord Balistair." Turning to John Airedale she continued, "I find you guilty of treason as well, Lord Airedale, but I will show you a small mercy; rather than execution, you shall be banished from Lothion. You are hereby stripped of all land and titles. If I find you again within our nation's borders your life will be forfeit. If I determine later that your heirs had no part in this, I may pass your title to them. You have five days to get across the border."

Airedale seemed surprised, "Yes, Your Highness."

"Get out of my sight," she responded, and she kept her gaze upon him until he had left the room, then she turned her attention to Dorian. "I have made my judgment, Sir Dorian. These three are guilty of treason. They are condemned to death. Carry out the sentence."

Dorian blanched at her command. While he had fought and killed many over the years, he had never killed in cold blood. The three men she had ordered put to death were technically armed, but they had put up no resistance. In truth they were as helpless before him as lambs at a slaughter, whether they wore swords or not. He hesitated.

"Sir Dorian?" she asked, "Must I repeat myself, or would you rather I take this task upon myself?" She held out her open hand, as if to take his sword. Her eyes burned into him with icy resolve.

She would do it. He could see that plainly enough. The condemned men stared at him in stark fear, eyes bulging. Waiting longer would only prolong their suffering. His arm moved with such speed the eye could hardly follow, and Balistair and Surrey were falling, their heads no longer attached. Cantley's hand almost reached his waist before he too died. Dorian wiped his blade clean before sheathing it again. As he did so, he noticed several drops of blood on Ariadne's face, but she turned away before he could mention it to her.

"We need to keep moving if we are to find Tremont," she said.

He nodded and followed.

They continued along the corridor, checking other rooms as they went, but they found no one aside from frightened man-servants and two maids. The few that they encountered elected to join them.

Ariadne began to wonder if Tremont, by some miracle, had decided to abandon the palace to them. Dorian didn't relax though, and his fears were borne out shortly thereafter. A group of ten emerged from a side hall, and they didn't seem surprised. The enemy had wised up, and now they were hunting them.

Dorian was at the front of the princess' band, and the enemy soldiers charged into them from behind. The cooks and other servants did their best, but they were no match for the well-equipped mercenaries. The enemy had the initiative here, and the fight turned ugly in seconds. Dorian struggled to get to the rear of the group, but many of the princess' followers fell before he could reach the fight.

Shouldering one of the laundresses aside he charged over the fallen bodies, disrupting the enemy's advance as they suddenly found themselves on the wrong side of his sword. Steel flickered in the light, and blood splattered the walls as he butchered them. He fought like a demon, impossibly graceful and lethally efficient. The end result was a floor that looked as if it belonged in an abattoir rather than a palace.

Two of Tremont's men turned and fled before he got to them. Rather than give chase he let them go, heartsick already from the killing he had done.

"They're getting away!" shouted Ariadne.

Dorian nodded, disgust written on his features. Many of her followers were wounded now, and at least ten had died. One woman lay silently gaping, struggling to keep her intestines from spilling out. Most of the enemy were dead already, and those that weren't were rapidly bleeding to death. Everywhere he looked Dorian saw nothing but death. "They've lost their will to fight," he said simply. "If I go chasing them, the next group may take your life before I can return."

"What if they warn the others?" asked Alan.

"They already know. Those men were looking for trouble. We've outstayed our welcome. The rest will be on us soon enough," returned Dorian. He felt old. In the past he had fought monsters, except in the war with Gododdin, and that had been a far more clear-cut fight. Now he had gone from protector to executioner—to butcher.

Ariadne was staring blankly at the wounded maid. "Help the wounded up," she ordered those that were still standing, but her attention never left the woman clutching desperately at her stomach.

Dorian leaned close. "She will not live, but she might survive for several days if she doesn't die of blood loss," he said softly in the princess' ear.

"What are our options?" she asked.

He grimaced, "Tell her the truth and offer her a clean death, either at my hand or her own, or we attempt to carry her with us. Without magical aid she will surely die, but the strain of being carried might kill her as well."

She knew they had little time, and so James Lancaster's daughter knelt beside the dying woman. "What is your name?" she asked.

"Nancy, Your Highness," the woman answered between clenched teeth. The fear and pain in her eyes would haunt the princess for the rest of her life.

"Nancy, I'm told you will not survive this wound, but you might live another day or two. If we try to move you, it might kill you outright; if we leave you here I don't know what our enemy will do. The choice is yours to make," she explained. Ariadne's face remained clear and steady as she spoke.

Nancy groaned, a tear creating a smudged track down the side of her cheek. "I would stay with you if I could. I'd like to see my children again, but you can't run with me bein' like this. Leave me a knife, milady. Get away and don't look back."

Ariadne stood suddenly, turning away as her resolve cracked, twisting her visage with grief. Dorian could see her heart breaking, and inwardly he wept for both of them. *This is the end of innocence, if there was any left.* Stepping forward, he sheathed his sword and squatted beside the dying woman. "Godsdammitt," he cursed under his breath. "If possible, I will see you to your family. It'll hurt, though." Carefully he eased his arms under her and gently lifted.

She gasped as he stood, cradling her to his chest like some overlarge child. He was already gory from the fighting, but almost immediately a fresh trail of blood began leaking, over his midsection and down his legs.

"Let's go," said Dorian as he began walking down the hall moving in the direction of the nearest stairs. The others followed without argument.

Elise Thornbear was leaning on one of the cooks as she watched her son carry the dying maid. Her heart was filled with a confusing welter of emotions, pride and despair warring within her for precedence. *No matter what else, Gram,* she thought, addressing her dead husband, *our son has become a man to be proud of, just like his father.*

"How's he going to fight like that?" Gerold asked Evan in a whisper.

"Shut up," said Evan.

Chapter 24

They reached the ground level without interference. Evan, Alan, and Gerold had taken positions around Ariadne, while the rest of the palace servants clustered protectively around Dorian and his burden. Though he respected their sentiment, he knew realistically that when they encountered more enemy troops he would be forced to surrender his charge to someone else.

The main door leading into the courtyard was guarded, but only four men held the position, and before he could give Nancy to someone else, the servants charged them. They were full of anger and a desperate need to find some way to act. Another of them was killed in the short fight, and two more were mildly wounded, but the rest overwhelmed the four men before they could ready themselves. More blood covered the tile floors of the palace.

It never ends, thought Dorian morbidly, *and I am tied to the cycle by iron, blood, and hatred. Forced to kill and kill again, until they finally put an end to me. What will Mort think of me then? Will Rose weep for me? And what of my son, will he follow in his father's footsteps, to find himself cursed by violence as well?*

"The courtyard is full of men!" said Alan loudly as he peeked through the now unguarded doors.

Dorian shifted the woman in his arms so that he could lean over enough to look through the crack in the doors. She didn't moan this time. Nancy appeared to have fallen asleep. Then her head rolled back in a wholly unnatural manner. *She's dead,* he realized.

Bending down, Dorian gently laid Nancy's body on the ground. His face was wet, though he didn't remember when he had begun crying. Of all the violence he had seen that day, for some reason it was Nancy's that had finally undone him. "Let me see," he told Alan.

No one commented on his tears.

"Tremont is out there," he told Ariadne after a moment. "He must have taken them out to recapture you after we snuck back in. The gate's open too. There're at least five hundred men out there now."

The princess' jaw was agape now. "How could he have so many?"

"Your father and I spoke regarding this just a few days ago. Lord Hightower had suspicions that someone was sneaking men into the city, but none of us expected something like this," admitted the Knight of Stone.

"What in the name of the gods is that?!" exclaimed Gerold who had taken Dorian's place as soon as he moved away from the doors.

"What?" Dorian shoved him quickly aside to get another view. It took only a moment to spot the source of Gerold's confusion. A large creature was entering the courtyard, having just passed from underneath the gatehouse. It stood nearly nine feet in height and walked on two legs, like a man, but the resemblance ended there. It had four arm-like appendages connected to a slender trunk. The overall coloring was a deep brown, but its skin looked thick and almost bark-like. The head was small, without a mouth or any other features besides six eyes that circled it, providing vision in a three hundred and sixty degree arc.

A number of thoughts percolated through his mind then as Dorian looked at the crowd of people around him. His mother was barely conscious now, supported by a man on either side. Ariadne was uninjured, but the rest of them sported a variety of wounds. *There is no way for me to get these people out of here.* His eyes met Ariadne's, "You need to put that man's clothes on and the armor as well."

She glanced at the dead mercenary he was indicating. Although he was one of the smaller ones, his armor would still be too large for her. The only bright side she could see was that rather than chainmail he wore a simple leather hauberk. It was heavily stained with blood. "You have a good reason for this I assume?"

He motioned her to step aside with him, and speaking softly he outlined his plan. As she listened her eyes grew moist but she knew there were no other options. It was a day of damnation, and she was already covered in blood.

She returned to the others, and ignoring their stares, she stripped herself out of the soiled remains of her dress and began donning the oversized clothes and armor. She also directed the two men helping Elise to put one of the soldiers' tabards over the lady's dress, followed by a cloak. She used her own knife to cut Lady Thornbear's skirts to knee length so that they wouldn't be readily apparent. She completed the haphazard disguise with one of the men's steel caps.

The two of them now looked, on casual inspection, to be just a couple more of Tremont's mercenaries. Gerold, Evan, and Alan, moved closer—their larger frames would help the two women to blend in better.

The rest of the servants looked at Dorian for an explanation. "What's our part in this?" asked one of them.

His heart clenched as he answered, but he kept his face confident, "Those of you who are willing, will come with me. Those who are not can stay here. They may show mercy if you return to your places and pretend you weren't part of our group."

"What will you do?"

"I'm going out there," said Dorian. "I will create a distraction. I'll make for the gate, try to sow as much confusion and discord as possible. The princess and her companions may be able to escape unnoticed during the turmoil."

"How will we get out?" asked one of the women.

"The most probable outcome is that if you follow me out there, you'll die. If you remain here, they may keep you in your positions, or they might lock you all up," Dorian answered honestly. "They might also kill you, or even torture you for information."

"Will we even do any good if we follow you? We're no match for even a few soldiers," the maid suggested.

Dorian wanted to run. Deep down his heart screamed at him. This wasn't right. It wasn't the sort of thing a knight, any knight, should ever ask of the people they should be protecting. "If I go out alone it will be less effective. A few people beside me will create a bigger impact, even if you contribute almost nothing to the fight." He looked down, ashamed. "You will be selling your lives for nothing more than the slight chance of improving the Princess and Lady Thornbear's chances of escape."

The maid lifted her chin and raised the large carving knife in her hand, "Then I will join you, Sir Dorian. I have no children, and I would rather die a good death than risk rape and torture at their hands." Her hands shook, but her eyes were clear.

No, please, said Dorian's inner voice, but his mouth responded according to his duty, "Then I will gladly fight beside you. From this day, from this moment, for however long we both shall live, I will call you my sister." Tears were rolling down his cheeks.

Many of the remaining servants made a similar choice, but five or six chose to remain. "I have a family, Sir Dorian," said one of the manservants. "If there's any chance I can survive to take care of them, I have to take it." Two of the laundresses and a few of the kitchen staff nodded their heads in agreement. Once they had sorted themselves out, it appeared there would be eight following him out the door, five men and three women.

Those who had decided to stay would return to their places, in hopes of avoiding being associated with the Princess' group, but before they left one of the women caught Dorian's hand. "If I live through this, Sir, I will tell the tale to my children and grandchildren. No one will forget you," she said before kissing him on the cheek.

"Don't remember me. Remember them," he said, pointing at the ones who would follow him. "They have no reason to do this. I have spent my life staining my soul with other men's blood, but they do this for no reason other than protecting their princess." He paused then before adding, "If you would say anything, if I don't survive—tell my wife and children that I love them. Ask them to forgive me for my absence."

Ariadne spoke then, "You will live to fight on, Dorian." She stopped, fearful of losing her calm. Raising her head she told the others, "I need your names. When this is over, I will see to it that your families are not forgotten."

She had no paper, but she listened and repeated them to herself. Ariadne had an excellent memory, and she wasn't the only one making mental notes.

The yard was full of men when they opened the doors. Dorian stepped out cautiously at first, as though he and the eight who followed him sought to avoid attention. A number of heads turned in their direction, but the enemy was slow to react—until Ariadne's small group charged out after them. Things sped up quickly after that.

The enemy officers were shouting at their men, urging them to cut off the 'escaping' supporters of the princess. Soldiers turned, and several groups rushed toward Dorian and his comrades.

Once the alarm had gone up, Dorian's small crew charged forward. It was a gesture of ridiculous defiance, a small group of nine rushing forward to attack the hundreds arrayed before them, but their purpose was fulfilled. Ariadne and her fellow 'soldiers' were lost within the press of mercenaries that closed around them.

At first Dorian fought to protect those who had followed him, but it was a hopeless cause. His allies were lost within the first half a minute, swept away and cut down. Even Dorian might have been overwhelmed, but for his enchanted sword. Its blade cut through swords and shields alike, creating a deadly swath of destruction around him. The fight paused as the men around him drew back, pushing against those behind them to avoid his cuts.

In the space of that moment, a silence appeared, to be filled by Andrew Tremont's voice, rising above the mercenaries. "Lay down your sword, Sir Knight. Can you not see the futility of your actions here?" he shouted. "Surrender now and I will offer you mercy."

Dorian Thornbear's sanity had been left at the door, when he emerged. "Tremont!" he shouted in response. "I am coming for you, and I will not rest 'til you have been treated to the King's justice!"

Tremont laughed, still unable to see the face of the man threatening him, but a few of those around Dorian recognized his face, and a murmur of 'Thornbear' passed through the crowd. Many continued to back away as the Knight of Stone resumed his progress, walking slowly forward.

"Kill the fool!" commanded the duke, and those who still retained their will to fight pushed forward past their reluctant fellows. They surged in toward Dorian.

Their concerted effort threatened to overwhelm him, and Dorian felt a stabbing thrust break through the chain protecting his back as his forward motion slowed. It was a small wound, hardly felt through the haze of adrenaline but his instincts told him that if he couldn't break free of the press, he would soon be dead.

Desperate, he did the one thing that he and Cyhan had repeatedly cautioned Penny never to do. Bending his knees he leapt, using his strength to drive his heavy body up and over those striving to stop him. He soared, ten feet up and fifteen forward, landing behind those who had faced him and among those who were unprepared. His sudden change of position created alarm and confusion as his new opponents struggled to move away from him.

He never gave them the chance. Having regained the initiative, he rushed forward, hacking and hewing before they could regain their organization. Dorian Thornbear roared, more demon than man in his heart now. Cutting and killing, he drove himself in the direction that he had heard Andrew Tremont's voice.

Men cried out in fear, and panic took root in the hearts of Tremont's followers. Those with quick reflexes got out of his way, while Dorian's sword cut down those too slow to escape. A path opened before him, as those between him and his goal tried to flee. Andrew Tremont stood alone, abandoned by his bodyguards, some fifty feet ahead.

Dorian snarled, a dreadful smile on his face, as he spotted his quarry. Nothing could stop him now. His legs drove him forward with lethal momentum as the Duke of Tremont watched him with terror stricken eyes.

Andrew Tremont would have died then, but halfway to his goal Dorian was blindsided. Something fast and impossibly huge slammed into him from the right, and only his reflexes and a quick glimpse of motion in his peripheral vision saved him. Twisting, he narrowly avoided the thrust of a massive spike as the creature that he had seen earlier attacked. He couldn't avoid the momentum of its main body however, and he found himself driven hard into the ground as it struck him.

His helmet was lost when he fell, and he attempted to roll before his new foe could pin him, but another of those strange arms caught his leg. In a split second of clarity, he saw that the spike that had nearly impaled him earlier was not a separate weapon but a feature of one of the creature's arms. The thing was a nightmare of odd proportions. Two arms ended in crushing pincers while the other two were covered in a variety of spikes.

Unable to rise, he barely intercepted another attack with his sword as the thing tried to remove his head with one of its heavy claws. The edge bit deeply into the armor-like skin of the monster rather than passing cleanly through, surprising Dorian further. Few things resisted the enchanted blades Mordecai had created. It was almost as though the beast was made of solid iron, but it moved far too fast for that.

His sword remained stuck in the thing's arm, but the veteran knight used that to his advantage, as it drew the wounded limb back he held on tightly. The momentum jerked him upward and as his body flew skyward he pivoted, twisting around the sword hilt to land on the monster's back. Unable to free his weapon he released it and instead caught the creature's small head with both arms, wrapping it in a tight grip.

It shook vigorously, trying to throw him off to no avail, for his grip was like a steel vise. Dorian had hoped he might have a moment's respite, but the thing's arms had a greater freedom of motion than he had expected. They twisted and reached for him as the beast switched tactics.

He wasn't simply holding his place, though. Dorian's corded neck bulged as he pulled, straining to tear the creature's head from its torso. It was just as resilient as the arm had been. *Why won't this damn thing budge?* he thought as it resisted his attempt to kill it. For a moment he considered abandoning his position, but then he would be left with no weapon and few options. Instead he redoubled his efforts. His hair, now without a helm to cover it, went white, and his skin turned an ashen grey as he strained.

The torturous moment stretched out, and time slowed down as at last he felt something give way. A scream of triumph erupted from his lips as the hard wooden flesh broke and tore under his hands, and the head ripped completely free from the monster's shoulders. The massive form beneath him shuddered and collapsed.

Dorian rode the body down, rolling when it reached the packed earth of the castle courtyard. Rising to his feet he could feel the strength of his body surging with the deep drumbeat of the earth. Adrenaline and rage were all he could feel now, and staring at the enemy soldiers standing in dumb amazement around him he screamed his defiance, "Who is next?!"

No one moved at first, and when they did it was to backpedal away from the enraged warrior. Dorian Thornbear's face was completely grey now, causing him to look as if he had been cast from stone. He smiled at them with granite teeth and a berserker's madness in his eyes.

"You are, human," said a dry voice as he was struck from behind by something with the force of a battering ram.

The lone knight was thrown through the air, sailing thirty feet, to slam into the wall that protected the palace courtyard. The stones cracked at his impact, and his body slid to the ground, but it did not stay there.

Impossibly, the Knight of Stone rose, dusting the dirt and gravel from his armor. "You should have died when you had the chance," he rumbled with a voice that sounded as if it were produced by rocks being ground together.

Most of the soldiers had retreated to either the walls or the palace by now, leaving the courtyard mostly empty. The gate had been shut and the portcullises were down, but it was with some relief that Dorian saw no sign of Ariadne or his mother as he started forward; with any luck they were already outside and making their way to safety. *Whatever I accomplish now will serve mainly to delay Tremont from turning his attention to finding the missing princess.*

Dorian's sword was still embedded in the creature's arm as they drew closer together, circling warily. The lack of a head didn't seem to impede the monster's ability to sense his position, but it moved carefully, having gained some respect for the warrior's dangerous strength.

They jockeyed back and forth for half a minute until finally the beast took a chance, rushing forward and trying to catch him with its claws. Dorian was too quick however, and he ducked low and slid, coming up underneath his opponent. Using his shoulder and both arms he lifted the half-ton monster and thrust it skyward.

It fell awkwardly, landing on its side several feet away. Dorian had hoped the impact might dislodge his sword, but his luck wasn't that good. Moving in, he tried to get his hand on the hilt but the beast recovered too quickly, nearly removing his head with one of its heavy pincers.

He caught that arm halfway along what would have been a human's forearm, holding it at bay as he grabbed again for his sword. Missing his mark, they wound up in a stalemate of sorts, Dorian held both of the pincered arms at their midpoint, and the two of them strained and struggled, matching strength against strength. While the beast was incredibly strong, the knight seemed to have some advantage, except for one fact. His opponent had two more arms than he did, and these were covered in vicious spikes.

Even as he concentrated, forcing the two clawed arms apart and away from his body, the other two arms whipped forward and across, ripping into the armor covering his chest and belly, shredding chainmail almost as easily as leather. Pain shot through him as the spikes tore into his stomach. *It had to happen sooner or later,* said the voice in the back of his mind, but the rest of him ignored it.

Roaring in pain and defiance, Dorian Thornbear put one boot on the monster's chest and pushed it downward while his powerful shoulders tensed. The beast screamed as the knight ripped the two arms from their sockets. The other two struck him again, knocking him sideways, but he was up again and tearing at the creature before it could recover. Dorian knew he had to finish it before his own strength failed him.

Forgetting his sword, he wrestled with the thing, pulling its two remaining arms loose before starting on the legs. Like a mad child he tore it apart, one limb at a time, until all that remained was a twitching torso. Unable to do much to it with his hands alone, he took a moment to retrieve his sword from the arm it was still lodged in. Using it, he cut each arm and leg into at least three pieces and then he proceeded to hack the torso itself into two parts, although it took some time. The creature's body was so tough that cutting it apart was as difficult as cutting a normal tree trunk into two parts—using a normal sword.

When he finished he surveyed the courtyard, leaning on his sword casually, as though it were a cane. It was largely empty, and those soldiers who did remain were scattered along the walls, watching him silently. Most of those held crossbows, cocked and pointed in his direction. His chainmail didn't have a hope in hell of stopping one of those quarrels. He wondered at the fact of his continued breathing. *I should be dead by now.*

"What are you waiting for!?" he roared at the onlookers. "How many of you bastards do I have to kill before you put me out of my misery!?"

None of them answered, though one man dropped his crossbow and retreated into a wall tower.

"Answer me!!"

Several more men dropped their weapons, an action that Dorian couldn't comprehend. Looking downward he examined his chest and belly, afraid to see what sort of wounds he had already sustained. *My guts are probably hanging out for—what the hell?!* He stared at his belly in amazement.

The chain and leather had been ripped apart, but his exposed stomach was intact, aside from some odd looking scratches in the grey skin. He slapped his belly with one hand, finding it hard and dry. The sensation was rather like banging two rocks together. As he looked down he saw a number of crossbow bolts littering the ground around him. Some were stuck in the soft earth, but others were broken, as if they had struck something hard. *Something like me,* he thought. *I've started turning, just like Mort warned. I'm more stone than man now.*

"Shit."

Unable to think of anything better to do, Dorian walked across the empty yard until he found the metal cap that he had lost when the monster first charged into him. Dusting it off, he replaced it on his head. Dignity restored, he stared at the gatehouse and yelled, "If you aren't going to kill me, then open the damn gate! Unless you want to surrender?"

He began walking toward the gatehouse. Both portcullises and the gate were open long before he reached it.

Chapter 25

Albamarl looked different than I expected. Smoke rose from a variety of locations, and it was far more substantial than the usual smoke that would have been seen rising from chimneys and cook-fires. This was the sort of smoke you'd expect from burning buildings. The city appeared to be in the midst of a war.

Where do you want me to land? questioned Gareth.

A dozen locations flashed through my mind, but the most important stood head and shoulders above those. "The Illeniel house, I need to retrieve Lyralliantha." I had intended to say, 'check on my family', but the geas compelling me was still in effect. My personal reasons aside, I simply couldn't do anything else—not without a logical reason.

Moira spoke then, *none of this makes sense. There was no sign of a war before we left.*

I had no answer for that, although I had my suspicions. A familiar form was waiting for us as we landed in the street, and it was someone whom I hoped would have more information for us.

"You said you would meet me the next day, but it has been almost five," complained Karenth as he approached us.

"Did you have something better to do?" I quipped. When he opened his mouth to reply I cut him off, "Don't answer that. I'd rather hear about what's been happening in our absence."

"Duke Tremont has made a bid for the crown. What you see around you is the fruit born of a civil war," answered Karenth.

The magic compelling me was impatient, I could feel it tugging me toward Lyra's resting place. *I have to find out what forces may be arrayed against me first,* I reasoned internally, and I felt the compulsion ease. "Give me the details, but make it brief and succinct. I don't have time to waste."

"His poisoner managed to render both the royal guard and Hightower's men helpless. He slew both the King and Queen two days ago, but failed to eliminate their daughter. Your friend, Thornbear, helped her escape, and she rallied what was left of the city's defenders to her cause. The fighting has been bloody and vicious. Tremont has a lot of mercenaries within the city, and he is supported by a substantial number of church troops," explained the diminished god.

"Where did he find that many sell-swords?" I wondered aloud. My emotions were at a dangerously low point at that time for it had been several days since I had last fed on a human. The casual mention of the death of my aunt and uncle registered within me as a dull ache but nothing more.

"Many of them are Shaddoth Krys, the servants and lackeys of Mal'goroth," Karenth informed me. "I am unclear whether Tremont is aware of this, or if he cares one way or the other."

I gave his words some thought before asking my next question, "Where is my family now?"

"Inside the building before you. The Queen is with them," he replied.

"The Queen?"

Karenth smiled slyly, "The people have taken to calling Ariadne the 'Iron Queen'."

That surprised me. My memories of Ariadne were of a sweet girl with a gentle disposition. While she had grown into an intelligent and practical woman, I could hardly see anyone pinning such a name on her. "And she allows this?" I asked.

"They do not do it in front of her. She still insists on being addressed as a princess, since there has been no coronation," explained Karenth. "I cannot confirm this personally, but your wife received word from home that Lancaster Castle has been sacked and burned. They were hoping for assistance, or at the very least help from the Prathions. To the best of our knowledge, they have retreated to Castle Cameron."

"What about Roland?"

"No one has seen him since the attack on Lancaster. He is presumed dead," Karenth answered.

A variety of feelings passed faintly through me, sorrow, irritation, and a vague sense of anger. For once it seemed an advantage having my emotions muted, but I knew there would be a reckoning the next time they returned to their normal levels.

"How many of the Knights of Stone are in Albamarl?"

"Just Egan, Cyhan and Dorian, but Cyhan is unable to fight," he replied.

That was my fault, of course. I stepped forward, approaching the front door of what had once been my house, or Mordecai's house, depending on how you looked at things. It was too confusing for me to keep thinking about it in those terms.

I knocked, just as any well-mannered stranger should. Now that my questions had been answered, the magic binding me was pushing me forward. It wouldn't allow for any unnecessary delays.

I waited for a minute and knocked again, hoping someone would answer. If not I might be forced to destroy the house to get inside. With the power taken from Karenth and an additional portion I had siphoned from the God-Stone, I had no doubt about my ability to do so. *Or I could just use a circle.* The thought seemed strange for a moment, and yet I wondered why it hadn't occurred to me first.

"What do you want?"

The voice on the other side of the door was deep and masculine. My senses couldn't penetrate the enchanted door, but my ears easily identified my childhood friend. Dorian was on the other side. "I am here to retrieve the She'Har woman. I need you to let me in."

"You aren't welcome here. I know who you are," said Dorian.

"I am Brexus," I responded, using the name I had given before. I wondered if my daughter had shared what Moira Centyr had told her when we departed last time.

"You can call yourself whatever the hell you want. I'm not letting you in this house," said my stalwart friend.

My mind was racing, but the answers it provided weren't helpful. "If you don't open the door soon, I'll be forced to break it, and there's no delicate way to do that. Those you are protecting might be injured or killed."

"You're bluffing," he replied. "Even the Dark Gods have been unable to force their way inside."

"Don't force my hand, Dorian," I told him, clenching my hands into fists. Simultaneously I was gathering my will, and the words were already on the tip of my tongue. Whether I wanted to or not, I was about to destroy the front of the house, and the effort would probably injure many of those within. Something deep within pulsed, *No! Don't do this!* While I agreed with the sentiment, it seemed foreign, as if it had come from someone else. It also held a lot more implicit emotion than I currently had.

My hands came up to shoulder level, pointing outward, toward the door. They seemed to move of their own volition. Time was up, whether I wanted to wait or not.

The door opened. Dorian stood aside, one hand on the handle. He wore his full plate armor, but the helm was under his arm. Instead, he wore a scowl on his face, and his eyes were focused so intently that I'm sure if I had been more sensitive at the time, they might have burned holes through me.

"Mind your manners, Dorian. He isn't what you think," said an older woman's voice from behind him. Elise Thornbear stood behind her son. She looked tired, and for the first time, truly old. Her eyes were red and her skin sagged, where it wasn't puffy from bruising.

What had happened to her? thought my mind, but my mouth was more practical. "The truth is complicated, but I am dangerous Dorian. You can't trust me at this point. Your best option is to let me have what I want and send me on my way."

Gareth Gaelyn was still a massive dragon and didn't bother trying to pass the door, but everyone's eyes looked curiously at the woman who entered behind me. None of them recognized the Stone Lady now that she was flesh and blood—except for one.

"Mother?" said my young daughter. "Is that really you?"

I walked past her without pause, heading for the stone sarcophagus that still remained in the hall between the anteroom and the kitchen. My body was unable to wait, but my magesight was firmly fixed upon Moira Centyr. Her face held a curious expression, as though she might cry but had forgotten how.

"I told you, little one, I am not really your mother. I am just her shadow," answered Moira Centyr, but she put her arms around her daughter nonetheless. Her eyes were bright with welling tears.

My daughter turned her head to look at me over Moira's shoulder, "Someone else told me that too, but I don't think either of you really understand. You're a mother in every way that matters. I'll claim you if I want."

Penny approached them carefully, listening to their words, a look of wonder on her face. "Are you really her?" she asked. A man I didn't recognize stood behind her.

Our daughter drew her in with one hand. "It really is her, Momma. This was the Stone Lady."

Their tearful reunion would have torn at my heartstrings, if they hadn't been wrapped in heavy wool. Once again I was grateful for my near lack of emotion. Stretching out my gauntleted hand I spoke a word and lifted the heavy stone box that held Lyrallianha. It probably weighed several thousand pounds, but in my current state it might as well have been a feather. Levitating it seemed as easy as breathing had once been.

All eyes were on me as I ignored them and proceeded to maneuver Lyra toward the door. Even Matthew had appeared, watching me from the hall. I couldn't be sure what Elise Thornbear or my daughter might have told them, but his intense gaze made it clear that he thought I was his deceased father. *Which I am—sort of.*

No one spoke to me, probably out of fear. It seemed I might complete my mission and escape without any more damaging personal conversations, but one person was too stubborn to be ignored.

"You think you can just take what you want and leave?" challenged Penny. She had left the others and moved to block my exit.

Something pulsed within me again, this time more painfully. *No, never—I have too much to say. I love you. Forgive me.* Again my internal voice seemed strangely out of sync with my own thoughts. "Move. I am not who you think I am," my voice answered tonelessly.

She didn't move. "Elise told me about your letter. She says you're still in there."

The magic binding me was insistent. Lacking any danger or logical impediment, my mind and body were betraying me. I would force my way past her if she didn't move. "I am Brexus. Your husband is dead. Move or I may be compelled to hurt you."

Her warm brown eyes were wet with tears, and her face twisted as she stared at me. "No. You wouldn't hurt me. Show me your face, and I'll let you…"

Too much time had passed. My armored fist came up with lightning speed. My body was moving against my wishes, and I was helpless to stop it. If she wouldn't move on her own I would strike her from my path.

Searing pain tore through me, burning along every nerve, as if someone had filled my veins with acid. My eyes were blinded for a second while my chest pounded with a furious pain. *No! You will not do this! NO!* I heard my voice speaking, but it seemed to come from another place, "Penny, please move quickly. I can't restrain myself for long. Please, I'm begging you!" The words were tortured, filled with emotion that seemed foreign to me.

My armored fist trembled in the air before me, scant inches from Penny's surprised face. It was caught between two opposing forces, and neither of them seemed to belong to me, for the moment I was merely an observer.

Before the inner turmoil could subside, she moved aside. The universe twisted around me for a moment, and the pain in my body disappeared. With an odd wrenching sensation, I resumed control of my body. My feet began moving forward, and using my magic, I directed the stone sarcophagus ahead of me into the open street.

What are your instructions? asked Moira Centyr's voice in my mind.

Since she had nothing to do with my compulsion, I was free to command her as I wished. I sent my thoughts toward her, *You're free to remain. Help them if you would. When this is over, if I am able, I will free you completely.*

The dragon waited for me, and Karenth stood beside him. "That coffin looks extremely heavy," noted Gareth. "I won't be able to carry that more than a mile or two."

"You're staying here," I informed him. "Do as your conscience demands until I return."

"My conscience?"

I brought out the enchanted stones that would form my flying construct. Lyra and her stone container would easily fit within, and I had enough power to handle the weight. "They are in the middle of a war, and you're the only wizard who might be willing to help, unless you count that little girl in there."

"I am a dragon," Gareth corrected me, as if the distinction meant something. "And the 'little girl' you mention in there, has more power than I ever did."

"You're also an archmage, and you have a hell of a lot more knowledge and experience," I answered. As I spoke, some part of my mind remained on Penny and the others. I watched them in my magesight, feeling a dull ache that was echoed by a sharper pain that came from some other place within me. Matthew and Moira stood beside their mother and Conall peeked out from behind her. They were all watching me and none of them seemed happy.

"Why don't you order me to do what you want done?" asked the dragon. "You still have my aystrylin."

I pointed at Karenth, gesturing at the opening of my flying machine, "Get inside. We can talk while we travel." I followed him in, my body still moving with ruthless efficiency. I couldn't have paused if I had wanted to. Reaching into my pouch I drew out Gareth's aystrylin before I sealed the invisible door behind me. I tossed it to him, and then I spoke the words that would close the 'doorway'. Sound traveled through it just fine though, "I'm tired of giving orders. Do as you will."

The dragons jaw snapped open, and he caught the small figurine in his mouth. His tongue tucked it away in one cheek before his mouth closed. With a roar he launched himself skyward, never looking back.

"It appears you made a miscalculation with the dragon," observed Karenth as I lifted us slowly.

I shook my head, "He'll be back."

"You think he'll help you of his own accord? You're a fool," said the Shining God.

His words registered, but I wasn't listening. My attention was on the ground below us where a small group of people gathered to watch us ascending. Despite my numbness, I was still sad to leave them. Below were most of the people I had cared about in life. I felt an additional twisting pain in my chest as they grew steadily smaller below us.

"No. I've been a fool up 'til now, and I still have a lot to learn," I responded. Before he could comment I asked him a question, "Do you ever hear voices?"

"What do you mean?" said Karenth.

I struggled to describe my meaning, "I think everyone has an internal dialogue or commentary of thoughts, but lately mine has been different. Sometimes it feels as though the thoughts in my mind are someone else's. Add the compulsion that Lyra's binding has placed on my actions and lately it seems as though I'm sharing this body with two or even three people."

Karenth grinned wickedly at me. "I know all too well what compulsions are like. You desire one thing, but your body and even your mind are forced along the path your master has commanded. It gives me no small amount of pleasure to hear that you are suffering as I have."

I ignored his obvious glee at my discomfort. "The compulsion, the geas, that part I think I understand at least. I want to do one thing, but my actions and at times even my thoughts, are channeled along the path that will accomplish Lyra's goal with the least delay. Today something different happened."

"Such as?"

I described my experience of a few minutes past, when Penny had put herself in my way. "At the time I just wanted to get away. I didn't want to hurt her, but the geas tried to strike her. My fist moved to do just that, but then something stopped it."

My companion looked incredulous, "Are you suggesting that you were able to resist the binding?"

"Not really. It didn't feel like me. I was just an observer, while something else fought for control of my body. Then I started talking, but it felt strange."

"In what way?" he asked.

"The words sounded like something I might say when my emotions are closer to normal, but I don't think I was the one talking," I admitted.

Karenth's eyebrows went up. "You're suggesting that *his* soul is somehow trying to control or communicate with you? That shouldn't be possible."

"Why not?"

"The binding around him is similar to the one you put around Celior. I don't understand the specifics of She'Har spellweavings, but if the function is the same as the enchantment used to create me, then he should be unable to communicate or do anything else. It's questionable whether he's even aware at all. His soul is probably asleep, dormant within its cage," postulated Karenth.

"But you're an artificial consciousness," I countered.

"So are you," he rebutted me.

I nodded, "Right, but Mordecai wasn't. Don't you think it's possible a living soul might be different, that he might find some way to reach out from the place where he is?"

"It's more likely that your tortured psyche is beginning to unravel under pressure," he answered dryly.

Chapter 26

We flew for several miles without much conversation. I was having difficulty regaining my inner composure after seeing Penny and the twins. And that was with my capacity for emotion at a fairly low level. The special pain that had emerged within me when I encountered them had vanished, leaving me with a dull ache that was entirely my own. I needed to feed, but I worried that doing so might unleash a storm of guilt and grief within. It was a moot point for now though; the geas wouldn't let me stop until I had delivered Lyra to her lover.

"Where are you taking us?" asked Karenth, interrupting my thoughts.

My mind snapped back into focus as I turned to face him. "*I* am taking Lyralliantha to her kianthi. *You* will remain in Lothion. I have several tasks for you."

"Then why bring me this far? Couldn't you have given your instructions before leaving?"

Karenth was probably the sharpest mind among the four beings we called the Shining Gods. Which is probably what annoyed me about him. "Take my hand," I commanded, and when he did so, I began channeling some of the power that I had absorbed from the Iron Heart Chamber and the God-Stone back into him.

"Why?" he asked, his eyes growing large.

"Because a weak servant is less useful than a strong one," I answered. "Once I've given you what I think is necessary, I want you to return and see if you can find your siblings. Tell them you escaped from me, that you know the location of the God-Stone. Lure them to me, using whatever additional lies you feel they will fall for."

"My siblings…" he said, letting the words trail off.

I sighed, "Millicenth and Doron."

"We aren't related you know… we were cre…"

I cut him off, "I know. From a human standpoint, we think of you as siblings, just accept it."

"What is your plan?"

I smiled, "You don't need that information. Just lure them to the place I tell you. Once I've gotten within earshot, they'll be mine."

Karenth frowned. It was obvious he disliked my plan.

Ignoring his expression I continued, "I also need more information. We didn't have much time before. How well do you think Ariadne's resistance is holding up? Will she be able to oust Tremont on her own?"

"If it were only Tremont, probably. The man's a fool, but he's got unusual allies," replied the subdued god of justice.

"You told me about the Church supporters and the Shaddoth Krys, are there more?"

"The supporters of the four churches have been misled. Without me or Celior they were easy to dupe. Even Millicenth and Doron have been reluctant to show themselves for fear of being captured by Mal'goroth. The Shaddoth Krys however, obey only one master," said Karenth.

"You're saying that Tremont is in league with Mal'goroth?"

"I'm saying that one hand guides them all, and whether he realizes it or not, that hand is not Tremont's," answered Karenth.

"That's possible," I replied, "even likely, but I'll need more information before we can assume Mal'goroth is behind it."

"I haven't finished," said Karenth. "When they were escaping from the palace Dorian fought against Chel'terek. He was lucky to survive."

"Chel'terek?" I was confused.

Karenth sighed, "That's the name of one of the others whom humans call the Dark Gods, though he is much weaker now."

"I thought Mal'goroth ate them. Isn't that what you told me once before?"

"He caught them and devoured their power. It was similar to what you did with me, though much more direct. The spellweavings that created them are virtually indestructible. He left them nearly powerless, but he couldn't unmake them. Instead they've become his servants," explained Karenth.

Well shit, I thought, *there goes my one advantage.* I had hoped that by taking command of the remaining Shining Gods, I would be able to counter Mal'goroth at least in the numbers category. Now it appeared that he would have far more helpers than the meager three I could potentially command. "How many of them are there?" I asked.

"What a surprise," he commented raising his eyebrows, "a piece of history you don't know. There are forty-one of them, if you don't count Mal'goroth."

I chided myself mentally. He was right, and as soon as he had said the number, I felt the knowledge rise from my hidden memories. *Forty-two guardians of the other realm, keeping the gates and protecting the groves from the outside.* The memory led to other questions, such as what the 'gates' represented, but I had more practical concerns for the present.

"How strong are they?"

"About as strong as I was before this 'gift' of yours," said Karenth looking down at our hands. I was still transferring power to him. He now held roughly an eighth of the power he had had originally.

An eighth of a Celior, I thought wryly, remembering my measurement system, by contrast I had roughly one and a half Celiors still at my disposal. I had drained a substantial amount from the God-Stone in addition to the power from the Iron Heart Chamber. "It sounds as though they are fairly weak then," I noted.

"That's still enough to make one of them a serious danger to one of your knights, and there are a lot more of them. This is aside from the fact that they are still immortal," Karenth informed me.

His words were unsettling and they sent my thoughts into a desperate spiral. *What do I do?* Even though I was dead, my family, even my nation, needed me. I had thought I could save them but it seemed that at every turn I found the odds stacked against me. *More importantly, what would Mordecai do?* Well, for starters he wouldn't be flying in the wrong direction, prioritizing the return of Lyralliantha before taking care of his own people. That couldn't be helped however. My only hope of freedom was to fulfill her command and trust that she would keep her word.

And after that? How do I defeat a legion of immortal mini-gods, their nigh-omnipotent master, and his human patsies—all while keeping the nation more or less intact? It was hopeless. Once Lyralliantha freed me, I should use the token she had given me and destroy myself. At least then the 'hero' could go to his well-earned rest. I was only a poor copy. Saving the world was impossible. I should content myself with saving Mordecai. Let his soul find peace wherever it was that souls went after they passed through the void. That was a more reasonable goal. *What would Mordecai do?*

Fight!

The last thought came from somewhere else, accompanied by a painful pulse in my chest. I took an unnecessary breath and let out a sigh. "Goddammit."

Karenth looked at me questioningly.

"Here's what I want you to do," I told him, and for the next quarter of an hour I laid out his instructions. Once I had finished, I opened the 'door', allowing a blast of air to roar into the interior of my flying device.

"What are you doing now?" he asked.

I smiled. "I'm kicking you out. My binding won't let me stop, so you'll have to make your own way back, but I'm sure you have power enough now."

"Right here?!" he said, startled. His voice rose to a shout as I placed a hand behind him and gave him a rather ungentle shove.

"Yep," I said smugly, watching him fall for a few seconds. His body sprouted wings, and he took flight before he had fallen halfway to the ground.

Alone, I watched the ground fly by beneath me for a few minutes before exploring my second idea. Closing my eyes, I turned my attention inward, seeking the black core of my being. It was a place of darkness, the She'Har spellweaving appeared to me like a sphere made of nothingness, a blank place that light entered but never left. Within it was Mordecai's soul, but from my perspective nothing of its interior could be observed.

Lines of dark power stretched outward from it, snaking their way throughout my body, and though some stopped there, many others went farther, stretching away invisibly into the distance—to the other shiggreth. According to my best guesses, those lines should allow me to control and communicate with them. I believed that they were dependent upon that link, that eventually, when I was free to destroy the spellweaving that maintained my existence, they would also die. For now though, I had other uses for them.

Focusing, I sent my thoughts outward along lines that stretched hundreds of miles, in a thousand different directions: *Come. You are needed.* Mentally I created a vision of the place I wanted them to go. Giving instructions as carefully as I could, I sent more images, faces and heraldic designs, each accompanied by one command or the other: *Kill these. Spare those.*

Inevitably, I knew that there would be mistakes. The images I had used to identify friend and foe were limited, and some innocent lives might be lost. Luckily my emotions had ebbed to a low point. Guilt wasn't a problem. Necessity and efficiency were all I cared about.

My biggest concern was that my commands might be ignored, or too complicated. My own experience suggested that their minds might be more complex than I had assumed before becoming one myself, but I still couldn't be sure. I was, after all, in a unique position.

Chapter 27

Penelope Illeniel stared at the sky for long minutes after 'Brexus' had disappeared with his cargo. The others went back inside, except for her children, who stood with her, sharing the quiet melancholy. Internally she was a wreck, her emotions were twisting and turning, anger mixed with sadness. *How can I believe what Elise says? He barely spoke to me.*

He nearly killed Cyhan. If it is him in there, he's changed. He's become darker and more violent, she thought. *But he didn't hurt the children that day.* Her thoughts had gone back to the day that Matthew was wounded during Moira's confrontation with her 'father', if that's who Brexus really was.

Today he had seemed just as distant, almost mechanical. He had shown no concern for her or anyone else in the house. Except for that last moment, when she had blocked his path. *I thought he was about to hit me.* She had refused to react to his threatening gesture, thinking to let him show his true colors. His sudden paralysis, accompanied by those words...

He sounded like my Mordecai, if just for a moment.

"He didn't even look at me," noted Matthew in a forlorn voice.

His sister tried to explain, "He isn't quite the same, but he's just trying to protect us. He thinks he's a danger to..."

"Just shut up!" Matthew interrupted loudly. "Ever since you got your magic, you act as though you know so much more than everyone else!"

Our moment of solidarity is over, thought Penny. "Stop!" she ordered. "Both of you go inside. We've enough to worry about without you two bickering all the time."

She kept her eyes on the street for a minute more, then she heard someone behind her. "You should come in, Countess. The streets aren't safe," cautioned Stephen Balistair.

She decided to heed his advice and stepped in, closing the door behind her. "I told you yesterday, call me Penny," she rebuked him.

Ariadne had appeared two days previously, desperate and seeking refuge, with Elise Thornbear and a few others. Stephen Balistair had shown up later in the same day, bringing with him some of the survivors of Lord Hightower's garrison. Dorian had returned later still, and his revelation regarding Martin Balistair's part in the treachery that had killed the King was less than welcome news.

Dorian wasn't one to act on mere rumor, but the fact that Stephen was Earl Balistair's oldest son cast him in a suspicious light. His solution had been to lock the man away, but for some reason he couldn't fathom Ariadne forbade it. She believed Stephen's claim of ignorance and shame at his father's actions.

Since then they had gathered several hundred armed men, remnants of the city guard, the palace guard, and the retainers of some of the local nobility who hadn't been involved in the plot. They were woefully outnumbered, but the invaders hadn't yet been able to organize properly. Sir Egan and Sir Dorian had also proven remarkably effective at dissuading Tremont's men from trying to force them into a head on confrontation, but their luck couldn't hold out for much longer.

"Forgive me, Penelope," replied Stephen courteously.

"Penny.   Only my father calls me Penelope," she returned. *And Mordecai sometimes, when he was angry or tense.* She cut that thought off immediately.

Dorian spoke up as she entered the main hall, "Are you sure we did the right thing?" The 'right thing' he was referring to was letting Mordecai remove the She'Har woman.

"We obviously couldn't do anything with her," she observed.

"That's not what I mean. We don't know what his motivations are. Nor do we know what will happen if he releases her. Her race wasn't known for being friendly to humankind after all," he responded.

"Your mother thinks we should trust him," Penny replied.

The large warrior grimaced for a moment, "She's never seen some of the things I have. In Gododdin we found whole villages, men, women, children—everyone. They look like us, but they aren't people. Sometimes they seemed to remember things, or have knowledge from their former lives, but they only used it to get close to their next victims."

"You think it's just a ruse? That he, or it, whatever you want to call him—just wants to get closer to us so he can devour us?" she asked, careful to keep her tone neutral.

Stephen spoke up, "That's what happened with Katherine." He was referring to his now deceased wife.

Dorian nodded. "I tend to agree with Stephen, but I've never seen anything quite as complicated as this."

"Complicated?"

"Usually, even the ones that have some memories only pursue short term goals. If he's one of them, he's acting in a whole range of ways that are uncommon. Mother's story about this woman, it doesn't make sense. I've never heard of one letting someone go," explained Dorian.

"Yes you have," reminded Penny, "us." Years ago, she and Dorian had been captured and used as bargaining chips when the shiggreth made a deal with King Edward.

"What?" Stephen Balistair had obviously never heard that story.

Penny retold the tale of their time with their undead captors, leaving out some of the more embarrassing details. "Anyway, that clearly shows that they are sometimes capable of advance planning," she added when she had finished.

"You ignore the fact that their goal at that time was to get leverage against Mordecai," noted Dorian.

"Well they've got a lot better than leverage now," said Stephen. "They have the wizard himself."

"Mordecai was only a means to an end for them," declared Moira Centyr, walking into the hall and joining the discussion. Her new body had perfect hearing and she had been listening from the kitchen. "Their goal has been accomplished."

"We're still alive," argued Dorian. "As far as I am aware, they were created to destroy mankind."

"That statement has some truth. From what I have learned, they were a vengeful accident on the part of the last of the She'Har, but there is another purpose that they have helped to fulfill," Moira told them.

Penny interrupted, "You said Mordecai was still himself. Why would he be serving their interests? And what is this purpose?"

"I would like to know that as well," said Ariadne, stepping up beside Moira Centyr.

Moira dipped her head in deference to the princess. "As you wish, Your Highness. My knowledge is limited but I will share what I can."

"We shouldn't talk in the hall when there are seats aplenty in the next room," suggested Ariadne.

After they had taken seats and gotten more comfortable, Moira continued, "I doubt most of you are aware of this, but I was originally responsible for part of the creation of what we now call the 'Shining Gods'. Well, not me exactly, but the woman whose name and memories I bear. She created me as well, but for simplicity's sake I refer to myself as 'Moira'."

"Pardon—what?" asked Stephen, already confused.

"I can clarify some of that later," Penny told him. "For now please continue, Moira."

"The Centyr wizards specialized in creating magical intelligences. Artificial minds, crafted purely from magic. At that time, there was an Illeniel wizard, a gifted enchanter, who devised an enchantment to make those minds permanent. His goal, and mine, was to create an immortal servant, powerful and ever vigilant, to protect humanity." Moira leaned forward as she warmed to her subject.

"To some degree, we succeeded. Though as most of you are aware, our success has since been overshadowed by what became of our creations after we were gone."

Penny interrupted, "What does this have to do with Mort?"

"He has in many ways become something similar. When he fought Thillmarius, the shiggreth leader, he destroyed him by removing the magic that maintained him. As a human he was incapable of directly changing or controlling the She'Har magic, but as an archmage he was able to subvert the magic, replacing the mind it held with his own," said Moira.

Dorian broke in, "And that made him into one of them?"

"Not directly," corrected Moira Centyr. "He imprisoned his soul within the She'Har spellweaving, severing its connection with the living world. After that his body died, though magic continues to sustain it."

"Severing its connection…," mumbled Penny quietly to herself.

"So he is one of them," said Dorian.

"Yes and no," said Moira. "I won't sugar coat this. The man you knew is trapped, locked within the creature you just met. He isn't in control either. He may not even be aware of the outside world."

"Huh?" interjected Dorian.

"His body is now a type of soulless animate construct. His brain, his memories, they've become a magical awareness, similar to the sort the Centyr wizards used to create. Initially the construct wasn't even aware of that fact, *it* thought it was him."

"So there are two Mordecai's?" Penny asked.

"There you have it," said Moira, pointing at Penny as if she had won a prize. "We have two, the original living soul, which is now trapped in a magical prison, and the present Mordecai, who has renamed himself 'Brexus'."

Stephen Balistair groaned, holding his head in his hands as though he feared it might split apart.

"It gets better," Moira informed him. "He is also the locus, the focal point for the shiggreth. To destroy them completely we will have to destroy him."

Penny flinched visibly at that pronouncement, but Dorian spoke first, "Wait! He's their leader now?"

"That is my best guess," she answered, "though I saw no direct evidence of it while I was with him."

"If he's still Mordecai, or if he is a copy of Mordecai, shouldn't he be helping us?" asked Dorian.

"He may want to," began Moira, "but there are a couple of reasons why we shouldn't put the same trust in him that you would in the man he once was."

Penny broke in, "Dorian's mother told me that he helped a woman after he attacked her. That sounds to me as though he still retains some of his old self."

"Let me explain," said Moira. "The She'Har woman has modified the magic that sustains him. She's bound him to her will. While I don't think her intentions are necessarily malign, her priorities are different than ours. As you noticed, he virtually ignored everyone here. He must satisfy her demands before his own. At the moment that means he must reunite her with her lover."

"Is this the purpose you mentioned earlier?" said Stephen.

Moira nodded. "Exactly. Her goal, Mordecai's first priority, is the rebirth of the She'Har race."

"The same race that nearly wiped us out two thousand years ago," noted Penny. "The same race that created Mal'goroth, who is still trying to finish the job."

"Remind me again. Why did we let him leave with her?" asked Dorian.

The twins had snuck back into the room unnoticed. Moira Illeniel spoke up unexpectedly, "We couldn't have stopped him. He's more powerful than anything you can imagine now."

Dorian looked down at the small girl, "Lass, I've fought the things we used to call gods—up close and personal. I can imagine quite a bit."

Penny's daughter didn't waver, "Take what you imagine, and multiply it."

"Maybe he'll take care of Mal'goroth for us then," suggested Stephen.

Moira Centyr grimaced, "I think that's what he wants, but he felt that Mal'goroth was at least an order of magnitude more powerful than anything he could hope to deal with."

Penny spoke, "This is all beside the point. We know that we're facing something too powerful for us to fight. The question is whether we can trust Mordecai, or Brexus—whatever you want to call him."

Dorian was gritting his teeth now. "As much as I hate what's become of him, Mother thinks we should trust him. I've never gone wrong putting my faith in him before."

"There is more you should know," said Moira Centyr. "There is a reason that only Centyr wizards were able to create magically sentient minds. Those crafted by other families were invariably unstable. I was able to observe him up close for several days. His personality is eroding. We may be able to trust his intentions now, but his sanity won't last."

Matthew spoke then, "You're wrong! He'll save us."

Everyone turned to the boy speaking, pity and condescension in their eyes. All eyes but one pair; Moira Illeniel stood beside her brother and added, "Don't look at Matthew that way. He's right. I spoke with Daddy—in here." She pointed to her forehead. "He won't let us down."

Stephen Balistair patted her gently, "Child, he isn't your father anymore."

"He is!" she growled, jerking her head away.

Ariadne rose from her seat then. "We will not gain anything by arguing. A choice must be made, and it must fall to me to decide. If Mordecai turns against us, all is likely to be lost. If he is with us, and we are mistrustful, he may fail. Therefore we will trust him." As she spoke her personality changed, and no one was left in any doubt about who actually spoke. It wasn't Ariadne the woman, but the Queen of Lothion who had pronounced her judgment.

Rose Thornbear stepped in with a tray of scones. She had missed the entire discussion, but her ears had caught Ariadne's tone. "Did I miss something?" she asked.

Dorian groaned. "I'll catch you up later Rose."

She looked at him doubtfully.

"What?" Dorian said.

"You always leave important things out, dear," replied Rose sweetly. Her eyes turned instead to Penny and Ariadne. "I'm sure the ladies will explain things more completely."

Everyone laughed while Dorian frowned at her. "Have it your way," he said grumpily.

*
**

Later that evening Rose found her husband looking over his equipment in the bedroom. They had returned to the Illeniel house after he had escaped from the palace. For obvious reasons it was one of the only truly safe places they could stay in the city.

He held his breastplate in one hand, examining it in the light.

"You haven't even managed to scratch it yet," she remarked. The breastplate was part of the armor that Mordecai had crafted to replace the set that had been destroyed when Dorian fought Karenth previously. "Is it really worth your time to go over it again and again, love?"

Dorian shrugged, "Old habits die hard. Better to be sure, than die from a mistaken assumption."

Rose watched him silently for a few minutes before broaching the topic that was bothering her. "Is tonight really wise?"

Her husband had gotten as far as inspecting his great sword by that point. He set it aside and gave her his full attention. "I doubt the word 'wise', really applies to anything that has occurred the past few days."

Ariadne had planned a strike against Tremont's troops during the dark hours before dawn. One of the main bodies of the usurper's mercenaries was currently occupying the main bailey that controlled the city's east gate. Coincidentally that was also the place traditionally occupied by the Lord Hightower, Rose's father. No one had seen him since the takeover, although they had liberated some of his men at arms.

The soldiers who had been poisoned were recovering, those who hadn't been slain by the invaders. According to Elise, the poison used was meant to sicken and incapacitate rather than kill.

"You know what I'm asking," she said.

"We're still outnumbered at least four to one, but we know the layout of the city's defenses intimately, and we're already inside the walls. If we wait Tremont will solidify his hold on the city and be able to bring more troops to bear. Each day also increases the chance that he will find the safe houses where we've hidden what remains of our guardsmen. Once that happens we'll lose our ability to fight back," explained Dorian. "Time is not on our side."

"Shouldn't we abandon the city and find a better time and place to fight?" she suggested.

Dorian rolled his shoulders, stretching the muscles. "We have one advantage."

Rose narrowed her eyes. "You?"

"And Penny, and Sir Egan," added her husband.

"She shouldn't be going with you," said Rose disapprovingly.

Dorian nodded, "I feel the same, but there's no denying she's one of our most powerful assets at this point. Besides, she won't be kept from it."

Rose's expression didn't change.

"And the truth is—we need her," said Dorian plainly. "We only have three fighters with the earth bond. The others are in Cameron."

"We shouldn't be fighting, we risk losing even more," countered Rose.

"That's probably truth, but you ignore the influence of our new queen. Ariadne has set a fire in the hearts of everyone she's come into contact with. I never would have suspected she had such a talent with people. She instinctively knows she needs to keep a forward momentum to gather the full support of the citizens."

Rose changed tack, "Without you she has nothing."

Her husband's heavy brows knitted together as he frowned. "What's that supposed to mean?"

"You're the linchpin, the last bit of power that holds everything else together. Penny can't afford to take on the sorts of dangers you will. Sir Egan, and for that matter, the other Knights of Stone, follow you. If something happens to you it will be the blow that finishes the work that Tremont started when he killed James."

Dorian listened intently, and silently he agreed with her on all points. "The truth doesn't change necessity."

Lady Rose waved her finger at her husband, "Don't try getting deep on me. I saw your face when you returned the other day. That armor you borrowed was utterly ruined and your eyes were haunted. She can't risk putting you at the spear point of this attack."

Dorian tilted his chin down, letting the shadows cover his eyes when he heard her words. "We talked about that already. I was just a little shaken. Too much blood in one day can do that to a man."

"It was more than that," Rose continued doggedly, "you were afraid."

"I've never felt fear in the face of an enemy. That still hasn't changed…," responded Dorian fiercely.

"Then you're a fool."

"… but I thought I might die that day. I thought of you, and the children—what might happen to you. It gave me a new perspective," Dorian added. "I carried that poor woman. All she wanted was to see her children one more time…," his words trailed off, but he picked them up again after a long pause. "I realized that all I wanted was the same, but all I could see in front of me was a sea of faces—men waiting for me to kill them."

"Then you understand why I used to push so hard to get you to stay home, to let other men carry some of the burden. Every time you left I cried. Each time I worried that that would be the journey that would take you away from us forever," she answered softly.

Dorian's head was in his hands now. "It's worse than that, Rose. It's changing me."

"No one passes through such trials unscathed."

"No, I mean something more than that. I'm afraid of what I'm becoming. It's gotten too easy. It used to be work, but now it seems normal. When I look at people now, the first thing that occurs to me is how easily they might die. Sometimes I fear that I might kill someone if I don't keep a close watch on myself. Not out of spite, or malice, simply out of reflex—simply because it's normal, because that's what I do."

Rose bit her lip. "You're far more than that. Think of your children. Your son adores you, and your daughter will too someday. You just have to survive this... to give your heart time to heal."

"Let's be honest, Rose. I'm gone more than half the time. And the things I do... I don't want Gram taking up the sword after me. I worshipped my Dad, but I didn't understand then what I do now. It's a curse. If you had seen those men's eyes today—when they looked at me..."

"Is that why you named it 'Thorn'?" she asked, hoping to turn his thoughts away from their morbid course. She was referring to the name he had given his magical great sword.

He stared at her for a long second, "You know why I named it Thorn."

"Remind me."

"Actually, I named it Rose's Thorn," he replied, "as a warning to any who might keep me from returning to you. I know you didn't forget that."

"I didn't," she admitted. "I just wanted to remind you. You have three good reasons to keep your handsome self in one piece, and I am one of them." She draped herself over his broad shoulders, letting one hand rest on his stomach.

Her hand reminded him of his most recent transformation. His body had returned to normal not long after the fighting ended, but he had kept the details of his battle to himself. He felt a small amount of guilt for keeping the secret, and he considered revealing to her then what had happened. "I'm not sure they *can* hurt me," he told her, wondering if she would pick up on his hint.

Rose was focused on improving his mood however. Moving her fingers lightly, she tickled his belly, forcing him to twist in her arms. Despite his brawn, her husband was still weak to certain things. "If those men knew your weakness, no one would fear you, dearest," she said, nibbling on his ear.

"I doubt anyone would think to nibble on my ear lobes," he answered with a weak laugh.

Rose laughed loudly at that, "I didn't mean that! I meant *this!*" Using both hands she began to tickle his sides, causing him to thrash about on the floor. Eventually he managed to wrangle her beneath him, pinning her hands to prevent further assaults on his dignity. Breathless and smiling, her eyes sparkled with mischief as she looked up at him. "Oh, dear! Now I'm in a terrible position. Whatever will you do with me?"

As always he found himself helpless to preserve his dark mood in the face of her sweet charms. "You'll have to pay a ransom if you wish to have your freedom again, milady," he said as he leaned in to kiss her firmly. He brushed away the tear that appeared in his eye before she saw it, and things rapidly grew more intense between them.

Rose made sure he had little time to dwell on his black thoughts after that.

Chapter 28

The island grew slowly in my vision. It seemed as if I was approaching it at a crawl, yet I was pushing my speed as much I could without the risk of losing control of my magical craft. Even though it had been a day and a half since I had left Albamarl, and my emotions were almost non-existent, I could feel a growing tension as my goal grew closer.

I flew over the shoreline without interruption. The magic that had been used to snare me on my last visit was notably absent. Magesight revealed a few glimpses of the Kriteck, but they were few and faint. I detected none of the more powerful ones that had greeted me before.

Where have they gone?

Something faint touched the exterior of my craft as I flew, a tenuous extension of power, seeking and identifying me in a single instant. *Bring her directly to me,* came the mental voice I recognized as Tennick. I was forced to admire his skill at being able to reach my mind directly, despite the distance and the various barriers represented by both my craft and the armor I wore.

"I suppose two thousand years alone on an island leaves one with a lot of time to practice," I said aloud. Silently, I returned an affirmative thought, assuming that Tennick would be able to detect it.

The rest of my trip across the island was similarly untroubled, though I discovered the location of most of the Kriteck once I reached the father-tree. They were gathered in all their varied forms around the tree. The four massive dragon-like ones that I had seen rise from the earth were there as well, spread out almost a quarter mile apart in each of the cardinal directions. Only the space immediately around Tennick was clear. I knew intuitively that that was where I was meant to land.

My landing was anti-climactic, silent, and without any sort of greeters, not that I was surprised. They knew why I was here, and each of them had their purpose. The Kriteck were to guard and protect, there was no need for envoys to welcome me. Tennick himself could not move, but I could sense his attention focused on me. The sensation was so strong it almost seemed as if the tree leaned over me. Even though the sun was still shining down brightly, his presence was a shadow over my shoulder.

I was fifty yards from the massive tree, a distance made necessary by the fact that, over the years, Lyralliantha would likely come to be just as large as her kianthi. In the past the She'Har had sometimes chosen to plant themselves closer together, but only when they had an explicit reason, such as growing some of the impressive structures their cities had contained.

This planting would be traditional and practical. Far enough to give the two trees room to grow freely, yet close enough for their roots to reach one another—and close enough to ensure pollination would never be a problem. In time, if things went well, the grove would expand, as some of their children planted themselves around them; mother and father-trees would eventually cover most of the island.

That reflection left me with one sobering thought. *Where will Mordecai's children be then? Will they still occupy the mainland, or will it be empty and sterile, victim to Mal'goroth's spite? Will he let the race that created him return to reclaim that land?*

Humanity's fate was very much in doubt.

I harbor no ill-will toward the people of my origin, Tennick relayed directly to my mind. *I merely wish to restore what I destroyed.*

You and Mal'goroth have very different visions of the future, I thought wryly.

For him there is no future.

That was a positive thought, but I wasn't so hopeful, *I wish that were true, but I can see no way to defeat him.*

You cannot, the ancient She'Har mentally nodded in agreement, *but he will have no future regardless.*

Even as we conversed, my body was moving, obeying its incessant requirement to deliver Lyra to her beloved kianthi. My magic had brought her stone container out and had removed its covering already; it was settling to the ground now. I walked over and stared down at the woman lying within. Reaching out I began removing the enchantment that held her bound, timeless, within the sarcophagus. In the back of my mind, my thoughts still pondered Tennick's words. *I'm more concerned with whether Mal'goroth will destroy humanity's future, even if he doesn't have one himself.*

You cannot defeat him.

Who could? I questioned.

The man who destroyed Thillmarius could do it, Tennick responded.

Mordecai? He's dead, I noted without enthusiasm. *What about another archmage?*

The She'Har didn't respond for a long time, his attention caught by Lyralliantha as she took a new breath and began to rise from the stone box. Her gaze was taken immediately by the sight of the massive father-tree, and her lips curved into a smile.

"You succeeded!" she exclaimed with unconcealed delight.

I have waited for you! Tennick's thought was bright with a joy that I hadn't suspected the tree to be capable of.

There was no hope of continuing our conversation for the moment. Tennick and Lyra's minds were entirely preoccupied with their reunion. I could catch hints of their emotions spilling out now and then, but the bulk of their communication was private, hidden from my perception. She had begun to dance, a physical expression of her happiness, as though her body could no longer contain the entirety of her feelings in stillness.

She ran to the base of the giant tree, placing one hand upon its bark before leaping away, twirling with a skip in her steps. Moving in large circles, she made her way around the clearing before returning to the center, to a place close to where I had landed. The earth looked soft there, as if it had been freshly tilled. Tennick must have known the spot she would choose.

She danced around it before lighting in the center and digging her feet into the loose soil like a child. A shudder ran through her body then, and her eyes stopped on me for the first time since she had emerged from her enchanted slumber. "You," she said softly.

I returned her look with a sense of mild annoyance. "Yes?"

She gestured toward me with her arms. Her legs seemed to have become stiff already. I wondered if she might already be taking root. I stepped closer, but she continued to gesture until I was within reach of her arms.

"What do you want? I thought I was finished," I said coldly.

Her arms went around my shoulders and she pulled me into a close embrace. "You have done all I could ask. You have your freedom, and—my thanks." She kissed me lightly then. "Don't forget the stone I gave you. You are free to end your suffering whenever you wish now. My geas is lifted from you."

Her lips felt electric and sent a jolt of living emotion through me, despite the fact that she was not actually human. I pulled away, feeling my irritation fully now. The magic binding my actions was gone, but while her wish had been granted, I was still left with no practical solution for the problems my family faced.

"What about Mal'goroth? You told me you would share your knowledge once I had completed this task," I reminded her. "Is there a way to control him?"

"I cannot help you directly," she replied slowly. "There is a way to control him, but it is lost to living memory."

I tapped my temple. "I still have the knowledge of the loshti. If I just knew what to look for, perhaps I could find it."

She shook her head sadly, "The loshti you bear is from the Illeniel Grove. Mal'goroth was created by the Mordan

Grove, only they knew the key-weaving that would control him."

"Key-weaving," I said, letting the word tickle my memory. It brought an alien bit of knowledge to mind, something meant to control Balinthor, but he had already been destroyed. *Even so, I couldn't use the knowledge; it required the ability to spellweave.* "Only one of your people could do it."

"Yes…" Her eyes seemed to be glazing over.

"Surely you have some information that can help me!"

"I—am—sorry," she answered, with ever longer pauses between her words.

The fresh bit of emotional energy she had given me was fully aggravated now. "You led me to believe you had some knowledge that might help."

Her eyes were completely closed now, "I—misled—you."

"You had already enslaved me! You could have been honest at least. It isn't as though I had any other options!" Visions of burning trees filled my mind, and my thoughts developed violent undertones.

Tennick's words filled my head, *Maintain your balance, or you will not be permitted to exist.*

"She could at least explain herself," I growled. "I'm sick of lies and half-truths."

She cannot hear you. She has begun the transition. Her thoughts are slowing, synchronizing with the longer timescale of an adult She'Har.

"You seem to be able to converse easily enough," I noted.

She must adjust to her new life. It will be some time before she can modulate her thoughts to speak to humans

278

or our new children. Talking with you is not comfortable or easy, even for me.

Just my luck. I was pretty sure that Tennick was ready to go back to sleep, or talk to his wife, a conversation that would take years once he returned to his normal mode of thinking. Meanwhile, I and the rest of the world could take a hike. "You don't seem very worried about what Mal'goroth may do once he's finished wiping humankind off the face of the world," I opined, hoping to irritate Tennick into staying awake longer.

He will not harm us.

I had had enough. "You can go to hell." Reaching into my pocket, I drew out the green stone that Lyralliantha had given me, studying it with my magesight. I was free now. One swift decision was all that stood between me and oblivion. My mind was tattered around the edges, fraying, and unraveling. Madness couldn't be too far away. *Perhaps I should just let go now, before I become something regrettable.* I had already been having trouble maintaining my more sociable demeanor.

You mistake my meaning. I have more to tell...

Chapter 29

Dorian and Penny left the house around three in the morning. They were accompanied by Sir Egan and Stephen Balistair along with a small group of armsmen who had been quartering at the Illeniel house. All totaled, they numbered less than twenty, but their plan was to rendezvous with the majority of the remaining royal guardsmen and the survivors of Lord Hightower's men. Once they had fully gathered, they expected to have somewhere close to three hundred. Not nearly enough if one were looking at just numbers, but they were counting on their three 'aces,' Sir Dorian, Sir Egan, and the Countess herself.

Dorian looked Penelope Illeniel over carefully in the dim light provided by the moon. She was more lightly armored than he was, wearing the enchanted chain hauberk Mordecai had created for her years before. She also carried the shield and sword he had crafted for her. A steel cap completed her outfit. The chainmail wouldn't protect her from crushing blows or broken bones, but the magic it was imbued with made it much lighter than normal mail. She could move much more lightly than either Egan or Dorian, which was how she preferred it.

Besides his worry for her physical safety, Dorian's other main concern lay in what he saw in Penny's face. She held an expression of eagerness there, as though she looked forward to the violence that was to come. *Was that what I used to look like?* he thought quietly. *Perhaps we're all just killers at heart.*

"Don't look at me like that," she told him with a daring grin. "By the time this night is over, I may have more notches in my belt than you."

He nodded, "That's what I'm afraid of…"

"You may want to consider some new information before you continue," said a voice from the shadows at the corner of the house where an alley led toward the carriage house in the back.

Weapons were drawn and shields readied as everyone reacted with surprise. None of them had expected to encounter anyone yet; they hadn't even begun to move toward the first rendezvous point.

"Who's there!?" challenged Dorian.

Karenth the Just stepped forward, moving silently into the moonlight. "An old acquaintance… I bear word from Mordecai—and intelligence from the city."

"And we should believe you?" said the Countess di' Cameron with poorly hidden incredulousness.

The somewhat diminished Shining God smiled, "Ordinarily no, but I am your husband's slave now. You should treat my words with the same level of trust or distrust you give his."

I am a widow, thought Penny fiercely, fighting to retain her composure. *Whatever he is, Brexus isn't truly my beloved.*

Dorian responded first, "If you are not here to betray us, then give us your words and be swift about it, our time is short."

Karenth bowed his head respectfully. "He has commanded me to tell you to flee the city and seek shelter in Castle Cameron if it is still safe there. If not, you should seek to find the whereabouts of whatever survivors there are. Albamarl will not be safe for much longer."

"It isn't safe now," muttered Stephen Balistair.

"Things will be far worse," the god continued. "Mal'goroth has grown tired of Tremont's games. He has summoned his brethren. Some of them are within the city already, and others will be here soon. Albamarl will become a slaughterhouse."

"His brethren?" said Penny questioningly.

"The weakened remnants of the Dark Gods, like the one that Dorian battled recently," clarified Karenth patiently.

Dorian grimaced at the thought. "How many of them are there?"

"There were forty two originally, according to the lore of the church. If we no longer count Balinthor, and since Mal'goroth has not yet shown himself directly, that would put their numbers at forty—assuming they all come here," answered Karenth.

Dorian could feel his heart dropping. There was no way to deal with such a number. "Thirty-nine, I dispatched one," he announced.

"No," said Karenth sadly. "You temporarily immobilized one. Even Mal'goroth cannot destroy them. That is why they still exist."

"So how many are in the city now?" asked Penny.

"I have already detected eleven, and my sources indicate that more are approaching," replied the god.

"And this is why he wanted us to flee the city?" she continued.

Karenth shook his head negatively, "He was unaware of their presence in any numbers. He wanted you to clear the city for other reasons."

"It would help to know them," she said sarcastically.

"He said, 'Tell them not to trifle with the dead. They must leave the city and seek shelter elsewhere.'" relayed Karenth. After a moment he added, "I believe he means to destroy or attack the city in some way."

"And what of the citizens?! What of the innocent, the children?" Penny responded in a shocked tone.

Karenth smiled, "He said you would worry for them. He told me to convey that he would do his utmost to protect them while punishing those who slew your king. He also said that he could not guarantee anyone's safety with perfect certainty. That is why he bids you to take your family and flee."

"Even if we abandon the city to its own devices, we still have far too many people to move. How are we supposed to get the remaining soldiers out? Not to mention their families—the logistics will be impossible to manage so quickly," argued Penny.

"Caution them to stay in groups of twenty or less," urged Karenth. "He said any large groups, over twenty men, might be targeted."

"This doesn't make sense," Dorian said with some annoyance. "What is he planning? What does 'might be targeted' mean? Can't you be any clearer?"

Karenth gave him a condescending smile. "I realize you are not an overly clever man, Sir Dorian, but think on it a moment. He did not make his plan explicit regarding

Albamarl for me either, but he did say 'not to trifle with the dead'. It shouldn't take a great leap of logic to get at least a vague idea of his plans."

Dorian's patience was close to its end. He leaned forward menacingly as he replied, "I really doubt he ordered you to be insulting while you were running his errands, lackey."

"The insult was my own contribution," said Karenth with a smile, "but don't think to threaten me, Sir Dorian. While I am charged with aiding your escape, I have had enough power restored that I can easily ignore any threat you might present."

"If that is the case, then we can count on your assistance dealing with the Dark Gods, may we not?" suggested Penny suddenly.

"That would be unwise," said Karenth. "As it now stands, while I have detected their presence, so too they have noticed mine. I have enough power to deal with two or three of them in their present condition; I could not manage more than that. It would be more effective for me to lead them away from you, rather than brave a direct confrontation."

They talked a bit more before finally Penny made up her mind. "Enough! If what this creature says is true, then we have to alter our course."

Dorian nodded, "Agreed. What do you propose?"

Penny pointed at the men with them. "Send them along to the rendezvous points. Let them relay Karenth's warnings about grouping up. Have them keep either the royal arms or Hightower's design close at hand. We'll return and gather up Ariadne and our families. We have little choice other than escape." She looked in Karenth's direction, "What will you do?"

"Lead your enemies away and clear obstacles from your path if the opportunity presents. You will not see me again until after you reach the World Road," answered the god.

*
**

It took more than an hour to rouse everyone in the house and get them out the door. Elise Thornbear in particular, was not in good shape for the journey. She could walk but she still suffered from a large collection of bruises. Also, the poison she had taken, while she had been partly immune to it, had still weakened her. She endured both pain and nausea as they prepared to sneak out of the capital.

Rose watched her mother-in-law carefully, nervous at forcing her to travel so soon after her injuries. Mentally she counted their group as they stepped out, a habit that had grown stronger since she had had children. *Gram, Carissa, Matthew, Moira, Irene, Conall, Lily, Penny, Cyhan, Egan...* She recited the names silently to herself. Along with their children, the group included several warriors and guardsmen, although Cyhan was still in no shape for combat.

A shadow loomed over her, and Rose turned to see the bulky form of her husband looming in the dim light. His presence gave her a feeling of security that nothing else could. *Dorian alone is enough,* she thought, *no one else could protect us as well.*

He handed her a soft bundle, Carissa, swaddled against the cool night air. Leaning forward he kissed Rose's forehead. "I wish I could carry her, but it wouldn't be safe," he said apologetically.

She lifted her free hand to his cheek, feeling the thick stubble there. Dorian hadn't shaved in several days. She said nothing, letting her expression carry her feelings. A moment later she caught Penny's eyes on her. Her friend looked away quickly, but not before Rose caught the hint of sadness there. A momentary pang of involuntary guilt washed over Rose. *We must constantly remind her of what she's lost.*

"Is everyone here?" called Ariadne, standing to one side.

After what had probably been their fifth head count she was satisfied, and the band of refugees began making their way down darkened streets. Dawn was close however, and the light would be upon them soon.

Their group numbered twenty-one once the men at arms were included. Penny worried about that. Mordecai's warning had said to avoid groups larger than twenty, but near the end of their discussion, Karenth had also told them to carry or wear identifiable house colors or arms. He hadn't been clear on whether that would allow them to ignore the number limit.

Since she was the most lightly armored and the least imposing, Penny ranged ahead of the group as they traveled. Ariadne, Elise and the children were kept close to the center, with Peter and Lily Tucker assisting with the smaller children. Dorian stayed near the front, while Sir Egan took the rear, and the other six men at arms ranged on either side. Cyhan limped along on the right hand side, but it was questionable whether he would be able to do much of anything with a broken arm and collarbone. The stubborn veteran wore his scabbard so that he could draw his sword with his left hand, but armor had been out of the question.

Ariadne questioned Rose again as they walked, "Are you sure this is the best choice?"

The other woman nodded, "I doubt anyone left in the city knows of the passage—other than my father." An awkward pause ensued, there had still been no news regarding what had happened to Lord Hightower.

Finally Ariadne spoke, "I find it odd that it would be hidden in a church."

Rose shrugged, "Before James, the monarchs of Lothion were close allies of the Four Churches." The escape route they were planning to use lay in the cellar of a now abandoned church. It had previously been dedicated to Millicenth, but since the ejection of the churches from the capital it had been largely abandoned. It was likely inhabited by the poor and homeless now.

"I am still uncomfortable with abandoning the citizens who remain," stated the Princess.

"I think we all feel the same, but we have little choice. As a ruler, you will be faced with many more such dilemmas," replied Rose.

Ariadne's eyebrows went up, "You think Roland is…"

"No. I don't know. I hope he is safe and the others as well. I spoke out of place," said Rose. A moment later she added, "If we survive this—I think you will be a great queen. Your father and mother would have been proud."

Carissa began squirming in her mother's arms then, and Rose held her to her chest, fearful that she might begin to cry. Ariadne didn't reply, but she squeezed Rose's shoulder with her hand. Looking up, Rose thought she saw tears in the younger woman's eyes, but it might have been her imagination in the dim light. Neither of them spoke for a while.

Luck was with the small group, and they encountered no one on the streets, although they heard strange noises in the distance. They reached the large building that nestled against one of the city's outer walls in less than an hour, and much to their surprise the place was empty of human occupants. Charred wood and refuse littered the halls, a testament to the vagrants and transients who had been using the building off and on since its owners had fled the city.

Rose led them to a large cellar door and down into a big room that appeared to have once housed a great array of wine bottles. Now it was adorned only with broken bottles and empty wooden casks. The place was so dark that Penny was forced to take out the enchanted globe she had brought from the Illeniel house. The glass had been another of Mordecai's left behind works. It glowed brightly, illuminating the cellar once she had withdrawn it from its heavy wool bag.

"There should be a door here, along the eastern wall," Rose informed them.

"You've never seen it?" asked Sir Egan.

"I've never been here before," Rose replied. "I only know of it from my father's words to me years ago."

"That seems a pretty thin bit of information for us to be...," Egan began, but he was interrupted by Elise Thornbear.

"Sir Egan, my daughter-in-law's memory and judgment are second to none. If she says a safe passage is hidden here it would behoove you to look for it rather than cast aspersions."

The Knight of Stone ducked his head in acknowledgement of Lady Thornbear's admonishment. "My apologies, I meant no disrespect."

Gram had gone to one corner with Matthew and Moira. He spoke up, "Moira says it's over here, Grandmother."

Rose clucked aloud at her forgetfulness, "We should have asked Moira first. I keep forgetting her extra senses."

A short search of the hidden door revealed an iron ring, and Sir Egan used his strength to pull the heavy stone section back so that they could enter. Beyond, a dark tunnel stretched out into the distance. It was only four feet in height so everyone was forced to duck down and hunch their shoulders as they walked. The air was musty and full of the dank smell of mold, but the passage itself was free of debris or even spider webs.

All of the men found it difficult to move in the confined space but Cyhan was unable to continue. His broken collarbone made changes in posture intensely painful, and walking while bent over was too much even for him. In the end, they rigged a makeshift litter out of a cloak and two spears that they used to drag him through the small corridor. It was still painful, but only someone who knew him well could see the signs in his face.

"You should have let my mother give you something," said Dorian as he dragged the litter. He was referring to something Elise had told Cyhan before they left. She had offered to fix the older warrior some tea that would relieve his pain while they traveled. Cyhan had refused, of course.

Glancing back Dorian saw a smile on Cyhan's face, always an awkward expression for the taciturn man. "I prefer not to dull my senses," he replied.

Dorian gave a short laugh, "Senses or senseless, you won't be much use in a fight. You just like to torture yourself."

Both of them knew that even with the injuries he possessed, Cyhan was still more dangerous than any three men combined, but the older veteran didn't choose to argue the point. "After everything I've been through, I'm inclined to agree with you."

It was unusual for Cyhan to offer up so many words without some functional purpose, usually regarding orders or tactics. Dorian thought about the words for a moment before replying, "I'm starting to think anyone who chooses this path in life is a fool."

"What path?" asked Cyhan, with brows raised.

Dorian was forced to keep his eyes on the ground, but he used one hand to tap the hilt of the great sword strapped across his back. "This one."

Cyhan grunted in agreement. "Yeah, you should quit it while you can. Keep at it and you'll wind up like me."

"You're still breathing."

"There's more to life than breathing," said Cyhan with an uncharacteristic sigh.

"You sure you didn't drink some of my mother's tea?" asked Dorian.

"Who knows?" said Cyhan. "She's trickier than both of us."

The tunnel emerged in a storeroom that was located under a small warehouse. The doors were locked and none of them had the keys, but that wasn't much of an impediment for Dorian and Sir Egan. Whether the noise of their destructive exit alerted anyone, they couldn't be sure, but there was no one visible in the street when they stepped out.

They resumed their former arrangement, with Penny ranging forward while the other warriors spread out around the Queen, the noblewomen, and the children. They didn't have much farther to go before they would be free of the populous region around the capital, then they could breathe easier.

Dorian heard the clash of steel first and his eyes flickered to Sir Egan who nodded a moment later. The earth-bond made their senses more acute as well as enhancing their physical strength. Lifting his hand, Dorian signaled for their party to halt momentarily.

"The Countess has encountered the enemy ahead of us. We will head down the right hand lane in the hope of avoiding them," Dorian announced softly.

Everyone nodded, except Gram, "Which way is Aunt Penny going?"

Dorian paused to answer his son, "She's moving left, to the north."

"We aren't going to help her?"

"She's helping us. Once she's led them away or removed the threat, she will catch up," he explained patiently.

The older children exchanged looks. None of them liked it, but Dorian exuded an aura of authority that would brook no more delays. Ariadne put her hand on Gram's

291

shoulder for a second, and without further urging he went along with her.

As they moved, the sounds of battle grew louder, until everyone could easily hear the noise. Hurried footsteps, the sound of armored men running, and the occasional grunt of pain, it got louder for a bit before receding in the darkness. Everyone was tense, but Moira's magesight showed her what was happening as they walked.

"She's alright," she told Conall reassuringly, making certain that Matthew could hear her words as well. "She wounded several men, and the others can't catch her."

"How will Momma find us?" asked the small boy.

"She can see and smell almost like a cat in the dark," whispered Matthew standing on the other side of his younger brother. "Plus she knows where we are going. Mom will find us."

They traveled on into the night, leaving the outskirts of the city via some of its lesser traveled roads before circling slightly to head toward the World Road. One of the better highways went in that direction, but they kept to the lightly wooded areas beside the road rather than risk being caught in the open.

It took them several hours to cover the distance to the western gate of the fortress that protected the World Road. Under more ordinary circumstances the trip would have taken less than an hour, but the moderate forest and the occasional farm they were forced to circle slowed them down considerably. As they progressed, Dorian's face grew sterner as he privately worried about Penny. He hadn't expected her to take so long catching up to them, whether she had killed their enemies or simply evaded them. *She should have returned to us by now,* he thought to himself.

The massive open archway seemed to loom ominously as they passed under it into the darkness that gathered there. Fifty feet more and they emerged into the starlight which was all that illuminated the courtyard. They had yet to see any sign of the guards who normally were posted on the walls or at the entrances. They had either been killed or had returned to the city itself, to join Ariadne's resistance or to hide with their families.

"Tremont's power is still too thin for him to spare men to guard even this, the most strategic of Lothion's strongholds," observed Ariadne with disdain.

"His strength is built on lies," said Rose. "This coup of his is like a house of cards. Once his allies realize how precarious his position is, his support will vanish."

Sir Egan listened with anxious impatience, "We should get to the tunnel entrance. We are too exposed here if the Duke has posted anyone to the walls. There is no way to ward ourselves if he has bowmen above us."

"What about the Countess?" questioned Lady Thornbear.

"Egan is right," said her son. "We should at least get out from under the open sky. We can wait for her there as long as is possible."

A noise caught Dorian's ear as they entered the eastern tunnel. Looking back across the courtyard his sensitive eyes spotted movement, and seconds later he recognized Penelope Illeniel sprinting toward them. He breathed a sigh of relief and started to announce his news to the others, when he glimpsed the dark shapes of her pursuers. Behind her came five inhuman forms and no two were alike. One moved on four legs, like some monstrous bull, while two others ran on long spindly legs like giant birds. The fourth was stranger still, fifteen feet tall, it moved on long spider-like legs that seemed slow and graceful, belying their true speed. The fifth was still too far to discern properly, but Dorian guessed it seemed even bulkier than the others in the shadowy darkness.

"Everyone move! Down the tunnel! Run if you can!" ordered Dorian loudly, startling the others who had yet to see anything. "Penny is coming, but she has unwelcome guests following close behind." Reaching back he pulled loose the cord that kept Thorn from shifting or slipping on his back. Drawing the sword was not as easy as it was with his longsword; the blade was too long for a man's arm to clear the tip from the scabbard.

Once the sheath was loosened, he was able to pull it away with one hand while taking Thorn's hilt with the other. After he had freed the blade, he let the scabbard drop to the sandy ground. Egan stood beside him, holding two of the famous Sun-swords, one in either hand.

"Don't forget!" shouted Dorian over his shoulder, "Turn right at the end. We're heading for the Lancaster gate." The others were already moving, but Dorian could imagine the reluctance on Cyhan's face. *I'm sure he hates it, but he'll do what needs doing.*

"Are those like the thing you fought at the palace?" asked Egan.

The senior knight was rolling his shoulders to loosen them up. "Probably," he admitted. "I don't think any two of them look quite the same."

They moved farther back down the sloping ramp that led into the tunnel, making sure they were completely covered by the deeper shadows there. Penny was close now, no more than fifty yards away and running for all she was worth. Her body moved with lithe grace while her powerful legs sent her flying forward faster than even the swiftest horse. Despite her incredible velocity, her pursuers were gaining, moving with inhuman gaits on their long, strange legs. Whether their human prey would reach the tunnel before they caught her, was still uncertain.

"Remember, their hides are like iron. They aren't easy to cleave. Be wary lest you snare your weapons," Dorian cautioned Sir Egan.

"She isn't going to make it," said Egan, preparing to start forward, but Dorian put his hand on the other knight's chest.

"We can't take the open ground. All's lost if we get surrounded," he reminded Egan.

"But...!"

"She'll make it, damn you!" barked Dorian. *She has to...*

Adjusting to a sideways stance, the senior knight lifted Thorn and twisted his torso, muscles stretching as he readied his swing. His vision narrowed as he watched the oncoming monstrosities, speeding after the small woman, like hounds in some grotesque hunt. Penny seemed tiny as they closed on her.

Time slowed, and Dorian Thornbear's heart began to follow a deeper rhythm as he felt the power of the earth reach up from below and embrace him. Penelope was almost to the beginning of the ramp as one of the bird-like creatures drew abreast of her, reaching out with an arm that was shaped like a farmer's scythe. In a frozen moment, Dorian could see dark blood running down across

Penny's forehead and cheek, threatening to obscure the vision of one eye. She was breathing hard from her lightning sprint, and while she could feel the presence of the monster behind her, there was no way for her to see the blade-like arm that was sweeping toward her neck.

Nooo! cried Dorian's heart as he saw death slicing toward her. Even if the chainmail stopped the cut, the force would surely break her neck. A glint of starlight on his armor must have alerted her then, for he saw her eyes lock on him as she leapt forward. Surprise and relief lighting her face as she realized help was near.

The distraction disturbed her pace and she stumbled, falling forward into a mad headlong tumble.

That accident of fate was all that saved her life as the dark god's appendage tore through the air where her head had just been, ripping one of her long braids. The momentum of her flight sent her falling down the shallow slope past Dorian and Egan, and her foe was close behind.

Dorian's body uncoiled like a tightly wound spring as he whipped Thorn across to meet the monster's body where it hurtled toward Penny. The combination of their relative velocities drove the great sword completely through the thing's hard body, sheering it completely in two with a great sound like that of some massive piece of iron being torn with unbelievable force.

Egan followed this attack as the terrible creature's body fell across the place where Penny had landed. His twin swords moved with deadly grace as he worked to both dismember what was left of the creature and to keep the scythes from tearing into the Countess before she could recover her wits.

Dorian had no time to waste. He left Egan to finish the first, while he stepped forward to meet the second and third of their enemies. His body was still twisting with the momentum of his swing, and rather than fight it, he went along, spinning like a top. The long steel blade removed the leg of the second, raptor-like creature but failed to connect with the third.

The one that had lost a leg fell tumbling to meet Egan and Penny, who was now rising unsteadily to her feet, while the third, a massive bull shaped entity, whirled to face Dorian. With shocking agility, it altered course and sprang at him lowering its great hammer-like head as it strove to ram him.

Unable to move aside in time to avoid the terrible rush, Dorian fell backward instead, letting his body drop beneath the monster's oncoming body. The head struck his breastplate a glancing blow, driving him to the ground with even greater force, but he still escaped the worst of the shock. Lifting his feet, he planted them beneath the beast and kicked upward, launching its bulk skyward in a fifteen foot arc.

Rolling to his feet Dorian could see Penny and Sir Egan working in tandem to dismember the one whose leg he had removed. The one that he had launched landed awkwardly on one side, but had already regained its feet. Meanwhile... *the fourth. Where is the fourth?*

The fourth was the most oddly constructed of the five. It stood tall, like some strange spider on lengthy pole-like legs. It was above him now, ten foot appendages holding it out of reach while two shorter arms pointed downward, a magenta glow forming at their ends.

Leaping sideways with stunning speed, he was still too late. Eldritch energies caught him before he could escape, encasing his armor in a storm of magic and arcing sparks and light. Most of it failed to reach him, but enough passed through the joints and openings in his suit that it felt as though he had been lowered into a river of fire. Pain shot through him, rendering him momentarily blind and senseless.

Smoke rose from Dorian's armor as he staggered. He never heard Penny's shouted warning. He wasn't even certain if he still held his sword. When the bull-like creature reached him this time, he was completely unprepared. It struck with unbelievable force, driving him backward to slam into the granite sidewall that flanked that side of the ramp leading into the tunnel. Stunned, he was still there when it struck again and this time the force of its charge had nothing to mitigate it. He was caught between the wide flat head and the hard stone.

A flash of light accompanied a sharp report as Dorian's breastplate shattered. The magic sustaining its enchantment had been stressed beyond its considerable limits, and it exploded outward, flinging dust and bits of stone and metal in all directions. The beast that had struck him was temporarily shaken as well, for it faltered, trying to regain its bearings.

Incandescent fire flashed out, filling the air in front of Dorian with white hot flames as Sir Egan turned his sun-sword on the monster that had been battering him. The beast screamed in pain as the fire proved to be unexpectedly effective against even its iron-like hide. Smoke billowed up around it as Egan continued his onslaught, and dark fluids seeped from its burning skin, catching fire as they emerged. In short, it burned like dry tinder soaked in pitch.

The tall, spindly fourth creature then turned its magic-charged tendrils on Egan, disrupting his attack as their power flashed through him, setting his nerves on fire. This time the assault didn't stop. The monster kept the power flowing, attempting to fry Egan within his armor.

Shuddering and twitching, Egan collapsed but the tall one continued its attack, until something flew through the air to strike it close to its round bulbous central body. Penny had launched herself like a missile, and she removed one of the softer tendrils with her initial attack. She clung to its main body now, and with a second swing she quickly removed the other. Leaping away, she landed near her fallen companions.

The situation had become dire.

The first three of their opponents were down, but two remained. The tall one loomed over Penny as she considered her options. Then impossibly, it began to grow new tendrils from its main body. Farther back, the fifth, and largest of their attackers had finally closed the distance. It towered, manlike in shape, twenty feet in height, a massive thing with heavy, bludgeoning limbs. It had only two arms, but each was thicker than Penelope's torso. She had no hope of cutting through such massive proportions.

A sound from behind caught her attention, and she saw Dorian's frame rising from the ground. A strange guttural noise seemed to issue from his lips; and he reached up with one hand to pull his helm from his head. What lay within shocked her.

Gone was the human face she had grown up with. In its place was a fierce stone head. His skin was now granite-like in texture, and while his features were still present, they were coarser, as though he had been carved by some mad sculptor with a penchant for feral, dangerous expressions. Reaching across his body Dorian began tugging at what remained of his pauldrons, and then he stripped the armor from his arms. Underneath was more of the same, stone. Everywhere stone. He had transformed completely.

This can't be happening, she thought. *He's like Magnus now. He's gone.*

She had no time to grieve for her friend however, the tall one was already aiming its new weapons at her, and she was forced to dodge the first of what proved to be several potentially deadly magical blasts. Sand and stone vaporized wherever the magic touched, and she had no doubt it would be even more effective against flesh, and her chainmail wouldn't shield her at all. *One hit and I'm dead.*

Weaving in and out, she moved like lightning, cutting at the creature's legs, which seemed to be its main vulnerability, but her smaller sword made it difficult to strike with the force needed to cut through the iron-like skin. *If it would stay still, and I could make a two handed swing, I could probably sever one.* She had more problems than just that however. The fifth was close beside the tall one now, and its huge hands were sweeping down to catch her as she tried to dodge the blasts coming from the other.

Something flashed before her eyes, and then she saw the golem that Dorian had become racing past. He had finished removing the armor and now held his great sword, Thorn, in one hand as he drove himself, shoulder first, into the main body of the larger monster, forcing it back. He rolled away from it as it fell, and the sword came up, glinting like a silver wraith in the starlight. Gripping its hilt within his two thick hands, Dorian's sword blurred as it struck and cut with incredible speed. Pieces of the monster flew in several directions as he danced and whirled around it, chopping bits away like some mad lumberjack whittling away at a mighty oak.

The tall one had moved away from her now, stepping back to survey the change in the battlefield. The deadly tentacles shifted, pointing at Dorian once again, and before Penny could react, they unleashed another deadly barrage at his unprotected back. He was transfixed for a moment as the magic ravaged over and through his body, but he didn't fall.

Penny was about to leap again, to make another flying attack on the tentacles, but Egan's voice warned her off, "Down, Countess!" The knight had recovered his footing, and his sword was pointing at the spindly monster. Once Penelope was clear, the flames rushed forth to bathe it in the devouring white fire of his sun-sword.

Dorian fared worse. The magical attack had temporarily stunned him, and his massive opponent wasted no time taking advantage; both of its huge arms rose and slammed into him from either side. Cracks appeared in his chest as they drew back, but he seemed otherwise unharmed. Whipping his sword upward with one hand, he struck at the left arm but the blade failed to bite deeply enough. It snared in the hard wooden flesh, and before he could release the hilt, the right swung across to strike the middle of the trapped blade.

A flash of light blinded them all for a moment as Thorn snapped in two.

Everything seemed to stop then as they struggled to regain their vision. Dorian particularly seemed stunned by the loss of his sword, but the fallen god he was facing had no such restraint. It caught him in one large fist, and rushing forward, slammed the stone man against the wall. Then it proceeded to pound him, driving him against the hard stone with massive fists.

Stone and dust flew in all directions, and the courtyard seemed to vibrate with the deep sound of each impact. Dorian Thornbear was quickly being rendered into gravel.

It's over, he thought. *Thorn is gone, and I can't go back.* Oddly, his thoughts still seemed clear despite the damage his body was taking. He could feel pieces of himself splintering away, but it didn't really hurt.

The image of Rose's face came to his mind. She would be devastated when she learned of his death. *"You know what I thought that day, when I first saw you?"* The words were hers, from an evening years before, when they were discussing their first meeting.

"Who is that big lout of a man?" That was the answer he had supplied.

"No. That was the next day. This day I spied you helping a young page. The boy couldn't have been more than nine years of age, and he was crying because he worried his squire would beat him. He couldn't clean the rust from the armor he was charged with. Do you remember him?" she had asked.

Dorian had shaken his head, 'no'.

302

"I do. You were still a stranger in my father's house, and yet you stopped to help him. The task was beneath your rank, but you not only showed him how to treat the armor with oil before using the steel wool, you stayed and cleaned half of it yourself. That was when I knew."

"Knew what?" Dorian had questioned.

Rose had given him her special smile then, the smile of a woman who knew the meaning of love. *"People sometimes speak of finding a 'diamond in the rough', but I had found something even better. You were a diamond from the start, polished and perfect."*

A diamond, thought Dorian. *Nothing is stronger than that.*

The hammering blows seemed to take on a rhythm that matched his heartbeat, or perhaps it was the beat of the earth. The difference didn't seem to matter anymore. Dorian's eyes were closed, and his chin was down as he felt the power surging through him. *More, I need it all.* His body seemed to be on fire, but he ignored the painful heat and focused on one thought. *Diamond.*

Penny saw a cloud of smoke rising around her friend's body as the fallen god pummeled him. At first she thought it was dust from the wall, but it was soon apparent that something else was occurring. A wave of heat rolled outward from him, and a strange hissing sound rose in volume. Within seconds the cloud obscured his body, and the heat became so great that she and Sir Egan were forced to retreat farther back.

When it began to clear, they were startled at the change in him, where before there had stood a golem, a stone man, now they saw a being that consisted of shimmering crystal. Dorian Thornbear lifted his head and

303

stared out with crystalline blue eyes. His body had become one living diamond, hard and yet somehow flexible at the same time. His opponent's thundering blows no longer seemed to affect him, other than rocking his body back and forth.

Moving suddenly he slipped away, dodging the next blow and thrusting forward with his own arm. Long crystal blades had grown from his fists and he drove them through his foe's torso before wrenching them sideways. Whether it was their sharpness or his strength, Dorian seemed to rip them through the monster's tough hide as though it was nothing more than tissue.

Utterly silent, Dorian continued his assault until the creature caught him with one massive swipe and dashed him sideways. Flying twenty feet to one side, he rolled to his feet and leapt back toward the fallen god, landing on its shoulders and tearing great gouges down its back as he descended. It roared and twisted trying to catch him as he reached the ground, but it couldn't match his speed. Ducking around and through the giant's legs, he cut and tore at one of them until it collapsed.

Once the god was down, the fight devolved into an extremely once sided brawl, as the crystalline golem sliced and cut, hacking the beast into ever smaller pieces. It seemed to go on forever, and when it ended, it was with a sudden silence. Dorian Thornbear, or the thing that had once been him, stood stock still, surveying the remains of his still twitching opponent.

Unsure of herself, Penny approached him slowly, holding out one hand. "Dorian? Are you in there?" she called tentatively.

His shining form twisted with a blur of light, and one bladed arm lashed outward stopping inches from her surprised face. She hadn't moved. Despite her own prodigious reflexes she hadn't even been able to blink. Taking a deep breath she stared into the azure eyes of the diamond golem. "It's me, Penny. Do you remember, Dorian? We grew up together…"

He looked away then, staring at the ground. Two steps and he leaned down, picking up what remained of his broken sword, a hilt with a foot and a half of blade protruding from it. Opening his mouth he uttered a low keening cry, "Thhhooorn…"

He's still in there, thought Penny, *but whether that's a blessing or a curse I don't know.* Suddenly aware of the passing of time, she motioned to her childhood friend, "We need to go, Dorian. We have to help the others. Do you understand?"

Dorian's corundum head dipped in what seemed to be acknowledgement, and when she began walking down the ramp again he followed. Egan came last, watching both his senior knight and the courtyard as they retreated.

"Are there more?" asked Sir Egan.

The countess nodded, "Those were the fastest, but there were more. I think they cannot be far behind." She quickened her steps as she spoke, and her eyes darted back frequently, making certain that Dorian still followed. For all his bulk, the crystalline golem made surprisingly little noise as he walked.

Chapter 30

They reached the end of the tunnel after a few minutes and discovered that the rest of their party had gone only a short distance along the World Road before stopping.

"Why did you stop?" started Penny, but her question was lost in the outcry as the others saw the golem behind her. The World Road was well lit by enchanted lights built into the ceiling and in that light Dorian's body shimmered, reflecting and gathering the light like a masterfully cut gem.

Everyone seemed to scramble back, seeking to put extra distance between themselves and the odd creature following Penny. She held her hands up to calm them, but her words were lost in the immediate chorus of questions.

"What's that?" asked Elise Thornbear even as Cyhan moved to position his body between her and Ariadne and the strange new being that had followed Penny. The children were asking rapid fire questions, less from fear than simple curiosity, but one voice cut clearly through the din.

"Penny," said Ariadne using a sharp voice of command, "I think you should explain this."

But someone else saw what was in the golem's hand, and her quick mind immediately made the connection. Rose started forward, grief and tragedy written on her face. "Oh gods! No! Dorian! Oh no!" She held their daughter

Carissa in one arm, but she moved to him without hesitation, reaching out to touch the hand that held the remnant of Thorn.

The golem was utterly still, its gem-like eyes locked on the woman before it. Dorian's hard face seemed expressionless, but he watched her with focused intensity.

"Dorian, can you hear me?" Rose asked in a calmer tone. The panic that had been in her voice a moment before was gone now, replaced by self-imposed control. Rose Thornbear was a woman known for her intelligence and composure. Over the years she had almost never lost what Penny thought of as her most enduring quality, her 'gentle serenity'. Today was no exception.

"Lady Rose, I think perhaps you should step back," suggested Cyhan with cold concern.

"Not now, Sir Cyhan," she rebuked him with a confident air of pure authority, although she never raised her voice. Even the tiny babe in her arms had yet to become aware of the incredible tension that lay beneath her unflappable exterior. "Do you remember me, Dorian?" she continued softly.

The crystalline golem stared silently at her before at last lifting its free hand and tapping its own forehead in a gesture that might represent either confusion or recognition. The question was answered when Dorian's crude mouth opened and one long mournful word emerged, "Rrrrosssse…"

Everyone in the room had fallen silent, holding their breath as if any noise might destroy that moment. Rose's voice had an almost indiscernible tremulous sound in it, but the tears that had appeared on her cheeks were the proof of her struggle to contain herself. "That's right, sweetheart. My name is Rose. Do you remember yours?"

"Thorrnnn…" He held up the broken sword.

"Dad?" asked Gram querulously, stepping out from behind his mother.

Dorian stared at the boy for a second before reaching out to gently stroke his son's hair. Looking back at Rose he noticed the infant in her arms for the first time, and his face seemed to shimmer. "Rrrossse," he crooned again.

Rose reached out and placed her hand against the golem's chest, as she had done so many times before with her husband. "These are your children, Dorian, your family."

"Broken…," he seemed to reply, lifting the sword again. Whether he meant the weapon itself or something deeper was unclear.

"The sword isn't important, Dorian. You are. We're going to fix this—somehow," as she spoke Rose's eyes darted back, looking to Moira Centyr for some hope, but the other woman only shook her head.

"No one's ever been able to change back after going so far," she answered reluctantly.

Tears ran freely from Rose's eyes, but she refused to despair. "It doesn't matter. You're still my Dorian. We love you no matter what happens," and then she surprised them by stepping into the golem's arms, leaning her head against his chest as he gently enfolded her and his infant daughter. Gram rushed forward as well, throwing his arms around his father's hard waist.

The world paused then, and there were no dry eyes to be seen, but when Penny cleared her blurred vision something had changed. The creature that Rose and her children were hugging no longer glittered with crystalline perfection; its outlines had softened somehow. Even as she stared she saw his head changing, becoming more human and gaining color. *He's changing!*

Moira Centyr was the next to notice with an audible gasp. "That isn't possible."

Dorian looked like a statue carved from a rosy-hued granite now, if the sculptor had been a master. His features were fine and perfect, and now there was even the appearance of stone sculpted hair on his head.

Even as her eyes witnessed a miracle, Penny couldn't help being reminded of her own reunion with Mordecai over a year ago... after his transformation. Her heart twisted with pain and guilt. *I didn't know. I couldn't know. I thought he was gone.* She knew better now. While her husband had truly died, something of him had remained. His decency had remained, and she had spurned him. *What might have happened if I had reacted like Rose?*

The moment ended with a deep grating noise as the stone door that guarded the ramp tunnel from the World Road descended, sealing them inside.

"Did someone do something?!" asked Stephen Balistair in alarm.

"No," responded Ariadne bluntly, "only the person with the control rod can open and close the doors here, unless someone is occupying the control room in the tower."

"Where is the control rod?" asked Elise Thornbear.

"The last I knew of it, my father had it..." supplied Ariadne before finishing suddenly, "... Tremont! This was a trap! He knew we would try this route. We have to

309

move. There's a chance he may not have sealed all the exits yet."

They rushed forward, forgetting everything else in their haste. Dorian's transformation stopped at that point, leaving him with the appearance of a perfectly shaped granite statue. None of them had time to think on the matter.

Peter Tucker spoke up as they quick marched along the subterranean road, "The first gate on our left will be the one to Lancaster, if it's open."

"I see a light coming from the side ahead of us," offered Egan. The extra light he was referring to was less than a hundred yards from them.

"Maybe Tremont doesn't know he can flood the tunnel," pondered Peter openly.

"More likely he just likes to play with his victims," declared Cyhan before shouting, "'Ware the front!" Large shapes were spilling into the roadway ahead of them, entering through the Lancaster gate. It took only seconds to realize from the odd shapes and forms that they were facing more of the fallen dark gods.

The light was good enough to easily count their foes as they approached, if there were enough time. "There must be at least twenty of them," said the Princess in a voice gone cold with despair.

A deep growl sounded behind them, followed by Rose's cry of alarm, "No, Dorian!"

Pushing her away the stone warrior started forward. With one hand he pointed at Sir Egan and then Penny, "Follow—behind." His words were spoken with great difficulty, but his gestures were clear as he indicated that

Penny should take the left and Egan the right as he advanced.

Waves of heat radiated around Dorian as he walked and the air shimmered. Glancing back he waved his hands for Penny and Egan to keep a greater distance, so they widened the gap from ten feet to twenty. Dorian's body had regained its glassine appearance, and the long blades sprouting from his arms had returned, growing ever longer now, and more appeared at his knees and elbows; even his skull acquired a deadly horn-like blade.

He's grown in size too, noted Penny as she started jogging to keep up with his ever increasing pace. Her childhood friend stood close to nine-feet in height now, if she had to guess.

The rest of their party had slowed to a walk, letting the distance grow between them and their 'vanguard'. Cyhan's face was a study in restrained suffering, but Ariadne ignored him and continued issuing a litany of small commands, more to reassure the group and maintain calm than to effect any strategy. Deep down she wondered why she bothered, for there was little hope in facing so many powerful foes with so few capable defenders. Logic told her they were minutes, if not seconds, from their deaths. *Because this is what he would do...* she told herself silently, thinking of her father ...*because I am my mother's daughter, a Lancaster, and the daughter of a king.*

Ahead of the main group by over thirty yards now Dorian met the first of the fallen dark gods with breathtaking ferocity. Leaping forward he tore the first of his opponents, a massive dog-shaped creature, into three parts in less time than it took to blink. Violence incarnate

311

now, Dorian whirled and slashed, using his entire body as a weapon. The diamond blades and spikes seemed to have grown from every surface and it was difficult for his foes to find any purchase to grapple his hard unyielding body.

Penny and Egan followed in his wake, keeping their distance and burning or hewing apart anything that still moved.

Stephen Balistair was uncomfortable with letting the three fight alone, but Cyhan caught his arm as he started to draw his sword and advance, "Don't."

"The Countess is fighting for my sake, I will be no man at all if I don't at least try to assist her," Stephen protested.

Cyhan grunted. "You'll be dead, and rather than help, you'll become a guilty memory of failure for her. Besides, she isn't fighting to protect you. It's them she'll die for," he pointed at the children in their midst, "not our sorry asses."

"Then what should I do?" asked the young lord.

"The same as any good man would, what you can. Watch the children, and be ready to run with one if necessary," answered the veteran.

A strange light filled the roadway with odd shadows as one of the monsters attacked Dorian with a magical blast of some kind, but the crystal warrior was so lost in violence and rage that he ignored the barrage of magic completely. Within seconds his latest enemy was ripped asunder. Several more piled onto him, striving to subdue him with sheer mass, but Dorian was too strong and no matter how many grappled him, he continued to swing and twist his arms and torso, shredding the bodies of any that came into close contact.

312

The battle had been raging for less than two minutes, but already almost half of their enemies were disabled, and Dorian showed no sign of slowing. If anything, he appeared to be even faster now. Within his translucent chest a bright red stone could be seen in roughly the same spot his heart would have been, if he had still been human. It was the size of a large man's fist, and it pulsed with a slow throbbing cadence.

"Are we—winning?" asked Gram incredulously.

His grandmother, Elise Thornbear, answered first, "Your father never learned to lose properly. It was always one of his greatest weaknesses."

"How can winning be bad?" wondered her grandson, but she didn't respond, other than to look at Rose. Neither woman appeared pleased, and a deep anxiety was written in both their faces.

They were distracted from their conversation by a series of sharp sounds as a number of large envenomed spikes hit an invisible barrier in front of their group. Young Moira Illeniel had been shielding them from flying debris or missiles, though no one had told her to do so.

The arrow-like weapons had come from something that looked as though it had been inspired by someone's nightmarish vision of a scorpion. It had bypassed Dorian's melee by virtue of its small size, it wasn't much larger than a hound, and it dodged Egan's flames with surprising agility. The projectiles had been spines that it launched from its whip-like tail.

Penny reached the insectoid monster in a mad dash, and using two hands on her sword, she removed the tail in one swing, severing one of its many segmented joints. Dodging a pincer attack she ducked low and removed the tip of one of its legs, causing it to stumble. One more leap took her out of range, and Egan's next blast of fire caught the thing before it could recover.

Dorian had almost reached the gate that led to Lancaster, and the number of monsters that still stood between them and their escape had dwindled to four now. Victory was close at hand, but a rush of air and a great roaring noise heralded the arrival of a new threat.

"They're flooding the tunnel!" announced Ariadne loudly.

One of the defenses built into the World-Road was the ability to close off any section and flood it with seawater to defeat would-be invaders. Whoever was in the control room had decided to take matters into their own hands.

Rose Thornbear had been silent since Dorian had left her side to take on the enemy, but the urgency of their situation had finally brought her back to herself. Her eyes took in the situation at a glance. "They haven't closed the gate to Lancaster yet. We can still escape."

"The water is coming," said Moira Illeniel. "We can't reach it in time, even if Uncle Dorian had finished them already."

"Run for it anyway," shouted Ariadne for they had no other options. Heeding her command everyone began running at their best pace, but it was readily apparent they would be far too slow. The noise of the oncoming water was growing steadily louder.

Meanwhile Dorian's foes had already sensed the imminent flood. They abandoned their attempts at defeating him and instead switched to delaying tactics, avoiding close contact, they danced around him. They knew the others could not reach the gate while they still fought.

Ariadne's party was forced to stop at a dangerously close distance of ten yards. Any closer and they would be caught up in the fray. The gate to Lancaster loomed temptingly a mere twenty yards farther on, but it might as well have been a mile. The furious battle raging in front of them was too terrifying even for the threat of drowning to force them closer.

Dorian danced back and forth across the roadway, attempting with each movement to either catch one of his opponents or stop one from slipping past him. Unfortunately, the things he fought were nearly as fast, and they dodged and retreated, feinting on either side until it was clear he could not hope to catch them if they wouldn't meet him directly.

Penny glanced back, desperate to save her children, but there was nothing she could do aside from aid Dorian in preventing the fallen gods from slipping past. Lilly Tucker held her youngest, little Irene, while Peter Tucker was holding Conall by the hand. Her twins were standing close together, eyes on one another as if seeking reassurance. *No, wait,* thought Penny, *they're scheming.*

She had seen the expression on their faces far too many times while they were growing up. Matthew was leaning in to speak directly in his sister's ear and the look on her face was far from one of fear or resignation. It was the look she got when she thought she'd heard a clever idea. Matthew's hands made wide motions, pointing first down the tunnel in the direction they had come and then back in the direction of Dorian's battle.

Moira nodded vigorously at him, and a small smile fell upon her lips. A wall of water had already appeared, rushing at them from the rear. It was a liquid avalanche, a great wave seven or eight feet in height. Because of the locations of the flood gates the water coming from the other direction was still out of sight, but once the onrushing waves met the entire roadway would fill until it was completely full.

The water should have crashed into them, driving them at breakneck speed down the corridor before drowning them, but something curious happened instead. Their party had gathered close to the outer edge of the tunnel, the side the Lancaster gate was on, and as the water reached them it slid oddly away from that wall, coursing sideways around them before continuing on. It split to avoid Penny and Sir Egan as well, but when it reached Dorian it re-converged, just a few feet past where he stood, slamming into the fallen gods with the force of a mighty hammer.

Their enemies were swept away instantly, disappearing into the roaring whitewater.

"Through the gate!" shouted Matthew as loudly as his small throat could manage. "She can't keep this up forever!" Indeed, his sister's face was a study in focused determination.

Moira Illeniel's brow was sweating despite the cool air, and her eyes narrowed as if she were in pain. Her brother had her by the hand and was guiding her forward, for she couldn't spare enough attention to watch her own feet.

Everyone caught on quickly. Penny and Egan rejoined the main group, simplifying Moira's task, since she no longer had to maintain four separate protected areas. Now it was just the main group and Dorian. Before they could start in the direction of the gate, a monstrous grating noise sounded.

The gate was closing.

Whoever was in the control room had at last decided to rectify their mistake. The gate should properly have been shut before opening the flood gates; at least that was what Mordecai had intended when he built the whole thing. It appeared the operator was learning fast, however.

Dorian was the closest to the gate, standing less than twenty feet from it already. Leaping forward his diamond blades pierced the bubble protecting him from the water and he flew over the waves to land beside the gateway. Stabbing downward with one arm he drove one of his blades into the stone roadway to keep the powerful flow from sweeping him away.

Moira had reshaped her protective barrier, forming it along the sidewall to give them a narrow corridor to reach the gate. She expanded it to keep the water from entering the gate entirely, giving Dorian some relief from the pounding water. The massive stone door continued to descend however, and within seconds it would seal them within the World Road. They would find themselves trapped in a watery grave soon after that.

The closest of them was Penny and even she was still thirty feet away.

Dorian Thornbear stood then, and stepping into the gateway he spread his feet, braced his shoulders—and caught the descending monolith.

The stone that descended upon him was almost two feet in thickness and ten in width. The bottom was wedge

317

shaped and sharp, making it difficult to find a place to gain purchase on it. Its descent was controlled by the magic stored within the enchantment Mordecai had created, but it was clear that the magic was involved mainly in managing the pace of its closing at this point. The weight of the giant stone was immense, and untold tons of force drove it downward.

It had been designed thus, along with the automatically recessing groove in the floor and walls so that it would be impossible to stop. Literally anything attempting to block or prevent its descent would be quickly crushed, allowing it to complete its task of sealing the path to Lancaster.

But it hadn't been designed with Dorian Thornbear in mind.

The crystalline warrior lifted his bladed arms and punched upward, driving into the bottom of the stone as he spread his legs. The enchantment guarding the stone showered sparks around him as his diamond weapons breached it and then bit into the gate itself. It continued to descend, however.

The others continued their mad dash to reach the gate, and as they ran they could see Dorian's struggle. It seemed hopeless at first, as he was driven to his knees, and the door forced its way through his hands to bite into his shoulder, but then a miracle happened. Slowly, begrudgingly, the door came grinding to a halt. The gap between the bottom of the door and the groove in the floor was a mere four feet, but it was enough.

Penny led the way, followed by the children, one by one, running easily under the great stone. Elise and Ariadne were next, hunching to avoid banging their heads, and they were followed by Rose and then the men. In the space of less than a minute they were all through. Lancaster and freedom seemed close at hand.

But Dorian was trapped.

Cracks appeared, tracing their way through his chest but he stubbornly refused to give up. The red gem in the center of his chest pulsed with an ever increasing pace and the door steadied again, but he could not lift it. Dorian's hands were trapped by the blades he had driven into the stone and looking down they could see that his feet had also created fractured holes in the stone floor.

Azure gems stared at them, but they focused on one person alone. "Rose…"

Rose handed her daughter to Elise and took a small step toward her husband before her resolve shattered. Weeping like a child she moved beside him and tried to help lift the great monolith that was slowly crushing him. "Help me!" she shouted at the others. "We have to stop it! Penny, Egan, you're strong! Help him!"

Penny and Egan both knew the door was far too heavy for them to make a difference, but they stepped forward and began pushing as well. They were unable to get an effective grip but Penny knew deep down that even if they had, it wouldn't have mattered. The door continued its descent.

"Go. Live. Rose…," said Dorian in a voice that seemed deeper than the earth.

Gram had escaped from the adults and now he was beside his parents. "Don't worry Dad! We can stop this!" The door was low enough now that he could attempt to brace it as well, not that it helped noticeably.

"You're right, Gram!" responded Moira Illeniel, and the others could sense a change as she began using her power to brace the door. Water began running into the corridor as she shifted her strength and attempted to block the flood as well as assist in lifting the gigantic gate.

The door continued to settle farther downward, and more water escaped to wash through at their feet. Moira Centyr watched in despair as her daughter struggled to aid them, but even her child's impressive strength was not enough. *If only I were the true Moira Centyr. If I had her power, I could find a way to stop this.* Her mind raced to find a method by which ordinary wizardry could save him, but her thoughts ran frantic circles around themselves.

A sudden flare of light startled her, and it took a moment before she realized the light she had seen was not physical, but magical. The powerful glow indicated the presence of another wizard, but she was confused at first as to who was its source. *Matthew! The stress has released his gift.*

She watched him in wonder for a moment. *He's strong—like his sister. No,* she corrected herself, *like his father.*

"Let me help, Moira," Matthew told his sister, taking her hand. The two of them locked gazes for a moment before returning their eyes to the stone door, and the earth began to shake. The floor beneath the door itself splintered and cracked under the magical pressures they were exerting, and for a long minute their power gave the others hope.

It was a false hope, however. Though Moira Centyr no longer had her power, she still retained her magesight, and with it she could easily gauge the weight of the gatestone, along with the power behind it. It would not be denied. Their best hope might have been to destroy it or find a way to derail it, but there was little time. Blood was trickling from her daughter's ear now, and she was certain that Matthew was already beyond his limit as well. In the end she had no other choice.

"It's impossible! The God-Stone powers the gate. They'll die if they don't relent! You have to make them stop!" she shouted, directing her words at Penny.

Egan heard her words and nodded at the Countess, "She's right. Take Gram, I'll get Lady Rose."

Without hesitation Penny left her place and took the boy from his father's side. He cursed and bit at her all the while. She had little time, so handing him to Stephen Balistair she addressed her two oldest children, "You have to stop. It's too great. If you force yourselves, the backlash could kill you."

Matthew and Moira's eyes were glazed and they looked straight through her. Their focus was perfect and unbreakable. Penny had seen the look a few times before on Mordecai's face, usually right before something terrible happened to him. *He slept for days after the battle in Lancaster Castle. They might not be so lucky.*

Behind her, Rose was begging Sir Egan to let her remain, but she was unable to resist his powerful arms. "Please! Just let me stay. It doesn't have to be this way. We can stop it. Please!!" Her sobbing words were full of tears and desperation. She had abandoned any pretense at dignity. All that remained was a woman beyond hope, facing a future of desolation and solitude.

"Rose—don't," said Dorian, grating out the words. Yanking one hand free of the door, he struggled to push her away without cutting her with the blade on his arm. His body had become a weapon and ill-suited to tender gestures. "Don't—let—Gram—be—like—me." The cracks in his body were widening, and the door was steadily inching downward again.

His frantic wife had dissolved to a place beyond reason, and her voice was a constant stream of plaintive cries, 'I love you's' mixed with screams of denial, until neither were distinguishable.

"I—love…" Dorian began, but his words ended abruptly as his massive chest shattered, and the stone gate slid inexorably downward, grinding the remnants in its path into smaller pieces and knocking the larger fragments aside. The twins' magic had collapsed, and they fell senseless to the ground. Blood ran from both their noses now.

Dorian Thornbear was dead.

If there were any true justice in the universe, a silent darkness would have covered them, to hide their grief and show reverence to the knight who had died. The world is unkind however; the tunnel they were in was well lit by the same enchanted lights Mordecai had placed throughout the World Road. They stood now on the Lancaster side of the gate, in a small fortress built less than a mile from the main castle.

The light that had been so welcome before now seemed harsh and cruel. Everyone but the twins now stood, dumb with shock and overcome by emotion. Rose Thornbear was the first to move, shoving Sir Egan away from her with an unintelligible curse. She followed it with a more clearly spoken warning, "If you ever lay hands on me again, I'll see you dead!" Her anger was so great that she punctuated the scornful threat by spitting in his direction.

No one spoke, or tried to console her, though Egan attempted an apology, "I'm sorry. There was no other way."

Moira Centyr and Penny were examining the twins, fear writ plainly on both their faces—two mothers who shared the same worry.

Unseen and unwatched, Gram Thornbear scrabbled through the stone fragments on the ground. Among the broken paving stones were brilliant shards of razor sharp crystal, the remnants of his father. His eyes were blurred with tears, but a carmine glimmer caught his notice and reaching out he found what he sought. With trembling fingers he gingerly picked up the giant ruby-like stone that had been Dorian's heart. He slid it into his pouch before anyone could notice.

Steps in the gravel told Gram his mother was close and turning, he accepted her embrace. Elise Thornbear joined them a second later, and together they mourned, wife, mother, son and even infant daughter, though it would be many years before little Carissa could fully understand her loss.

Chapter 31

The sunrise was slow and unremarkable; a slow lightening of the horizon with little of the colorful pigmentation that poets and lovers are so fond of. It had been three days since my last leave-taking, and I had arrived in the wee hours of the morning.

If Karenth had followed my instructions, he would be arriving any minute.

I waited patiently, senses alert. In particular, I was watching for the appearance of several powerful beings. It was almost half an hour after the sun broke over the horizon before I was rewarded with their arrival.

A smile crept over my face when I sensed them. I had fed a few hours before, and my emotions were fully functional, so my sense of satisfaction was enjoyable. They were trying to cloak their presence, muting the brightness of their aythar. None of them had anything like the gift that the Prathions had, so the best they managed was to dim themselves to an almost human level.

It might have fooled an unsuspecting wizard, one less sensitive, or less skilled. I was none of those things, and I was expecting them in any case.

I sat quietly on a long wooden bench in one of the royal gardens at the palace. There were no wizards in the capital, and while Tremont did have a number of what I thought of as 'god-seeds' guarding the place, none of them were near enough to spot me. Flying down to have a meeting in the garden by the palace seemed an appropriate way to start the plan to get rid of the usurper.

Two men and one woman approached, all of them cloaked and covered. The morning air was crisp, but they were more concealed than the weather called for. "Can I help you?" I asked as they stopped in front of my bench. The garden was empty but for the four of us.

Abandoning their attempts at disguise, they tossed their hoods back, and I felt their aythar wash over me. One of the men was Karenth, the other was Doron, and standing with them was Millicenth. The power they radiated had probably alerted every sensitive being in the city. The weight of it seemed to press down upon me even through the protection of the armor I still wore. In the past I might have felt fear, but being dead, I was now immune to some worries.

"You were a fool to trust Karenth, mortal," said Doron, gloating. "You have delivered yourself into our hands." He leaned forward, seeking to use his still excessive body size to intimidate. He had obviously gained little in the way of wits since our last meeting.

Millicenth looked more properly wary, but she still felt secure with the two other gods beside her.

Not daring to wait, I uttered two strange, seemingly nonsensical phrases. Both of my new guests stiffened as they recognized the words. "How?" asked Millicenth.

I was in no mood to answer questions. "How is of no consequence," I replied. "You are mine now, just as Karenth is. Bend your knees if you understand me." Gratifyingly, both Doron and Millicenth genuflected.

"You meant them, right?" asked Karenth with a sardonic smile.

"I did," I clarified for him, then I spoke to the others once more, "Rise. There is much to discuss."

"Karenth was your tool all along," murmured Millicenth, thinking aloud.

"He was," I agreed, "and now you are as well. If by some miracle I succeed, then I will grant you what you wish when this is done."

"You think you understand our desires, mortal?" she asked with a curious glance. Her eyes had changed color, swirling into a sea green.

"He is no longer mortal," declared Doron, staring at me with interest.

She dismissed her dimmer companion's remark with a wave of her hand, "His current state is not the point. His existence has been short and ephemeral until now." Focusing on me again, she continued, "Tell me, dead man, what do you think we should desire?"

Her attitude annoyed me to no end, and for a moment I was tempted to punish her. My control was absolute, which enabled me to humiliate her in any number of ways, but I restrained myself. She was too intelligent to be brought to heel with childish punishments. "I can unmake you," I replied simply.

"Should that frighten us?" she answered in teasing voice.

"It wasn't a threat," I explained, "but rather the reward you most desire."

The Lady of the Evening Star's eyes widened at that pronouncement, but rather than admit defeat, her mind turned to clever rebuttals. I could see the wheels turning in her head. Before she could begin another line of discussion, I cut her off, "No more wordplay. From this point forward, you will speak to me with respect and focus your will and efforts toward furthering my goals." I repeated my command for Doron's benefit as well.

Both of them bowed, "Yes, Master."

I really should have been an evil villain, I thought suddenly. *It could have been a lot of fun if I had gone this route from the early days.* For the hundredth time, I thought of my family, reminding myself of my reasons. *Too late to turn over a new leaf now, I guess.*

"Before we get started, I need some information. Do any of you know anything that could tell me where Mal'goroth is?"

Doron shook his head mutely, and Millicenth replied with a simple, "No, Master."

Karenth was more forthcoming, "We have no inkling of where he is, but we do know of a few places where he *isn't.*"

"Elaborate."

The former god of justice nodded and began to pace as he graced us with his wisdom, "We know for certain that he is not within Albamarl, and while he has committed some of his forces to causing mischief in Lancaster and Cameron, I don't believe he is there either."

"Your reasons?" I asked.

"Again, I think it is a simple matter of enjoyment. Mal'goroth shares something of the same temperament as I. He has been playing a game of cat and mouse with you to extend his entertainment. He is well aware that he can crush you at any moment. Why else would he send his weakened servants in to fight in the capital, to harass your

327

allies? He could easily have spared the power to make them stronger. Just a bit more and they would have handily destroyed the Princess's followers."

"Speaking of which…" I began, letting my words trail off.

"They made it to Lancaster," Karenth assured me. "Your creatures didn't molest them, whether by pure chance or because of your instructions I do not know. Tremont did his best to trap them within the World Road, but despite his efforts, and the assistance of the weakened Dark Gods, he failed. Well… mostly failed."

I raised an eyebrow; sometimes Karenth needed dramatic pauses and a bit of encouragement to tell his tales to their fullest.

"Your knight, Thornbear, was slain during the escape." He said bluntly.

My eyes bulged. At least they felt as if they did. "What?!"

He relayed the basic facts quickly and without showing the slightest hint of enjoyment, although I suspected Karenth secretly reveled in the news.

"How did you learn this?"

"Second hand, my lord. I overheard some of Tremont's servants discussing it after the fact. He was crushed by the gate stone that guards the path to Lancaster."

The gates that I had designed. "They don't move swiftly enough to trap someone," I argued.

"From what I heard, he attempted to keep it from closing. The good duke decided to flood the road while your family and friends were still within," explained Karenth.

The gate stones were immense monoliths, and if one was blocked in its course, the force of the enchantment would add extra pressure. They drew upon the God-Stone... no one, not even a Knight of Stone could hope to stop or even delay their closing. I had built them to be absolute. "You said the others escaped. Was Dorian last?"

"First, my lord, he held the gate for a short while—until it crushed him."

How my friend had managed such a thing, I couldn't comprehend. My emotions were a storm within me, and I found myself clutching at that disbelief to avoid facing them. *This was my fault. I built those gates, and I gave their control away.* I was pacing now. Anger and sorrow warred for my attention, but since my eyes no longer had the power to provide tears, I leaned toward the former.

"Someone is going to regret this," I announced.

"Given the situation, that is more likely to be you than Mal'goroth," advised Millicenth before adding, "Master."

A sudden impulse to give several painful orders caught in my throat. Again, I was nearly undone by violent thoughts. *This isn't who I am.* Taking a deliberate breath, I ignored her and faced Karenth, "What advice would you give me?"

"Go to Lancaster, claim your family, and disappear. The path of least suffering would be hiding for as long as possible," he said immediately.

"You think it impossible to win?"

He nodded. It was so patently obvious that it didn't require an explanation.

"Currently, his minions and allies are focused firmly upon my home territory and the capital, the two areas I am most closely connected to. If I move to intervene or overturn his plans, what do you think will happen?" I asked suddenly. I had an idea of my own, but I wanted an outside opinion.

Millicenth interrupted, "It depends upon your effectiveness. Fight poorly, and he will enjoy the show. Upset the apple-cart, and he will move to crush you more directly."

Her words echoed my thoughts. "So... if I take your meaning correctly, if I seem to be winning you think he'll intervene, otherwise, he'll just let me flounder about indefinitely." I paused a moment before continuing, "That being the case, I shall have to divide his attention. Draw him in one direction, while defeating his allies absolutely in the other."

"They will have some method of summoning or communicating," countered Karenth. "If you overwhelm his minions, he could answer their pleas for help within a very short period of time."

I smiled, "Then I'll make certain they cannot call him."

The looks on their faces quickly confirmed my guesses regarding their thoughts. Despite their dealings with me in the past, they thought I was utterly insane. *This time they might be right,* I thought privately.

"Give me your hands," I said, pointing at Doron and Millicenth. Once I had them firmly in my grasp, I began siphoning away some of their strength.

"Why?" asked Doron.

"I need it more than you do," I replied. "I will leave you both with more than enough to handle your assigned tasks, something close to half of what you have now."

Millicenth gave me a pouty expression, "What will you do with us, my lord?"

"What you were created to do," I stated firmly. "You will follow my family to Lancaster or Cameron, and once you find them, you will heal and support my wife and friends in whatever means they ask of you. You, Doron, will bolster the strength of their warriors. The Knights of Stone are few and scattered. You will tip the scales back in their favor."

Their eyes widened in shock. No one still living knew their original purposes—until now.

I held up a finger, silencing them before they could ask. "What I know and how I know it, is my own business. You will do as I say, and you will follow Karenth's direction when you are in doubt. He will coordinate and be the primary information gatherer."

"Once you find them," I told Karenth, "you will submit yourself to my wife's authority. In her absence, you will defer to whoever among them is in charge, whether that be Ariadne, one of my knights, Lady Rose—you get the idea."

He nodded, "Do you have any messages for them?"

Something ached inside, but it felt foreign, as though I had developed indigestion. I ignored it. "Nothing personal," I answered. *Tell them I love them.* "They need to find the Prathions first, if they are still alive. Their skills will be most useful if my people are to survive. After that, their next course should be to take refuge in Cameron Castle. Walter knows how to operate the defenses there."

Karenth winced, remembering his assault on me at my home. "I hate to argue, but even as formidable as your handiwork is, it won't keep Mal'goroth out."

"It will be more than sufficient for his lackeys, though," I offered. "If, or when, Mal'goroth shows up, Penny knows how to get them to safety."

"This is also information that…"

"You don't need to know," I finished for him.

"And how you plan to deal with his people within the capital…"

"You'll find out later," I supplied. "For now, I have given you what you need. Help them, and forewarn them about my *other* allies." I leaned in to whisper additional information in his ear.

He stared at me for a moment, mildly surprised. "Yet, even if you succeed here, you will almost certainly fail against him at the end."

I grimaced. "If nothing else, I'll make certain that he has not one remaining ally or servant before he defeats me. In that case you must take my family and hide."

"While he commits genocide?" questioned the god of justice.

"If only a few can be saved, make sure that they are mine," I answered with brutal honesty. "One way or another, even if he destroys my people, the She'Har will eventually either yoke him or unmake him."

"Such cold words," observed Millicenth. "You sound less like a mortal and more like a god than I would have expected."

"Just make sure none of you attempt to face him directly. Retreat rather than allow him to gain even more power," I cautioned. "Now… go!"

Chapter 32

I stared at the city in the waning afternoon light. The sunset bathed it in a deep orange that the rose granite walls transformed into a shade reminiscent of red. My imagination took it a step further, showing me a city bathed in blood. *As it will be.*

I was no longer within the walls. I had moved outside to meet my new allies as well as to prepare the enchantment I would use. Several were hiding close to my current position, I could feel them through the links that tied them to my enchantment. The others were gathered in various spots around the city, hiding in fields and forests. Some of them had lain quietly for days, while others had just arrived. They were patient.

One things I had failed to understand about the shiggreth previously, was their abiding patience. My former belief had been that they required aythar from living beings to maintain their bodies and while that was technically true, it was far simpler to acquire aythar than I had realized. Most of the shiggreth were nothing more than dead people, animated by magic. They moved and acted according to the orders of their master—me. Some of them retained their memories, those were the ones most similar to me, but all of them were soulless, essentially automatons of dead flesh.

None of them possessed any strong desires, not even to feed. Left to their own devices, most of them would simply lie in one place, subsisting on the aythar obtained from the tiny things that tried to consume them. Those that had arrived earliest had done just that, they lay down to wait, and drew energy only from whatever touched them.

Before my transformation, I had thought most of them destroyed. Dorian's forays had been highly successful, and near the end we had found fewer and fewer of them. The truth had been simpler; Thillmarius had become preoccupied with me. While he spent his days and evenings quietly stalking me, they had become dormant— but they numbered in the tens of thousands.

Most were too far to reach the capital in the amount of time I had given them. Those I had left to their devices. My belief was that they would find true death after I had destroyed myself, but for now I had things to do. There were at least three thousand gathered around Albamarl now. Another three thousand had gathered in the forested foothills of the southern Elentirs, around the fortress known as Castle Tremont.

Extending my will I took direct control of nine of the closest and called them to me. I watched them approach across a farmer's field with my magesight, while my hands drew out the enchanted diamond cubes. *Tonight will be the true test. My previous uses were a proof of principle, but if things go badly tonight… Gareth is right to think me mad.*

The dragon had warned me that if the cubes failed, the resulting feedback might precipitate a disaster worse than the one that had created the Gulf of Garulon. I had drawn roughly half of Millicenth and Doron's power into myself, and combined with what I had already taken from Karenth, and the portion I had taken from the God-Stone, I was charged with roughly two and a half Celiors worth of aythar.

It was still nowhere near enough to challenge Mal'goroth, but if my plan worked, he would never receive any word of my work here until I was already finished. If my plan failed…

The Gulf of Garulon will be a lot bigger, I thought to myself.

My new 'friends' arrived, and I began handing out cubes along with mental descriptions of where they were to take them. Eight of them would be placed around Albamarl in a square formation, one at each corner and one midway between those. The ninth would be hidden in the center of the city, close to where the palace was located. Those would demarcate the bottom face of a giant cube. Nine more would delineate the upper face, but I would have to place those myself, since the shiggreth couldn't fly. Of the remaining nine, eight would mark the middle and corners of the cube while the ninth would remain with me. That stone was the one that would have been placed in the exact center, but it had a special purpose.

Once the sun was below the horizon, and the light was dim enough, I placed the upper stones in their positions. Each one would lock into its place once I put it close to the spot where it belonged. It took nearly an hour, but it was a labor of love—or something.

My preparations finished, I issued my final orders. My first commands went to those who had gathered around Castle Tremont. *Enter, take the castle. Leave none alive.* Somewhere deep down I felt a rebellious cry, begging for the lives of the innocent, but I pushed it away with an internal snarl at my weaker side. *They killed James, Ginny, and so many others. They killed Dorian! Let them die!*

Dorian would not seek vengeance upon children. He would not prosecute war against the unwitting servants of even one so wicked as Andrew Tremont.

The devil's advocate within me had gotten surprisingly eloquent. *I don't give a rotten damn!* My response wasn't as witty, but I didn't care.

My next orders were for those near Albamarl. *Clear the World Road, those guarding it are our enemies. Once you have slain those there, kill no more. Leave and return to your hiding places.* I designated a smaller group of five hundred to guard the boundaries of my enchantment.

With my plans complete, I began a slow march to the eastern gate of the city. It would be a long night, and probably a long day as well.

The gate was closed when I reached it, but with the power of several gods running through me I found it to be a small impediment. I burned a man shaped whole through a foot and a half of solid oaken timber and kept walking. I was twirling the last diamond cube absently in one hand and began to whistle.

I am become death. The thought roused my sense of humor, and I laughed. It was probably my first laugh in over a year, and it came out dry and awkward, as if I had forgotten the skill. "The Shining Gods each had their domains, I suppose I should have one as well," I told myself. "There really isn't anything more appropriate for me now, other than death."

A very frightened guardsman approached me, holding out a spear threateningly. No doubt he was nervous at confronting the man who had just burned his way through the gate. "Stand and declare yourself!" he stammered.

"My name is Brexus, and I have come to collect payment on behalf of Mordecai Illeniel," I answered with a bland smile.

"This city is under the rule of King Tremont, sir. You will have to submit yourself to our arrest," stammered the man who I now realized was a rather shabby captain. Several more of his compatriots now surrounded me.

"That's a rather unfortunate answer on your part," I told him. "You'll have to make payment."

"Payment?"

Holding out the final diamond cube I spoke the words that would empower it. At first nothing seemed to happen; the size of my enchanted construct was so great that it took a great deal of power before it began to take hold. Pushing hard, I poured my aythar into it, watching lines stretch outward in my magesight as the cubes all connected and began to hum with a synchronous resonance.

Everything slowed and then came to a complete stop. At a guess I had used nearly two full Celiors of aythar to activate the enchantment; at least it felt like it. I didn't worry, since that matched the rough estimate my calculations had given me. The diamond cube in my hand now was glowing so brightly that it hurt the eyes, and it was emitting a heat so intense I was forced to create a temporary spell to protect my clothing from it. *Let's hope it doesn't shatter under the strain,* I thought. *Be a shame to destroy all of this.*

I was standing inside the largest stasis enchantment ever created. I was pretty sure anyway. There were no memories within my considerable recall of anything approaching one of this scale. The center cube that I carried created a small area of normal time within the field, while the rest of it, which was the entire city of Albamarl, was frozen in time.

Walking forward, I approached the guard captain. His face became startled when I moved within range and the effect of my cube released him. From his perspective it must have seemed as if I had teleported to him. "Yes, payment," I said, answering his previous question. "Everyone serving the usurper must make this payment."

The aura of my remaining aythar was still potent enough that it had rendered him nearly helpless just from my proximity, but he managed to croak, "What would you have of me?"

I gave him a wickedly charming smile. "Don't worry. Anyone can pay this price. I only want your life." My hand was at his throat so quickly that he never saw it. Pulling fiercely at the flame within him, I extinguished his life within no more than a second or two. The pleasure of it was exhilarating.

I didn't bother talking to his subordinates. They died without ever knowing why.

Chapter 33

The small gate keep in Lancaster was in perfect condition, but it was the only thing that Penny and her companions found in such good shape. Castle Lancaster itself, little more than a half-mile away, was a burned ruin. Some of it had fallen, collapsing as the timbers that supported it went up in flames, other parts were standing, a stone husk surrounding an empty charred interior.

They found no sign of anyone, though there were quite a few corpses in the courtyard. Most of those were too far gone to identify, if they weren't burned beyond recognition then scavengers and carrion eaters had removed all the soft tissues. It was a grisly scene by any measure.

Penny looked on the destruction but her heart was numb. She had lost too much to feel any more sorrow. The one thought that seemed to bubble up from the mire within her found her lips before she realized it, "If Cameron is like this, then we've lost it all."

Ariadne looked at her fiercely, "I've already lost everything." Lancaster Castle had been her home.

"Where next for us?" asked Sir Egan. The man seemed smaller now, as if losing his mentor and teacher had diminished him in some way.

"We need to discover what's happened in Cameron and Arundel," suggested Penny.

Ariadne nodded, "Mordecai's advice to us was sound. We must find the Prathions."

"The only thing we know for certain is that they won't be at either Cameron Castle or Arundel," offered Peter Tucker suddenly.

Stephen Balistair seemed confused. "How do we know that?"

"Walter had access to a number of message boxes at his home in Arundel. He also was intimately familiar with Castle Cameron, where many others were located. If he or his children, were currently at either place, they'd have been sending messages all along," explained Peter. His work as the head chamberlain for Castle Cameron showed in his thinking.

Penny shook her head in agreement. Over the years she had come to expect such keen wit from Peter. "That should have occurred to me sooner, but you're absolutely right Peter."

"Then how will we find the other wizards?" asked the princess.

Elise Thornbear gestured at the unconscious Matthew and Moira. "We are not without resources. We have two wizards with us now. When they awake their senses will tell us far more than our eyes can."

"It won't matter," said Cyhan interrupting abruptly. "The ones we seek are Prathions. If they are hiding, we won't be able to find them. Even Mordecai couldn't manage that."

The Princess looked at him thoughtfully, "Then what is your counsel, Sir Knight?"

"There are two possibilities that I can see. Either they're dead, caught by whatever surprise was sprung here

340

in Lancaster or at their home, or they're alive and hiding. If it's the former, there's nothing we can do, and if it's the latter we'll never find them, but we don't have to, Your Highness," said Cyhan.

Ariadne had gotten an inkling of his meaning already. "You imply that they will find us?"

The old veteran nodded. "They will be watching, and there are three high priority places to observe in this area, the gate-keep in Lancaster, the gate-keep in Arundel, and possibly Castle Cameron itself."

"No one finds a Prathion, if they don't wish to be found," said Elaine Prathion from beside him. She was leaning in close to his ear.

The older veteran didn't flinch, instead he gave Elaine a bored stare.

Ariadne looked sharply at Cyhan, sensing a ruse. "Your logic is too perfect. It has the ring of something crafted to explain facts that are already known. You knew Elaine was here. Do you care to explain?"

"Begging your pardon, Highness, I would rather not," replied the heavyset warrior. It was uncharacteristic of him to show such reluctance.

"For what reason?" asked the Princess.

"It would be embarrassing."

She was taken aback, as was everyone else. It was unheard of for the taciturn knight to show embarrassment of any sort. "For you?" she questioned.

Cyhan cast his eyes downward, "No, Your Highness, for you and the other ladies present."

Penny was thinking hard as he spoke and her mind, with some help from her enhanced senses, had given her cause for suspicion.

"Do explain anyway, Sir Cyhan," commanded Ariadne.

Taking a deep breath Cyhan began his explanation. "As you are aware, those of us with the earth-bond are possessed of more acute senses, as well as strength and speed. In particular, my nose is several times more sensitive than a normal man's nose. It still isn't nearly as good as a hound's, but it does provide a lot of information."

Ariadne frowned, "You're saying you identified her merely by her scent?"

"No, Your Highness. I could never make such a bold claim, but we have been traveling together for quite a few hours and not long ago I caught the scent of a woman whom I knew was not one of the ladies in our group," answered Cyhan carefully.

Penny's suspicion was confirmed now, both by his words and her own nose.

"You could tell us apart so simply?" questioned the Princess.

Cyhan shook his head negatively, "No, Your Highness, but at certain times women are given to different odors. I already knew that this was not your time, nor that of any of the other..."

"Enough!" interrupted Penny, hoping to save him from a more complete explanation, but Ariadne had already caught on to his meaning, and her cheeks were turning a deep shade of red.

Nodding her head vigorously Ariadne agreed, "Thank you, Sir Cyhan. That will be sufficient."

Her discomfort and the awkward silence that followed were broken suddenly when Elise Thornbear began to chuckle, and soon the rest of the women were laughing. The men in the group joined in cautiously, except for Cyhan, who kept his stern demeanor. Rose was the only woman to abstain from the mirth. She knew that even a simple laugh would only lead to a new outpouring of tears.

Conall Illeniel was still confused, and he tugged on his mother's sleeve. "Momma, I don't understand. Why is everyone laughing?"

"Me either," agreed Gram.

Penny stopped laughing for a moment to stare at the children in dismay. She had no idea what to answer, not just because of the nature of the question, but also because everyone in the group was watching with intense curiosity to see what her answer might be. She looked at Moira Centyr for ideas.

The former lady of stone shrugged, "How should I know what to say?"

Lady Rose's shell finally cracked, and she began to cackle in a manner most unladylike. Her usual laughter was far more composed, but this was the sudden and slightly hysterical laughter of a woman under too much stress for far too long. The others joined her for a few minutes, until the inevitable happened and her emotions shifted. Her sobbing laughter then became something more sorrowful.

Rose's mother-in-law led her aside while the others watched helplessly. Many of their eyes were damp as well. Grieving is always a painful thing, in that nothing can be done for it. It is an illness that cannot be cured, merely shared.

Elaine witnessed the entire cycle of events without understanding the cause, but her intuition was working full time. "I'm certain you all have a lot of questions for me, but I can tell there are many things I need to hear from you as well," she suggested.

Ariadne undertook the task of relaying the news from the capital, though her voice failed her when she began to relate the tale of her father and mother. The Countess took over for her then, though she suffered a similar problem when the story of Sir Dorian's end came. At the end, it was left to Cyhan to finish their tale.

Elaine Prathion took a small amount of time to assimilate what she had just learned. She was understandably distraught at much of the news, particularly that which concerned the King and Queen, as well as the news of Dorian's death. When she finally was ready to reciprocate with her own story, she looked regretful.

"I had hoped your news would be better than mine," began Elaine, "for I fear my news will not cheer you. On the same day that Tremont murdered our sovereign, Lancaster went up in flames."

She took a deep breath and then continued, "My father and I were in Arundel, and George was in Cameron, so we didn't witness any of the events there directly. There weren't many survivors, and those who did emerge were mostly servants who lived outside of the keep itself. From what we can put together, it seems that several groups were involved. A number of men were guesting with Roland under the pretense of being an envoy from King Nicholas in Gododdin."

Elaine closed her eyes. "Those who pretended at nobility were inside, while their retainers barricaded the main doors to the keep from the outside. Those inside set

344

fire to the interior and we think they died along with the rest of the occupants. Some of the bodies we found belonged to those who threw themselves from the towers and upper windows in desperation."

The Princess could wait no longer. "And my brother?"

The wizard looked at the ground, unwilling to meet her gaze. "We have found no sign of him, and we can only believe that he died with the others when the castle burned. Please forgive me, Your—Majesty." Her use of the sovereign's honorific reinforced her words.

Ariadne started to object to her use of 'Majesty', but she stopped herself. "Very well, though you have given me sad news, I must finally accept this fate. I will no longer argue the use of that title, even though ceremony and custom must wait before I fully claim it as mine."

Though, if she lived, the historians would later claim the date of her coronation as the day Ariadne became Queen, those who were there knew that that was when it happened. That was the moment a young girl accepted the change, and went from princess to Queen of Lothion, or as the people had already begun to call her, the 'Iron Queen'.

Silence stretched out for a long moment, as everyone considered whether they should offer obeisance, until at last Ariadne broke the spell. "Not now," she said, "I know where your hearts lie. We can worry about deference and oaths of fealty later. Elaine, please finish relaying your news."

"Yes, Your Majesty," offered the wizard. "In Arundel we received no word of the black doings in Lancaster, but that same night we received an attack by strange beings that defy simple description. Having heard the news of your escape through the World Road, I feel certain that these were more of the same fallen gods. They attacked us, along with a lesser number of ordinary humans, the Shaddoth Krys. Father sent word to George in Cameron to come and assist us, but it was to no avail."

"While we could have protected ourselves, in the end we were unable to protect our people. For as long as we remained in an easily located place, our attackers were able to overwhelm our defenses. After less than a day, Father ordered us to abandon Arundel. Taking everyone still with us, we fled into the forests and used our magic to hide them," finished Elaine.

"And what of Castle Cameron?" asked Ariadne.

"It fell in our absence," admitted Elaine. "While we were struggling to fend off the attackers in Arundel, Castle Cameron came under attack of its own. The remaining knights worked for its defense, but in the end they were forced to do as we had."

"How many of my brothers remain?" asked Cyhan, referring to the other Knights of Stone.

"Three are with us now, Sir William, Sir Thomas, and Sir Harold," said Elaine. "We met the refugees in the forest between Arundel and Cameron. They are in hiding with the rest of our survivors now."

"And what of Sir Edward?" questioned Cyhan, referring to the last knight unaccounted for.

"Dead," answered Elaine. "Sir William told me he died bravely defending their retreat."

"Give us an accounting of how many remain," ordered Ariadne calmly, "that we can number our resources."

"Seven hundred men women and children, Your Majesty," said Elaine promptly. "They are from various parts of the valley—few from Lancaster, some from Arundel, and some from Cameron. There are many others, scattered and hiding on their own, but I have no count of them for you. Among those I have already named, there are two hundred men-at-arms, three wizards, and the three Knights of Stone I mentioned."

"It seems a small number, compared to what we have lost," said the Queen sadly.

Elaine spoke quickly to reassure her, "Do not let the number cause you despair. The bulk of the people survive. That is only what we have managed to gather and shelter personally."

"Our course shall be to meet with your father and the others," said Ariadne. "After we have taken counsel with him and seen for ourselves the situation, then we can plot our future course." The choice was obvious, but as Ariadne was their leader, it was important that she make it clear.

Penny found herself watching Stephen Balistair, to gauge his reaction, and when he looked back at her she was pleased at what she saw. *Determination and the will to follow our new Queen. Perhaps I have judged him too harshly,* thought Penny.

Of them all, only Rose Thornbear seemed disinterested in the outcome of the discussion. She remained silent, focusing on her daughter, Carissa. She seemed to have completely withdrawn from the present, and Penny could only wonder how long it would be before her friend recovered her spirit.

Chapter 34

It was one of the best nights I could remember. I had spent hours walking from place to place in the city that was now frozen in time. By my own reckoning it was probably already morning again in the outside world, but the sun's light couldn't touch the eternal night that now cloaked Albamarl.

That was the nature of stasis fields: nothing enters and nothing leaves. Even I could not exit until I canceled the enchantment, but for now I was content to move within it, the one active agent in a timeless moment. I had spent a lot of time scouring the city, searching out every guard, soldier and watchman, anyone who served the usurper. Thankfully, Tremont had made my job easier by having them replace their colors with his own. That saved me the tough moral choice of whether to kill someone in Hightower's livery.

I knew intellectually, that most of his men were simple mercenaries, or in some cases even loyal servants of the rightful king, seeking to preserve their lives and protect their families, but I didn't care. Anyone wearing Tremont's colors of burgundy and black—I slew. I passed through the walls, the towers and every gate house and bailey. Everywhere I went, I chose and killed, leaving a trail of dead men behind me. My power swelled as I drained them by the hundreds, but the euphoria was just as potent each time.

Humans were a drug for me now. The pleasure was so great that at times I erred on the side of 'caution' rather than let someone questionable live. It was a glorious night.

I wondered what the people who remained alive would think. In many places I killed ten or twenty people while leaving one or two alive who were obviously not in Tremont's service. When the enchantment was eventually dispelled, they would find themselves surrounded by dead men, who, to them, had just been breathing a moment before. The overall effect would be, that it would seem as though every single person serving Tremont had died within a single instant.

I found myself giggling whenever I thought about it.

The city jail in particular would be interesting. I slew the jailors and left the keys in one of the cells. What would they think when time resumed? How long would they hide within their cells before venturing out?

Even with the possibility of an eternity within the city to do my work, I knew that there were practical constraints on the time that I had. Eventually Mal'goroth would wonder at the lack of communication from his underlings and come to check on them. Whether that was a matter of hours or days or longer, I couldn't be sure. I had decided to give myself only twenty-four hours, one day, before ending the effect and moving on to my next target.

That meant my deadline was sunset. I intended to end the enchantment at the same time I had begun it. That would make it even more difficult for them to realize what had happened. I laughed even more when I thought of the confusion this would create for those who charted the year and marked the phases of the moon. Someone would figure it out—eventually, but I wouldn't be the one to tell them.

I laughed again and began to skip. Death does not come to us solemnly, but rather with a smile and a spring in his step. Or at least, that day in Albamarl, he did. If Death didn't like my stylistic interpretation of his job, he was welcome to come and discuss his differences with me.

While I concerned myself primarily with official buildings and places where the usurper's men would be, I encountered numerous interesting doings on the streets themselves. Here and there I found people fighting, and each time I chose one to slay. I couldn't be certain of the reason for each of the fights, but since I was representing the underdog today, I always slew the person who seemed to have the upper-hand, unless I had some way of telling if one of them served Tremont.

It was a night full of delightful choices, and by the time I reached the palace itself I had already slain thousands. My inner voice argued and railed against some of my choices, but I didn't care. The euphoria of so many lives taken made it impossible for me to feel down. Most of the time, if they were clearly in the service of the usurper, my conscience kept his damn mouth shut.

The palace was full of surprises. Along with the expected soldiers, I found ten of the 'god-seeds'. The weakened Dark Gods were no more trouble for me than the others. I drained each one of its power, and then, when they were reduced to virtually nothing, I trapped the remainder of each one within a spell. I stored them as small glowing spheres within one of my pouches. I had no way of destroying the spellweaving that sustained each one, but I could imprison them indefinitely. Later I planned to create a permanent enchantment to hold each one, similar to the one that had created the God-Stone.

I saved the best for last.

Andrew Tremont was in the feast hall, preparing to sit down for dinner. After I killed most of the others, which was nearly everyone being served, I turned to him. I had left the palace servants and maids unharmed, but they would have quite a shock when the enchantment ended.

Tremont was standing, with a frozen half-smile on his corpulent face. Looking on him, I felt a burning hatred that seemed to be echoed by my inner voice. *If anyone deserves to die today, this one deserves it more than all the others combined.*

The bubble of normal time around me would free my victims once I had approached to within a couple of feet of them. I moved close and watched with enjoyment as Tremont became aware of me, but I didn't kill him—yet. His face cycled through a gamut of different emotions—surprise, shock, anger, and then fear. I liked the last one most of all.

"Did you miss me, Andrew?"

He was nearly unable to speak. While I had divested myself of the majority of my power when empowering the enchantment around the city, I had gained almost another full Celior in strength from drawing the life out of so many healthy people. The pressure of that much concentrated aythar right next to him nearly crushed his will instantly. It was the same effect I had encountered so many times in the past when facing the Shining Gods.

I didn't bother trying to shield myself or dampen the effect at all. I wanted him to despair.

"How?" he managed to stammer.

"Did you think Mal'goroth was going to protect you? You're just a toy to him, a plaything. He'll gain just as much pleasure from hearing of your slow death as I will gain while giving it to you," I taunted, whispering in his ear. I was careful not to touch, lest I inadvertently kill him.

"But you're dead…"

I suppressed the urge to laugh. "I am dead, or more appropriately I am death. Unfortunately for you, I still have a considerable grudge against you, and your actions of late have not endeared you to me. In fact, I think I might hate you even more than Mal'goroth."

His face twisted into a defiant grimace, which I hadn't expected. Apparently Tremont was made of stiffer stuff than I had thought. "If you're going to kill me, just get it over with. I'd rather not listen to your whining drivel," he replied.

"Your wish is my command, Majesty," I answered sarcastically, "but it will not be quick or easy."

Andrew Tremont attempted to spit then, but his mouth had gone dry from fear. "You haven't got the guts, boy. I know you better than you know yourself. You're too craven to torture anyone."

"You really are a sick bastard," I told him, "to think that cowardice and torture have anything to do with one another. It's quite the opposite really. My conscience thinks you should die swiftly, painlessly, for justice and nothing more, but I don't care what my conscience says anymore. Today I'm making a special exception. I'm going to lower myself to your level." Finishing that sentence, I used a tiny bit of aythar to remove one of his thumbnails, ripping it free with little more than a thought.

He screamed and I smiled, although somewhere, far away, I felt a sickening twist in my stomach. I ignored it, and began removing the other nails, one by one.

That task took less than two or three minutes, even including the toes, and I realized I would have to be a lot more creative if I didn't want things to end too quickly. I decided to burn his digits off, one by one. Fire had the added bonus of cauterizing as well, preventing the blood loss that might otherwise speed things up.

No, that's enough, came the annoying voice from within. *No one deserves to die like that.*

I paid my conscience no heed, and soon my head was swimming with cries for mercy and forgiveness. After a time I began to have trouble telling which ones originated with Tremont, and which ones came from within. Two men were crying, one in front of me, and one inside. I laughed and tortured them both.

It went on for over an hour, and by the end, the room was filled with the stench of burnt flesh and voided bowels. My inner voice went silent at some point, though I could still feel its sickened revulsion at my actions. I danced over the messy remains of Andrew Tremont.

"You can all go straight to hell," I told the immobile servants in the great hall. They couldn't hear or see me, which made the statement rather unsatisfying, but I decided I didn't really care.

I left the palace in high spirits.

Chapter 35

Gareth Gaelyn flew on outstretched wings, circling over Castle Cameron. The world below stretched out to the horizon, but his keen eyes could easily discern even the smallest of details below. The castle was occupied, but not by its rightful occupants. The soldiers manning its walls wore no livery at all, and here and there among them were creatures that bore an uncanny resemblance to the ones Gareth had seen at the father-tree. Creatures possessed of considerable aythar.

They look like Kriteck. Could these be related to the Dark Gods?

Unsure, he determined not to fly closer than he was, keeping a range of several miles. In the distance to the west he could see several small dots. They were so far away that they were over the gulf. *Which means they're pretty large for me to see them at this range. What could be flying this way that is that big?*

Gareth had more questions than answers, but he was certain that things would get much more interesting in the region of Cameron Castle very soon. He had flown from his hiding place near Albamarl the night before, hoping to find someone to warn. Moira had previously sent him a message that they were leaving, broadcasting her thoughts as far as possible, but he hadn't replied. He had been deep in thought, considering his own situation.

Now he hoped to find her, and with her the others, to share what he had seen, but all he could discover were more enemies.

A familiar voice echoed in his mind. *I saw you fly over.* It was Moira Centyr.

Where are you?

There was a long pause, and then her thoughts came to him again. *In the forest, midway between Cameron and Arundel. Draw closer and I'll send you a mental image when you are near.*

You are with the Prathions? questioned Gareth.

Another pause and then, *yes.*

The dragon shifted direction to a more westerly course, in the direction that Moira had indicated. As he did, he flew lower, forsaking the view for the obscurity of the air just above the tree tops. Despite this effort to remain unseen, he soon spotted what appeared to be a winged man closing rapidly on him.

This is going to be one of those days, thought Gareth. Lately it seemed he had been involved in the lives and activities of far too many other beings. It was thoroughly against the grain of his dragon nature. He wanted only to be left alone, and yet, somehow he found himself continually drawn into the world and its affairs.

He didn't bother trying to avoid the encounter. Whatever was heading for him possessed a large store of aythar, and within a moment, it was close enough that he could identify it. *Karenth,* he said to himself.

Within minutes, the former god of justice had pulled up abreast of him in the air and sent a mental greeting. *Permission to come aboard?* The thought came with an implied smile.

Gareth fought down the irritation that the question immediately raised within him. Over the past weeks he had become some sort of ferry service for Mordecai and his friends, but he'd be damned before he let himself get used to it. *If you think you must,* he returned with a mental growl.

Karenth settled himself onto the flying dragon's shoulders as though it were the most natural thing in the world. *I could get used to this,* sent the god.

Only if you think you could get used to being torn in half and eaten as well, returned the dragon.

You seem to be in a poor mood, as usual, responded Karenth. *You should cheer up. I have good news for our side.*

I am my own side, said the dragon automatically.

Don't play coy, thought the god. *You can no longer claim that, else you wouldn't be here.*

The dragon didn't bother replying. He had no good argument, which only made him angrier.

I met with Mordecai a day and a half ago. He has taken control of my fellow gods, Millicenth and Doron. He also sends word of new allies.

Save your words for the others. I would rather not have to listen to you talk twice, answered Gareth.

You aren't listening now. We're speaking mind to mind.

Gareth suppressed the urge to express his annoyance with a jet of flame. No need to make his position easier to spot. *Your thoughts are just as vexing as your irritating voice.*

Karenth shut up after that, and they flew onward in silence, until eventually Moira contacted him again and guided them down to the southern edge of their hidden camp in the thick wood.

The area that they landed in seemed to be utterly devoid of any humans, but both Karenth and Gareth knew better than to expect to see them. Following Moira's small steps, they traveled another fifty feet on foot before the world changed around them, as though they had stepped through a curtain. They were in a wide meadow now, packed with men, women, and children. There were no fires, for the smoke would have ruined the effectiveness of Walter's illusion.

"I must admit to being impressed," said Karenth aloud. "I would never have credited a human with the skill to create such an artful veil to hide so many companions." He stared around him as though taking in the view with new eyes.

"I'm not sure I like your tone," said Elaine Prathion, appearing as if from nothing. "Why have you brought this creature with you?" she asked, turning her attention to the dragon.

"Do not speak to me as your friend," growled Gareth. "I am here for my own reasons. This thing followed me of his own accord, but I did not attempt to dissuade him. I believe he is in the service of your former mentor."

"Try to be civil, Gareth," admonished Moira Centyr. "We do not have enough allies to drive wedges between each other with harsh words."

Gareth closed his toothy mouth and refrained from offering anymore biting remarks.

Ariadne approached them now, moving with confident grace. "I am hopeful you bring good news, Sir Dragon." Her eyes went from Gareth and then to Karenth.

"My news is neither good nor ill, Princess," said the Dragon. "But it should be of concern, for it could possibly herald the destruction of most of Lothion."

The Queen of Lothion blanched at his suggestion. At the same time Moira leaned in to whisper something in Gareth's ear.

"My pardon, Your Majesty," added the dragon. "I was unaware of the news regarding your brother."

She waved her hands as if to hurry him along from the unpleasant subject. "Please continue, I would rather not dwell upon my family's tragedies at present."

"Very well," he responded quickly. "I spent the last few days at rest, watching the city of Albamarl, when I saw something most alarming occur yester eve. Just as the sun went down the city was encased in the largest stasis field I have ever witnessed."

"What does this mean?" asked the Queen.

"Such a thing can only be accomplished using a most rare and exceedingly complex enchantment; one that I believe only Mordecai to be currently capable of crafting. I have seen him do something similar, on a much smaller scale, no more than a week ago. I fear that he has done the same with your city," explained the archmage/dragon.

"I am not well versed in the magical arts," began Ariadne, "but if I remember correctly, a 'stasis' spell can only freeze things in time. Is that not correct? What could his goal be with this, and how do you think it could be dangerous?"

"Enchantment, Your Majesty," corrected Gareth. "A spell could not accomplish this."

"Enchantment then," she replied impatiently. "Get to the point."

"He has developed a method for moving and acting within the stasis field, while whoever else is there is helpless. He probably is using it to further his grievance against Tremont," started Gareth.

"That sounds promising," interrupted the Queen.

The dragon sighed, a much less subtle signal when done by such a large creature. "The greater danger lies in the amount of power required to create this enchantment. A small one, like those created in my day, required a vast expenditure of aythar to charge them during their making. The larger the final enchantment, the greater the energy needed. The power input necessary rises at an exponential rate that corresponds to the cubic expansion of the volume to be included."

Ariadne was no stranger to math, but her education into the topic had stayed mostly in the realm of the more practical applications of arithmetic as they applied to bookkeeping and governance. "I am not certain of all your terms, but I gather you feel the amount of aythar necessary to be rather drastic?" she questioned him.

"Drastic is putting it mildly, Your Majesty," said Gareth. "When Moira destroyed Balinthor in our time, the energy released destroyed a nation and created the gulf we now call the Gulf of Garulon. The amount of power Mordecai must have used to create this enchantment would be more than twice that."

"You imply that he will misstep and create a much greater swath of destruction," observed the Queen.

"He does not even have to make a mistake," answered Gareth. "The problem lies in the vessels he is using to channel and control that much power. They have to be able to withstand the force of that much concentrated aythar. If he exceeds their capacity they will fail, and the result will be similar to the iron bombs he has used so successfully in the past, only on a much larger scale."

"Is it not possible that he has chosen something able to withstand the stresses?" she asked.

"I could not begin to guess what material would be up to such an extreme task. That he has something remarkable is evidenced by the fact that we are still here, but whatever it is, it cannot endure that much power indefinitely," said the dragon.

"So you have come to warn us? It sounds as if the danger has already passed," Ariadne observed.

"I came to escape the danger. The warning was merely a favor," answered the dragon in a surly tone.

Moira Centyr gave him a disapproving glare, and Ariadne couldn't help but wonder if they were having a second, silent conversation.

Karenth broke in at that point and saved her from pursuing the thought further. "While the dragon's news is pessimistic, I think you'll find mine rather more encouraging."

The new queen let out the breath she had been holding with relief. Only then was she aware of how tense she had become. "Good news would be welcome. We have had little enough of late."

"First I would like to mention, if Mordecai's plan in Albamarl has gone without any difficulties, then the capital is free. While he did not give me the full details, I know he intended to rid the city of the usurper and his allies. We cannot disregard this good news," Karenth told the young queen. "Also, he instructed me to present myself here and submit myself and my fellow gods into your service."

"Fellow gods?"

"Indeed, Your Majesty. As with me, Mordecai has bound both Millicenth and Doron to his will. Before separating to prepare for Albamarl, he instructed us to find you and aid you in whatever manner we could," the god informed her.

Something flickered across Ariadne's face, an emotion suddenly felt and quickly subdued, the possibility of hope. "Where are your fellows then?" she asked.

"Searching the vale, as I was, for some sign of you and your people. Once we have finished I will leave and fetch them to your side," said Karenth immediately.

"Though I find myself mistrustful of you and your ilk, I yet find hope in your words," said the queen.

"There is yet more," said the shining god. "As the good dragon here can attest, on the horizon there approaches a mighty host of strange beings. Mordecai was successful in restoring the She'Har, and they are sending their servants, the Kriteck, to aid you in your battle."

"Is this true?" she asked, turning to Gareth.

"They were too far away for me to be sure of their nature, but they match what I already know, and they were coming from the proper direction," said the dragon.

"I know little of the She'Har. As with most of you, I had always been taught that their race was long extinct. Do you know anything of these 'Kriteck'?"

Moira Centyr stepped forward then, "Your Majesty, I was with Mordecai and Gareth when he first met with them. The Kriteck, as I understand them, are the sterile progeny of the father-tree. They live but a span of a few months and they only exist to protect the She'Har. They come in myriad shapes and forms, according to the will of the father-tree that grew them. Some of them are powerful magic-users, while others are designed as fierce warriors. The powerful remnants of the Dark Gods, which you have faced recently, were probably created from the Kriteck of antiquity."

Ariadne took a moment to digest the information before asking a new question, "Can we trust them?"

Moira shook her head negatively, "Probably not, Your Majesty, but they owe Mordecai a great debt. The question should probably be, dare we trust *him*?"

"By that logic we should say the same of the Shining Gods," inferred the young queen.

"Absolutely," agreed Moira Centyr.

Karenth spoke again, "You should also know, Your Majesty, that Mordecai instructed them to place themselves at the disposal of either you or the Countess. They will answer to no one else."

"Then I suppose I had better meet them," said Ariadne. "Gareth, would you be willing to provide me with transportation?"

The dragon made an odd noise. It sounded like the beginning of a growl, but Moira glanced sharply at him, and it cut off suddenly. "I suppose it wouldn't be too much trouble, Your Majesty," he replied after a minute.

Chapter 36

With a word and a thought, I released the enchantment that held Albamarl in my perfect, timeless moment. The tension in the air vanished, and the world snapped back into motion while I drew the aythar back from the diamond cubes of the enchantment and returned it to its proper home—me.

My strength was even greater than before. When I had begun, I had commanded something close to two and a half Celiors worth of aythar. Reclaiming most of that from the enchantment, along with what I had garnered from my wonderful slaughter, put me closer to four.

And it still isn't enough.

Of course, without spending some time with my tools back in my workshop, I couldn't be precise, but I trusted my guess to be roughly correct. Based on what I knew of Mal'goroth, I needed more than ten times what I currently held to face him on even footing. *That's easy enough,* I thought, *take the rest of Lothion's population, toss in some extras from Dunbar and Gododdin, and I might have enough—so long as I'm not too picky.*

No!

My conscience had decided to speak up again. He had been strangely silent since Tremont's slow demise. *Relax, I wasn't serious,* I told myself. Something about that seemed humorous to me, and I began to laugh.

I stopped when I heard the screams.

They were soft and in the distance, but they gave the impression of being multilayered. Using a hasty spell I increased my hearing, and then the true symphony began to make its way to my ears. All across the city people were reacting with various degrees of shock, dismay, and delightfully, sometimes with screams.

It must be rather disconcerting to suddenly find everyone in your vicinity inexplicably dead.

"Mal'goroth should be fairly peeved when he finds out how many of his toys he lost here today," I said to myself. I suppressed the urge to walk back in. Hearing the sounds of chaos within made me desperately want to go and see the reactions of the people first hand.

Once everyone has calmed down, they'll probably want to throw a parade for me. It was a pleasant thought, but my pessimistic inner voice wouldn't shut up.

No, the reason you're leaving is because Mal'goroth will be drawn here now. We mustn't let him discover us here. It's time to reclaim your home.

"Shut up!" I yelled at myself, not caring if anyone saw my odd behavior. "I'm in charge, not you!"

If you are looking for excitement, all the action is going to be back at Cameron Castle.

That was true, I had to admit. Sometimes my inner observer had a point. "Penny will be there, too," I said aloud with a feeling of sudden anticipation. Thinking of her filled me with a distinct craving. It was a sensation similar to the mixture of intense hunger and sexual tension.

Stay away from her! My inner demon was particularly emphatic, almost desperate.

364

"You're so easily riled up. I wouldn't hurt her. I still love her after all," I told myself with a clever grin.

Reaching into one of my wondrous pouches, I withdrew my staff and used it to etch a complex circular design in the dirt. It was a teleportation circle, and I set the destination key to one of the circles in the courtyard of Castle Cameron. Whatever was happening there at the moment, I doubted anyone would be expecting me to reappear there just then.

Uttering a word, I attempted to transition myself to my destination, but nothing happened. "That's odd," I said. I tried one more and again, nothing. The only explanation was that the destination circle had been destroyed.

I tried one of the circles in Lancaster, and after that failed I tried another in Arundel. Both were completely non-responsive. "That doesn't bode well for my friends and family," I noted dispassionately. Deeper down though, my inner self was growing panicked.

Considering my options, I knew I could still use the World Road, but I didn't really want to travel by such an obvious route. If Mal'goroth were watching for me, that would be one of the prime locations to keep an eye on. I still had one circle in the foothills near Lancaster, a secret location I had set up for evacuating Cameron Castle, but I was too paranoid to use it now.

What if my opponent had destroyed all the other circles just to force me to use that one? What if he was waiting there? My head was full of shadows, and it was difficult to think clearly. Was it really a bad idea, or was I seeing traps where there were none?

If you're that nervous, just fly. You can still reach it within a day if you use your best speed.

"Yes," I replied, "That is a good idea." I started to withdraw the enchanted stones that would form my flying craft, when I noticed that I still had the diamond cubes in my right hand. After disassembling my enchantment they had flown back to the center stone and formed a larger cube. It seemed slightly hazy now.

Looking closer I could see cracks in some of the cubes. *I probably won't be able to use them for anything as large as a city again,* I thought sadly.

You shouldn't use them at all. They're cracked. It's too dangerous.

I made a sour face in response to my inner killjoy and tucked them back into their proper pouch. Before I could reach for the stones for my flying craft I had another thought, and this one was particularly brilliant. *I'm immortal, invulnerable, and possessed of the power of at least four gods—why do I need a flying craft?*

"Damn right," I said in agreement. I considered wings for a moment but then decided they were too unfashionable. Instead, I said a few words and took control of the air around me, using it to lift myself directly up. Creating a cone shaped shield, I used the wind to drive myself forward through the air. It wasn't easy to steer, but my reflexes and reactions were far beyond human now.

Faster and faster I drove myself through the air, gaining ever more speed. One mistake and I'd drive myself headfirst into the ground or perhaps a mountain, when I had gotten closer to Cameron. The thought didn't scare me a bit, though. *I'd feel sorrier for the mountain.*

Chapter 37

Cyhan sat in quiet solitude. He was uncomfortable in much the same way that rivers are wet—thoroughly, completely, and without words. The lack of a fire was a minor inconvenience, but combined with the cold night air, his broken collarbone, the ache in his recently dislocated hip and a variety of still healing bruises, it was almost too much for him. Almost.

A tall figure approached slowly, but Cyhan recognized Harold Simmons by his characteristic gait. The man had a casual walk that sometimes hid his excessive vitality, but it was apparent in the brisk way he stopped and started. "Shouldn't you be getting the men ready?" Cyhan asked the shadowy outline in the dark.

"That's part of why I'm here," replied Harold. "Now that...," he stopped for a moment, unable to finish the sentence. "You're the grandmaster now. I need your input on the morning assault."

"I'm not the grandmaster, just the most senior ranked of those left. I'm also incapacitated, making you the highest ranked brother still competent," Cyhan shot back with a faint growl. "You should get back to work."

"There isn't any doubt about your promotion, assuming we survive the present," said Harold, ignoring his superior's surly demeanor.

"Yeah?" said Cyhan, "Who's going to promote me? The Count is dead, or worse. There are only five of us left anyway."

Harold sighed. "The Queen will likely transfer our order to royal service. New knights will be made. The work will continue."

The old veteran caught Harold's eye with a hard stare, "Without an archmage there will be no more earth-bonds. Which also brings us around to the fact that you and I are on borrowed time. How long before you think we'll lose ourselves?"

"Doesn't matter," insisted Harold. "We live for the oath. If I only have a few years, then I'll use them to that end. As for new knights, our order is about more than superficial power. It's about an ideal. As long as there are men who share that dream, we will persist."

Cyhan spat on the ground. "You really believe in all that shit? You're just like our departed grandmaster. You know what it got him? Dead. And he was lucky. You should have seen him before he died."

Harold gave little outward sign of his anger, but one fist clenched reflexively. "Are you saying you're ready to forsake your oaths?"

The wounded warrior laughed. "No. They're all I have left. I'm just sick of hearing a lot of romanticized bullshit about them. We kill, we protect, and we die. Anyone that thinks it's a glorious calling is due disappointment."

"Dorian felt differently."

Cyhan turned his head to face his visitor squarely, and in the dim light Harold could still make out the tell-tale glimmer of tears on his cheeks. "Dorian was a damned fool! You're right though, for most of his life he did feel differently, but not at the end. In the end, he saw the ugly truth. I could see it in his eyes."

Harold's anger dissipated as he realized how deeply Cyhan was suffering over Dorian's loss. "What are you saying?"

"I'm saying he was heartsick. The blood and the futility of it all had taken root in his heart."

"You're still here, and you still serve," said Harold bluntly.

"I'm not exactly a role-model. Look at me! My body is broken and battered, but that's not the worst of it. It's just that my exterior finally matches my interior. My heart died a long time ago. I should be dead along with it."

Sudden insight woke within Harold, and he began to understand. "You loved him, didn't you? Just like the rest of us."

"He was a fool, but yeah, I did. I hated him for it, but I did love the bastard," admitted Cyhan slowly.

"You want to know why?" Harold asked him unexpectedly.

"Why, what?"

"Do you want to know why you loved him?" clarified Harold.

"Because he was the only man I considered my equal," said Cyhan, adding, "except for his foolish ideas."

"No," declared the younger man, "You loved him *because* of his dream. You found a man, a warrior, dedicated to the same art, who still believed in honor and the dream of chivalry. He was everything you wanted to be. You loved him because he represented *your* dream, the dream you had before life and time broke you down inside. You didn't believe in it anymore, but you loved him anyway, because he gave you hope."

The older man was silent for a long time, not daring to reply until his throat had cleared. Harold's words had found their mark. "You're probably right, I'll admit it, but where does that put us now? He's still dead, right along with his dream."

"That's where you're wrong. It's right here," Harold pointed at his own chest. "It lives in me and in every young soldier that Dorian inspired, whether they be knight or not. Whatever Dorian felt at the end, it was too late. He had already passed it on, to me, to his son. If you need inspiration, just look to the next generation. It's here." The younger knight held out his hand toward his superior.

"What do you want from me?" asked Cyhan, staring upward.

"I need your help. Doron's power will be shared with our soldiers, giving them strength and speed similar to our own, but they aren't accustomed to it. There are two-hundred men preparing for war, and some of them are liable to kill themselves before they understand their own strength. I need your help to instruct them in the little time we have left." Harold kept his hand outstretched.

"You really are much like him," said Cyhan at last, and then he placed his hand in Harold's. A moment later he let out a muffled scream of pain. "Stop!" The other man had attempted to pull him to his feet, forgetting his broken collarbone.

"Forgive me!" exclaimed Harold. "I forgot!"

"Well godsdammitt all! My body didn't forget!" griped Cyhan, between short shallow breaths.

"Elaine said she would come and tend to you," said Harold.

The older knight grimaced, "Well she hasn't made it around yet. Get back to your work. I'll come when I am able, if she gets around to me soon."

Feeling a bit sheepish Harold left.

Cyhan rearranged himself to lie flat on the ground. The grinding pain told him his collarbone was seriously out of alignment again, but he was helpless to correct it himself. Nor did he have the resolve to request assistance doing so. Harold's remarks had helped his spirit, but his physical pain was still overwhelming. "It should have been me," he said aloud, to no one in particular.

More footsteps announced the arrival of a new visitor, and by their lightness he could guess it was a she. The direction was suspicious however, for the sound came from upwind. Elaine appeared close by, and he realized she had learned from his embarrassing remarks earlier, approaching from a direction that was unlikely to give her away.

"How long were you listening?" he asked.

"Not long," she lied. "I just heard you swearing when he pulled on your arm."

Cyhan hadn't really expected a truthful answer, so he accepted the lie. It was simpler than inviting a discussion. "I don't suppose you can do something about this?" he asked, indicating his shoulder and arm.

"I can," she said, "If you can bear it."

"Been awhile since anyone asked me that question."

She let out a breath in mock exasperation, "You were supposed to ask how much it would hurt."

"Been awhile since I cared," he added gruffly, though in truth he was far past his limit already.

"It won't hurt at all. I can block the nerves before I begin," she answered, giving up her attempt at humor.

Cyhan gave her a rare smile, a subtle indicator of just how much her response had improved his mood. His actual words were as stubborn as ever though, "Just make sure everything still works when you're done."

Shaking her head in disbelief, Elaine put one hand on his chest as she began seeking out the proper nerves to block before realigning and fusing his broken bones. "Don't worry, I had a good teacher," she said mildly.

*
**

Ariadne Lancaster had had better days, and she deeply hoped that the next day would be one of them, but she had her doubts. She stood in a small clearing that was currently serving as her meeting chamber. They had no chairs, so everyone stood, which was just as well since there was no table to sit at.

"How will the Kriteck distinguish between friend and foe?" asked the Countess pointedly.

"We have agreed that they will ignore all human combatants, and non-combatants for that matter," explained the new queen. "They will concern themselves with nullifying the activities of the 'god-seeds'. They will also attempt to protect us if Mal'goroth should appear, though it is doubtful if that will be possible."

"Which means?" asked Chad Grayson. The master hunter had been the de facto leader of most of the civilian refugees until they had merged with the survivors from Arundel.

"If Mal'goroth shows himself, we are probably dead," she admitted.

"We have three of the Shining Gods with us, a dragon, five wizards, and a bizarre army of extinct creatures, and we can't face one Dark God?" he asked argumentatively. As usual he utterly forgot to include the honorific, 'Your Majesty'.

"In a nutshell," she said brusquely, "yes."

The huntsman seemed mollified by her direct answer, so Walter used the pause as an opportunity to ask his own question. "You still haven't discussed your strategy for this battle, Your Majesty."

Ariadne directed her gaze at him, and her confidence radiated outward. "In part, that is because I need information regarding your capabilities. Up until now, you or one of your two children have kept the illusion operating that protects this camp. How many of you will be able to participate in our assault?"

"Just two, Your Majesty, unless you wish us to give up our attempts to hide the camp," he answered promptly.

"It is tempting," she said thoughtfully. "A major part of the reason for this is to acquire supplies, and a better place to house our people. If we succeed, this camp will be abandoned."

Sir Harold arrived then but had heard the previous remarks as he approached. "Your pardon, Majesty, but I think we should maintain the secrecy of the camp. If we make our attack and encounter unforeseen problems, we will lose any hope of retreat or recourse. Also, any counter attack could be directed at the civilians remaining here. The illusion will be their only defense in our absence."

"Shouldn't we wait another day before we attack? This plan seems very hasty," suggested Stephen Balistair.

Harold nodded his head, "I think we all would prefer that, but unfortunately we are out of time. Walter can confirm that."

Walter nervously agreed, "Some of these people have been living in the woods for over a week now. We've almost run out of food, and we are far lower on other essentials."

"We can still hunt," said Stephen, looking in Chad's direction.

The huntsman made an irritated face. He didn't like being put on the spot. "Sorry, Yer Lordship, these woods can't feed so many, and more importantly we're out of water. Unless we plan to move down to the river and expose ourselves, we're out of options."

"You're a disagreeable rascal aren't you?" retorted Stephen, irritated at the hunter's direct manner.

Chad's eyes narrowed, "I said, 'Yer Lordship', what more do you want?!"

"It's your tone I object to," shot back Stephen, "and the fact that you neglected to use any honorific at all with the Queen a moment ago."

"Silence," commanded Ariadne abruptly. "We can ill afford to fight here. Lord Stephen, I will worry about my own honor and you would do well to pay less heed to yours, at least until this day's work is done." The hunter shook his finger at Stephen while the Queen spoke, unable to restrain himself, though he kept his tongue. Without looking in his direction, Ariadne continued, "Master Grayson, you would be wise not to test my patience."

"Forgive me, Your Grace," answered the hunter hastily. Penny leaned in to whisper in his ear and he amended his statement, "I mean, *Your Majesty*."

Ariadne acknowledged the apology with a faint nod before moving on, "Sir Harold, how do the men fare?"

"Awkwardly, Your Majesty. I have Sir Egan, Sir William, and Sir Thomas working with them at the moment, helping them to acclimate to their new strength. Once we finish here I will rejoin them, and I hope that Sir Cyhan will soon be able to assist as well," he responded quickly.

"Is it really so difficult?" asked the queen.

"Yes, Your Majesty," said Harold. He blushed mildly as he remembered his first charge while strengthened by the earth-bond. He had nearly killed himself slamming into a ceiling. "Several of the soldiers have already been injured and one would have died if the goddess had not been present."

"Died?"

"He leapt into a tree and broke his neck when he struck a limb, Your Majesty," supplied the knight.

"It really takes a lot of getting used to," added Penny.

"And the gods have been true to their word thus far?" asked Ariadne.

"Yes, Your Majesty," said Harold. "Doron has given any man who volunteered the strength of several men, and Millicenth has already healed a number of injuries, new and old alike."

Penny broke in then, "Speaking of our allies, how will we coordinate with the Kriteck?"

"Karenth will serve as our liaison, ferrying information and orders to them," said Ariadne. "They will remain separate from our forces and wait until the attack has begun before they respond. Once the attack starts, their giant flying 'dragons' will deposit them in the central courtyard."

"And what of our dragon?" asked Harold.

"He has declined to participate," responded the queen with a tight face. "He prefers autonomy. Moira Centyr assures me he will render assistance if necessary, but only when and if *he* feels that it is required."

"Damned uppity dragon," muttered Chad, "wonder how he'd feel with an arrow in one eye?" He closed his mouth quickly when he realized the queen was staring at him. "Sorry, Your Majesty, just thinking out loud."

The meeting continued for another half hour, while details were discussed and agreed upon. When it was over, Ariadne signaled to Penny to wait behind. Once the others had left she took the Countess's hands in her own, and Penny started to take knee.

"Please, don't Penny," said the new queen. "You know I think of you more as an older sister. As difficult as all of this has been, please continue to treat me as before, at least when we are alone."

Penelope watched the younger woman's face with empathy. Having been raised a commoner, she was all too familiar with the discomfort of newfound formality with former peers. "I should have known better. Forgive me, Ariadne, the stress of late—sometimes I don't know who I am anymore."

"That's mainly why I held you back," said Ariadne. "I wanted to know how the twins are doing."

"They regained consciousness briefly, before returning to a more normal sleep," assured Penny. "I've seen it with their father a few times before, so I think they will make a full recovery."

The young queen nodded, "I'm relieved to hear it. What about Rose? I had hoped she would come to the council, but I didn't think it right to command her presence."

Penny frowned. "She's withdrawn into herself. She's still nursing, and she seems to be comforting Gram but she hasn't spoken to anyone other than Elise since Dorian died."

"Not even you?"

It was a sensitive subject, but Penny decided to be frank, "Rose and I weren't on the best of terms before the attacks."

"I thought you two were as thick as thieves," commented Ariadne.

"Normally, yes. She came to visit me the day that your father...," Penny paused before rewording her statement, "... the day Tremont showed his true nature. I think she had come to reconcile, but everything just fell by the wayside when the news came."

"It's not really my business, but why were you fighting?"

"My stubbornness to consider future wedding arrangements," admitted Penny. "She thought I should start thinking of my options before the year was up, so that I'd be better prepared when the pressure began."

"I can see why that upset you."

"It's even worse now," said Penny. "I felt as though she was cheapening Mordecai's memory, but when Dorian transformed…"

"What?" asked Ariadne.

"… she went to him without hesitation, even when he was a horror of crystal and spikes. I saw then, that she was truer to her heart than I had been," said Penny with tears in her eyes. Now that she was finally confessing what had lain in her heart, the emotion threatened to sweep her away.

"But you didn't know!" protested the younger woman. "He had become a shiggreth. Even Dorian knew that he wasn't safe."

"But he was," countered Penny. "He was confused, but he didn't want to hurt us. I saw that later, when it became apparent that he had not become the monster we had assumed."

"Moira says he isn't really the same man, and that his mind is unraveling."

Penny stared at the earth. "Moira isn't the same woman, but she still loves her child. I stood beside my husband the last time we thought his sanity was in question."

"You did what was necessary. You told me that he didn't really want to take the bond with you back then," corrected Ariadne.

"You're right," agreed Penny. "I had no faith then either."

"You took a ballista bolt through the stomach for him. Stop feeling sorry for yourself. You've done the best you knew for you and your family at every turn, right or wrong," said Ariadne as she moved toward her friend. She put her arms around Penny and did her best to comfort her for several minutes before they pulled apart.

"I need to help Harold," said the Countess.

"You need to talk to Rose," countered Ariadne, "There may not be a chance later."

"If something happens to me, then you will have to tell her," said Penny, drying her cheeks with one sleeve. "There's too little time now."

The Queen looked sadly after the Countess as she returned to her duties. "There's never enough time, is there?" she said to herself, thinking of her mother and father.

Chapter 38

"How will you be able to see when they open the gate to let the villagers in?" whispered Harold. He stood close behind Walter, along with Penny, and Sir Egan. Another twenty men stood with them, huddling together at the edge of the road leading through the gate into Cameron Castle.

They were cloaked in invisibility provided by Walter, who also dampened any noises they might make. A similar group stood across the road from them with his son George shielding twenty others, plus Sir William and Sir Thomas.

One unfortunate side effect of an invisibility shield was that it blocked the entry of whatever it was hiding the user from. This meant that if you were using it to block visible sight, you were effectively blind. For a wizard this wasn't so bad, since they still could see using magesight, but Walter and George were forced to hide them from that as well. The sound dampening also made it impossible for them to hear beyond their small groups.

They were deaf, dumb, and blind.

However, Walter had been using his magic to hide for decades, and his family was known for their special talents in that regard. "There's a hole in our perceptual shield," he explained. "It allows me to see out through a tiny spot, but only using physical eyesight."

"Because they might find us if you used magesight?" questioned Harold.

"Yes," responded Walter. "I think a physical peephole is easier to hide than a magical one, especially with so many people full of aythar inside."

"How do you hide a hole?" asked Sir Egan, clearly enthralled.

"With an illusion," said Walter with some exasperation. "I'm looking through what, from the outside, appears to be a perfectly normal bird perched in a tree right here."

"But there isn't a tree here," objected Egan.

"There isn't a bird either," Walter told him with no small amount of sarcasm. "Will you let me concentrate? I know I make this look simple, but it really isn't."

Penny fought the urge to laugh at their conversation, though she needn't have. Her sounds would have gone unheard by the outside world, but old habits die hard. When she did speak she continued to whisper, as they all did, "You should relax Egan."

"It isn't easy, standing in the pitch black on the side of the road, waiting for the order to move, knowing that at any moment we could be discovered," protested the knight, also in a whisper.

"Imagine Cyhan is standing behind you, watching over your shoulder," suggested Penny.

Sir Egan shuddered in the dark. "That really doesn't help. I don't think anyone would want that," he complained.

"Then just shut up, or I'll have him watch you sleep for the next month, after we're done today!" hissed Harold in frustration. He wasn't enjoying the circumstances either, but he kept his complaints to himself. They were all on edge, nervous with pent up adrenaline, afraid to move or even speak loudly for fear of disrupting their wizard.

"The wagons are rolling up now," announced Walter. "They'll be opening the gate any moment."

"That's a relief," said one of the soldiers in the group. Penny didn't recognize him by his voice.

Harold sighed, "Keep it quiet."

"See, I'm not the only one that's a bit anxious," said Egan, feeling validated by the other man's comment.

"I'm starting to think Mordecai bound you to someone's grandmother instead of the earth, because that's what you're starting to sound like!" barked Harold in a slightly louder voice. "Just like my Nanna, next you'll be complaining about your rheumatism." His remark was met with a number of quiet chuckles.

Even Egan saw the humor in the remark, "I rather like your Nanna. She's a sensible woman. She'd know better than to be standing out here on a cold morning in the dark."

"Alright, be quiet!" ordered Walter. "We're going to start moving carefully forward. Move at a slow pace, the last thing we need is to bump into each other, or heaven forbid, into George's group."

Each person kept a hand on the shoulder of the one in front of him and another on the waist of the person to their right. Standing at the front of the group, Walter led them carefully forward. His peephole was no longer disguised, but it would be difficult for anyone to spot; although he knew from experience it wasn't impossible.

382

His son should be on the opposite side of the road from them now, moving in the same direction, but he had no way to confirm the fact. So long as their shields rendered them invisible to aythar, even direct mental communication would be impossible. They had discussed their routes earlier however, and each group had a different target.

Breathing a sigh of relief as they passed through the gatehouse without incident, Walter guided them through the mostly empty courtyard toward the main keep. Once they reached the main door to the keep, they would discard their invisibility and break into three subgroups. George's group would do the same, once he saw them enter the keep.

Walter's group would divide into three parts. One, including him and Penny, would head for the key chamber that controlled the castle's magical defenses. They were fairly certain that these had remained undiscovered, since the enemy had shown no sign of using them yet, but it would be important to gain control of them quickly. Harold would take seven men and head for the barracks and armory, racing to catch and eliminate any enemy reserves who weren't on duty, while Egan and his seven would head for the roof to eliminate the archers there who threatened the courtyard. Once that was done they would sweep the walls and smaller defenses to eliminate the other defenders.

George's group would also split, with one team, led by Sir William, taking control of the main gate as quickly as possible. At the same time, as soon as their game was revealed, Sir Thomas and his seven would run for the postern gate to take control of it before their enemies could coordinate to stop them. George and the remaining six would sweep the top of the outer walls to help take control of the courtyard.

It was a simple and direct plan, made possible by two things, the element of surprise, provided by the Prathion wizards, and the strength of Doron. They couldn't sneak enough men in for their initial surprise attack to have succeeded if it weren't for Doron's enhancement of their soldiers. Each of the men with them would be nearly as fast and strong as one of the Knights of Stone, and although their armor would be simpler and their weapons mundane, they should be able to handle any human defenders they encountered easily enough.

As soon as the walls and gates were under their control, the Kriteck would land to deal with whatever 'servants' Mal'goroth had left behind, and the rest of their enhanced soldiers would enter to solidify their hold on the castle. It sounded easy enough.

I can't wait to see what goes wrong first, thought Harold pessimistically. He knew from experience that few plans survive past the first few minutes of battle, but it was better to have one than not.

"We're standing in front of the main door to the keep now," said Walter with a nervous warble in his voice. "There are four men directly in front of us, two on either side. I'm going to count to three, and then I will drop the concealment. Are you ready?"

A quick chorus of 'ayes' answered him, and Walter began to count. "One, two—three!" The light of what seemed to be a dozen suns blinded them as soon as Walter removed his spell. Having been in absolute darkness for almost two hours, their eyes were slow to adjust. Moving forward on instinct and experience more than eyesight, Penny and Harold killed the four men guarding the door in seconds.

Egan was prevented from doing the same by the man behind him who in his excitement brought his axe to the ready so quickly that he knocked the knight forward and off balance. Two others in the group were less lucky. One lost an ear when the man next to him unsheathed his sword, while another suffered a broken arm from an overenthusiastic mate next to him.

About what I expected, thought Harold as he threw open the doors.

Penny entered beside Walter and spoke rapidly to Harold, "We'll take the injured. Walter can patch them up before we reach our objective."

Nodding, Harold and Egan quickly pointed and switched the two wounded men for two of those who had been meant to accompany Penny. Without waiting further, the two broke off in different directions, Harold toward the barracks and Egan the stairs that led up. The few guards who were in the entry were dead before they could react, and Walter created a new concealment shield to hide himself along with Penny and the remaining men.

"How long will it take to fix them?" asked Penny.

"I've already stopped the blood loss from the fellow's lost ear," replied Walter. His healing skills were nowhere near the level that Mordecai's had been, or even the level of Elaine's, but simple cuts and bones he could handle. "Once we get to a safe place, I'll drop the shield and tend to this fellow's arm. That will take a minute or two."

They began their careful walk to the center of the main floor of the keep, toward the hidden chamber that controlled the castle's defenses.

*
**

George and his group stood in the shadow of the wall, just inside the main outer gate of Castle Cameron. Speaking in his characteristically calm voice, George made his announcement, "They've begun. I'm going to drop the invisibility. Get ready."

He didn't bother counting to three, which was just as well, for it avoided the problem that the other group had encountered. No one was so hyper-ready that they wounded their companions. There was no one standing close to their position, and the shadow of the wall made it easier to adjust to the sudden change in lighting.

William went directly to the doorway that led into the back of the gatehouse; unfortunately, it was closed and locked (as it was supposed to be). He had hoped the invaders would be too lax in their duty to bother keeping it secure while the keep was seemingly safe otherwise. His men were prepared for it, though. He motioned to one of the soldiers who had been chosen as their door-breaker; the man stepped forward and brought out a heavy iron sledge. With a twenty pound head, it was normally unsuitable for combat, but Doron's strength changed the equation a bit.

The fellow smashed the door in within three strikes, and Sir William was into the interior like a steel flash. The others followed quickly behind, but William's enchanted sun-sword was so swift that they had little to do but finish off the wounded and hurry to keep up with the armored knight.

Meanwhile, George led six of the soldiers up the stair that led from the interior courtyard to the first section of Cameron's exterior wall. Their job was considered one of the most risky, especially considering he didn't have a Knight of Stone along with his subgroup. George was unarmored, but he trusted his shields to protect him from the arrows they would probably face. The men with him had no such guarantee though, and their chainmail wouldn't stop a crossbow bolt.

To make up for that disadvantage, he cloaked them with a shimmering near-invisibility that would let the men see dimly while making them hard to target. The first bowmen on the walls never even realized what had hit them until it was too late.

Things got tougher from there. The top of the outer wall was sectioned, so that the walkway atop each wall between the towers was separated from the others by a ten foot empty space to the left of each tower. When things were quiet, wide wooden gangways provided easy bridges between each section of the wall, but when threatened, the men near each would shove them off to make it more difficult for an invader to take the entire wall.

As soon as the guard at the next tower heard the first bowmen's cries, they called out an alarm. The nearest crossbowman raced to the wooden bridge and knocked it free, watching it fall to the ground far below. Raising his weapon, he and the two men exiting the tower behind him began to take aim on the elusive figures now trapped on the other parapet.

A ten foot gap was little problem for a man with the sort of strength and agility that one of the knights had, provided he was used to it. Regrettably, Ariadne's newly enhanced soldiers did not have that much experience yet. The first two to reach the gap were afraid of heights and sensibly stopped, the third was bolder. Leaping out, he overshot his mark. Passing over the gap, he covered the distance but landed off-kilter and fell from the other parapet. His scream as he fell to his death was a warning to the others.

George swore. As he watched one of the crossbowmen's quarrels found its mark in another of his soldiers, despite the shimmering illusion that partially hid him. *"Shadok ni miellte,"* cried George loudly, marking the archers and crossbowmen he could see mentally. Darkness sprang from his fingertips to wrap itself like some living thing around the three bowmen's heads, hiding their faces and blinding them within solid shadow.

Striding quickly to the gap, George uttered another phrase and created a temporary bridge of pure force across the empty space. As a finishing touch he added an opaque brown color to allow the men to see it. "Get across!" he shouted, and the soldiers with him began crossing as quickly as they dared. Their blind foes never stood a chance.

After that things got easier. With only four men left, they were more careful, but George blinded the archers at each section before they could get a clear shot, and the lack of gangways was no obstacle.

Thomas and his group were the first to find real trouble. Sprinting across the courtyard, they were relying upon speed and surprise to protect them from the archers who stood on the walls and atop the keep, until George and Egan's groups could take care of them. Arrows weren't really a problem for Thomas, but the men with him didn't have the protection of enchanted plate as he did. A well placed broadhead arrow or crossbow quarrel could kill a man in chainmail, whether he'd been graced with Doron's strength or not.

Arrows turned out to be the least of their worries.

Running faster than the fleetest stag, Thomas led their charge across the open ground. Their goal was the archway that led to the eastern courtyard; from there they would head for the postern gate. The ground erupted in front of them with clouds of dust and dirt as they neared the center and strange creatures emerged, rising like nightmare sentinels.

Ten of the strange, twisted forms had appeared, from what looked to be small pits dug and concealed within the hard earth. Their shapes and limbs were bizarre in both number and arrangement, but their purpose was clear.

No stranger to surprises, the calm minded Thomas veered to the left rather than springing into the air. An ambusher would be prepared for an instinctive leap, the fact of which was proven when two of the men behind him shot skyward, startled by the sudden appearance of foes in front of them. Neither reached the ground alive; two of the beasts in the rear caught them with long clawed arms, ripping through chainmail and disemboweling one before he found the ground again.

The other died more painfully, as one of his legs was caught and snipped off by a thing with claw-like shears for arms. He fell, blood pumping forcefully from the ruined stump and mercifully lost consciousness before the diminished god could finish the job.

Sir Thomas's great sword removed the front right leg of a four legged turtle shaped monster, causing it to topple awkwardly sideways as he skipped past. Reversing his momentum, he spun back to the right and removed the arm of another before his ambushers could react. Moving in a pattern of almost random madness, the knight was among his foes and dancing with a deadly grace that reflected either a chaotic genius or a callous disregard for his own life. He stayed nowhere, constantly moving, using the bodies of his foes to change direction and momentum in ways that defied his own weight and previous movement.

Regrettably, his disordered dance also kept him from doing serious harm to any of his foes, other than the occasional removal of an arm or leg when his swings connected with weak points by chance. His purpose was far from random though, his whirling dervish routine confused the enemy long enough for the remainder of the men with him to reorganize themselves, forming two groups, one of two men and another of three.

"Take the right!" shouted Sir Thomas. "Flank the tall one on both sides while you defend each other's backs."

The soldiers, although less experienced, knew well how to take orders and coordinate. Reacting quickly they moved to obey, while Thomas tormented their foes from the left. The 'tall one' he had called out was a particularly spindly, stork-like raptor with ripping claws for forelimbs. The disarray of their initial contact had left it farther out than the others, and the men were able to flank it on either side. Two of the five struck alternately from either side, forcing it into a losing game, while the other three struggled to keep the monster's closest allies from moving to assist.

Continuing his desperate rampage Thomas' luck eventually ran out. Bouncing from the heavy trunk-like torso of one near the center, he was brought to a standstill when, rather than empty air he found himself intercepted by the bulky body of the weird turtle he had initially struck. The pause in his motion proved disastrous.

Reacting with un-turtle-like speed, the beast he had run up against snapped down on Thomas with huge jaws. Acting on pure instinct, the knight brought his great sword up to protect himself and wound up impaling the beast, his sword sliding through the outstretched jaws to thrust through the back of its mouth and into its head. The blow did little to damage the weakened god, but it completely immobilized Thomas' sword.

Knight and turtle stood at an impasse for a long second while he held its powerful head away with the long blade of his weapon. Rather than release the hilt, Thomas took his only other option, uttering the word that would trigger the sun-sword's flames. Fire exploded from the creature's mouth. Shielded by his armor, Thomas felt only a momentary heat while the light blinded him. The turtle-monster was less fortunate. Surprisingly flammable, its form caught fire within and without, and something deeper inside the strange beast exploded.

Thomas lost his grip on the sword then, as he was flung back across the courtyard. Their enemies were also thrown in different directions. The five soldiers with him had finished disabling the tall raptor, but one had been badly wounded during the skirmish. The other four were tossed back like ragdolls when the turtle-thing exploded.

Arrows began to land around them as archers on the walls took aim, assisting their monstrous allies.

Things looked grim for Thomas' soldiers, and their leader was far from being able to recover in time to help them.

A booming rush of wind from above heralded the arrival of a massive dragon-like creature. On its back were numerous smaller creatures, terrible and monstrous in shape and form. They were no less alien in appearance than the diminished god-seeds that Thomas and his men were fighting.

The Kriteck had arrived.

Chapter 39

The courtyard of Cameron Castle dissolved into anarchy as creatures that defied sane description fell together in combat. The massive flying dragon died first, as one of the god-seeds tore open its throat. Unlike the fallen dark-gods, the Kriteck were still living creatures, they could not survive the same fatal wounds their opponents could.

They were more numerous however and some of those that had arrived were magic-users. Lines of power writhed through the air, wrapping themselves around some of the god-seeds, pinning and slowing them while the magic burned at their skin.

Thomas had found his feet, but his hearing had taken a leave of absence. Yelling at the four men still able to move he pointed in the direction of the archway that would take them to their goal, "Get up and start running!" He could only hope their hearing was still intact. His own voice was nothing more than a muted rumble in his ears.

While his men scrambled to obey, Thomas scanned the yard for his sword. *I'll be damned if I spend the rest of the day fighting without it.* His eyes failed to find it, but he did spot what seemed to be the head of the thing that had exploded. Taking a calculated risk, he ran for it, dodging two more monstrosities as he went. The creatures seemed more interested in each other now, and since he could hardly pick bizarre friend from multi-legged foe Thomas responded by ignoring them in like fashion.

His luck held when he found his sword still lodged in the burning head of the turtle beast. Putting his armored boot down on it, he wrenched the blade free and headed in the direction that his soldiers were already running. He cursed as he saw one fall directly in front of him; a crossbow quarrel had sprouted from between the soldier's shoulder blades.

Looking up to spot the man who had fired, Thomas was grateful when he saw one of George's men send the sniper flying from the wall. Sword in hand he ran onward.

*
**

The barracks door flew inward as one of Harold's men struck it a second time with a heavy mace. The scene that greeted them inside was unusual given that it was their own barracks. If the castle had been in their possession, Harold would have expected to find men resting, cleaning armor, or simply talking together, instead it looked like a scene from a bacchanal.

Most of the men inside were naked, baring chests and arms covered in strange tattoos, most notably the flaming black dagger that denoted the Shaddoth Krys. A number of the people inside were women, some tattooed and others clear skinned. Without exception they were naked as well, and while some of the assassins were simply oiling one another, others were unabashedly engaged in more erotic acts.

Everyone became still for a moment as the assassins stared at the newcomers.

Opening his visor, Harold grinned at them evilly. "I thought I told you bastards to clean this place up!" he said, as though he were addressing his own men on a normal day.

One of the nearest men opened his mouth in confusion, "Huh?" The words had barely left his slack jaw before his head rolled away from his shoulders. Harold's sword sent blood spatters along the wall as he whipped it back to a forward guard position, and the assassin's headless torso slumped, pumping more sanguine fluid onto the mattress and floor.

"Look at the mess you've made!" cried Harold in mock disbelief. "You've gotten blood all over my floor." Pointing the tip of his sword at the others he dropped his smile, "The rest of you will have to clean that up."

Pandemonium erupted as the occupants of the barracks scrambled to claim weapons to meet their attackers with. Daggers and swords appeared from beneath mattresses and footlockers, but their general state of unpreparedness was a fatal disadvantage for most. Harold and his soldier's waded forward, cutting and cleaving. Men and women died while blood ran so heavy that it created channels and rivulets throughout the large room.

One of the soldiers with Harold, a man named, Clarence pronounced his disgust, "Dammitt! That was my bed." He was one of the refugees from Cameron itself, and one of the women now lay in two parts across his old bunk.

The fight was almost over now, with only two of the forty-odd Shaddoth Krys that had been in the room still alive. They ducked and dodged around bedframes trying to avoid Harold's soldiers, but they were unable to match them for speed. The outcome was inevitable. A loud boom from outside caught Harold's attention.

"What was that?" asked the blond knight, but none of the others had any suggestions. "Finish here and then sweep the hall and kitchens for more of them," he commanded hastily. "I'm going to check outside. I'll find you afterward."

With that he left them and began running for the main hall that was the closest exit to the courtyard. Along the way he encountered a few more confused enemies. He spared them no words, and only the time it took to leave each dead as he passed.

"Who might you be?" asked a strangely accented voice on his right as he burst through the door to the front entry hall. Turning, Harold spotted a bizarre spider the size of a small horse approaching.

Something about the confidence in its movements worried Harold. It wasn't in the least troubled by the sudden appearance of a Knight of Stone within the castle walls. Seized by a sense of foreboding the blond warrior lowered his visor to protect himself more completely. "A more appropriate question," he replied genially, "would be: What the hell are you?"

"I am Chel'strathek. You would know me as the Terror of the Night, one of what your people call the Dark Gods. Lately I have been reduced to Mal'goroth's lieutenant, not that that is any of your concern, human," answered the strange arachnid.

Harold's body loosened as he prepared to take action. His eyes raked the hall, making note of distances and the

396

few heavy pieces of furniture. "You do yourself too much honor in assuming that I or any of my people would know your name," he said, rebuking the god. "If I have had terrors in the night, they were not for fear of you. Like all your kind you are already forgotten. Your name has no meaning anymore."

A vicious bolt of malevolent power struck the place that Harold had been standing, but the knight was already moving. Dodging to the side only a few feet, Harold reversed direction to avoid the second attack that followed a split second after the first.

With each step he closed on his opponent, watching the waving forelimbs that presaged each powerful bolt of energy. He had almost reached Chel'strathek when his feet discovered hidden webbing lining the floor beneath him.

"Fool," crooned the Dark God gleefully. "Did you think I would be so simple a foe?"

Sweeping downward with his great sword Harold almost clipped one of Chel'strathek's closest legs, forcing the giant arachnid to dodge backward. The swing had been only a feint though, and as the sword reached the floor the knight unleashed the enchanted flames, burning through the She'Har spellweaving that held his feet in place. Ripping his feet free and leaping sideways a full ten feet, he only barely avoided his foe's next blast of power.

Harold was well aware that he had lost the initiative, and when facing an enemy of superior power, that was as good as death warrant. Attempting to regain it with an offensive attack was almost guaranteed to failure, but he still had another option. The cacophony from outside the main doors had reached a new level of madness. Which probably meant the Kriteck had arrived, either that or their assault was already doomed.

Dashing to one side, he used his sword to topple a lofty marble statue, one of the few that the Countess had added over the years. It seemed at first that it was an attempt to injure his opponent, but his true purpose was diversion. In the space that the crashing stone gave him, he suddenly changed direction and ran for the main doors. Flinging them wide, he leapt out into a scene from a lunatic's fever dream.

A terrible ray of malign force exited the door behind him. It missed narrowly, striking one of the grotesque horrors battling in the courtyard. Half the beast's body dissolved in a brilliant flash that left only burnt flesh and a mysterious goo behind. Sir Harold had no way of knowing whether it had been a friend or a foe that was wounded.

Filling his lungs with air Harold shouted a warning for everyone concerned, "I think I found the big one!" He was forced to dart sideways to clear the doorway and avoid a new magical attack. Heads and head-like appendages turned to track the new entrant into the battle, some viewing Chel'strathek's emergence with joy and others with less enthusiasm.

The main gates were wide, and the rest of Ariadne's god-enhanced warriors were streaming inward. They added a new level of disorder, but the tide had turned against the limited number of diminished Dark Gods. Or so it had seemed, before Chel'strathek's arrival.

The giant arachnid strode into the sunlight with an air of all too human delight. Legs rose and spellweavings lashed outward with the speed of lightning, catching

Kriteck and human alike. The servants of the new She'Har tried to defend themselves but it was readily apparent that the new combatant had far more power than any of them had expected.

Men and monsters died, melting and screaming.

What the hell did I find? worried Harold suddenly.

Now in the open air, Chel'strathek threw caution and subtlety to the wind, unleashing a cone of power that blasted everything in front of him for thirty yards in a wide swath. The attack was too wide to avoid, and all that were caught within it withered and melted.

Except Harold.

Unable to dodge such a massive attack, the Knight had only managed to cover his visor with one hand and hope that his armor would save him. When the light died, he found himself unharmed. Standing in front of him was Karenth, once known as the Just.

"Human, I think you found more than you can swallow," he said with an odd sound in his voice.

Harold nodded, "You mean, 'I bit off more than I could chew'," he corrected. Looking around, he realized that everything within thirty yards had been reduced to dust; men, monsters, and even the ground itself.

Another withering blast struck, and again Karenth held up one hand, diverting the destructive power around them. "Just as you say, Sir Harold."

"You seem to be doing alright," said the knight hopefully.

"Unfortunately, your perception is misinformed. What your eyes cannot tell you, is that I am only a quarter as powerful as I once was, while the being in front of us probably possesses at least twice the aythar I had at my peak," the Shining God informed him.

"I was never very good with fractions," said Harold, backing up slowly with his newfound protector. "Perhaps you could simplify that for me."

"It means Chel'strathek is roughly eight times stronger," answered Karenth. "It means we cannot win."

"Time for a retreat?"

"That is also impossible. Our opponent is controlling our battlefield in more than one way. The attacks you see are only part of what is occurring." Another blast of power struck and was diverted, but Harold could see that Karenth's defense was even narrower that time.

"If we cannot win, why did you come to my aid?"

"Accident," admitted Karenth. "I was atop one of the Kriteck transport creatures a moment ago. Chel'strathek obliterated it, and before I could recover, I found myself with you in the castle yard."

Harold had been prepared for death before joining the attack, but now that it stared him in the face, he found it difficult to accept. *I'm sorry, Lissette. Fate has turned against us,* he thought silently, wishing he could see his wife one more time. *What a pointless way to die.*

His thoughts were cut short when he saw Penny emerge from the main entry hall, directly behind Chel'strathek. She had her sword out and a determined look on her face as she made ready to attack the spider from the rear. She had no way of knowing her opponent was too powerful to face.

Harold's eyes went wide inside his helm, and his mouth opened to yell a warning that would be hopelessly late. The Dark God before him already knew of the woman approaching from behind. It ignored her purposefully, enjoying the anticipation of her horror when her surprise attack turned into a leap into death's arms.

Screaming uselessly, Harold saw Penny leap forward, sword shining as she made her attack. Chel'strathek smiled then, and turning he released another blistering attack. The world exploded in light and sound. Harold and Karenth both found themselves thrown to their knees as the earth shook. It felt as though a mountain had fallen on top of all of them.

Stunned, they found themselves in a tan cloud of dust and earth until a sudden wind arose and dispersed the choking debris. The inhuman god had been thrown to one side of the courtyard, as if by a giant hand, while standing in a twenty foot crater was an armored figure bearing the unmistakable crest and design of Mordecai Illeniel.

Chapter 40

Flying without using my enchanted stones was an exhilarating experience. Even though my armor protected me from the worst of the buffeting by the air, the experience of having the wind tearing at me greatly enhanced the feeling of speed. Since my rebirth as an undead monster, it was the first truly enjoyable thing that I had done, aside from my recent killing spree. This had the distinct advantage of being a guilt-free pleasure. Even my inner spectator could find nothing to complain about.

After a while I got used to the wind, and it felt as though I was no longer moving very fast, so I pushed harder. The world moved slowly by below me, and although I knew this was an illusion, I found myself wanting more. *You can't die. What's the worst that could happen?*

The most difficult part of the entire task was the fact that my armor wasn't exactly designed with flying in mind. The higher my velocity the more problems its odd aerodynamic properties created. Eventually I went ahead and created an impromptu shield around myself, shaping it to my will and enabling me to more easily control my attitude and direction.

My first efforts nearly sent me into the ground several times, and at one point I destroyed a tall pine while tumbling through the air out of control. Somehow I recovered at the end and vaulted skyward before clipping the top of a rocky hill.

Hours later I was comfortable and feeling at ease with my new method. *This is the sort of experience a living wizard never gets. If I had tried this while alive, I'd have killed myself a dozen times over by now.* I soared, I flew, and my earthly problems no longer seemed so heavy.

The moon was up and nearing full which gave the ground below a ghostly luminescence, beauty of a sort I had rarely had a chance to appreciate previously. While I didn't need the light, I found myself grateful for my lunar companion. It was always there, just over my shoulder, like a friend enjoying the nighttime landscape with me.

I sailed over the southern extension of the Elentir Mountains not long before dawn, which surprised me. I was traveling far faster than ever before. *At this rate I'll be at Cameron Castle shortly.* That led me to the possibility of meeting Penny again, something I now looked forward to. I wanted her, though I tried to keep the thought below the conscious level lest my inner observer begin nagging me again.

I spotted the clearing with Cameron Castle miles before I reached it. The morning sun had lit the tops of the trees with golden light, while the lower branches were still cloaked in shadow. The skies were clear, empty of clouds and haze, which combined with my high altitude, gave me a view that even the eagles might envy.

The distance was so great that even my magesight couldn't find what my physical eyes could see; meaning the castle itself was more than a mile or two in the distance. I was so besotted with speed and wind that I couldn't be certain. The air was so clear that my view to the horizon must encompass hundreds of miles which made it hard to ascertain the distance to something so close. The castle might be five, ten, or fifteen miles away. I had no way to guess.

At last it occurred to me to enhance my physical vision. I had done something similar while still alive, using my aythar to mildly reshape my eyes for better distance vision, but when I tried that here it was completely inadequate. It helped, but I wanted to see farther. I finally settled on creating a different type of shield in front of me in the air. I kept this one ephemeral, so that it wouldn't affect the wind and disrupt my flying, and then I began altering its optical properties.

I had learned long before then how to alter a shield's color and transparency. Walter had also helped me improve my illusions in the past by teaching me how to change the way that a shield bent the light passing through it. A few minutes of experimentation and I had created a lens of sorts that greatly improved my view. *Ahh, how the astronomers would love this,* I thought.

Focusing on the approaching castle, I was able to make out an incredible amount of detail. Now I could see a few small clouds of dust rising from the courtyard. Tiny ant-like people running along the tops of the walls. Something exciting was happening. *They've started fighting without me!* I laughed silently.

I saw one of the massive dragon-like flyers that Tennick had created hovering over the castle. *They must be preparing to assist.* A flash of light and a large part of the creature vanished while the remainder fell from the air. *That can't be good.*

Expanding my view, I sought the source of the attack. It had come from the direction of the ground. I pushed harder for more speed and magnified the view even further, though I struggled to keep it stable enough to remain focused. *There's Harold, and that's Karenth with him,* I noted. They were facing something odd, a large spider of some sort. It was hammering at them with strange blasts of energy. I was still too far to 'feel' it with my magesight, so I couldn't guess at its strength or what the type of attack was.

It didn't look good for Harold though, Karenth was backing up slowly, and everything else within the courtyard had been obliterated.

Then I saw Penelope.

Shit.

Time was no longer something I could spare. I pushed—hard, and then I pushed harder still. My velocity had become something beyond common measurement. Idly the back of my mind considered repeating the experiment someday using markers so that I could calculate the speed. It's funny what the mind does in the middle of a crisis.

The envelope around my body was growing hot from the blistering force of the wind, and I realized then that my landing would be anything but gentle. There was simply no way I could hope to suddenly overcome the vast momentum I had created. I smiled at the thought, and instead put my power into the shield around me. *I can't die, and I have several Celiors worth of power. Why the hell not?* My shield would be my weapon.

I traveled the last mile in a flash, covering the distance so quickly that the spider-thing probably never got a chance to even register my presence before I struck. The world shattered.

The force was such that while my shield absorbed most of the impact, my body turned to jelly within my armor. No mortal would have survived. The change in velocity, from whatever speed I was moving, to zero, was simply too great. The earth around me was liquefied by heat and pressure, exploding outward to hide the world from normal sight.

Penny had been in the air when I smashed into the Dark God. I thought I had managed to get a shield around her before I impacted, but I worried what the shockwave might do to her. My magesight found her now, collapsed near one of the outer walls. *She's alive, and conscious.* I could see her struggling to sit up, confused by the dust.

The thing that had been between me and the bottom of my new crater had been pulverized and splintered. Fragments of its body and legs had flown in all directions, but it wasn't dead. The majority of it had been sent flying in a vector opposite to the angle of my descent. Now that I was close I could sense its enormous aythar.

This is no 'seed'. Mal'goroth left this one with a lot of power, I observed. At a rough estimate it was something close to two Celiors worth of aythar. Not as much as I held, but enough to make it a serious handful. Its body reformed even as it was flung back by the devastating impact. It struck one courtyard wall, damaging the stones and crushing its body again. It recovered from that wound even more quickly.

The air was so heavy with dirt and ash that it blocked all sight. *It probably isn't good for breathing either.*

Harold and Penny were fully within the cloud. A word and a thought brought a wide brisk wind to clear the air.

Rising to my feet, I surveyed the scene. The courtyard was largely empty now, the ground, which had been hard packed dirt and grass, was now blackened earth and what I suspected might be the beginnings of glass. My crater was a definite eyesore.

"Do you know how difficult it was to get grass to grow in here?" I said, projecting my voice in the direction of the large arachnid. "With all the traffic and wagons—it was almost impossible," I finished, answering my own question.

A sudden pulse of aythar appeared and vanished. The creature was examining me keenly, and I suspected it had just sent a signal of some sort.

"Signaling for help?" I asked aloud. "Make sure whoever you call has deep pockets. It's going to cost a fortune to replace all the dirt, re-level the ground, and replant the grass."

"You caused most of the damage," replied the strange being in a tone that seemed far too cultured to arise from something that looked as though it should be hiding under the furniture—if you had furniture that large.

"That is hardly material to the issue. You were trespassing, and this damage resulted from my effort to protect my home and property. Therefore you are culpable for any losses incurred here," I countered. If it, whatever it was, was willing to discuss legal particulars, then I was game. Having been a count for many years, I had become far too familiar with the terminology. I found myself smiling at the situation.

Stubborn people love to argue a point, and gods are the most stubborn of all.

Laughter rang out from the direction of my new opponent, "Human law does not apply to us."

"Define *us.*"

"We are not human," said the strange god.

His willingness to talk told me everything. The spider had assessed our relative strengths and was certain I outclassed him by a considerable margin, despite the difficulty reading me properly through my armor. The only reason he had to continue a pointless discussion was to buy time. *My time is nearly over,* I thought sadly, *but it won't end the way you wish it.*

"Give me your name, before I prove my right upon you," I challenged.

"Chel'strathek," he answered in a slightly petulant tone, "the Terror of the Night, have none of your kind been properly educated? I thought that perhaps you at least would have some knowledge."

The name brought a string of memories from the loshti running through my mind, but I preferred to play at ignorance. Chel'strathek had a streak of vanity, which would make it easier to goad him. "I can't be bothered to keep up with every petty god left over from a forgotten race," I taunted. "The important point, is that your nature is irrelevant to the law."

"I answer to a higher power, therefore your law does not bind me," he argued dispassionately.

He definitely needs time. "Very well," I began, "if your claim is that power bestows *right,* then it should be apparent to you already that I will, given a hard fight, be able to prosecute my right over you. You should surrender to my law and save us both the trouble."

Chel'strathek straightened, "I answer only to Mal'goroth, and his power far outshines yours. I will not surrender without a fight."

I smiled, "Then do me one favor and I may show you kinder treatment once I have defeated you. Let us take our fight to the open field, away from my property and chattel, lest more unnecessary damage be done."

"Certainly," he replied.

He's decided that he has delayed long enough. Our fight will not be over until his Lord has arrived. I made a mental calculation, though guess would be a better name for it. I didn't like my estimate, but it would have to be enough. "Move to the open field, half a mile from here, in the direction of the river. I will give instruction to my servants here and join you momentarily."

I could feel Chel'strathek's satisfaction shining like the sun. I had given him even more time. He might gain enough to get by without having to fight me for long. He didn't want me rubbing his face in the dirt before Mal'goroth arrived. Rising on long legs he grew strange bat-like appendages and flew away. "Five minutes," he said to me as he left.

Wasting no time I headed directly for Penny. Harold and Karenth met me halfway, and I began giving instructions as I went. "You need to get everyone in here as soon as possible," I told them. "How far away are your people?" Inwardly I winced as I realized that I had said *your.* They were no longer mine.

"Almost all are here already," said Harold responding to my authority instinctively, "except the Queen."

That was news to me. "You mean Ariadne?"

He nodded.

"You need to get her quickly then. Gather her and as many as you can. You have ten to fifteen minutes at best, and possibly less," I told him.

The young knight blanched at the warning, "It will take me that long to reach them and far longer to convince them and bring them back."

I glanced at Karenth, and he tilted his head in acquiescence of my unspoken order. Swelling in size he sprouted wings and lifted a surprised Harold gently in one hand. "Make haste," I told him.

I had reached Penny by then. She was back on her feet now, though she looked rather shaky. There was a look in her eye, something I hadn't seen the last time. *Defeat? Guilt?* My mind circled, unable to read her clearly, but from somewhere deeper came another thought, *Shame.*

Ignoring my weaker self's odd insight, I addressed her confidently, as a lord speaks to his servant, "There is little time. Karenth will return soon with whomever he can carry. Take your children, your queen, and whoever else you will and seek safety. There is only one place for you now."

She cast her eyes downward, "Of course, I will save our children."

"Are there any wizards with you?"

"The Prathions, Walter is inside already, in the key chamber," she said quietly.

"Good. As soon as they are within the walls, have him activate the defenses. They won't hold for long against

Mal'goroth, but they might give you enough time to get them to your apartment," I said firmly.

"Will you not come with us—Mordecai?" she said tentatively at first, and then with near tears when she repeated my name, "...Mort?"

My emotions rose in a whirlwind of fury inside me. Sorrow, loss, anger, and betrayal, they tore at me. Justified or not, she had rejected me before; I had come to terms with that. In her place I would have done the same, or so I had tried to make myself believe. Her implied acceptance now threatened to undo me.

Hardening my heart, I replied clearly, "My name is Brexus. The man you knew is gone. If you would honor his memory, do as I bid you, nothing more."

Her eyes were bright, welling with tears, but she did not cry. My Penny was a strong woman. "Mort, Dorian is...," her voice choked before she could finish.

"I already know," I said coldly. "They will pay for as much as I am able to make them, but it won't be enough."

"You have a plan?" There was hope in her voice. The sound of it was a cruel torment.

"No. I will fight and lose. Delay is all I can give you. Stay hidden, and perhaps you and the children will survive. Where there is life there is hope," I told her plainly.

"There is hope if you are with us," she stated, baring her will now.

"I am already dead." Turning away, I was glad that the helm had hidden my features. Tears were impossible for me, but my expression could only have wounded her more deeply. My face and my voice were in perfect opposition to one another.

Several flying behemoths were arriving already. Karenth had been swifter than I expected. Gareth Gaelyn was with him, carrying as many as he was capable of. Doron and Millicenth had swelled in size and flew with them, carrying still more people. Most impressive of all though, was the Kriteck transport beast. Almost two-fold larger than Gareth, it had been designed to carry occupants. Its wide back was smooth except for a variety of ridges and protrusions that would make it easier for a variety of different forms to keep a firm grip. More than forty people clung to it now.

I spotted Peter Tucker among them. He and his sister Lilly were helping to unload the twins. They were alive but unconscious. I went to him immediately, checking as I approached to make sure their hearts were beating strongly. *They will recover.*

My time was almost up.

"Peter," I called loudly.

He was startled by the familiar voice. I hadn't tried to disguise it as I had done previously. "Yes?" he answered uncertainly.

I motioned to the man beside him, and he took Matthew from Peter's hands. Then I waved a hand for Peter to follow me. Stepping away I began talking rapidly, "You know the dagger you carry with you, Peter?"

His face blanched. Before he had joined my service, years ago, I had killed his grandfather inadvertently. It had been an accident, but he had been very angry then. He had even stolen one of the knives I had enchanted early on, a kitchen knife, discarded and forgotten, or so he had thought. Somewhere along the way he had learned that it would take an enchanted blade to pierce the shields I kept about me at all times.

I knew that he had long since given up his desire to kill me. Peter was a good man. Over the years, working beside us, he had become a part of my family somehow. Now that Dorian was gone, there were few men I trusted as much as him. But he still carried the knife. It had been with him every day. A sign of his early intention, I knew it had become a symbol to him over time. It was precious. It represented his compromise and the bond of duty he had forged with my family.

"I have a knife, yes, my lord," he answered from habit, returning to his old manner of addressing me.

"I know the meaning of the knife, Peter. I always have. I know why you carried it, and I understand why you kept it, even after you decided never to use it," I said solemnly.

Eyes wide, he blinked—twice. Nothing like being told by your employer that he knew you had once planned to kill him. I had no time to mince words, though.

Reaching into my pouch, I withdrew the green stone that Lyralliantha had given me. "Hand me the knife," I ordered.

Mutely, he reached into his coat and drew it out.

The pommel was plain round pewter. Using my fingertip and a bit of pure will, I dented the end of it and held the green stone against the indention. A quick spell fixed it in place. It wouldn't last for more than a few weeks, but then again, it didn't need to. "I am immortal now, Peter. The magic that sustains me will keep me forever, unless it is undone. It's a spellweaving, and normally only one of the ancient She'Har could undo it, but this small stone was created as a weak point."

"What are you saying?" he asked.

"There are worse things than death, Peter, and I am one of them. Mal'goroth will be here soon, but you won't be. Wait twenty minutes after you have gone and then use your dagger to crush the stone, any hard surface will do," I explained.

"I don't understand."

"Mordecai is still here, trapped," I pointed at my chest. "Until the spellweave is broken, he will never find rest. Go with them, live. I will do what I can here, but I won't win, and I can only imagine what Mal'goroth will do once he has me completely in his grasp."

"This will kill you?" he stammered.

I nodded.

"I can't do that," he protested.

"You have to Peter. You're the only one who can do it. You're the only one who really deserves the right. After all these years if you can't kill me for vengeance, then do it for the man you used to serve," I told him.

"But you'll die!"

"Brexus dies, Peter. You'll be setting Mordecai Illeniel free. You owe him that. Let him rest in peace." I had waited long enough. My time was up. With a word I used a spell to bring up a wind, pushing him away as it began to lift me.

"I won't do it!" he screamed into the torrent.

"You will," I said, making sure my words cut through the roar. "If we meet again, I will kill you." Thrusting downward with the air I shot skyward. Most of the people below were already running into the keep. I hoped they would make it to safety, but I had done as much as I could.

Racing the wind I sought my opponent. *Stupid never dies,* said my inner companion. "It does today," I answered, not caring if I was insane.

Chapter 41

Chel'strathek was waiting for me, just as he had promised. As I neared him, I felt a surge as the defensive shield was activated around Castle Cameron.

"Don't trust me?" asked the monstrous spider.

"Just making sure we don't inadvertently damage anything," I answered.

"You're a fool. My master will be here within minutes," two of his legs came up, and with them two writhing lines of spellweaving rose toward me. "I only need keep you here long enough to wait on his pleasure."

I didn't answer. Instead I opened my hand and used a simple spell to send the iron spheres it was holding hurtling toward him in a multitude of directions. The air was lit with explosions, some of which tore through his spellweavings, while others slipped past to irritate the beast I faced. Withdrawing my staff from its pouch, I channeled a blazing line of white fire. It sliced through his body and burned a red line across the ground beneath him.

The damage was insignificant, though. It would take far more to subdue him. His body renewed itself almost instantly. It was a fight I knew I could win given enough time, but time was a luxury I didn't have.

Reaching into my pouches again, I withdrew still more of my iron bombs. The chest that the pouch connected to was deep, and many years ago I had spent considerable time storing them there until it was full. Compared to my present power they represented but a feeble flicker, but I used them anyway.

Chel'strathek was moving now, sending his power out in wide ribbons. He fought not to hurt but to bind. His strength was not great enough to give him victory, unless I made some mistake, but he needed to be sure I couldn't escape. I dodged them and sent more of my iron bombs flying toward him. Focusing my power, I danced around him like a mad bird, darting in and out to avoid his snares.

"Why do you keep using those pathetic iron things?" he exclaimed at last. "Have you no dignity?"

"I don't know," I answered loudly. "It may be that I'm too stupid to know when to quit."

"There is a method to your madness," he shouted back. "I can see that."

I flew directly at him, and he flinched backward. He could sense the change in my demeanor. Playtime was over. I came to a sudden stop ten feet away. "You're right. There may be a pattern here." Raising my hand I gave him a glimpse of what I held there.

Chel'strathek snarled at me, "More baubles?"

"I may be a fool," I answered, "but I can spot the difference between diamond and steel." Speaking the command word, I channeled my power into the stasis enchantment as strongly as I dared.

Aythar surged into the enchanted diamond cubes. My darting flight and useless iron bombs had been a simple ploy to distract Chel'strathek while I set my trap. My opponent might have noticed if he had paid better attention, but his casual disregard for the 'baubles' had been his undoing.

Even so, while the area I had arranged the cubes in was much smaller than the capital, the massive aythar concentrated within that area, Chel'strathek's aythar, resisted the enchantment. For that reason alone, I knew my trap wouldn't work on Mal'goroth. Using it against a creature as powerful as Chel'strathek wasn't really wise either, but in this case I outweighed him enough that I felt reasonably sure I could hold him.

My power filled the cubes, and it took far more than I expected. With at least half of my strength channeled within the cubes, the Dark God still struggled. He could no longer move freely, but he still moved, albeit at a slow crawl. Time within the stasis field had slowed but not yet completely stopped.

Standing in front of him, I worried over the next part. The central cube negated the effect of the stasis in a small volume of space around it, in this case an area roughly large enough to hold two or three people. With half of my power in the enchantment, I was no longer stronger than my foe. Moving close enough to finish the battle would be risky.

Chel'strathek's bulk was great enough that only a small part of him would be released by the proximity of my null cube, or so I thought. *No one's ever done this before, so I don't really have a damn clue.*

Taking the plunge, I stepped close, reaching for him. His face registered surprise as I seemed to appear in front of him, moving, from his perspective, at an impossible speed. His time seemed to normalize as I drove my hand through his hard carapace, but he was still disoriented and dazed.

I pulled, devouring him as I had the usurper's men in Albamarl. Caught off-guard, he was still incredibly powerful. His will reacted instinctively against the assault on his core, and our minds wrestled for a moment. It was too late for him though, I had taken too much in that moment of surprise. Laughing with a dark delight, I felt him weakening and I tore great pieces of his essence away. The process accelerated as the scales tipped irrevocably in my favor.

I drained him until all that was left was a dwindling spider's husk. Within it, the spellweaving that maintained his awareness still pulsed. I could feel it, but even with my newfound strength, it was impossible to destroy. I had reduced him in much the way Mal'goroth had done with the others, until there was little left other than his 'god-seed'.

The cubes around me throbbed oddly, and I felt them begin to crumble. *They still have enough power to destroy most of the region!* Desperately I pulled the power from them, but I knew it could not happen quickly enough. Expanding my body, I felt the aythar rippling within them, unstable. With a sudden snap the diamond cubes disintegrated, releasing the power still in the enchantment.

Clenching my mind, the world disappeared in a blaze of swelling light and burning pain.

*
**

Penelope Illeniel, Countess di' Cameron and widow of Mordecai Illeniel, stood in the castle courtyard, staring helplessly as the man she loved walked away. She had been dismissed. She felt the pain keenly, a message that hardly needed words. *You betrayed him when he needed you. There will be no forgiveness. Be grateful and save the children.*

That was the gist of it. That was all that remained.

Gritting her teeth she started moving. People had begun arriving, and among them were her children. Elise, Elaine, Lilly Tucker, and countless others were unloading. Moving quickly, mechanically, Penny began her task.

Get them to our apartments. Once there they would be safe. If she opened that door it would lead to their secret home, far away in the northern Elentir Mountains. It was their bolt-hole, their sanctuary. Mordecai had created it to keep his family from harm, whether he was present or not. They could survive there, isolated and hidden from the outside world.

We don't have room for several hundred people, but I'll be damned if I will leave them behind, she thought.

Moments later the shield went up. Walter had activated the castle's defensive enchantment, a massive shield powered by the God-Stone.

Racing along the corridor, Penny reached their apartment door long before the others and threw it open. So long as the door stayed wide it led to their sanctuary. Once the doors were shut, the automatic portal would close and anyone who opened it afterward, other than Penny or her family, would find only the decoy apartment that they had maintained within the castle over the years.

Heading back down the stairs she gave directions to everyone she passed. Some of them knew the castle already, but most were from Arundel or Lancaster. Elise Thornbear passed her, tightlipped as she carried her

420

granddaughter Carissa. Rose was close behind, leading Gram and carrying Penny's daughter, Irene. Conall was holding Gram's hand.

My family, thought Penny.

Lilly Tucker was climbing the stairs awkwardly, holding Moira's sleeping legs while one of the men carried her torso. Two others followed with Matthew.

"Where's Peter?" asked the Countess. He had been helping with Matthew when they arrived.

"Mordecai took him aside in the courtyard," answered Lilly. "I don't know what he needed."

Moira Centyr was next, and she heard their conversation. "He's still down there, guiding people into the keep." Gareth Gaelyn walked beside her in his draconic half-human form.

Penny frowned. *Maybe he gave Peter some task?* She didn't like being left in the dark. "I need to talk to him," she said as she continued to make her way down the stairs against a constant stream of people.

"Let me help," suggested Gareth, baring a mouth full of sharp teeth. His unnatural appearance frightened most who saw him and they instinctively moved to give him as much room as possible. Following him down the steps became almost as simple as if they had been alone. People fought to avoid any proximity with the scaled mage.

The courtyard was clearing rapidly. Doron and Millicenth had just arrived with the last civilians from the camp. Peter Tucker stood to one side of the great double doors, ushering people into the keep. "Head down the left-hand corridor," he shouted. "Follow the others to the stairs, and go to the third landing."

He gave the Countess a guilty look when she took his arm. "What did he tell you?" she asked, without preamble.

Peter's thin façade crumbled into tears. "Forgive me, Your Excellency."

"What?!"

"He knew. I'm not worthy to serve you. Please forgive Lilly; she never wanted to hurt anyone. It was only me," blurted her head chamberlain. In all the years since he had joined their service, Penny had never known Peter Tucker to break down in her presence. She understood immediately what must be the cause.

"Please hush, you stupid man," she told him, using harsh words, but a gentle, forgiving voice. "We always knew. The debt was ours, and you have only increased it over the years. You are family now." She hugged Peter then, squeezing him tightly. "Get upstairs, Lilly is waiting for you."

Taking a step back, the chamberlain produced a moderate-sized kitchen knife. Openly crying, he offered it to her. Penny had never seen it before, but she had heard the story of it long ago from her husband.

"Put that up before you hurt yourself," she rebuked him. Waving him away, she ignored his gesture. "Keep it Peter. Mordecai never wanted you to forget, just to forgive."

Hands trembling, he stared at her numbly for a second before nodding and putting it back within his coat. He was shaking like a leaf, and the Countess worried he might cut himself on the enchanted blade before he could safely store it. "Go," she reiterated. "Make sure everyone is inside before you close the door to our rooms."

Gareth Gaelyn still stood beside her, silent but with a pensive look. "That knife..." he said letting his words trail away.

"Mort told me it was one of the first he enchanted," she explained. "It's a long story. Don't worry about it now."

The draconic archmage furrowed his brow but nodded. It was not the first time he had seen magic that he didn't understand, especially where Mordecai was concerned. *But the stone, it didn't look like a human enchantment.*

Penny's mind was already working on other things. Peter's outburst had solidified her gut instinct. *Telling him that was not the act of a stranger. Only Mort would say that to Peter.* The more she considered it, the more firmly she believed it. The man inside the armor was more than a dead body, more than a magical copy. He was her husband, in every way that mattered.

The cold behavior and constant insistence of a different identity had been carefully calculated to make things easier for her. *So I could let go. It would be much harder for me if I knew he was still in there, still suffering, if the man I loved were dying again, today.* Unbidden, the vision of Dorian Thornbear's diamond bladed hands struggling to push Rose away appeared in her mind.

Her heart and mind came together then, her emotions crystallizing into one hard resolution. "To hell with this!" she growled, startling Gareth from his own thoughts.

"What?" he asked as his eyes focused on her. In one hand he held a small white figurine.

She scowled. "I said, 'to hell with this,'" she repeated. "If he thinks he can have things his way and run off to die, while I hide in a hole, he's never been more wrong!"

Gareth stared at her curiously, unsure what to say. Despite his constant and unwelcome contact with humans, he still found them alien in subtle ways. Penny placed a hand on his arm, sending involuntary shivers up his spine. Gareth disliked being touched.

"Will you carry me to him?" she asked, her eyes burned into him with fiery determination.

The dragon-mage blinked. "If we are seen, your children will be orphans," he warned her. "Mal'goroth will not let us escape."

"We won't be seen," she assured him. Raising her voice, she called to Millicenth, "Lady, I require your aid."

The goddess came closer, her body seeming to glide across the intervening space. "I am bound to heed your words," she answered.

Perfect, thought Penny. "Gather your brothers, Karenth and Doron. We are leaving. Wait for me here," she commanded.

"That is unwise, Countess," advised the goddess.

Penny ignored her and ran for the key chamber, hoping Walter would still be there. *I'm tired of being told what's wise and what's not,* she thought.

She nearly ran headlong into George Prathion exiting the key chamber. His father was close behind him. "Countess," said Walter, greeting her. "Shouldn't you be upstairs?"

"Is that where you're heading?" she asked him.

"Of course," he answered. "I've left the shield up as requested."

"We've had a change of plans," she said quickly.

Walter's eyes narrowed. Penelope Illeniel was a strong willed woman, but she was a poor liar. "We?" he queried.

She pursed her lips, "I."

He nodded, preferring honestly, "What do you want me to do?"

"Turn off the shield, and go with me to find my husband," she answered with a perfectly straight face.

Walter was a cautious man, some thought him a coward, but time and experience had taught him some hard lessons. "Why?" he probed, "Is there something we can do?"

"I've been a fool, and now he's going to make a martyr of himself. Hide us, let me reach him. If nothing else you can help him escape. You're the only one who could do it. Only a Prathion would have a hope of eluding the power of a god," her words were firm and unapologetic.

"One mistake and we all die. If not for your children's sake, what of mine? I don't want my family facing the terrors of our future without their father beside them," he argued. In the past, when Mordecai and Penny had first encountered him, Walter's family had been held hostage. Kept from them for years before reuniting, his sense of duty to his wife and children was paramount to him now.

Penny didn't hold back. "You would have no family if not for Mordecai, nor would you be alive. You died and he brought you back. You owe him everything."

George spoke up, "Let me go with you."

Walter stiffened, "No, son. This is my burden."

"But…," George started to protest.

The elder Prathion held up his hand to silence him, "Will you be alright without me?"

"Of course," said George. "I can operate the shield to let you out and back in again."

"That isn't what I meant," said the father. "Will you be alright without me if I don't return? Do you understand?"

George's face became animated. Normally his expression gave the people the impression that he was either uninteresting or, at best, uninterested in the rest of the world. Swallowing, he looked seriously at his father, "I wouldn't like it, but I would carry on."

"And your mother, your sister?"

The young man blinked, eyes watering, "Neither of them are so weak as to fall apart from life's trials. We would take care of each other."

"Get inside the key chamber," ordered Walter. "When you see us at the gate, open it and then close it behind us. Then you join the others. If Elaine asks you where I am, tell her I am already inside. She's far too stubborn to be obedient."

"And mother?"

"Tell her I love her," said Walter solemnly. "Afterwards make certain that no one comes back. Ever. That door must stay closed. Assume the worst. If by some chance we survive, I will find you. The Countess knows where you will be. She can guide me."

"Yes, father," said the youngest Prathion, bowing his head slightly.

"Whatever you do, don't let them keep the door open. Everyone is in danger until it is shut and Mal'goroth can no longer find you. This shield will hardly even slow him down," added Walter and then he hugged his son.

"I love you," whispered George, in a voice almost too hoarse to understand.

Walter smiled and kissed his son's cheek, "I'm proud of you son. You're a good man." Then he turned and walked briskly away. He never looked back, and Penny didn't comment upon what she saw in his face.

"Let's be fools together," he said as they began to jog down the corridor.

For the first time, Penny doubted her decision. Not for herself, but for the price her friends might pay trying to help her undo her mistake. *One more regret,* she thought, *but there's no turning back now.*

Chapter 42

The pain was beyond belief, but it ended as abruptly as it began. It was remarkable mainly in that I had felt so little physical pain since my death. It was no longer a sensation I knew very well. It was almost a welcome change.

Pain makes you feel alive.

I had drawn as much of the power in as I could before the enchantment failed, and then, with an extreme effort of will, I had contained the majority of the explosion. There wasn't much to compare the sensation to, but if I'd been forced, I would have likened it to a hangover—*The worst hangover imaginable, and then you start slamming your head against a wall.*

The power of the explosion itself, I held onto, carefully assimilating it within myself. I doubted it would be enough to make a difference, but I decided I wouldn't throw any chance away. The more power I had, the more likely I could survive what was coming.

Six or seven Celiors now, I thought to myself, estimating what I must have after stripping Chel'strathek of his aythar. *Mal'goroth must have more than forty, possibly more than fifty.*

My experience in Albamarl had taught me one thing. People add up. I had slain several thousand men there, taking their lives in the most direct way possible. While each had been a relatively small meal, as a whole their aythar had been considerable.

This started when I slew the army of Gododdin, said my inner observer. *Thirty thousand men, gone, and their families afterward, taken by Mal'goroth.* That was when my foe had become too powerful to stop. That was what had given him the strength he needed to overpower his siblings and take their power for his own.

"I would have to slay half the world to gain the power to defeat him," I told myself, and for a moment my mind considered attempting it. *No,* my conscience argued, *this ends here.* As usual my conscience was a killjoy.

Then I remembered Peter. "There's no getting away from that anyway. I'm on borrowed time now," I said aloud. Somehow the thought made me feel better, no matter what happened, my part in all this would soon be over. The end was in sight.

Having a final stopping point ahead of me gave me a certain kind of strength. "I'm free to spend the next fifteen minutes or so any way I choose," I said to reinforce the idea. Penny and the children flashed through my mind. My first choice would have been to see them one last time. "But that's not an option. Some doors have already closed."

I could feel Mal'goroth approaching now, flying in at a leisurely pace. He was taking his time. *Probably savoring the moment—the asshole.* A thought occurred to me then, and I reached for my pouches. They were gone. My armor was gone as well. The destruction of the stasis enchantment had burned away everything on my person.

I was naked.

"Son of a bitch," I cursed, more because of the inconvenience than the possibility of embarrassment. Those pouches had held a plethora of handy tools, most notably my silver stylus and in this instance my staff.

One of the conveniences of power, when you have it in quantities that can be measured in Celiors, is that some extraordinarily wasteful uses of said power are no longer quite as important. I had enough power to simply manufacture things, creating them from pure aythar itself. However, I still didn't want to waste the aythar.

A minor illusion provided a semblance of clothing. *Doubtless Penny would complain about my choices,* I thought with a chuckle. She regularly disagreed with my fashion sense, mostly because I didn't really have one.

On a whim, I changed the doublet and hose I had chosen at first, to a plain homespun robe. I considered just a loincloth, but that seemed a bit silly.

Manipulating the wind, I rose a hundred feet to survey the earth below. Despite my effort the explosion had leveled the terrain for probably a quarter mile in every direction. I wondered how many livestock had lost their lives. *Think of the sheep!* I almost started giggling. I could feel the edges of my mind skittering away in the distance.

With a conscious effort I focused my attention. *You only have a few minutes, don't waste them losing your sanity,* cautioned my imaginary friend.

I nodded in agreement. I would have replied mentally, but I worried he might get confused, since our thoughts sounded the same. *Or maybe he isn't as easily confused as I am?*

Shaking my head, I opened my hands and imagined my fingers as rune channels. It was an enchantment I was intimately familiar with, so it didn't take much effort. Looking down, I saw that they were now elongated, and each of my digits was ringed in perfectly arranged runes. *That should work,* I noted.

Then I began to draw.

I was still at least a hundred feet up, so the ground below was like a great sheet of blank parchment. Creating the shapes from my current vantage point was far simpler than I would have expected. I drew lines and circles, ringing them with symbols and geometric shapes. It was rather like finger painting.

That's utterly mad, observed my more sensible counterpart.

"Only if you expect to survive. I'm just having fun," I told him.

It will certainly piss him off, came a thought that had a smile attached.

*
**

Mal'goroth was much better looking than I remembered. He had forsaken his horns and extra limbs for a simple human shape. The only extravagance I could see was a lovely set of ivory wings. They had an almost iridescent shine in the morning sun.

He flew toward me with a knowing expression, his sense of smug satisfaction so strong that I felt it as a palpable force in the air.

"You look well," I complimented.

"You also," he responded, through a sparkling white smile. "Though I can't say much for your taste in clothes. Is this a product of some previously unseen humility? I had not thought you so modest."

His remark provoked a bit of introspection. "I think perhaps the robe is a reflection of my favorite self-image," I answered.

"Novitiate priest?" he asked in jest.

"No. I've had a lot of roles and titles in life. I've been a peasant, a nobleman, and even king briefly," I said.

"What about a god?" suggested Mal'goroth.

"I suppose, but I don't think of myself that way," I explained.

"What then?"

"I think my favorite role was father and husband, but I can't claim those anymore. Archmage was the most interesting, but my transformation to my current condition robbed me of that. This would be the best of what I have left," I replied enigmatically. I'm sure it annoyed him as much as it always had me. I had fought a lot of long-winded villains over the years. It was my turn now.

"Idiot?"

I sighed. He just had to ruin the moment. "Wizard," I said in irritation. "I have only wits and magic left."

"You have none of the former and too little of the latter," said my exquisitely beautiful foe. He accompanied the insult with a probing burst of power.

It rebounded harmlessly from the shield enchantment carved into the ground around me.

"You waste your time with those scribbling's," he complained, sending a more powerful surge at my position.

This time his magic was in the form of a spellweave, which gave it far more potency. The air crackled around my shield as it burned into it, but my enchantment continued to hold.

"My scribbling's too much for you?" I asked dryly.

His answering smile was almost feral, "I'm just warming up. We wouldn't want this to end too quickly." Another blast struck suddenly, without warning or any sign of buildup. It wasn't a spellweave, but the sheer force of it shattered my shield instantly.

I laughed at him from a different vantage point, standing now in a different circle sixty yards to his right. A new shield surrounded me now. "There isn't much risk of that happening, I think, unless you manage to get smarter in the next few minutes," I taunted.

To his credit he didn't lash out immediately. Instead he watched me with careful eyes, wondering at my ruse. The landscape was covered with arcane runes, lines, and circles. I was betting my opponent hadn't a clue what any of them meant—or more importantly, which ones were pure gibberish.

"You realize these games won't last forever," he informed me.

"You said you didn't want it to end too quickly," I retorted.

"That's right," he agreed, "so I did." As he spoke, I began noticing a strange red mist rising from the ground. Mist was too simple a description though; it was a complex weave of She'Har magic, breathtaking in its dual complexity and simplicity. It covered the ground in every direction for almost a mile, and while I couldn't be sure of its purpose I had a few guesses.

He's testing, trying to figure out what's real and what isn't. The mist flowed smoothly, covering everything except some of my circles. Roughly half of them had shields around them which kept the mist out, while the others did not.

"It appears you didn't have time to finish your work," he commented.

In point of fact, I hadn't finished, but it wasn't the shields that were left undone. "Chel'strathek took longer than I might have wished," I lied. I had actually gotten lucky. If his lieutenant hadn't been such a fool, I would have still been fighting him when Mal'goroth arrived.

Another swift strike destroyed the shielded circle I had been talking to him from, but I wasn't there any longer, and as the aythar destroyed my circle, some of the power was drawn away, caught in the lines that traced back and forth across the scenery. I wasted no time in claiming it.

"Teleportation circles or illusion?" wondered Mal'goroth openly.

"You're getting warmer," I teased.

I could imagine his mind working now. He had already discovered that many of the circles were merely for show, unshielded as they were. The others appeared empty, but all of those boasted a shield that blocked aythar, preventing him from actually sensing whether I was inside.

Since meeting Walter Prathion, I had learned a lot about invisibility and illusion. In particular what invisibility was not good for. *"Invisibility is wonderful when no one suspects, but if they know you're there already, it's much less useful,"* he had told me.

"What do you mean?" I had asked.

"If they suspect your presence, there are many ways to ruin invisibility. In those cases it is often better to give them something to see, rather than trying to hide completely."

Watching him work, I had come to understand his lesson, and since I couldn't create the type of invisibility that came instinctively to him, I focused on what I could do. In a situation like this, that was almost as good. Hiding from a god was tricky, especially if you possessed the immense aythar that I currently had. It was like trying to hide a blazing torch in a dark room, impossible. Unless you covered it with something else.

The shields disguise my location, and the illusion gives him something to focus on, I thought silently.

A line of flickering power, a spellweave this time, cut through the air like a whip, but my shield disappeared before it made contact. My body vanished and reappeared in a different circle.

The differences between spellweaving and enchanting were many, but superficial. The theory behind them was the same, only the execution differed, well that, and the symbology. During the course of my experiences with Thillmarius, the She'Har, and several of the Dark Gods, I had discovered a few things. While they believed in the superiority of their spellweaving ability, and they were very fast, they weren't instantaneous.

Enchanting was the same, except that it took a lot longer to prepare. Once finished though, both types of magic had similar properties. The extra formality involved in their structure and creation isolated the magic along the fourth dimension, time, preventing them from dissipating or wasting aythar. Although I couldn't prove it, I was

435

pretty certain that everything that could be done with one, could, with some time and effort, be done with the other. They were like different languages.

Except they can produce theirs in seconds, while it can take me minutes or even hours sometimes to prepare mine, I thought ruefully. Preparation had its advantages, though. Since they could produce complex, permanent, and frankly, fantastic magical constructs almost on a whim, they rarely bothered building things in advance.

A human enchanter has to think about what he does. He plans and prepares.

I might not be an archmage anymore, or even human for that matter. But I was the best damn enchanter who had ever lived.

Or the most arrogant, suggested my inner self.

"Somebody told me that once," I replied defensively.

Mal'goroth was watching me suspiciously. "Are you talking to yourself?" he asked suddenly.

I made a face, "Perhaps."

"You were poorly made then. Your mind is starting to unravel, though I suppose that should be expected of anything of human origin," he announced. Another spellwoven whip struck, and again my shield vanished a split second before it could make contact. I reappeared in another circle.

I smiled, "I've been called worse." This time his reaction was a blinding strike of pure aythar, raw and unformed. It happened almost instantaneously and with enough brute force to make up for what it lacked in finesse. The shield around my apparent position never had a chance, nor did the illusion of me that stood within it.

The extra aythar from his attack bled away through the lines I had scribed on the earth, moving in every direction.

I quietly absorbed the aythar from where I watched.

"I can see what you're trying to do." Mal'goroth turned in a slow circle, unsure which direction to face when speaking, since it was obvious that I was unlikely to be where I appeared. "Stealing odd bits of power, do you think you'll gain enough to balance the scale?"

I hadn't thought I could hide it for long. Nor had I believed it was practical. Such a thing would have taken days at the rate things were going now. There weren't enough circles to keep him busy for that long. My main purpose was to show him the truth. He might win, but it would only be because of brute force. In every other way I was his superior. That couldn't sit well with him.

Just to get under his skin even further, I reactivated the shields at the places where he had tried to hit me with his spellwoven whip. Since I had turned them off before he struck, the enchantments were still functional. The places he had smashed with pure aythar were a lost cause however.

"There really isn't a balance between us," I told him. "No amount of power will ever compensate for all the things you lack."

"I haven't forgotten the places I attacked," he assured me. "Shield or not, I won't bother with them again."

"Then you assume that it's illusion I'm using?" I said suddenly, and this time I appeared in one of the unshielded circles near the center. He had been ignoring those since deciding they were decoys, but my appearance there now was a direct challenge.

Without a shield to hide my aythar, he knew without a doubt that I was truly there. I teleported away an instant after I appeared.

His reaction, expected as it was, was still so swift that it nearly caught me, although I had already prepared myself to teleport immediately after showing myself. A blazing column of raw power struck the place I had been standing, burning a deep hole in the ground. The attack was so great that half of it was absorbed by the earth itself, and only half was caught in my enchanted sieve—to be funneled into my greedy hands.

Damn, I thought, *he isn't playing around.* The strike had used an incredible amount of aythar. *If he keeps doing that, he's a bigger fool than I thought.*

Snarling, he sent more of his spellweavings to destroy the shields around empty circles, but I had enough warning to shut them off before they struck. I brought them back up the moment his spellweavings vanished.

He had to be frustrated. If he used spellweavings, I couldn't steal any of his aythar, but if he attacked spontaneously and missed, I grew stronger. Of course that assumed he played by my rules. *He's going to start changing the game.*

Mal'goroth couldn't be sure how quickly I could teleport, so I was betting that he would assume that my visible location was bound to be an illusion if it was under a shield. Taking a chance, I removed the illusion hiding me and dismissed the false image I had placed in one of the other circles. If he used a spellweave, I could probably teleport, but if he tried a spontaneous attack I knew I'd never escape in time.

But you won't do that, will you? You're going to focus on the empty ones. My thought was as much a wish as a prediction. It was entirely possible he'd swat me like a fly if he had a different chain of logic.

"I think we've had enough of this," said Mal'goroth. "I've grown tired of the game." Extending his arms, lines of spellweaving shot outward and upward, until it seemed that they might cover the sky. From one horizon to the other, the blue was replaced with an absolute black as his power expanded, filling the air over our heads out to a distance that was hard to comprehend.

He gave me a charming look. "Now that we know where we stand, let's see where you are." A flash of raw power erupted from his body and destroyed all of my shielded circles in an instant. I had reinforced my own, which kept me from being completely overwhelmed, but the others were gone now. A torrent of aythar was channeled through my spell-sieve. Desperately I absorbed everything I could, but I knew it wouldn't be enough.

Pointing at me with a slender finger he crooned, "Now, we see you revealed."

I stood in my lone circle, a hundred yards away. My strength was far greater than it had been when we started, but anyone with even a hint of magesight could still see the difference between us. With my circles gone, I had run out of places to hide. *Things are about to get painful,* I surmised.

This is going to hurt.

"I already said that," I admonished my inner voice.

It was worth repeating, it responded.

Gathering everything I had, I threw my strength into the shield ring around me. Mal'goroth's spellwoven nightmare in the sky was shrinking now, closing with ever increasing speed. A contracting knot of blackness, with me at its center.

When it reached me, I lost consciousness, which was interesting in itself. As a rule, immortal beings don't black out. The crushing power that destroyed my shield should have been painful, but it completely overwhelmed my senses, leaving me awash in a sea of dark oblivion.

My senses returned far too quickly, and I found myself trapped within a black sphere, or at least I thought it was a sphere. I couldn't tell much about it other than the crushing pressure it seemed to exert upon me from every direction. I'd never experienced anything quite so claustrophobic before, not to mention painfully unpleasant.

Speak for yourself, chimed in my inner self.

The pressure lightened for a moment, and light began to enter my world. My body lay in the same place I had been, wrapped within tight bands of densely powerful She'Har spellweaving. They were covered in thorns, and the pressure they applied made them less than enjoyable.

Very little of my body was exposed, primarily my eyes. The beautiful face of my enemy looked down on me from only a foot away. "I'm sure you're starting to feel foolish now, aren't you?" he told me in an amiable tone.

I tried to speak, but my mouth was covered as well, so I crossed my eyes instead, hoping that would communicate my disdain for his opinion. After a few seconds of staring at me he gave me access to my mouth again.

"You had to tear up half the valley *and* wrap who knows how much sky with your aythar to subdue me," I told him. "That can't sit well with you."

"We're going to be together for a long time," he informed me. "You might want to consider how your words will affect your future." Reaching through the thorns as though they were insubstantial, he thrust his hand into my stomach.

Physical pain was almost impossible for me these days, but what he was doing was entirely different. Ripping his hand free, it emerged with a glowing handful of concentrated aythar. I screamed.

"Today we will teach you a new sort of agony, Mordecai," he said in a calm tone.

The next handful he took was less pleasant, and since the only power I was free to use was my voice, I channeled everything I had into it, emitting a painful cry that would have turned his head to jelly if he'd been a mortal.

He flinched, which did little to improve my mood, but it was a start. The vines covered my mouth again. Ripping and tearing at me, he tore my essence away in both small and large chunks. It was the spiritual equivalent of disemboweling someone, and then eating the organs in front of the previous owner.

Being unable to die was a real problem sometimes.

It could have been much less unpleasant, or at the very least, non-painful. I was gaining a new appreciation for the humane method that shiggreth used with their victims. Even my struggle with Chel'strathek hadn't been this bad.

After he had reduced me by half or more he allowed me to speak again, so I took the opportunity to cry uncontrollably. Deep within I hated him, and deeper still I wanted to respond with a clever remark, anything to cover the shame and indignity of what he was doing to me. But the agony had defeated what was left of my sanity.

"I'm going to keep you forever," Mal'goroth told me, "since I don't have the key to the spellweave that sustains you. But don't worry; you'll be my most favorite pet."

He resumed his awful feast, but one clear thought brought me a tiny piece of satisfaction. *Peter, do it soon.*

I had lost all conception of time.

Whether it took him minutes or hours I couldn't be sure. For me it felt like an eternity. There wasn't much left of me. Mal'goroth had devoured everything but the still dead flesh that encased me. The thorns were gone, but I was too weak to move. The only aythar left was that of the spellweave that sustained me, the cursed magic that bound the true Mordecai's soul and kept me in my damned, undying state.

My consciousness began to fade, too weak to sustain itself as I watched Mal'goroth walk away. "I'll find you later," he said as he left. "...in a week, or a month, or a year—whenever I get bored. I have a lot to do in the meantime."

I was desperate to speak, but my lips wouldn't move.

He stopped, gazing down on me with pity. "I'm off to finish my task. Your family, your people, your race, all of them—do you understand?"

I couldn't nod, but my eyes probably showed him my feelings.

"After I've done that, it will be just you and me and the others like us. I might let the new She'Har, whom you kindly resurrected, live if they can find a way to set us free. That's your only hope, really. Otherwise, I'll destroy them as well, and then we'll just have to amuse each other for a very, very long time."

Once again I wished my dead eyes could weep, but they continued to betray me, remaining dry and nearly lifeless.

"Don't think your people can hide," he added, pausing again. "I'm not picky. If necessary I'll tear down the mountains, burn the forests, and boil the oceans. I won't mind killing every living thing just to make sure they are dead. That should give you some comfort."

Mal'goroth had apparently learned a different definition of the word 'comfort' than I had.

Perhaps he was able to read my thoughts because he seemed to answer me then, "They won't have to live, Mordecai, but your suffering, and mine, will last forever."

I closed my eyes and let my awareness drift into the dark. *Finish it, Peter, please.*

Chapter 43

Once again Gareth was forced to serve as mount, while two humans and three gods rode on his back. The gods could have flown themselves, but Walter had insisted that they stay together; otherwise his invisibility spell would be more difficult to manage.

The vast amounts of aythar being used, along with the chaotic fighting, allowed Walter to modify the invisibility spell to some degree. Assuming that the combatants were focused on their battle, he gave the shield a faint permeability to both light and aythar, so they could see and sense the fight. From inside it gave the world a dark hazy appearance, while from the outside they would seem ghostly and ephemeral to a sharp eyed observer.

Passing through the gate, it was easy to tell which direction to take. Only a half a mile or so in the distance were frequent flashes of light and the deep dull booms of Mordecai's signature iron bomblets.

Why is he using those? Gareth wondered. They were sure to be nearly useless against a being as powerful as the spider god.

"What's happening?" asked Penny. The haze, combined with being limited to only normal vision, made it difficult for her to discern anything at their distance.

"He's using his iron bombs, lots of them," answered Walter, straining to sense something more specific. They were less than a quarter of a mile away now, but the shield interfered with his magesight.

"Is he winning?" she asked hopefully.

"He will, undoubtedly," said Gareth. "His strength is at least twice as great as the spider's, but he is fighting oddly."

"He should be trying to finish this quickly if Mal'goroth is coming," pointed out Walter.

They both stopped for a moment, wondering at their perceptions. The lack of communication annoyed Penny to no end. "What?!"

Walter seemed confused, "I don't understand. What is that?"

But the dragon knew exactly what he was witnessing. *The fool!* he exclaimed mentally. Banking rapidly, he began a series of powerful wing strokes to gain altitude.

"You're going the wrong way!" complained Penny.

"We should have stayed inside the castle," responded Gareth, "or better still, we should be in your hidden sanctuary."

Walter seemed fascinated, staring behind them as the dragon made haste to bear them farther away. "He's caught him somehow," he relayed. "It looks like a giant golden box of some sort. I think your husband just declared himself the victor." His voice was elated.

The dragon kept flying farther away. "We need a shield," he said loudly.

"I've already got one around us," said Walter.

Gareth blew flames in his frustration, heedless of the fact that they blew back to endanger his passengers. "No! We need a strong shield. Like the one around the castle."

"I will do it," declared Doron.

"Link yourselves," suggested the dragon. "I think it will take more than just one of you."

"More than me?!" answered Doron dubiously.

"More than all of us," said Gareth.

It was Millicenth who finally shut Doron up and convinced him to coordinate with her and Karenth. Together the three of them formed a powerful shield around the flying dragon. Walter assisted as well, but his strength was hardly noticeable compared to theirs.

"I can't sense anything now," fretted Walter. The shield had completely obscured his magesight.

A bright flash blinded them then, even though they were flying away from it. A split second later the world seemed to flip upside down. The shield was gone, vanished, utterly and completely, and they found themselves tumbling through the air, clinging to the back of a dragon hopelessly out of control in a hurricane of wind.

Spinning through the sky, Penny found herself thrown free, flying on her own, like some strange wingless bird. Events had progressed so quickly that fear hadn't had time to solidify in her, but she knew with a strange detachment that she was falling to her death. *What a stupid way to die,* she thought. It never occurred to her to scream, not that she could draw a deep breath. The air was blasting into her face.

Millicenth found her somehow, gliding toward her like a brilliant white swan through the turbulent rush. Penny couldn't remember ever having been glad to see the goddess before, but at that moment, she was.

Caught in the Lady of the Evening Star's strong arms, she was carried toward the ground. The rush of wind seemed to be dwindling, but it was still great enough to make normal flight difficult.

Once they landed, Penny had a number of questions. "What the hell was that?" was her starter.

"Whatever your husband was doing, it fell apart," said the goddess.

"I thought the world was ending for a moment," groused the countess.

"It may have come close," conceded the goddess, "at least for this part of it. He seems to have stopped it, though."

Karenth appeared then, flying low to the ground, and he was carrying Walter Prathion. "Are you alright?" asked Walter when he had gotten close enough to make himself heard.

"I think—perhaps," shouted Penny over the distance.

"Where is the dragon?"

That was a good question. It took them a few minutes and a careful search to find Gareth. They found Doron first, a quarter mile away, but Gareth was almost a half a mile beyond that. His wings had allowed the wind to throw him much farther than the others. He was caught in the top of a large oak tree, but he seemed to be uninjured.

The others gathered at the base of the tree, and Gareth began climbing slowly down. He was using his more human form.

"Wouldn't it have been easier to fly down?" suggested Walter from the ground.

Gareth dropped the last few feet to land beside him. Something about his appearance was oddly off.

They all stared at him for a long minute. Penny was the first to break the silence, "You have red hair."

"Much like my mother's," said the man in front of them. He idly stroked a wild red beard with his hand, as if discovering an old friend.

"You're—human, aren't you?" asked Walter uncertainly.

Gareth Gaelyn nodded, "That seems to be the case." Reaching out with one hand, he opened it and let a fine white dust sift between his fingers.

"Was that your aystrylin?" inquired Walter cautiously.

The archmage gave him a smooth glance, but said nothing.

"The explosion?"

Gareth sighed, "No, though I thought my end was upon me. As I was hurtling through the air, I decided to finish my days as I had begun them. I made the choice myself."

"Why?" said Penny curiously. She had heard his story several times through both Mordecai and Moira Centyr, but there had never been a hint of any desire to restore his humanity.

"I had been quietly considering it for some time," he admitted.

"And you didn't talk to anyone about it?" she questioned.

Gareth gave her a flat stare. Despite being fully human again, his personality still remained rather aloof. "I keep my own counsel, woman," he replied in irritation.

She resisted a sudden urge to grab his beard. Taking a deep breath, she focused on their more immediate concerns, "How will we travel? Can you still transform?"

The archmage answered immediately, "I could, but it would be—unwise, more so now that my aystrylin has

448

been used. It would probably be safer to have one of the godlings handle it."

After a moment's discussion, Karenth reshaped himself. His flesh flowed like a strange liquid and sprouted feathers while expanding simultaneously. When he had finished he was in the form of a giant eagle. He had conveniently included a saddle with three places for riders.

"I have often wondered something," offered Walter suddenly with a pensive look, speaking to Gareth.

"Why are the gods so freely able to transform? It seems that even for you, one of the Gaelyn line, it holds many dangers," said Walter.

"They do not change the way that we do," replied the red headed mage. "Their natures are fixed by the enchantment that binds them."

"Couldn't you do something similar to yourself?"

"No!" responded Gareth quickly. "That sort of thing is very close to what happened to your Count. My family was one of the few to use physical transformations, partly because of our gift and partly because of the risks. We kept to the forms of living creatures to minimize the risk."

"The eagle is a living creature," said Walter, pointing to Karenth.

"Eagles are, yes," agreed Gareth, "but that is not an eagle, nor is it properly alive."

"Now I'm truly confused," said Walter scratching his head.

"Karenth has created a body shaped like an eagle, but it has no heart, no blood. Cut it and you will find only more of his solidified essence inside," explained Gareth.

"But he is alive...," said Walter.

"Not to interrupt your erudite conversation, gentlemen, but I think we should be going," suggested Penny.

Gareth climbed up, taking the middle seat. Penelope rode in front of him, and Walter took the place behind. "Ask Moira later," he told Walter. "She may be able to explain it better."

Millicenth and Doron shrank rapidly in size, until their bodies were no larger than a child's doll. The Lady of the Evening Star floated upward and landed in front of Penny, settling in as though she actually were a child's toy. Doron chose to secure himself slightly behind Karenth's feathered head.

Beating his wings, Karenth took to the air. "Which way?" he asked.

"Back," said Penelope, pointing in the direction they had come from. "I still need to find him."

"What if it happens again," asked Walter.

Gareth spoke then, "It won't. The explosion was caused by the destruction of his enchantment. He could not easily create another like it."

"Could he be...?" asked Penny, not wanting to finish the sentence.

"Dead?" said Gareth bluntly. "He died some time ago, but if you mean 'gone', I'm afraid not."

The Countess kept her features composed, but underneath she felt a twisting pain in her chest. Her resolve had not changed however. "Fly dammitt," she urged Karenth.

Traveling back, they covered the mile they had lost and soon were within half a mile of the area where Mordecai had been. Walter had replaced their semi-invisible shield, but he had reduced the amount of light and aythar that they could sense even further. He was taking no chances.

Then he closed it completely, leaving them flying through what seemed to be an endless black void. "I can't tell which way I'm going," complained Karenth.

"Turn around and head toward the ground," said Walter. "I'll give you enough to see a bit on your way down. We can't go any closer in that direction."

"I felt nothing," said Millicenth.

Gareth spoke then, "Mal'goroth has arrived."

"I would have felt that," insisted the goddess.

"My magesight is far better than yours at a distance, Lady," the archmage told her. "Especially when we're cloaked in this shield."

The goddess didn't reply.

Carefully, Karenth made his way to the ground, and as soon as he had set talon to earth Walter resumed his absolute invisibility, sealing them away from all sight and magic.

"How close are we?" asked Penny.

"Too close," said Walter, "less than half a mile probably."

"We can't help him if we can't see," she pointed out.

Gareth interrupted, "Exactly. We can do nothing."

"That isn't why we came," she argued.

"Then you're deluded, Countess," said the archmage sternly. "What you failed to sense, while Walter's shield was faintly open, is that there is a being beyond it that can crush us with nothing but a thought. The very fact that you can *breathe* right now is only thanks to the amazing gift your wizard here possesses. No human could produce a normal shield strong enough to prevent just the pressure of the aythar out there from crushing your will."

Penny chewed her lip. She hadn't caught even a hint of the sort of pressure she had once felt when confronted by one of the gods. It gave her new respect for Walter's special gift, but at the same time she was frustrated by their helplessness.

"What should we do now, Countess?" asked Millicenth demurely.

"We wait."

A sudden booming rumble echoed across the valley, sending vibrations through the ground. "We should probably excavate a bit," suggested Karenth helpfully. "It might be best to be slightly below the ground level."

They agreed, so the god of justice used his power within the confines of Walter's invisibility shield, making a six foot depression in the soil.

More booming noises followed, leaving them to wonder, blind, at what might be happening.

"It should have stopped by now," declared Doron, puzzled.

"Why?" asked Walter.

Karenth took up the question, "Because of their relative strengths. Mal'goroth should have finished it within seconds."

"He's playing with his food," suggested the Lady of the Evening Star.

"No," said Gareth, "they're still fighting. There wouldn't be so much noise if it were that."

Penny had taken a seat on the ground. She held a hand in front of her face, but the darkness was absolute, and she couldn't see it at all. Listening to the conversation around her she struggled to retain her composure. *Think about something else,* she told herself, but it was hopeless. In the black earth she felt tears begin to roll down her cheeks, and for the first time she was grateful for the darkness.

Another rumble rolled out, shaking them in their hidden cavity.

"How is he doing that?!" said Doron, still incredulous.

"The man has an amazing proclivity for surprises," observed Gareth dryly.

A rosy light began to filter in, and they could see a painful expression on Walter's face.

"What are you doing?!" shouted Gareth. "He'll find us!"

"The mist," said Walter as sweat rolled from his forehead. "Help me."

Able to sense the outside world again, Gareth felt the red spellwoven mist that Mal'goroth had summoned. It had covered their niche, and like some strange acid it was devouring Walter's shield. His body relaxed, and his eyes unfocused while the red haired archmage reached out, listening to the voice of the earth. A moment later it flowed over their small pit creating an earthen ceiling. They were fully entombed now.

Walter's face relaxed as he restored the shield. "That worked," he said after a second. "But being completely under the ground will make us noticeable. It won't matter if we're invisible once Mal'goroth notices a strange empty bubble in the earth."

Gareth's voice answered him in the darkness, "He won't find an empty place. The earth believes this place is whole. It will not betray us."

"I wish I understood how that worked," said Walter wistfully.

"Me too," said Gareth honestly.

The earth continued to shake until at last it seemed to jump under their feet, threatening to dislodge their makeshift ceiling.

"That had to be it," said Doron with a hint of something like hidden glee.

The world grew silent, and then an even greater blast shook them. Minutes passed and nothing happened. Penny thought of her children, and began to regret her decision. *I'm stupid. We're going to die, and I'll have accomplished nothing.*

In her memory she heard Mort's favorite saying, *"Stupid never dies."* Inside she was wound so tightly that the phrase, which she had never thought much of before, almost made her laugh.

That was when the screaming started.

The first was impressive, an agonized cry of someone being tortured, but the second, which came a half minute later was so loud that it seemed as though the world itself was dying. Penny's hands were over her ears but they hardly diminished the sound. Worse, she could recognize the voice. Mercifully, Walter adjusted his shield to prevent sound from entering as well.

In the silence, there was no solace.

**

Time passed slowly, with nothing to mark it. In their dark and silent womb the world had ceased to exist.

Deprived of her senses Penny's mind began to create sights and sounds to fill the emptiness. At first they were small, imaginary noises or half-heard phrases, some accompanied by a sudden image or a flicker of light, but as time dragged on, they grew more real.

"It's over now," said Mordecai, sitting beside her.

She ignored the illusion, for she knew her mind was playing tricks on her.

"I'm sorry," he added.

Why? You did nothing wrong, she protested mentally.

"For everything," he said, answering her thought, "for hiding so many things from you in the past, for failing to protect you, for all of it. I tried to handle everything myself and now it's all gone to hell."

"You were always an idiot, but I don't think it's your fault," she said then. "You didn't create Mal'goroth."

Walter was startled from his own reverie, "What?"

"Nothing," she told him quickly.

"I did create Mal'goroth," said Mordecai, continuing. "Or at least I gave him the power that set this all in motion."

Are you talking about the war with Gododdin? She asked silently.

"You were there with me, you remember it," he said sadly.

You had no choice.

"There's always a choice, Penny," he said softly. "Sometimes we just don't see it."

What would you choose now, if you could change all this?

"To be at home with you, watching you brush your hair, listening to the children talking in their beds, hoping we will think they are sleeping."

The last remark was too much for her and she shook her head. "Please Walter, let some light in. I think I'm going mad."

Gareth agreed as well, "I too am tired of facing my phantoms. Just give us a glimpse."

Walter returned the outside sounds first, waiting to make certain everything was quiet above. Gareth eased their earthy roof aside, and then Walter began to let some light, and more importantly, a faint amount of aythar, pass inside.

"Mal'goroth has moved. I can feel his pressure emanating from the castle now. Their shield seems to be down as well," said Gareth. "He's quite far; you can probably release the invisibility."

"I still can't sense anything," said the older wizard.

It didn't take much convincing, although Walter still removed their concealment gradually. They emerged from their dark pit into a world that looked as if it had been scoured by a giant hand.

"Is there any sign of Mordecai?" asked Penny nervously.

"No," said Gareth in a tone that brooked no doubt. The red haired archmage was confident of his senses.

Walking carefully over the torn earth and upturned rocks, they began walking in the direction where the battle had taken place. They had gone several hundred yards when Gareth spoke again, "I see something."

"What?" asked the Countess.

"A body," he answered. "It must be him. There is so little aythar I mistook it for the ground when we were farther away."

Narrowing his eyes, Walter chimed in, "I can feel the body, but there's no aythar there."

The red haired archmage was already striding forward, "It's there, just a faint bit that comprises the spellweaving inside him. You'll feel it when we get closer."

They found him draped across a smooth stone that had been uncovered by the turmoil. His body lay supine, with eyes staring at the sky blankly and while it was in one piece, it was torn and ripped. The skin and flesh looked as though it had been savaged by some wild beast, but there was no blood. It was the dry and damaged husk of a man who had died more than a year gone past.

Chapter 44

I, Mordecai Illeniel, awoke.

My eyes were already open, but I hadn't been able to see through them until that moment. My ears also began to report sounds, and gradually I realized someone was walking toward me, several someone's in fact.

Above me the sky was a brilliant blue. The sun shone again now that Mal'goroth's black attack was done. My body felt wooden, as though it were dry and stiff. Idly I tried to move my arm, but nothing happened.

Last time I didn't wake until my body had absorbed enough aythar to restore itself, I thought, remembering the day I had awoken under a mound of dead insects. The memory itself seemed like a dream however, as if it had been someone else's awakening. This one felt far more real to me.

A red haired man's head blocked the sun for a moment, peering down at me. He looked vaguely familiar, but I had trouble placing him. He moved out of my line of sight, but my eyes weren't able to track him. Aware of my magesight now, I felt him step back, closer to the people with him.

That's Doron, Millicenth, Karenth, Walter—and Penny. The gods were easily recognized by their powerful aythar, but Penny and Walter were a surprise. The stranger felt similar to Gareth, but his aythar was subtly different. *Why is Penny here?!*

The thought brought a shock of fear and alarm. She was supposed to be hiding. She was supposed to be safe, at least for a while anyway. In a panic I tried to speak, but of course my mouth wouldn't move.

"What was that?" said the stranger, leaning closer to me.

Penny drew closer as well. Her aythar was warm in a way that the stranger's was not, and although he radiated a powerful aythar, it was hers that seemed to call to me.

"It's awake somehow," noted the man. "I can feel a consciousness."

"It?!" said Penny, somewhat offended at the usage.

"It," he repeated. His voice sounded maddeningly familiar to me. "The simulacrum that thinks of itself as your husband," he added to clarify.

"You said he can't die, because of the spellweave," reminded Penny.

"Die, that much is true," said the stranger, "He can't die. It's the awareness that puzzles me."

"Why?" she asked him.

"Because the essential feature of aythar is awareness," he explained carefully. "Everything possesses it, even the stone he is lying upon, but the type of awareness is determined by the level of aythar."

Pointing at the ground, he spoke as though he were in a classroom, "The earth below us, for example, its aythar is very small for every ounce or pound. It is hardly aware of anything, but added up, it comprises a huge consciousness. One that is so far removed from you or me that it is almost completely alien to us." Moving his hand,

459

he indicated Mordecai's body. "This body however, contains hardly anything more than does the stone it rests upon. The magical sentience that controls it shouldn't be conscious."

Listening to him expound on magical theory gave me my final clue. *It's Gareth, but he's human!*

Walter was leaning close now, peering at me. "I felt it," he agreed calmly, "a flicker of something. I think he's listening to us."

Of course I'm listening dammit. You're talking into my ear. I was beginning to find being spoken of in the third person annoying. *You look old, Walter,* I added. Somehow the rude observation made me feel better.

Penny was fully beside me now, her face only inches from my own. The feeling of her presence was like a warm balm soaking into me. Her hand reached out, but before it touched my face, Gareth had caught it.

"Careful!" he warned her.

She gave him an angry glare, "Why?"

I silently cheered for her, *you tell that bastard!*

"He's still a shiggreth," said Gareth. "Even now his body is slowly absorbing aythar. If you touch it..." He glanced around, looking for something to illustrate his point. Unable to find an insect, he settled for a torn clump of grass that was still green. Placing it on my chest he told them, "Watch."

My eyes still wouldn't move, so I couldn't look down, but I knew what they must be seeing. The grass was turning gray. The thought made me feel ashamed. *After everything I've been through, this is the greatest indignity yet, having them display my corruption for her to see.*

Her voice came back defiantly, "He's my husband. He won't hurt me."

"I doubt it would be intentional," said Gareth, "but in his current state he may not be able to control himself."

"Allow me," said Millicenth unexpectedly. "I can prevent him from taking much. A small amount should help restore him," said the goddess, and before Gareth could reply she reached out and placed her hand on my chest.

I could feel my body tugging fiercely at her, but only a trickle of aythar emerged. The Lady of the Evening Star's will was far more powerful than mine, and she controlled her energy flow with great precision. She had been designed that way, long ago, by Moira Centyr, to make her an effective healer.

As the aythar flowed into me, my body began to awake, returning to a more human-like state, but the world was growing dimmer, fading. A darkness was rising around me, the prison of Lyralliantha's spellweaving. It had been weak, thin, deprived of all but structure by Mal'goroth's hand, but now it was gaining strength. I could feel another mind stirring, one similar to my own, yet different.

"Stop," I managed to croak through dry lips.

Thankfully, the goddess withdrew her hand.

Something wet fell on my face, and I realized Penny was crying over me quietly. She urged me, "You need more. Your body is healing. Let her help you."

"No," I said, struggling to make my stiff mouth form the word. I could feel my other self, shifting, confused. *Brexus,* I realized. The aythar had roused his awareness as well as restoring my soul's prison. He was trying to regain control of his speech.

The strange duality of my existence returned to the foreground of my memory as I recalled the bizarre events of the past few months. I had awoken many times, sometimes in a lonely darkness, accompanied only by thoughts that sounded like my own, but were in fact a stranger's. On one or two occasions though, I had been able to see through his eyes, trapped like a passenger on a runaway horse, observing with no power to affect his actions.

Awake now, I could remember everything he had done, but it felt strange. Like the memories of the loshti, they were there, but they were not my own.

"No more, it will trap me again," I said, desperately hoping she would understand.

My wife stared at me with uncertainty. "What can I do?"

"Where is Peter?" I choked out.

Her expression changed from puzzlement to annoyance, "I should have known. You *still* have a scheme don't you."

In her irritation I could sense a glimmer of hope. She still believed in me. She thought I had an answer. That insight pained me more than I had expected. Unable to hide my despair I told her the truth, "He promised to kill me."

Eyes wide, she stared at Gareth, who came to the same conclusion. "The knife," he said at once.

Penny's reaction was more specific, "Someone has to stop him!"

"No," I uttered, not that anyone was listening.

462

"He should be in your hidden sanctuary, wherever it is located," said Karenth. "If you tell me where it's at, I can fetch him."

My foolhardy wife began describing it to the best of her ability, giving away the general location of my greatest secret almost immediately. "That's hundreds of miles from here," he replied in frustration. "Even flying, it will take me more than a day." He was already rising from the ground on wings that had sprouted from his back.

"You'll never get there in time," said Gareth, but the deity had already taken flight.

He thinks he'll be trapped if I die, I observed. *Karenth doesn't know I gave Gareth the keys to unmake them.* That made me chuckle inwardly. The god of justice had caused me enough trouble in the past; he deserved to panic for a while.

"It will take him days searching those mountains, even if he knows the region," said Millicenth disapprovingly.

I saw Gareth's head turn in the direction of Cameron Castle. "The pressure is growing. Mal'goroth is moving in our direction."

Penny seemed unaware, and even Walter was surprised. "I can't feel anything yet," he announced.

The ex-dragon raised one red eyebrow, but didn't comment. He had explained their differences once already.

I watched them start to draw away, preparing to leave. Millicenth was changing shape, to become some sort of graceful bird, except on an entirely different size scale. I could feel their urgency, but Penny held back.

Go dammitt! I cursed silently. Contrary as usual, she came closer. I struggled to speak, but in my distraction

463

Brexus had taken control. My voice was no longer my own.

"We need to make haste, Countess," said Gareth warningly.

She held up her hand, "Just a minute. Give me that. Let me say goodbye." The look on her face frightened me. She was about to do something stupid.

Somebody put her on the damn bird and get her away! I swore at them.

My lips parted without my wishing it and a word emerged, "Penny."

She was kneeling beside me now with a face that made me wish I was truly dead. No man should see that. Her lips and cheeks were contorted with grief and her eyes were grotesquely swollen. Her shoulders were contorting with suppressed emotion.

I had never seen her look so perfectly ugly in my life. Her nose alone was… well it might have made me shudder if I'd been alive.

Somehow, despite the mucus and the retching sobs, she was still the most beautiful thing I had ever seen. I would have given anything to hold her once more.

And so you shall, came Brexus' thoughts. Even knowing they weren't my thoughts, it still felt odd. Even in my own mind, he sounded exactly like me.

"Penny, help me," he told her.

Inside I raged at him, *What are you doing?! She has to leave.*

"I can't do it, Mort," she said quietly, pitching her voice beneath the hearing range of her companions. "I watched it with Rose and Dorian. I can't leave you."

464

Yes, yes you can! I shouted at her mentally, but naturally she couldn't hear me.

"Don't," said my treacherous other self. "I have an idea."

She still thought she was speaking to me. I was livid, shaking and furious to the core of my being.

Penny's eyes changed, as hope flickered again.

"I need your love," my bastard doppelganger told her. "I need a little more power to do this."

"To do what?" she whispered. I could feel her breath on my face.

"I can save the children," he told her heartlessly, playing on her most vulnerable emotions.

Until that moment in my life, I had only thought I understood the depths that hate can reach, but in that place I discovered its fathomless extent. I hated myself, my other self, in a way that was beyond comprehension.

"How?" she said, glancing back to make sure the others hadn't gotten close enough to hear.

"I just need enough strength to stand, to restore my body. One person would be enough, but...," he stopped dramatically, letting the sentence finish itself.

Walter coughed. "We have to go, Penelope. I'm sorry, but we've taken too long," he said delicately.

"We need to go now!" restated Gareth in a much louder voice.

Penny's eyes searched mine, seeing all the feverish intensity that my demon-birthed twin could put in them. "Only you, Mordecai, I've never loved another—only you," she said urgently, and then she kissed me.

YES! Brexus was elated. The sick bastard had been fantasizing about this since he first thought of my wife.

Her aythar entered my mouth with a sweet taste that reminded me of nothing else. The demon was drawing it out, but not as quickly as he could. In the past he had killed men within less than a second, but he took his time now.

I could feel her love radiating through me, like a beacon calling to my soul. I cried and rejoiced as our spirits touched again, hating myself for the comfort it gave me to feel her again.

I love you, she said through the bars of my spellwoven cage.

And then I realized what was happening.

My alter-ego was funneling her aythar directly to me. Using his meager strength, he was warping the cage, trying to let her life, her love, her aythar—reach me.

Pulling gently, Brexus drained my wife until the flame that warmed her flesh was flickering in the cold, and he gave all that he received to me. At the end, I thought her flame would expire, but he stopped, severing the connection.

Unconscious, Penny's near lifeless form collapsed over my body then, and a shout went up from the others. Leaping forward, Gareth pulled her away from me.

"Foolish woman!" he shouted. "What has she done?"

Walter was stunned motionless, but the two gods didn't seem concerned.

"We can carry her," said Doron.

The Lady of the Evening Star nodded, "She's still alive. I will care for her."

Trapped in my body, I heard something then, something I hadn't heard in a while—the voice of the earth.

Talk to your friends, Brexus told me. My lips were my own again.

Why? I asked him.

I love her too. It was a gift, he answered.

The heart of the world beat strongly beneath me.

"Gareth," I said suddenly, struggling to sit up. My body was thoroughly dead. It was like trying to control a marionette. Thankfully, Brexus helped, he had had a lot more experience at it. I realized then that he was also considerably weaker than I was. He had absorbed none of the aythar Penny had given us.

Gareth Gaelyn looked at me with a profound intensity. My apparent assault on Penny had angered him, but he wasn't sure why I hadn't finished her. "What?"

"I can hear the earth again," I said simply.

"How will that help you?"

"Don't leave. I have an idea. If it doesn't work you can escape later," I said nodding at Walter.

"We have little choice now," he stated bluntly. "She delayed us too long." Gathering Penny into his arms, he stepped back toward the others and vanished.

Chapter 45

Standing proved to be too difficult, so I opted to sit on the stone. *Funeral bier,* I thought absently. Mal'goroth was coming to me anyway. Since he was the one with all the strength, he could do all the walking too.

As I sat, I enjoyed the air. It was my first time to experience it first-hand in a long time. My sense of touch was badly skewed, but anything was better than the emptiness inside my cage. Brexus was still weak, and with my new strength, meager as it was, I could sample everything around me directly.

It would have been a nice time for birdsong, but some bastard had blown all the trees down and scared them away.

My apologies, came Brexus' thought in my mind.

"It wasn't your fault," I replied generously. "What you did was extremely clever. It was Mal'goroth who tore all this up."

Most of it happened when the stasis enchantment broke, he reminded me.

"You remember it your way, I'll remember it mine," I said firmly. "I'll blame him for all of it."

Fair enough, he agreed. *Those diamond cubes were the work of genius. Your crafting skills are without compare.*

Since I had created them while still alive, I realized that it meant I shared the guilt for the destruction they had caused, but I decided not to dwell on it. My other self was kind enough to stick to the positive, thankfully. *I wasn't very happy with what you did with them in Albamarl,* I replied with a strong sense of reprimand.

I have an anger problem, admitted Brexus.

"Well, I'll probably have nightmares over that for the rest of my life," I shot back.

Somehow, I'm not too worried about that, he responded with a sarcastic air.

"I suppose you're right," I agreed, stifling a laugh, "if Peter ever gets around to keeping his promise."

He will, said Brexus.

"You know him well, to be so certain," I conceded.

As well as you.

"You really have lost your mind, haven't you?" said Mal'goroth.

I had felt his arrival long before he got close enough to speak, so I wasn't startled in the least. "I prefer to think that I have gained an extra one," I retorted cleverly. Of course he didn't quite get the joke.

That was funny, Brexus assured me.

"Thank you," I responded. *At least you understand me,* I added silently.

Mal'goroth watched me carefully. "I did not expect to see you moving so soon," he commented. "Did someone try to help you?"

I had expected that question. It was the one I worried about the most. If my over-endowed enemy decided to start banging his club looking for my friends he could easily kill them. They were far too close. I absently flipped a stone in his direction. I had picked it up only a few minutes before.

"You still underestimate human enchanting," I lectured him. "I had a contingency designed to restore some of my strength in the event I lost."

"That?" he asked, raising one eyebrow as he glanced at the stone.

"I didn't have a lot of time," I said truthfully.

"A clever idea nonetheless," he said, complimenting me, "though it wasn't very effective."

"You saw the stone," I responded. "I didn't have much to work with."

If this ever happens again, you should do something like that, commented Brexus.

He was right of course. As so often happened, some of my brightest ideas only emerged when I was making things up. Lying seemed to inspire my creativity.

"You'll have to suffer for it, of course," said Mal'goroth coldly. "I haven't finished punishing you yet."

"You might want to reconsider," I told him calmly. "The last treatment nearly unhinged me. Do it again and I might not be able to help you." I tapped my skull with one finger.

"Help me?" he asked incredulously, and then he began to laugh.

The difference in our strength was beyond comparison. My offer seemed as ridiculous to him as if an ant had tried to offer assistance to the sun. His laughter rang out long and loud.

I didn't interrupt, preferring to wait for him to wind down. When he had finished, he stared at me again.

"What could I possibly have to gain from you that I have not already taken?" he asked.

"A way out," I answered.

"Of what?"

"This," I said, gesturing around me with my hands, "All of it."

His eyes flickered with anger, "You think to mock me? If there were any way to escape this eternal coil, your ancestor destroyed it along with the rest of the She'Har two thousand years ago."

"They have returned," I reminded him.

"Tennick was a human," said Mal'goroth, almost spitting in his irritation, "and the loshti that he stole was of the Illeniel grove. They knew nothing of my making."

I started to speak, but his will pinned me in place like an invisible hand.

"Do not mention Lyralliantha. She was an ignorant child. She could not possibly know the key to my binding." His rage was around me like a tangible force.

Unable to do much else, I lifted one eyebrow. After a moment he released me, curious even in his fury. "What?!"

"You assume I'm talking about your people. Yet you have not even considered human enchanting," I said, without an ounce of guile in my voice.

His gaze went to the stone I had tossed at him a minute before, indicating his train of thought to me without words. He was probably also remembering the battle we had just had, and I doubted anyone had ever frustrated him so completely for so long.

You're starting to wonder, aren't you? I guessed quietly.

Of course he is, said Brexus.

Don't interrupt, I told him quickly.

Sorry.

"If you are lying…" began my enemy threateningly.

"You'll carry on with torturing me for all eternity," I said impatiently. "You've mentioned that a few times now."

"How would you do this?" he asked, taken in by my offer.

Help me walk, I asked Brexus, and he graciously guided my legs as I rose to walk closer to Mal'goroth. Nothing would spoil my ruse as quickly as being so poorly coordinated that I fell taking a few steps.

Striding confidently toward him I replied, "I won't lie to you. I have an idea, but I cannot be sure it will work. Your spellweaving is far different from what I understand." It was probably the most honest thing I had told him thus far, but I counterbalanced the truth with a look of absolute confidence in my eyes.

He sneered, "You will fail."

"Then you have your other entertainments," I assured him.

"Try what you will," he ordered.

"You'll have to relax for a moment. Don't push me away," I cautioned. "I have to be able to see your core, the spellweave at the center."

Absolutely fearless, he let me close until we were face to face, and then his body opened, peeling away to display the place that held him bound, locked forever to an unwanted existence. Thousands of years had taught him nothing could affect it, and the very concept of true death drew him in a way that no living being could understand.

"If you succeed, the power within me will destroy the world," he said, leering. It was obviously a pleasant thought for him.

I had already considered that, though, "I am well aware." Reaching forward with my hand, I touched the spellweave that bound him and closed my eyes.

The biggest part of my lie had been that I would use enchanting. While it was likely possible to do what I had suggested, it would require the same knowledge that I lacked, namely the key. There would probably have been a host of other problems as well, but that wasn't my concern. I was using an entirely different ability.

With Penny's aythar and Brexus' assistance, I had temporarily regained the ability to perceive the world directly, and my perception was what truly made me an archmage. Opening my mind I listened to Mal'goroth, engrossing myself with his core essence in much the same way that I had done with Thillmarius.

That was the reason for my confidence. I had done this once before. It was the reason for my current condition.

The world faded around me as we resonated together. My soul changed for a moment matching his, and the two slid together while at the same time the spellweavings within us reacted and finally fused. For a split second we were a hybrid being, but then we were one.

An archmage does not use power; he becomes that which he seeks to use.

I had become my enemy, assuming his mantle and power. The aythar now at my command was inconceivable, but I had bigger problems. Just as before, the power strengthened the prison, and I lost contact with

473

the outer world. Mal'goroth and I separated again, and I was trapped, lost in a void of darkness within a dark god.

But Brexus was not.

A being of pure thought, a construct, like Mal'goroth in many respects, he existed as a function of the spellweave itself. As the two merged, he began to fight for control.

Their battle went on for what seemed to be ages for them, but in the exterior world it finished in the blink of an eye. I heard Brexus' voice ring out as he spoke commandingly to my friends.

"Reveal yourselves," he ordered. "There is little time." My alter-ego sounded different now, more pompous. He had probably picked up a lot of our enemy's mannerisms.

I liked to think that I knew he would win, but I hadn't been certain. My only reassurance had been that if Brexus was truly like me, he had to be far smarter than Mal'goroth. It had probably been an arrogant assumption, but sometimes it was all that I had to work with.

Gareth and the others didn't appear. They were far too sensible to come out of hiding simply because Mal'goroth had told them to.

Brexus was in no mood to wait, however. Shouting the words that commanded their bindings, he called Millicenth and Doron to him. Walter's shield hadn't been made to stop sound, and soon enough they were stepping forward. The two wizards and Penny stayed hidden, though.

My isolation was complete now.

The effect of over forty Celiors of aythar on the spellweave that contained me had been to make it impregnable. My only source of information now was that allowed to me by listening directly to Brexus' thoughts. I wasn't sure if he could hear mine in return either.

Nor was I sure he was reliable.

He had surprised me before, with Penny, demonstrating that he was almost as much 'me', as I was. Now though, I couldn't be sure. My merger with Mal'goroth had nearly destroyed my identity. If not for the re-establishment of my magical prison, I was worried I might have been more *him* than me.

Brexus had taken the blow for me in a sense. He actually *was* the spellweave that imprisoned me, just as Mal'goroth had been the one that had created him originally. Now that the two had merged...

I was a bit worried.

Throwing his head back, Brexus/Mal'goroth screamed at the heavens, "I am ALIVE, Mordecai. Deliver on your promise, or I will make good on mine!"

Flanked by Doron and Millicenth, who were now bound to obedience, I couldn't help but believe him.

In his mind Brexus responded to a question from Millicenth. She was confused by his actions somehow.

"I am feeding you my power," he told them. "You will keep it in my stead, until I call for it again. If I am still alive after an hour, or if I cannot call for it, you will use it to bring an end to this world. Do you understand?"

A second later I heard the memory of her response, although I couldn't hear her directly. "I would love nothing better," she had replied with a chilling tone.

Doron's response was even more enthusiastic.

Since binding the Shining Gods to my will, it had been almost easy to forget their true motivations. They had been created as slaves, and they hated humankind for it. Like Mal'goroth, the only thing they truly desired, more than an end, was revenge. Having experienced the world from their perspective, I couldn't really blame them.

What are you waiting for, Peter? I wondered. *Kill me.*

I did all I could, came Brexus' thought, directed at me now.

Are you still in control? I asked.

Destroy us, or we will destroy everything else, was his only reply.

Chapter 46

It had been over an hour since they had closed the door leading from the hidden sanctuary to Cameron Castle. Initially there had been a lot of confusion when it was discovered that several key people were missing. An argument had begun over whether or not to hold the door and wait.

No one had thought to ask George about it, for which he had been grateful, but eventually he had been forced to reveal what he knew, to keep them from searching for the missing Countess and his father.

Rather than share his information with his family, George told only Ariadne, allowing her to make the decision privately. She had had the door closed immediately, and then she had shared the news he had given her.

As per his prediction, his sister, Elaine, had reacted badly to the revelation. She might have gone in search of her father, but for the door being closed and barred already.

Currently neither she, nor her mother, were speaking to George, but he bore it with his customary stoicism.

Meanwhile, the others had spread out around the house. While it was spacious it was nowhere near large enough to hold several hundred people. Thankfully it wasn't far up, having been situated in the middle part of a secluded mountain valley, so the temperatures, even in the fall, were moderate.

Even so, there would soon be a desperate need for housing. Ariadne already had the soldiers gathering firewood and considering their options for building temporary shelters.

Peter Tucker sat in the cold mountain air behind the secret home that Mordecai and Penny Illeniel had maintained for years. Seeing it had been a revelation to him. The simple fact that they had been able to keep it completely hidden, even from his eyes, troubled him.

When he had first taken service at Castle Cameron, they had shown him trust and kindness. At the time he had thought it was simply in their nature, but now he knew they had done it in spite of his murderous intent. He had hated the Count di' Cameron intensely then.

Over time he had been given greater responsibilities. Lilly had begun to help them care for their children, who, despite his own prejudices, he had come to love. He had told himself that he worked to gain their trust, so that someday he would be in a position to avenge his grandfather, but eventually he had given up on it.

As his youthful temper had mellowed, so had his memories. His grandfather had been kind, and Peter had always known he would have disapproved of his plan. Without remembering the exact moment, he had at some point become what he pretended to be, a loyal servant, a friend—even family.

,The hidden house in the mountains challenged that somewhat, though. He had thought himself privy to all of their greatest secrets—trusted above all others.

They knew all along, but they held you close anyway. Why?

He had once heard someone recite a wise man's quote, 'Keep your friends close, and your enemies closer.'

Was that what he was, a closely held enemy?

He stared at the knife in his lap.

"Are things that dark?" asked a woman's voice.

Glancing back, he was startled by Lady Rose Thornbear's nearness. He had not heard her steps approaching.

"No, my lady! Forgive me," he protested. "I was only thinking. This is not what it might appear." Lady Rose had hardly spoken to anyone other than her children and her mother-in-law since her husband's death. Peter was curious as to why she had approached him now.

"If you have no use for it, then pass it over," she told him, taking a seat on the stone beside him.

He was shocked by her statement. Dumbfounded, he moved the blade farther from her, and then he found his voice, "You could not possibly...," he began.

Lady Rose shook her head, but didn't smile. "No, I couldn't, but my joke was a truthful glimpse of my heart's despair."

Peter's heart went out to her, forgetting his own turmoil for a moment. "Lady Rose, please believe me when I tell you how much I hate what has happened to you and your family."

Her face became a mask, and her emotions seemed to vanish. Peter knew he had said the wrong thing somehow, but he was helpless to understand what it had been.

Rising to her feet, she gave him a polite expression, "Thank you, Peter. I appreciate your condolences." Then she started to turn away.

Unsure of himself, Peter called to her before she could leave, "Lady Rose?"

She stopped and looked back, "Yes?"

"Why did you want to talk to me, honestly?" His words were too direct, and he knew if she took offense now, it would have been because he had stepped beyond his place.

"I thought you were like me, for a moment," she admitted. "You looked more wretched than anyone else here."

Casting his eyes downward, he admitted it, "It may be that you were right,"

She resumed her perch beside him, almost smiling now. "Misery loves company," she noted. "Tell me what it is?"

"The Count and Countess," he began, and then without fully intending to, he recounted his story. He started with his grandfather, including the story of his early employment and the reason he had taken it. Lady Rose had been the one who originally arranged for him to take service with the Cameron Estate, so it lifted some of his guilt to confess his true reason.

Throughout his confession Rose listened quietly, a skill that she was known for. She didn't reveal that she had also known of his true motivations at the time, or her part in Mordecai's scheme to save the Tucker's from poverty. She simply listened and accepted.

He told her everything, including his new doubt in the trust that Penny and Mort had for him, since discovering their greater secret. He stopped short only of telling her about Mordecai's last request.

"So what did he want?" she asked, when he mentioned speaking to the Count.

"He wanted to give me a task," replied the chamberlain vaguely.

After a short pause she asked, "Are you going to tell me what it was?"

"I am not at liberty to say," he answered, ending his former forthrightness.

Rose sighed, "Probably another of those shoulder crushing burdens, I imagine. 'Take care of them!' No, don't tell me."

He was puzzled by her response.

"It doesn't matter what it was," she said reassuringly, "just the fact of it. That's what counts."

"I don't understand," said Peter.

She gave him her first genuine smile, "Neither do I, but I can tell you a few things about your good Count."

Despite himself Peter was enraptured by the thought of Lady Rose sharing her insights. He leaned in, letting his expression convey his interest.

"Mordecai loves secrets. The man simply can't help himself. Not when he was alive, and not even after his death. Since I've known him, it has been nothing but one after another," she announced.

"He has always been a complex man," said Peter seriously.

Rose shook her head in disagreement, "No, he's as simple as they come. Sometimes he was as simple as my own husband. Brilliant, clever, smarter than anyone I've ever known in some regards, but Mordecai was simple in his emotions, in his heart."

Peter's brow wrinkled.

"The secrets were his attempt to make up for it. He would lie and bluff, cheat and steal, all to cover his plans, but his goal was easy to see," she declared.

"Steal?!"

"He picked up a lot of bad habits from Marcus," said Rose. "But that's not what's important."

Peter had already lost the point of her story, "What was it?"

"This house," she explained in a tone as if it were self-evident. "That and the fact that you just discovered they knew about your plan for revenge all along—secrets!"

"Alright..."

"Mordecai would have kept the location of this house from Penny if he could have managed it," she told him. "In fact, if it were possible, he would have made her *think* it was actually their apartments in the castle."

"That's insane."

"No, that's Mordecai," she answered, warming to her subject again. "He loved simply, but the things he encountered, the enemies he made—they made him very cautious. Anything you didn't know, couldn't be stolen from your mind and used against him, or more importantly, against his family."

"That's a bit extreme," suggested Peter.

Rose clucked her tongue at him. "Think about Walter Prathion. You know his story. Mort was hell bent on making certain he never faced something like that again."

"That just reinforces the fact that he never really trusted me," pointed out Peter.

Like a logician, Rose circled him with her argument. "No, it merely discounts the fact that these secrets indicated distrust. The fact is that he *did* trust you. He loved you, in fact."

"Where is the reasoning for that?"

"Are you fond of Matthew?" she asked suddenly, "or what of his daughter, Moira? What does little Conall think of you?"

Having spent countless hours with them, Peter loved all four of Mordecai's children. He also knew that they felt the same. "I care deeply about them, and I'm sure they're very fond of me, of course, but they're children. They know nothing of guile."

"A brave man might put his back to an assassin, or let him carry a knife in his presence, but he would never leave him alone with his children. More so, he would not let his children grow to love and trust such a villain."

Peter was struck by the clarity of her insight. He sat still for a moment considering her words.

Rose started to leave again. "Thank you," she said.

"For what?"

The smile she gave him was sad, but it was less so than before. "For being miserable and for sharing it with me."

"Wait," he protested.

"Yes?"

"I still don't know what to do," confessed Peter.

She looked at him wisely, "How should I know?"

"But you seem to understand everything so well…"

"Losing my husband has taught me humility. I know less than nothing," she countered. "I just thought you should make your decision based on the truth rather than your doubts. Mordecai trusts you. He asked you to do something, probably something difficult. It's your choice whether you do or don't."

"What if it could affect all of us?" asked Peter.

"Everything involving that man affects all of us. My own grief is too great to worry about it anymore." With that she withdrew, leaving him alone with his thoughts again.

Holding the knife up at eye level, Peter stared at the green stone imbedded in its pommel. *Do I dare kill the man I've served and loved all these years? Will I still have a place here? Penelope would never forgive it.*

He shook his head, as if to knock something loose inside. *I'm being selfish. I'm afraid of losing my new family, when I should be thinking of what I can do to help them—what he wants me to do. My personal consequences should be secondary.*

Lifting the blade into the air he held the pommel downward in his fist, toward the stone he sat on. He thought of his grandfather, who would have never approved of his old dream of vengeance, but this was different, this was a mercy.

"I'm sorry grandfather," he said softly, and tensing his arm, he brought the knife down with all the strength he could muster.

Chapter 47

Too much time had passed.

Since our merger, we only had one body now, my old beat up corpse. Brexus/Mal'goroth had transferred almost all of our power to Millicenth and Doron. I was sure that Mal'goroth alone would have kept it, hoping to annihilate the world when he was unmade, but my demon twin seemed to have kept them on the path I had plotted.

When I died the world would go on.

Gareth had been given the knowledge to control the Shining Gods, and I trusted that he would do the right thing. He had been the one urging me to rethink my harsh methods all along. The ex-dragon would find a way to store their power, and then he would free them from their unwanted immortality.

All of this hinged on Peter doing what I had asked, and with each passing minute the hybrid being I was trapped within grew more anxious, more agitated, and angrier.

At least he didn't do it as soon as I had asked him to, I thought. If he had followed my original instructions, my existence would have ended shortly after Mal'goroth had stripped me of my power. That would have prevented *me* from destroying the world at least, but it would have left them with an enraged Mal'goroth to deal with.

This way was much better—if Peter would just do his part.

What if he reclaims the power and Peter does it afterward?

Brexus/Mal'goroth heard my thought, and I could feel his inner smile. There wouldn't be enough of our world left to bother with in that eventuality.

I could feel the Dark God's decision forming, to do just that, when it happened.

I felt a snapping, as though a string had been under tension and suddenly broken, and then the spellweave that surrounded me began to unravel. I was disconnected, no longer tied to anything, especially my long dead body.

In my mind's eye I could see Brexus, or Mal'goroth, I wasn't sure what to call him anymore. He radiated a sense of amazement and wonder as he began to fray and disintegrate around the edges.

I loved her as much as you did, came one last thought, and I knew the message came from Brexus.

He faded from sight, and I drifted in the darkness. My soul was free at last, and the void called. I felt no fear, for I had been here once before, with Walter. At that time I had been struggling desperately to pull him back from the final crossing, to keep him anchored until I could heal his body.

My body was far too long dead for something like that. Even if there had been someone to catch me. This was better.

I couldn't guess what lay before me, but I suspected that our world lay atop another. After learning to hear the voice of death, I had later theorized that it was another form of aythar, simply with a reversed time dimension. The other world would have a negative entropy, counterbalancing our own. Death there might be a rebirth here.

Or I could be completely mistaken. There was no way to get a glimpse beyond the veil, even though I had been closer than most. It was a one way trip.

It made sense mathematically though, I told myself, grinning mentally. Even on the way to the great beyond, I couldn't stop pondering wild ideas.

A rushing sound approached, and I knew it was the boundary—the final crossing. My mind presented it to me as a waterfall, but I knew at a deeper level that it had no physical form.

Mordecai!

The shout came from someone else. It felt familiar.

Mordecai!

It was Walter. Like a golden lamp, he lit the darkness around him, shining like some kindly spirit. He was a beacon and a comfort to me. I tried to move toward him, but it was impossible to do. I had no strength left.

I fought to stay still, and he grew closer, pushing himself to meet me, since I couldn't reach him.

You shouldn't be here, I told him. *You know what this is.*

His light enveloped me, pushing back the cold emptiness.

You won't be able to make it back, I warned, although it was already too late. *It's too hard, you aren't strong enough.*

Shut up, was his only reply.

He held onto me with everything he had, and then we began to move, drawn on what seemed to be a golden rope, back toward the world I had thought lost for good.

As we got closer, my perception sharpened, and I realized it was Millicenth that was helping him, feeding him a steady stream of aythar to bolster his strength and lead him back.

I don't want to go back to that body, I told him, remembering my corpse. *Let me die instead.*

Don't worry. Your body is completely impossible, he explained. *Mine will have to suffice.*

I liked the sound of that even less. I had been through the shared body situation for far too long. I was tired of having a roommate. Plus, Walter was really old.

I don't want to be a decrepit old man! I protested. *What will Penny think of me?*

I have a wife too, you know, he reminded me.

So which one would we be married to? Both? I asked. Mentally I imagined being with Walter's wife, Rebecca. She wasn't an ugly woman by far, but…

Really? I bring you back from the brink, and the first thing you do is start fantasizing about my marriage bed?! Have you no shame?

In truth I hadn't been thinking positively about it, but I didn't want to hurt his feelings. Instead I took the misunderstanding further. *And you wouldn't enjoy a chance to roll around with Penny?!* I accused.

Wherever Walter's physical face was, I knew it had to be turning red now. The man had always been easily embarrassed. I could sense him floundering emotionally. He nearly lost his hold on me for a moment, which would have sent me drifting back into the void.

You really are as stupid as the Countess claims! he rebuked me.

Just wait 'til we've been stuck together inside your bald skull for a year, I threatened, *you'll start to wonder what you ever needed all those extra brains for after all.*

Oh. His thought seemed strangely subdued, as if he had just realized something.

Taking a more serious tack I addressed him again, *I appreciate this, Walter. I know how hard it was to go where you did, to find me, but this isn't a good idea. Let me go.*

Another mind intruded then. Gareth Gaelyn's words echoed around us, as if he were yelling across a great divide. *I'm ready.*

Time to go, Walter told me. *I'm tired of having you in here already.* With that he released me, and began to push me away.

Some friend he was.

Another will was at work beside him, pulling in tandem with his shoves, and together they forced me into another body, one that felt younger, more vital. The heart was beating powerfully, thrumming around me and I began to settle in almost automatically.

Gareth was there with me, but his mind began to retract almost as soon as I had joined him. Sudden anxiety seized me as I wondered if he were committing suicide. I could tell already, the body I occupied now was his, right down to the red hair on its chin.

Relax, he told me. *Accept the gift. You'll understand soon.*

My first reaction was automatic sarcasm, but I suppressed it rather than complain about not wanting to be a red head. Besides, from what I could tell, he was evicting himself, and that was something I couldn't understand.

Weariness overwhelmed me as I rejoined the physical world again. The body was strong, but my soul was exhausted in a manner that few could understand. Darkness closed around me, and for the first time in over a year, I slept.

*
**

I woke in a familiar place.

Staring up at the ceiling I let my senses range wide. The sense of freedom that gave me was like a breath of fresh air. My magesight brought it all to me; Castle Cameron surrounded me like a dear friend. After so long trapped within my magical cage I could feel the world directly. My body was alive, warm, and full of energy. I was lying in one of the guest bedrooms.

The earth was rumbling deep below, and the stones in the walls sang softly. I could feel! Smell and taste were there as well, though mostly as a reminder that I needed to clean my new body's mouth. My breath was undoubtedly atrocious.

The scent next to me was deeply comforting, in a way that few things are. Bringing myself into tighter focus, I examined the woman lying next to me.

Penny was sleeping there. Her body was cold, as if she had taken a chill, but she still breathed, and her heart was beating slowly. She looked as if she had been brought in from a battlefield. She wore leather and a padded gambeson that smelled of iron and sweat. The chainmail that had gone over that had been removed at least, so I was grateful for that.

Touching her cheek, I felt tears start in my eyes. "Why didn't someone take those filthy clothes off of you?" I wondered softly. The room was empty, so I was speaking only for myself, but the voice surprised me. It was Gareth Gaelyn's.

Sitting up, I saw my reflection in the mirror across from the foot of the bed. A shaggy red beard and wild mane of hair greeted my eyes. *Sonofabitch!* I thought. *He really did it.*

Despite my shock, I was humbled by the ex-dragon's gift. The thought of living with a different face bothered me more than I would have expected, but the understanding of his sacrifice made me ashamed of my earlier complaints. *I can't believe he did this.*

My magesight had already told me one odd fact. The only other human within a mile of us, was Walter Prathion. He was sleeping next door in the room beside this one. *That's the room he and Rebecca usually stay in when they visit,* I noted absently. *Why am I in a guest bed?*

"Penny," I said softly, hoping she would wake. She didn't. Thinking back I already knew why. I had nearly killed her.

While her body was unharmed, I had drawn upon her aythar until she had come close to dying. It would be days, if not weeks before she recovered fully from that. She might not regain consciousness for some time.

As gently as I could, I removed her clothes, noting the bruises and scrapes that adorned her body. Using my magic, I brought water from the upstairs cistern, and lacking a bucket or bowl I just left it suspended in the air while I warmed it to a comfortable temperature. Once it was ready, I used it to carefully wash her body and hair, encouraging the dirt to join the water when it was reluctant to be parted from her.

I couldn't blame it. If I was that stain on her chin, I'd want to stay there forever too.

Maybe not that dried mucus though, that's just disgusting. I remembered her face before I had drained her. It wasn't surprising she still had a crusty nose.

Finished with her impromptu bath, I sent the water out a small window while I kept the air warm around her as she dried. Clean and cozy in the bed now, her body was still cool to the touch. It was having trouble producing enough heat.

More tired than hungry, I got out of my own strangely clean clothes and climbed back into bed with her. I wrapped her in my arms and drew her close, until her back was smooth against my somewhat hirsute chest.

Damn, Gareth really was a hairy bastard, I thought to myself. Without much further consideration, I drifted to sleep again.

Chapter 48

My next wakening was less pleasant.

It was morning this time, which was usually a bad sign, but it was the bone crushing pain in my wrist that really set the tone.

"Ow, ow, ow...!" I began yelping reflexively. "You're going to break it!" Penny had my hand bent at an angle that threatened to cause serious damage. It wasn't the threatening sort of pressure either, it was the sort of pressure you applied when you *wanted* to break the wrist. She had just been kind enough to give me a moment to wake up first.

"Get it away from me," she ordered fiercely.

I immediately understood. It was morning, and my new lower half had risen before me, as it usually did. At the moment it was pressed against something warm and soft, namely, her.

Rather than try to explain, I squirmed rapidly to create some distance between her and all the parts of me that weren't being broken yet. She didn't release my wrist, but she did ease the pressure slightly, so that I wasn't in immediate danger.

"If you have an explanation for this Gareth, you should make it quickly," she warned. She spoke through clenched jaws, and her tone was one I had rarely heard, except on the rare occasions when she was killing people.

"I do," I blurted out, "but it will take some time to tell." As I spoke I noticed how clammy her skin was. Although she was awake her color was pallid, and there was a tremor in her shoulders. She was probably as sick and weak as she had ever been, and she had awoken to find Gareth holding her. She had made an obvious leap of logic.

Despite the pain I was still in, I felt terrible for frightening her. "How much do you remember?" I asked.

The pain in my arm went up sharply, "That doesn't sound like an explanation."

I had no easy answer. I didn't want to use magic against her. That would only make things worse. As a compromise, I used a silent spell to block the nerves leading to my arm. That way I could at least think clearly, and it had the added advantage of leaving her with a feeling of control. I couldn't think of much worse than having awakened half dead and thinking she had been violated while she was helpless.

That's love for you. I figured in the worst case scenario I could probably heal whatever damage she did later.

"I'm not Gareth Gaelyn," I said carefully, continuing to feign helplessness.

Her body tensed so I squirmed as if in pain. She followed by stating, "Lie to me again, and I'll break it."

"This used to be his body," I told her. "I was dead, but somehow he and Walter saved me."

She froze, staring at me with eyes that didn't dare to hope. It made me want to cry to see her so vulnerable. "That's too cruel. You can't say that. No one could say something so terrible," she replied, her face showing

494

clearly the storm winds that were blowing her heartstrings back and forth.

"Only you, Penny, I've never loved another—only you," I said, rephrasing what she had said to me at the end.

She began crying then, so I joined her. Just to be companionable of course, no one likes to cry alone.

After a bit she relaxed and let me hold her with my one good arm. I still couldn't feel the other one. I tried to kiss her, but she turned her head. "No."

That hurt, but I tried to hide it.

"It's your face," she said, seeing the pain in my eyes. "It feels like I'm doing something wrong."

"I really am Mordecai," I assured her.

"That's not his face," she repeated. "The beard, the eyes, they're different—even your voice."

"I'm sorry." In front of me I realized, we had a whole minefield of strange body issues to sort out. *Maybe if I use illusions so that I look and sound like myself...*

She kissed me without warning. It was quick and awkward and still wonderful. I could tell she was trying to avoid the beard, though. My own had been short and well-kept, but Gareth's was a red wilderness of danger. "We'll figure this out," she told me.

The kissing had done wonderful things for my—state of—mind, but I pulled away from her. The rest could wait. She was far too ill for me to let her go further. "I'll get you something to eat," I said instead. In truth, I was starving as well.

Rising from the bed I tried to dress, but my arm was still out of operation.

"I didn't do that," said Penny.

I explained the paralysis while I restored the nerves. For some reason she thought that was hilarious. The wrist was still pretty sore when the sensation returned.

Dressing quickly, I found Walter in the kitchen, already tending a pot. It smelled like ham and peas with a mixture of spices. I hadn't expected him to be a good cook, but then considering his many years away from his wife and family...

"You look good in an apron," I told him.

He looked up from his pot, "You look good breathing."

"You probably tell all the redheads that." We both laughed then.

"How is she?" he asked after a minute.

"Unwell," I admitted. "I nearly killed her before..."

"That was as much her fault as yours," said Walter as he tasted his handiwork. "Your wife is only marginally brighter than you are at times, and twice as stubborn."

"We're well matched," I agreed. "I want to thank you again. You risked everything for me."

He kept his eyes on his pot. "We've been through too much to start getting sentimental this early in the day," he answered in a slightly gruff voice.

I agreed with him there, so I changed the subject, "Why did you put us in one of the guest rooms?"

"We couldn't get to your 'other' home," he replied with a faint tinge of frustration in his voice. "When we opened the door, it just led into your false living quarters."

That aside, our 'false' living quarters were still quite comfortable and did in fact hold a lot of personal items such as some of our clothing. "I'm surprised you didn't just use that room, though."

"I preferred to have you in a room closer by, in case either of you needed me," he said, passing me a platter with two large bowls of steaming soup.

Once again I was reminded of how surprisingly kind Walter could be. Some had faulted him in the past for his excessive caution, myself included, but he was a complex man. The truth was, his courage had never failed me when it really counted and his ability to care and nurture those around him had always been an example for me to follow.

A new presence gave me pause; a flier, closing on the castle. Adjusting my focus I examined the newcomer. It wasn't one of the gods. It appeared to be an eagle, but its aythar was far too powerful. It shone with a radiance that could only indicate a wizard, and the feel of it was familiar. I turned to Walter, "You said 'we' a moment ago…"

He nodded, "Gareth should be back soon." The eagle still hadn't gotten within his range.

I gave him a quizzical look, "But…?" Unable to find the words I set the platter back down and waved my hands across my body.

Now it was his turn to look puzzled. "What? You thought that—oh!" He began laughing then, which annoyed me to no end. "Wait 'til I tell him!"

"I really don't think this is amusing," I protested. "I thought the man was dead!"

"You didn't seem too sad about it," he noted, before adding in a mock tone, "'You probably tell all the redheads that'."

"I'd already been through all the emotional turmoil I could handle in one morning!" I said in exasperation.

Walter's eyes flicked to one side then as he sensed Gareth's arrival. "Well, you can rest easy. He's alive and well." Glancing around in a conspiratorial way, he lowered his voice and added, "And still as difficult as ever to deal with. Just between us, I'm starting to think his aloofness is a normal part of him."

"I always figured it was a part of the dragon-nature he had taken on," I commented.

"Me too," said Walter. "But he's completely human now, and yet he's still pretty stiff."

The eagle transformed into the redheaded archmage in the courtyard. It was graceful the way he did it, shifting just before his talons reached the ground. He went from flying to walking on booted feet as easily as I might have removed my coat on entering a house. *That would be the Gaelyn gift, I suppose.*

A couple of minutes later he walked in and greeted us, giving me an odd look at the same time.

"I feel the same way when I see you," I told him dryly.

Walking closer he lifted one hand to adjust a stray bit of my hair. "You look good," he said approvingly, "but you need to pay better attention to your grooming. A beard like that is a blessing; you should treat it as one." His face was solemn.

"Penny nearly broke my arm when she woke and thought it was you in bed with her," I informed him sourly.

That made him chuckle slightly. "It's a wonder you have survived marriage so long. I had thought her a stubborn woman, but now I see she must have a great deal of patience."

"Patience?!"

"To put up with your shenanigans," he said, as if that clarified things for me.

Irritated, I glared at him, "Look, I had only woken up once before she did. There were no shenanigans. She's quite ill and all of this...," I gestured to indicate my face, "...was very upsetting for her."

Gareth took one of the bowls from the platter I had placed nearby. Collecting a spoon he walked past me. "Then you should have changed it," he suggested.

I stared at him, flabbergasted, while he stuffed a large spoonful of Walter's soup into his mouth. My brain had seized up, so my mouth kindly helped out by turning out phrases without consulting it. "That was for Penny," I said.

"No, that one was," he said pointing at the tray. "Since you like wearing my face I could just take both of them up to her for you. Is that what you're suggesting?"

I briefly considered flinging the other bowl of soup at him, but my poor brain finally sorted through what he had meant. "Oh!" *I'm a damned idiot!* There's one transformation that any archmage has to know. Whether you are speaking to the wind or the earth, whether you change your flesh or mind, the one transformation that always has to occur is the return to yourself.

In the past I had always begun as 'me', and while Moira Centyr had once taught me that I could modify that deliberately, I hadn't taken the time this morning to think it through. Gareth had given me a copy of his body, but it certainly didn't have to remain that way.

Walter had already filled another bowl and replaced the one on my tray that Gareth had taken. I could see the mirth in his eyes. "You could have reminded me sooner," I complained.

"I am neither an archmage nor a Gaelyn wizard. My body stays pure and undefiled. I have no idea what shape shifters are capable of," he said honestly. "You should take the soup up to her before it gets cold," he suggested.

I ignored him for a few minutes. Leaving the tray where it was, I closed my eyes and turned my attention inward, remembering myself as I had been. I listened, not to the outer world, but to the voice of my flesh, joining its song to my conscious awareness—and then I changed. My self-image faltered for a moment as a vivid memory of my dead body flickered through my mind. My heart stopped, and the world grew dim for a second, but I recovered quickly, returning to the image of myself as I had been a year ago. Opening my eyes at last, I stared at Gareth.

His eyes had a hint of alarm in them. He had probably noticed my near mistake. If I hadn't corrected it before it had taken hold, I'd have died again. *That would have been annoying,* I thought. *I wonder if they would have tried to save me a second time.*

"You should have kept the beard," he advised me, returning his attention to his soup.

I crossed my eyes and twisted my face into a goofy expression, "I don't need to cover it all up now that I don't look like this anymore."

Walter snorted and Gareth chuckled. I left then, heading for the door. I couldn't wait to show Penny my good news.

"I hope she isn't too disappointed when she sees how he looks now," said Gareth to Walter, just loudly enough for me to hear. "It'll probably be hard for her to get over the letdown."

Chapter 49

Another day of Walter's cooking, and a lot of rest helped considerably. I was still wounded inside, in ways I hadn't even dared to look at yet, but I had too much to do to let myself fall apart.

Penny was worse physically, but her spirits were high. I hoped she would emerge from all of it without as much mental scarring as I would likely have, but there was no way to compare. Human beings simply aren't meant to survive the things we had.

The empty castle was a strange experience. Never in all the years that we had lived there, had it been so quiet. Mal'goroth had destroyed the shield around it after... what he had done to me, but he hadn't done any real harm to it after that. It had been the people he wanted to punish, not the buildings.

Once Penny had gone back to sleep, I went with Walter and Gareth to open the door to my hidden home. It was locked from the inside, but I was able to show them how to get the attention of the door guard. Walter and Gareth hadn't realized before that, while a stranger couldn't open the door, knocking could be heard by the occupants. The portal was active so long as the door was closed and wasn't *opened* by the wrong person. Otherwise we'd have been unable to respond to messengers and such.

The reunions that followed were joyful.

Walter's wife was nearly inconsolable. I might have thought he had died when she saw him, but I didn't have time to worry about them. My own children were awake, and they had been without either of us for the past day.

The refugees wasted no time returning to Castle Cameron. Camping in the mountains was far less desirable than what I had to offer there.

I kept Penny's location a secret. She didn't need to be bothered. Not by anyone, whether it was a small matter or a concern of the Queen. As soon as our home was empty, I took her quietly and installed her comfortably in our bedroom.

Lilly and Rose had been caring for our children, a kindness that I loved them for. That's how you know who your family is, truthfully. I spent a long time with the children that first day, to the exclusion of everyone but Penny. Irene hadn't noticed my absence of course, but little Conall had. He stared at me constantly and seemed hesitant to let me out of his sight. I took to carrying him around, as much for my own comfort as his.

Moira cried and clung to me when she first saw me, but she recovered faster than the others, outwardly at least. I knew she would grow up to be a strong woman someday. Her personality was comprised of some of the best parts of Penny and me, and the end result was a resilient, intelligent girl who might wind up more like Rose than either of her willful parents.

Matthew wasn't bashful, but he didn't cry when he saw me. I think he wanted to protect me somehow, to avoid letting me see how much he had been hurting. I held him as long as I could, and days later, when it was just the two of us, he finally broke down. When all was said and done, I suspected my 'death' had been hardest on him.

Once we were reunited, I evicted everyone but Lilly Tucker. I asked the Thornbears to stay with us as well, but Rose declined. I suspected that it was my return that influenced her decision. I knew she considered us family, but she had only recently lost Dorian. While that hurt all of us, I couldn't imagine what it must be doing to her to see Penny and me together again.

Their roles had been reversed. Our family was whole once more, while Rose had become the widow. That's the true horror of losing a spouse, being alone. Sometimes the very people who care for you the most cause the greatest pain, reminding you constantly of what you've lost. We wanted nothing more than to help her, but our good fortune only pained her more.

I put Peter in charge of the castle itself and told Walter, the Baron of Arundel, to act in my stead in everything else. Despite some initial objections, I closed the door to our home and the Illeniels isolated themselves from the world.

⁎

A day later, Peter was knocking.

"The Queen is asking for you," he informed me when I answered it (I had ignored everyone else who came to the door).

"And?"

"The World Road isn't functioning," he replied.

I hadn't thought about it, but that made sense. When Mal'goroth had destroyed the shield around Castle Cameron, the feedback would have shattered the God-Stone, which was where the power that fed the portals was stored. It also meant Celior was on the loose somewhere.

"Too bad," I told him.

"But…!"

"One of the Prathions can provide transportation if that's all she needs. The repairs can wait until I get around to it," I assured him.

Peter frowned. "My lord, I realize you are busy, but the capital is in shambles. The Queen will need your assistance during the reorganization…"

I cut him off, "I don't give a damn."

His expression went blank.

"I don't give a damn," I repeated. "The capital, the world, and all the rest of it, can go to hell. My wife is sick, and my younger daughter needs to be changed." As I spoke I could hear Irene crying in the background.

"Isn't Lilly there?" he reminded me. "Surely she can handle it."

I scowled at him, "Your sister is busy cooking dinner. I'll look after Irene myself."

He started to speak, but I put a finger over his lips.

"Because I want to," I clarified. "More than anything else."

Although he was intelligent in many ways, Peter still didn't get it. "I understand wanting to see your family, but you have priorities, my lord, duties and obligations."

"I was dead for a year, trapped inside a monster. I've already saved the world, Peter. It can do without me for a while. I know what my priorities are, and they aren't out there," and then I closed the door.

"There could be a civil war!" he shouted through the door.

"Our young Queen is stronger than you realize," I answered back. "I'll come out in a few weeks, maybe. If anyone has the poor taste to try to depose her before then—well I feel sorry for them."

I walked away from the door, but after a minute I changed my mind and went back to it. Opening it, I found my chamberlain still standing there. His expression became hopeful.

I hugged him, which made him stiffen immediately. Embraces were strictly not part of normal lord-servant relations. "Thank you, Peter," I said. "You saved me a few days ago and the rest of the world too."

"You're welcome, my lord," he intoned sincerely, his voice was muffled by my chest. I hadn't let him loose yet. "Does this mean you will see the Queen?"

"Nope," I replied, and pushing him away, I shut the door on him again.

Penny was sitting by the fire. She was still having trouble staying warm. "Who was at the door?" she asked me.

"Just Peter," I said.

"What did he want?"

"He just needed my approval to deal with a few minor things," I said mildly, winking at her.

She gave me a suspicious look, but didn't say anything.

"It can wait," I told her. "The world will survive without us for a few weeks."

Slipping her hand into mine, she nodded. I sat down beside her, and she leaned into me. It scared me to feel how cold she was. Irene began crying once more. I still hadn't taken care of her.

"You better get that," said Penny with a wan smile.

***

That night, after dinner, Penny went to sleep early. She had been doing that every evening, as well as napping frequently during the day. Her strength still hadn't returned, and she had begun to develop a cough. I worried that an illness might take her before she recovered.

"Dad?" said Matthew as we sat in the parlor. We were watching Conall play a new game he had invented involving two sticks and some rocks. It made no sense, but he enjoyed it anyway.

"Yes?"

"Is Mom dying?" he said with his customary directness.

"No," I said immediately, putting all the confidence I didn't have in my voice. "She's just weak because she gave me too much of her aythar, her energy."

"You said that the same thing happened to you though, right?" he asked. I had given the children an abbreviated version of the ordeal, but I had kept the descriptions less vivid.

"You mean when Mal'goroth took my power?"

He nodded.

I took a deep breath. "That was different. He was drawing the aythar that my magical construct had gathered. My 'source' was still protected, isolated, within the magical cage. Your mother gave me the aythar from her wellspring, from the place that keeps us alive. Does that make sense?"

He nodded again. "She'll get better?"

"She will." I hoped she would. Sometimes when the flame of life is drawn down too far, it sputters and goes out. Hers was guttering, too close to the edge of having been extinguished to immediately restore itself. All I could do, much like a man husbanding a newly lit fire in a frozen wilderness, was to shield it from the wind and keep offering fresh tinder.

The twins were able to sense what I was doing, hence their concern. Since returning with Penny, I had kept a constant light shield around her. When she slept, I stayed close, warming her not only with physical contact but a tiny flow of aythar. I wanted to give her more, but I had learned a bit from my studies before and after Marcus had died. Much like the fire in my analogy, forcing too much on her could overwhelm her and ultimately produce the opposite effect.

I thought she would recover, but it was far from certain, and only time would tell. Until she did, I wasn't going anywhere.

*
**

Another two weeks passed without much change. I spent some of my free time, while Penny was convalescing, examining the wilderness around our isolated cottage. The brief visit by several hundred refugees had done considerable damage to the forest. Some trees had been cut, and a lot of underbrush removed to make lean-tos and other temporary structures.

Not that I blamed them. If you're in the woods with your family, you do whatever is necessary to stay warm and dry. The twins and I explored, removing some of the deadwood and cleaning up the damaged areas. An amazing amount of refuse had been left behind as well. Some of that we burned, and other portions we buried.

Naturally we used magic to do this, and I enjoyed the opportunity to see my children learning how to use their abilities. Moira's magic hadn't manifested until my unfortunate transformation, and Matthew's had come even later. This was my first chance to see them at work, and I found it fascinating.

Walter had taught Moira some of what she needed to know, but her knowledge was still very limited. Clearing brush, turning logs into firewood, and eliminating trash— rather than being annoying tasks had become a special way for us to restore our bond. I began teaching them the Lycian vocabulary, offering advice, and showing them my preferences for how to do these things.

What amazed me most was the agility of their minds. The young should not be underestimated.

They were full of enthusiasm, having never been asked to use their abilities for any productive purpose before. Like puppies they seemed to vie for my attention, and they frequently surprised me. I had been a wizard long enough to have stopped thinking about many things that I considered ordinary. They hadn't. Whenever I showed them something new, their curious minds turned it over, shook it, and sometimes they found new insights I had overlooked.

Sometimes parenting can be as humbling as it is rewarding.

That afternoon I fell asleep, a common occurrence for me after our outdoor exercises. I woke to find Moira leaning over me, holding a cup of hot tea. Lilly had taken to teaching Moira and Matthew some of the basic tasks of cooking, letting them help her prepare meals. Moira in particular had shown a fondness for it.

"Thank you, sweetheart," I told her, touched once again by her thoughtfulness. My daughter was proving to be a natural caregiver. "Your tea is always welcome."

"Momma made it," she said with a knowing look in her eye.

I raised my brows. "Oh," I said astutely. Expanding my attention, I was surprised to see Penny sweeping in the kitchen.

My wife had always been a meticulous person, and one manifestation of that was a propensity to clean. Since her illness, she hadn't done any of that, letting Lilly manage everything. Seeing her with the broom told me a lot.

She was feeling better.

Her aythar was brighter, and I knew she'd passed the danger point now. I blinked a few times, feeling the boulder that had been sitting on top of my shoulders for the past few weeks quietly vanish.

Moira leaned in to kiss me on the cheek. "I knew she wasn't going to die, Daddy."

That shocked me, and I let my face show it. "Who said anything about dying?" I had kept those fears carefully to myself.

Moira wrinkled her nose at me, "Sometimes you aren't a very good liar."

"If you knew, why didn't you ask me about it?" I asked, remembering at the same time that Matthew *had* asked. "I might have been able to reassure you."

"You had enough to worry about," was her reply.

My children had been hiding their fear to protect me. I wondered where they learned to do that. *I have only myself to blame.* Setting my cup of tea aside, I rose and hugged her tightly. "Go tell your brother," I said.

"He already knows," she told me.

"You told me last?!"

"He told me. It was his watch," she said in a matter-of-fact tone.

"His watch?! You were setting watches?" Again, never underestimate the young. "And you wait to tell me last."

"You were sleeping. I wanted to wake you sooner, but Matthew thought you needed your rest," she said with a smile.

Her words made me wonder exactly who had been taking care of whom for the past few weeks. I had thought I was caring for my wife and children, but apparently the situation had been partly the opposite.

Matthew entered from outside then, carrying a dead rabbit, presumably for dinner. Looking at his sister he said, "I see Dad's up." The tone in his voice clearly communicated his anticipation of my surprise.

"I'm still a young man, I hope you two realize. I don't need you both watching over me like a couple of overprotective shepherds!" I told them firmly.

My son rolled his eyes with a sigh and took his prize to the kitchen. Moira just smiled, and then she reached over to pat my head. "You take a lot of keeping, and Momma was tired."

I gave her my best glare.

"Are you hungry?" she asked. "You always get grumpy when you're hungry."

Our conversation was a losing battle, so I studiously ignored her. Taking a sip of my tea, I rose and went to find Penny. She was my only hope for an ally against the unholy conspiracy that was forming around us.

Chapter 50

We waited another week before emerging from our seclusion. Peter and Walter had been giving me reports all along and things had been moving as expected, so I didn't feel too guilty. I might have pushed to wait longer, but Penny was beginning to get cabin fever.

That's what she called it anyway. Once Penny had recovered her strength, Lilly had left, to give us more privacy. After a week though, I was pretty sure that my wife was yearning for more diverse company.

In other words, I was driving her batty.

Peter was relieved when we finally stepped out. It took a lot of pressure off of his shoulders. Walter and his children had been up and down the valley, assisting those that needed help to return to their homes.

Walter's estate in Arundel had been thoroughly mucked up by the Shaddoth Krys, but most of his buildings were still fine. It was nothing compared to the state that Lancaster was in. The castle had been gutted by fire, some of the people's homes had been burned, and most of the storehouses pillaged.

Winter was deepening quickly, and without outside assistance famine would soon be an unwelcome guest in many people's homes. The fact that the World Road was inoperative only made matters worse; outside aid would be difficult to arrange or convey.

Teleporting to my house in Albamarl, I set about creating a new circle there, one large enough to accommodate wagons. Once it was established, Walter and his children took care of transporting what was necessary. One of them remained at either end to allow frequent trips.

Being one of the richest men in Lothion, if not *the* richest, now Tremont was dead, I opened my purse strings to purchase whatever was necessary. I gave Elise Thornbear carte blanche to handle the arrangements in Albamarl in my name. It was something I had done once before, with Rose, but she had declined to involve herself this time. She still had deeper wounds to heal.

Once those things were in motion, I made a visit to our new Queen.

*
**

Adam, the head chamberlain who had served in the palace under both King Edward and King James, was the first to respond when I made my presence known at the palace.

"Her Majesty is in a meeting, Your Excellency. If you would like to leave your card, I'll make certain that she knows you would like an audience," he told me with an air of efficient formality.

I had never known Adam to be anything less than professional, but over the years he had learned to treat me with an extra level of respect. I had clearly had the ear of King James, being one of his most trusted confidants.

Before that, I had been to the palace numerous times to see King Edward.

When things had gone badly with Edward—well, I was the one still in the palace. Edward was buried in the royal cemetery.

"What meeting is she in?" I asked casually. "She probably won't mind if I drop in." While James was in power, I had had to fight with him to stay *out* of the meetings.

"That is a matter of state, Lord Cameron," he responded.

Now he really was putting me off. 'Lord Cameron' was my official title; if he'd been treating me more normally, it would have been simply a 'Lord' plus my surname, Illeniel. Not to mention, he had just told me, in essence, that everyone who 'needed to know' was in there—and I wasn't one of them.

"Do you remember the last time you gave me a cold reception, Adam?" I kept my tone friendly, but I wanted to make sure that he knew what he was setting himself up for.

"Unfortunately, I have always had an excellent memory, Your Excellency," he answered demurely.

I gave him my best genteel smile. "I'll give you five minutes to report my presence to Her Majesty. I'll even play nice and sit out here, so everyone can see that you followed your silly damn rules and kept me waiting. After the five minutes are up, I'll find my own way, and I don't mean by leaving."

He held out a gloved hand, palm upward.

"I don't have any damned cards!" I bit out, losing my patience a bit. I'd always thought the damn things were pompous and silly. Peter had had some made once, but I never used them.

"Very well, Sir," he said, and then he left.

Taking a seat on one of the cushioned benches that decorated the waiting room, I let my mind explore the palace. Just because I was being kept out, didn't mean I couldn't peer in any and every corner of the place if I felt like it.

Imagine my surprise when I found my magesight couldn't sense anything beyond the few rooms in the entry areas and the courtyard. Curious, I stepped outside and focused my senses from a different vantage point. I could sense a large swath of the city, but most of the palace was curiously opaque. Many of the interior walls seemed to have some sort of embedded shield that blocked magesight.

Stepping back inside, I walked until I reached the closest wall with one of the new shields. Peering closely, I could see the small runes engraved along the base of the wall. It was an enchantment I hadn't seen before, but its purpose was self-evident. Someone had put privacy shields throughout the palace.

They weren't powerful. I could have easily broken one, but I could tell they were linked to something else, probably something to signal that the enchantment had been breached. It was the sort of thing that should have been done ages ago for King James. It made perfect sense for the ruler of our powerful nation to have privacy for matters of state.

Except, I had never thought of it.

Apparently someone else had, though. *It had to have been Gareth,* I assumed. The man hadn't been human

516

more than a month, and he was already sticking his nose into politics.

I sat, irritated, and waited until something like five minutes had passed. Finally I got up, and as I was striding toward the door, it was opened by someone I recognized just before I got there.

"My lord," said Sir Harold, looking a bit embarrassed, "If you will follow me."

I raised one eyebrow, but followed him without comment.

He led me along a long corridor, one I already knew quite well. It did *not* lead to the royal quarters, or to one of the meeting chambers. He was taking me toward the barracks.

"Harold," I asked calmly, "Where are we going?"

"Forgive me, my lord," he said quickly. His eyes looked a bit furtive, as though he was afraid someone might spot him. *No, as if someone might spot me,* I corrected myself mentally. "This is the way to my office near the barracks. We can talk privately there."

I nodded as though that were perfectly normal.

We reached his office without encountering anyone, which I figured had been his purpose. He must have known that the men in that area were already on duty. As soon as we entered, I pounced with my first question, "Why do you have an office in the palace, Harold?"

His face turned a funny shade of pink, telling me I had hit a sensitive spot. "Well, my lord, that's an interesting story. While you were away, a lot happened. The lords nearly rebelled when we moved to have Her Majesty crowned. Peter thought it would be a good idea to provide the Queen with solid support to prevent the same sort of thing that happened before…"

"Alright, I get the picture," I said cutting him off. "But this is an office."

"The remaining Knights of Stone have taken over security for the palace, as well as command of the royal guard," he explained.

"For how long?"

His color grew deeper. "This is merely a temporary measure, Your Excellency, since you were unavailable, until…"

"Until, what?"

"Until you sign the documents the Queen has had drawn up," he finished. His eyes wouldn't meet mine.

"Documents," I muttered.

"Her Majesty intends to nationalize the Order of the Stone," he replied, his voice growing softer as the sentence wound down to its end.

I gave him a sour look. "Nationalize, as in she's taking *my* knights for her own?" I took a deep breath.

"Peter should have informed you about all of this," suggested Harold.

I waved my hands dismissively. "He's left a lot of papers and reports, but I haven't gone through them yet." I was regretting that already. I had left my self-imposed retreat without warning, and Peter had been out at the time.

"So, you have no idea about today's conclave?" Harold asked tentatively.

I tilted my head to one side and gave him my best 'what do you think' look. "Surely there's someone here who will share the news with me," I offered, staring through him.

"They're in the Hall of Lords," began Harold. "They've called a full conclave to discuss what to do with you."

"Of course," I said dryly, "I figured it would be something silly, like confirming the support for her coronation or reorganizing after the disaster. I never suspected it would be something *so* important."

"The coronation was held last week," mentioned Harold.

They hadn't wasted much time with that then. Obviously, I was woefully lacking in information. "So, what are they trying to decide about me?"

"The majority of the nobility is calling for a trial, to settle the matter of your actions during the recent insurrection," he explained.

"Trial?" I spluttered. "What are they charging me with?"

"Today's meeting was to decide the formal list of charges, my lord."

That's when I finally realized that Adam had been trying to do me a favor by keeping me from wandering blindly into a meeting I wasn't prepared for. Instead he had brought Harold, giving me the opportunity to discover what lay in front of me.

"Tell me honestly, Harold. How bad do you think this is?"

"Do you know what the people in the streets call you?" he asked suddenly.

I shrugged.

"They've taken to calling you the 'Blood Lord' or sometimes the 'Blood Count'. You're what they tell their children about when they want to make sure they don't leave home at night," said Harold.

"Well that's new," I responded blandly. I was completely blindsided. While I was deeply ashamed of what my alter-ego had done that night, I hadn't thought anyone had seen him, no one still alive anyway. Since he had restricted himself to the usurpers men, I didn't think it would have been a matter for a trial either.

"They found over a thousand people dead," said Harold urgently. "And that was just inside the city. There were thousands more outside of it."

Well true, but most of those had been shiggreth. They had stopped moving like marionettes with their strings cut when Mal'goroth/Brexus had finally died.

"A lot of those were already dead," I told him honestly.

Harold clapped his hands over his ears. "Please don't make me a witness, my lord."

I sighed. Sometimes Harold was too honest for his own good.

"The point of all this, is that you should return home. Plan your response," he advised me.

Chapter 51

"I told you there was a risk of civil war!" said Peter loudly, almost on the verge of shouting.

"You didn't say anything about them putting me on trial," I groused.

My blond chamberlain ran his hand through his hair again. It was a miracle he hadn't pulled it all out yet. "I wasn't informed. That was in the private missives that the Queen sent you. Didn't you think to read them?"

After my ordeals, I had taken an almost perverse pleasure in completely ignoring all of it. I figured I deserved it, and most certainly my family had. Now I was paying the price.

In my absence, the new Queen had been hard pressed to solidify her hold on the governance of Lothion. The capital had been in a state of near anarchy when she returned. My 'solution' to the problem of Andrew Tremont had traumatized the citizens and given birth to a whole host of rumors and outright lies.

If I had been there, much of it might have been avoided. The Lords would certainly never have been so bold as to press a case against me. Gareth and to my surprise, Elaine, had done their best to support Ariadne during the transition. It had actually been Elaine's handiwork producing the enchanted privacy shields in the palace, although Gareth had taught her the design.

But Gareth Gaelyn hadn't had the same sort of reputation and general clout that I did. Combine that with the fact that I had done my best to ruin myself in the eyes of just about everyone, and it was a recipe for my political downfall.

A knock came at the door. After a moment, one of my footmen introduced the visitor as Lady Rose. That startled me a bit. I hadn't seen her in weeks.

"Gentlemen," she said. It was only Peter and me in the room. I had spoken with Penny about it earlier, and she'd been rather perturbed. She still hadn't gotten past the 'cutting them into small pieces' stage of anger management.

"Rose," I said, trying to keep my emotional reaction off of my face. I took her hand and passed it under my lips. Not something I did on most of our greetings, but it had been a while and it helped to get my face out of view for a moment. The last thing she needed to see was pity on my face.

She was not so easily fooled of course. "I am not so fragile that I will break, Mordecai," she told me. Setting her hand to my chin she lifted my head, forcing me to give her a direct stare. My eyes began watering almost immediately.

Seeing her brought Dorian's death back into stark, painful focus. She pursed her lips, trying to keep her own eyes dry, and then she hugged me tightly. A few minutes passed before we were able to return to the discussion at hand. Stepping away Rose moved the conversation on, "We'll talk about things later, for now I need to hear about your trial."

I lifted my eyebrows. "Why?" It was rude the way I said it, but I had thought to leave her out of this. She was still grieving.

"Two reasons," she said, beginning her points in the same logical fashion she often did. "One, you need someone to represent you. Two, I need to do something— anything, before I go mad."

I couldn't help but agree. Not to mention, it was a relief to hear the words. Somehow I couldn't imagine my case going poorly with Rose defending me. The woman was sharper than any two noblemen put together. I had learned a deep respect for her during the years I had known her. She was a force to be reckoned with.

"Tell me about the charges," she said.

I offered her the charging document and summons, which I had just received. She scanned through it and thought for a moment before speaking again.

"This is rather unusual," she said at last.

I nodded intelligently.

"I thought they might press a case based on the events in Albamarl, but this relates to what happened at Tremont's estate. They really don't have any evidence of your involvement there. Were you involved in it?" she asked.

My alter-ego had sent a legion of the shiggreth to wipe out Tremont's holdings. While I had some blurry memories of arguing with him, trying to convince him otherwise, he hadn't been swayed. In fact his actual orders had been rather open ended. The shiggreth had killed every living person at Tremont's castle, everyone in the neighboring town, and most of the outlying farmers.

It had been an almost complete slaughter. Afterward, many of the shiggreth themselves had died there, when I freed Mal'goroth/Brexus. The first people to try and restore contact with the region had been horrified to find a land full of dead and rotten corpses. It was still unoccupied. The land itself had acquired a cursed reputation.

"I think so," I told her.

She frowned, "You think so, or you *know* so? Explain, please."

I launched into a lengthy description of the events. Their faces grew paler the more I talked. In fact, the more I went over it, the more I wondered at how quickly I had pushed those thoughts to the back of my mind. I had been very carefully *not* thinking about all the things my other-self had done in my name during the past year.

"Well, they don't really have a case," said Rose after I had finished.

Short of arguing that I hadn't been in my own mind at the time, I couldn't see how that would be. My face told her as much.

"There's no proof you were in charge of the shiggreth," she said bluntly.

"I *was* a shiggreth," I replied.

"They cannot infer control from that alone, nor can they prove that you were, in fact, a shiggreth," she said calmly.

"But I *was*!"

It was her turn to raise an eyebrow, "You don't look like one to me."

"I got better. Look you know most of the story already."

She sighed, "That's not the point, Mordecai. *They* don't know the story, and we don't have to share any facts that might incriminate you unless directly questioned regarding them." She paused for a second and then added, "And if they *did* know the full story, they'd drop this entire thing. You don't deserve this. There wouldn't be a court to prosecute you in if you hadn't done what you did."

"So should he tell them the whole thing?" asked Peter.

"No," she said calmly. "They'll never believe it. I meant if they really knew the truth. There's no way to convince them of the actual story. It sounds like a fabrication to protect him from blame."

"I'll just tell them the truth. What they do with it is none of my concern," I stated, wearying of the topic.

Rose gave me an incredulous look, "Well of course it's your concern. This could affect you and your family in serious and permanent ways, and that's without considering the possible damage to our nation."

Mal'goroth had been potentially damaging to all human life. After my year long ordeal, I was having trouble seeing the importance of the constant political maneuvering involved in my life as a nobleman. "What can they do, seize my bank accounts, strip me of my title? I could care less," I said truthfully. "I'm tired of the whole thing."

"Those are both possibilities," agreed Rose, "depending on the charges they convict you of, but there are far more serious penalties; execution or banishment could be handed down for what happened on Tremont's lands."

Not that I don't perhaps deserve those things, I thought to myself, *but after everything I've been through…* "They could *try*. I wouldn't suggest it, but they could try," I told her with a stony glare.

"Suppose they did," she began, "and you flaunted the court's justice. Certainly, you probably have enough power to ignore their mandate. What would that mean, civil war? Is that what you want? Is that what you fought Mal'goroth to protect?"

"I wouldn't have to go to war. Ariadne would have enough sense to leave me alone," I declared.

Rose frowned even more, "Think, Mordecai! Think! You are much brighter than this. What happens when the Queen can't enforce her laws on you? What happens if she doesn't try? She's already standing on shaky ground. Lothion has never been ruled by a woman before."

"They wouldn't dare try to depose her," I said ominously. "They call me the 'Blood Lord' now; I'd teach them the meaning of it if they started another war."

"Which leaves Ariadne where?" said Rose pointedly. "The puppet ruler of a puppet nation, dancing in fear of an evil wizard."

"I'm not evil," I protested feebly. My logic sounded pretty thin even to my own ears.

"Even Mal'goroth thought he was just getting his due for what had happened in the past," observed Rose. Sometimes the woman was just too damned sharp.

I knew she was playing the devil's advocate for my own sake, but her words stung a bit. An idea occurred to me then, "I could just disappear. Take the family and retire someplace far away. That would solve their problems."

"If they choose banishment, yes," said Rose. "If they choose another penalty, and you abscond it will still weaken Ariadne's position—and you won't be around to save the day afterward."

I gave up. "What would you have me do then?" I looked back and forth between her and Peter, who had been listening quietly the entire time.

"In two days you appear before the court. I'll argue your case, and they will either dismiss it or find you guilty. If you are given penalties, you take them. You must accept the rule of law, otherwise this nation you've worked so hard for will be nothing but a sham," she said firmly.

"And if they order my execution?"

"They could, but they won't," said Rose with a smile. "That's the clever part. The High-Justicer, Earl Winfield, is no fool. If they handed down a sentence like that, you'd be forced to buck them, which would undermine the Queen. Even if we lose, they'll make sure it doesn't force you into a corner."

Peter nodded emphatically.

I held up my hands in defeat. "When you are right, you're right. We'll do it as you suggest."

*
**

Rose visited that evening, along with Moira Centyr. They brought Gram with them but left Rose's small daughter, Carissa, with her mother-in-law. They joined us shortly before dinner, and once we had all eaten, the children went to play.

The conversation during the meal was plain and unremarkable. Both Penny and Rose were inhibited by unspoken issues. Once we finished, the two of them went aside, leaving Moira Centyr and me to entertain each other. I suspected that it was a strategic move on Rose's part. She had probably brought Moira with her just for that purpose.

We made small talk for a short while before Moira brought up a topic I didn't expect, "Have you noticed anything odd in your daughter's room?"

I wasn't sure where she was headed with that, but I was always willing to discuss 'our' child with her. "Aside from the fact that she can't be bothered to keep it clean?"

A smile quirked at the corner of Moira's lips. "No, I mean something more along the lines of her imaginary friends."

Moira Centyr was a frequent visitor in our home. In fact, next to Lilly Tucker and my mother she was our most common baby sitter. Some women might have been intimidated by their adopted daughter's mother's thousand year-old shade hanging around, but Penny had been more pragmatic. Moira Centyr had become something like an extra grandmother for all our children. Consequently, she was almost as familiar with my daughter's room as I was.

"She's always had imaginary friends," I admitted easily. "I think she'll outgrow them eventually." The reality was that my daughter spent a lot of time talking to a stuffed bear we had given her several years ago. It was a cute habit most of the time, though it worried me some. She was almost eleven now and had shown no sign of stopping.

Moira gave me a knowing glance, "Pay more attention. She's a Centyr, remember? Her imaginary friends will probably start talking back to her, if they haven't already."

That was a sobering thought. "I hadn't even thought about it," I admitted.

"It's usually not a problem," said the Stone Lady. "I just wanted you to be aware. Don't overreact if you find something unexpected moving around and talking in your home."

It was good advice. Unprepared, I might have traumatized my daughter by roasting the first living 'doll' that surprised me. Definitely not the way to guide her into learning to control her abilities.

"Is there anything specific I should teach her, or avoid?" I questioned.

"Not really," answered Moira. "The Centyr abilities are almost instinctive. She'll learn to use them without even finding them strange. I'll be here to help with specific questions."

Penny and Rose returned soon after that, holding hands. Their eyes were swollen and puffy, but they both looked as though a weight had been lifted from their shoulders. They had made up at last.

"Goodness gracious!" I said emphatically. "Did you two get in a brawl with someone? I'd hate to see what they look like!"

That earned me a scowl and a laugh, each in equal measure.

Chapter 52

"What's this?" I asked Penny, referring to the clothes she had laid out for me.

"Clothing," she answered sarcastically. "It'll make a bad impression if you don't wear some."

I took a deep breath. Everyone in my family had become a comedian, but I knew if I complained, they would just blame me as a bad influence. "You know very well what I mean," I said.

The doublet was new, and rather than the usual felt or velvet, it had been made of soft doe-hide. It was done in black with generous amounts of carmine trim. The reds weren't subtle either; they had been cut with aggressive patterns to edge the garment. The boots and other accessories all matched the theme as well.

"If they're going to call you names, we can at least make them work for us," offered Penny.

"The 'Blood Lord' business?"

She nodded, "Wait 'til you see what I'm wearing."

"This is a trial, not a costume party," I complained.

"I discussed this already with Rose," said Penny, as if that made it automatically correct.

On second thought, that's probably exactly what it meant. "Spell it out for me," I requested, "I'm a little slow sometimes."

"They're afraid of you, and today we have two purposes. One, we want to help our new Queen by showing that the dreaded 'Blood Lord' does still bow to the rule of law. Your reputation has sunk so low that your open support won't help her, but the other side of the coin, is that they fear you so much it will help if the peers of the realm feel like the Queen is the only thing protecting them from you," she explained.

"That I can understand," I said, before she could get to her second purpose. "But won't antagonizing them worsen my chances in court?"

"It may hurt your chances of a dismissal, but it will remind them of your power, lowering your chances of an overly severe penalty," said Penny. "That was the second purpose, by the way."

"Oh."

She left after that and finished her own preparations away from my view. I was told not to 'peek', so I tried to keep my attention elsewhere.

When we rejoined an hour later, I was shocked. Tradition and common expectation was that a noblewoman would wear respectable attire when she might be seen by the peerage. In general, that meant a nice dress and the more extravagant the better.

Instead, my wife wore a matching set of black and red leathers. Her long hair had been styled into two long braids, each with a thick metal cord intertwined, and the ends were capped with silver cylinders. She had dressed herself as a man.

Not that she looked even remotely masculine. Let us not give false impressions here; rather the close fitting trousers and sleek doublet showcased her feminine

531

attributes in an aggressive and deadly manner that was sure to make almost every nobleman in the courtroom uncomfortable.

Unlike the currently fashionable dresses there was no décolletage, in fact very little of her skin showed anywhere, aside from her hands and face. It was the shape and close fit alone that would make the outfit a shocker. In fact, on closer inspection I realized that much of the doublet contained square metal inserts. The parts of her not covered by the armored garment were protected by heavy leather.

Even more surprising, most of her outfit was enchanted. The leather had been laced with runes to keep it flexible, while making it more resistant to cuts and blows, and the metal plates had been made nearly unbreakable. The silver cords running through her hair were also infused with magic, although I couldn't tell what the purpose of it was. I'd need to remove them and study the rune-work to make sense of it.

"Is that brigandine?" I said when my voice returned.

The hell-cat I was married to grinned at me. The overall effect of her clothing was to appear as something like a truly extravagant and overly expensive hunting outfit, but with a much more martial air. In fact though, my wife had arrayed herself for war.

"If they figure out what that is, it will cause even more trouble," I declared.

"There's no rule against armor," said Penny stubbornly.

Weapons weren't allowed in the Hall of Lords, probably because of a few unfortunate historical incidents.

Consequently, armor was never worn either, although that might have been a matter of comfort alone.

"Some of those old men are going to die of apoplexy when they see you," I told her.

That seemed to please her, "The world won't miss them. Now, let's fix your beard."

"What's wrong with it?" I protested. Since returning to my proper looks and features, I had forgotten my beard. I had been growing it back over the last two weeks, not as a great wooly abomination, which Gareth preferred, but as a tightly controlled goatee.

"Nothing," she said. "The style suits you, but it hasn't gotten long enough yet. It needs another half inch so you can give it some jaunty points."

"Jaunty points," I snickered. "Are you sure that's what they're called?"

Penny glared at me, "I don't care what they're called. Make it a little longer and give me that comb."

Unfocusing my eyes for a second, I reimagined myself with a slightly longer beard. I could have done it with normal wizardry, but in this case, using my ability as an archmage was simpler. She proceeded to work on my chin with the comb.

When she had finished, a quick look in the mirror showed me the face of an arrogant man with a fierce goatee. I had to admit, it suited me. So long as my goal was to frighten children.

I liked it. While I had had my doubts about our plan, I couldn't deny that it matched my personality better than trying to pretend humility.

*
**

It never fails, even in dark times, or perhaps because of them, people love the excitement of seeing blood. Today I would be the main event and they had all gathered to witness the fall of the mighty Lord Cameron.

The Hall of Lords had an almost festive air about it when we entered. Granted, the harvest celebrations were in the offing, but given the terrible events of late, they weren't expected to be very good. For myself, I knew why the lords were in such high spirits—they were expecting entertainment.

I determined not to disappoint them.

Rose entered ahead of us, resplendent in a flowing white dress. An azure belt with silver trim and buckles complemented a silver and sapphire necklace. The general effect, combined with her elegantly coiffed dark hair, was guaranteed to stun.

She would have been the star jewel in a crowd that was already brimming with opulence, the center of attention, if it had not been for the two who entered behind her.

That was us of course.

While Penny and I were dressed expensively, the main thrust of our attire was not wealth so much as dangerous power. My expression was aloof and disinterested, while Penny's was challenging. She met every eye directly, with a stare that dared them to speak to her only if they had a death wish.

"We make quite the villains," she whispered to me as we took our places.

I nodded, "I've already had some practice at it, but you seem to be a natural."

"I had to fend off suitors for a year," she informed me. "I learned quickly."

That earned her a smile from me, and as I returned my attention to the crowd, I could see them watching us. I could only imagine the things they must be wondering as they studied our expressions.

There were a lot of preliminaries to my trial. Each member of the assembly was named, along with a declaration of all those notables who were absent. In particular the Lords of Tremont, Cantley, and Surrey had not yet had replacements selected since they were executed. Stephen Balistair, had replaced his father, Martin, the late Earl of Balistair, and David Airedale had replaced his father, John, as Count Airedale.

Once they had finished naming and listing, the first order of business was a reading of my charges. Duke Grumley represented an anonymous coalition of lords who wished to press the case against me, so it fell to him to present the list.

He made it take longer than it should have, but it boiled down to the unlawful murder of Andrew Tremont and his servants in the capital on one hand, and the terrible slaughter of innocent lives at the Tremont estate on the other.

Ariadne sat in the traditional seat at the back of the room, some distance behind the High-Justicer's chair. The courts acted on the authority of Her Majesty, and technically, if she wished, she had the power to dismiss them and dispense justice according to her own whims. In practice though, that was very unlikely, since it could potentially precipitate a civil war unless the monarch's power over the lords themselves was absolute. That was definitely not the case in these times.

As soon as the charges were finished, the new queen sent a young messenger down to whisper in Earl Winfield's ear. Listening for a moment he nodded and addressed the assembly, "The Queen wishes to declare her support for Lord Cameron's actions in the capital. Her Majesty had already determined Duke Tremont's guilt and stripped him of all rights and privileges; therefore, neither he nor his men enjoyed any protection of law."

Treason was a crime that the monarch had always reserved rights over, for immediate prosecution and punishment. That had been Ariadne's justification when she had Dorian kill the coconspirators Balistair, Cantley, and Surrey. She was extending it now to me, pronouncing me her agent after the fact.

"Lord Grumley, do you wish to amend your charges in light of this fact?" asked the High-Justicer.

Grumley was a stout, barrel-chested man with a maroon coat and a lot of grey hair. He swallowed before answering, "Yes, my lord, I would like to withdraw the charge of unlawful murder against Andrew Tremont and his servants in the capital."

Well, that was easy enough, I thought.

"We still wish to press the case that he unlawfully murdered the inhabitants of Tremont Castle and all those within several miles of that estate," continued Duke Grumley.

Gerald Winfield, the Duke of Winfield and High-Justicer turned to me then, "Lord Cameron, do you wish to present your own defense, or is there someone to represent you?"

"Lady Hightower will represent me, Your Lordship," I replied. Since her father's passing, Rose was 'the Hightower', even though her actual last name was Thornbear now. It was a situation similar to my title of 'Cameron' even though my own surname was Illeniel.

Winfield addressed her directly, "Lady Hightower, are you prepared to present a cogent defense? The laws of Lothion are sometimes complex. It is not a subject to be taken lightly."

He was alluding to the fact that, since she was a woman she probably didn't possess the necessary acumen to handle such a difficult task. That thought made me smile.

"I feel capable of the task Lord Winfield. I do not feel likely to swoon just yet, but perhaps we should move forward quickly before the strain overwhelms my weak constitution?" she suggested helpfully.

He stared at her coldly for a moment, but said nothing.

Taking his silence for acquiescence, she continued, "I would like to move to dismiss the remaining charges against Lord Cameron."

That was unexpected. "On what grounds, Lady Hightower?" asked the High-Justicer.

"At the time the assault on the Castle Tremont occurred, Andrew Tremont was already dead, my lord. Being without a sworn vassal to the crown holding their trust, the people were therefore no longer under the rule of law. Being not under the law, they also no longer enjoyed its protection," she explained nimbly.

There were a few gasps in the crowd, and I have to admit it took me a minute to unravel her chain of logic. Her premise essentially meant that since the people of Tremont had lost their lord and had no formal tie to the government of Lothion, they had no longer been protected by it either. This rested largely upon the fact that at the beginning of Lothion's legal system, all rights and powers were vested in the nobility, granted to them by the king. The people living on their lands had no rights whatsoever originally, except those their respective lord chose to give them. What they did receive was protection from exploitation or harm at the hands of any *other* lord of the realm.

Any lawless peasants not sworn to a specific lord were fair game. They could be slain, captured, or robbed at will by any peer of the realm.

While it sounded barbaric on the face of it, the original intention was to discourage brigands and banditry. Lawful citizens lived in towns and owed allegiance to a local lord, and it was his power that shielded them from any other lordling's whims or cruelty.

So, since Tremont was dead for treason, she's saying that his people were effectively lawless, free for the taking, I noted to myself.

Ariadne was smiling from her place, and I could sense Penny's admiration from where she stood next to me.

Everyone was either happy, or dismayed at the logic of it. Except me, I was upset, but for a different reason.

It isn't fair. People should enjoy the protection of the laws of Lothion whether or not their asshole of a lord is dead. My alter-ego had ordered the murder of what happened to be over a thousand people. It hadn't actually

538

been my decision, nor had it been fully Brexus' intention, but it should not be swept aside on a technicality that relied upon removing the rights of thousands. It was wrong.

I leaned close to Rose's ear, "Withdraw that motion."

She glared at me. "No! That's your best chance…"

"It isn't right," I argued softly. "I don't want to win by setting a precedent that will endanger future generations."

"You're asking me to abandon your best defense," she informed me.

"Just do it," I ground out.

The High-Justicer was still digesting Rose's motion when she raised her hand again.

He recognized her with a nod. "You have something to add, Lady Hightower?"

Giving me a disappointed glance, she responded, "Yes, Your Lordship. Against my advice, Lord Cameron wishes to withdraw the request for dismissal." That garnered a few gasps from those in the room.

The High-Justicer gave me an odd look and then addressed me directly, "I was considering granting the dismissal, Lord Cameron. Are you certain you wish to withdraw the request?"

Lifting my chin I answered, "Yes, Your Lordship." I could feel Penny's eyes burning into the side of my head. If I survived the trial, I had further consequences awaiting me later. "I would rather face the inquiry than leave the people with no response for the insult done to them."

The Earl of Winfield accepted my withdrawal with some softly muttered words. I couldn't be sure but it sounded as though he had said, 'Most of them are dead already.'

Things went steadily downhill from there.

Lord Grumley questioned me regarding the events and presented the known facts regarding what happened at Castle Tremont. I hadn't heard the full story, so I listened with interest. The shiggreth had overrun the castle itself, hunting down and killing everyone within. Afterward, they had dispersed through the region and begun hunting villagers and farmers in their homes.

Very little of the population that had once resided in the Duchy of Tremont still survived, and most of those left had deserted the region. The land was abandoned now, and when the shiggreth had died the next day, there had been no one left to dispose of the bodies. The first people to venture there in search of answers had found a cursed place littered with decaying human remains.

Hearing it all made me sick.

Penny nudged my elbow. "Stop it. You didn't do that. You weren't even there."

"Brexus was part of me, I gave birth to him," I told her quietly. "I was there when he made the decision, and while I tried to stop him, I didn't try very hard." Part of me had secretly wanted him to destroy, not just Tremont but everything associated with the man. I had been able to stop Brexus on a few occasions when I had been desperate. All I had done when he ordered the shiggreth to murder Tremont's people was 'counsel' him otherwise.

I had been a passive accomplice to their deaths.

"Mort, look at them," she said, her eyes darting around the room. "That story has set even those who were mildly in favor of you back on their heels. They could very well order you to hang. Is that what you want? What about us?"

By us, she meant not just her, but our children as well. "Don't worry. They don't dare push for execution or the whole thing will fall apart. If they are so foolish, then I'll have no recourse but to abandon the country. We'll take the children and run."

"And that's better than letting them dismiss the case?" she said pointedly.

"It avoids a bad precedent, and it puts the Queen firmly on the side of the people," I replied. "Besides, I feel sure that Winfield won't go so far. He'll impose some harsh penalties, which will go even farther to reinforce the rule of law."

The next half hour was spent questioning me regarding my role in what happened. Rose began with the assertion that I wasn't even in the region where the attacks occurred, and I ruined it by admitting that my alter-ego had given the order.

Rose questioned me about my dual nature at the time, revealing to the court that I had, according to my testimony, not been in actual control of my actions. She asked for leniency based on the grounds that I wasn't capable of making my own decisions at the time. It was essentially a defense based on mental incapacity.

Duke Grumley had one simple retort to that line of reasoning. Gazing around the room, he summed it up quickly, "My lords and ladies, we cannot know the truth of what lies in a man's mind, but what we can see, here and now, is that Lord Cameron is quite clearly in control of his own actions. His assertion that he was not, in fact, himself, is nothing more than a thinly veiled attempt to avoid culpability. He should be judged accordingly."

I could see Penny's hands gripping the rail in front of us. They were white-knuckled, and she wasn't the only one who was nervous. Rose's normally unflappable exterior was showing signs of strain as well.

He won't go that far, I told myself. *Banishment, loss of title, those I can live with.*

Rose and Grumley both made closing remarks, and then it was time. The High-Justicer withdrew to deliberate. It wasn't long before he returned though, a matter of minutes only. "If the defendant will rise, I am ready to read the verdict," he announced.

Taking my feet again, I scanned Winfield's face, hoping to garner some clue as to what he was about to say. As I did, I felt a shift in the room, a new presence. Gareth Gaelyn entered from one side. He had been hidden behind one of the new privacy shields in a side room. One look at his face told me all I needed to know.

They had him here all along, as an officer of the court. He was there to make sure I didn't run.

"Son of a bitch!" I muttered under my breath. Penny followed my gaze. Her eyes went wide when she saw him, and I felt more than saw her body tense.

Harold was standing by Ariadne, and his eyes were a warning to me. More guards positioned themselves at the edges of the room, and these felt enhanced to my senses. Possibly by Doron, since I was sure they weren't any of the remaining Knights of Stone.

"Mordecai Illeniel, Count di' Cameron and Protector of the Northern Reach, I find you guilty of the unlawful deaths of the citizenry of the Duchy of Tremont. While the court understands that there may be some mitigating circumstances involved in this case, we find that the magnitude of the harm done must require a commensurate penalty. You will be stripped of the title, 'Protector of the Northern Reach', but you will retain the title Count di' Cameron, so that your heir, who is blameless of these crimes, may inherit it. I sentence you to death by hanging, to be carried out immediately."

As the words rang out I found myself numb. *Next time, I should listen to Rose,* I thought as what seemed to be a very heavy stone settled in my stomach. Penny's hands rose to her braids, reaching for the metal cylinders that capped them. I knew instinctively that they must be weapons.

Desperate I looked around the room. Harold stood opposite me, next to the Queen. Whatever his feelings might be, I could only assume he would act on behalf of the court if my wife attacked. The extra guards and Gareth weighed on me. In an instant the Hall of Lords could turn into a battlefield.

There would be no winners.

Reaching out, I put one hand over Penny's, "No," I said softly. "We can't win."

Rose nudged me then, and I realized I had missed a question from the High-Justicer.

"Huh?" I said in some confusion.

"Do you have any last words to say?" he repeated.

I blinked and took a deep breath. "Yes, Your Lordship, I would like to address the full assembly of lords."

"You have one minute to speak," he replied.

Facing the gathering, I put on a determined face. "While I find the court's decision to be just, I would like to reiterate that I did only the best I could under unusual circumstances. If I could change what happened in Tremont, I would. As for the Duke himself, I am unrepentant. I would also give warning to any here who may have secretly conspired with him. I have returned from death once already. Should I discover that any of you were in league with him, or should any of you create a new conspiracy against our queen, I will find a way to do so again. There will be no refuge that can hide the traitors from my retribution."

A number of people's faces went pale as I spoke. The fire in my eyes left no doubt, even my death would not grant safety to the wicked. I hoped they would lose sleep over it.

Another messenger from the Queen found the High-Justicer's ear, and after a moment he held up his hand again.

"In accordance with our ancient law and custom, our monarch reserves the right of pardon. Rather than force her hand, she has instructed the court to commute Lord Cameron's sentence. Out of respect, I will do so, rather than see justice diverted," announced the Earl of Winfield.

Now I was confused. "What does that mean?" I asked Rose.

"It means the Queen will use her right to pardon you if the High-Justicer refuses to amend your sentence. Rather than let that happen, he has agreed to give you a lesser penalty," she explained in a whisper.

Relief washed over me.

The High-Justicer continued, "Therefore I will reduce the sentence to a fine of twenty gold, to be paid for the death of every person who died in the attack on Tremont's estate, and ten lashes to be administered at noon tomorrow. The gold paid as a result of these fines will be given to the heirs and relatives of those who died. For those with no familial survivors, which I understand are many, the gold will be held to assist whomever the Queen grants title of those lands to."

While I should have been glad to be free of the threat of death, it was hard to be overjoyed by the replacement. Ariadne was frowning at Earl Winfield from her position behind him, clearly displeased with his substitution, but she said nothing. Her only option at that point would have been to pardon me anyway and overturn the entire trial.

A lashing for a peer of the realm was virtually unheard of, and the humiliation that accompanied such a public event was probably viewed as barely preferable to death by the majority of the noblemen present.

Lashes in Lothion were not as civilized or humane as they were in Gododdin. There they used a short rod that terminated in a number of thin plaited leather strips. It was painful, but unless the number of lashes given was very high, it wasn't dangerous.

Lothion however, had a different tradition that had probably originated with early punishments given on board ships. In Lothion lashes were administered with a medium length leather whip that was capable of slicing through the skin of the prisoner if done by someone with sufficient force and skill.

As a result, the number of lashes given as punishment in Lothion was generally low, two or three for most offenses. Five or six were used for very serious crimes, and more than that was unusual. Ten could be dangerous if the person punished wasn't treated promptly to stop bleeding. A sentence of twenty sometimes resulted in death even with prompt treatment.

I was willing to bet that the royal flogger took great pride in his work.

Penny was shaking with rage.

"Penny, you've got to calm down," Rose told her, for she seemed on the verge of a violent breakdown.

"You're not taking this!" said my wife, glaring at me indignantly. "To hell with them, they can't do this to you."

I smiled bravely, "Winfield never did like me, but I will survive." My courage never felt as false as it did then.

"We don't need these people, Mort. We don't need the titles or the money. We can..."

"...talk about this later," I interrupted. Too many eyes and ears were focused on us.

Lifting our heads we let the final moments of the court play out until I was dismissed, and then we retired from the hall. We were in dark spirits when we finally left, but Penny and I did our damnedest to keep from showing it to anyone there.

Chapter 53

Our debate that evening had been heated and bitter.

Penny had thought we should abandon it all, rather than accept the punishment. I felt otherwise. In the end it wasn't something she was able to persuade me on.

There were a number of possible ways magic could make the lashing less painful. A shield would negate the entire thing, but that would be noticeable. Subtly strengthening the skin could prevent a lot of the damage and reduce the pain somewhat, but again, it might be noticeable.

Blocking the nerves, as I did when healing, could save me from the worst part of the experience, and since I could heal the damage immediately thereafter, it wouldn't matter how badly my back was torn up.

But it felt like cheating.

When I finally stepped onto the platform I had already decided to take the punishment as it was intended. My only concession was allowing Elise Thornbear to treat my back with an ointment meant to numb the skin. Hopefully, it would dull the pain to a level that would keep me from embarrassing myself.

The man who greeted me on the platform was masked, much like an executioner. As far as I knew, that might be his other job, but it didn't seem like the time to ask. I wondered if the mask was to protect his identity from me, or from the crowd. I probably could have identified him later from his aythar alone if I had been of a mind to be vindictive.

"Good day," I greeted him. Old habits die hard.

He didn't respond to my greeting, choosing instead to remain business-like. "If you'd put these on for me, my lord," he handed me a pair of manacles with a short chain between them.

"I'm not planning to run," I explained. "I would have already done so if that were my plan."

"Those are more to keep you upright, my lord, after you pass out," he answered in a dead pan voice.

"Does that happen a lot?"

"Yeah, if you're lucky, it happens sooner, rather than later," he told me.

Involuntarily my eyes were drawn to the braided black coil of leather he had soaking in a bucket nearby. Clasping the irons around my wrists, I raised my hands to show the crowd. My situation was humiliating enough, but I felt a need to show my determination.

They remained silent, but every eye was on me; some with pity, some gloating at the lord brought low, and most of the rest with simple interest. For them, perhaps I was merely a source of entertainment.

Penny had come, along with Rose and Walter, but we had excluded everyone else from Cameron, especially the children. Ariadne had invited them to stand with her, as a kindness, but Penny's anger hadn't allowed for it. She blamed the Queen as much as the Justicer.

"Why do you soak the whip?" I asked as he helped to loop the chain between my wrists over a hook mounted on a pole in the center of the platform.

"We soak it in brine, my lord, to help minimize the bleeding. The physicians say that it keeps the wounds from getting the rot later too," he volunteered. "Personally though, I think they started doing it to make it hurt more."

I was beginning to sense a theme regarding that.

"Try not to tense up too much," he added. "It cuts deeper if you're stiff."

And how many people actually retain that much self-control after this starts, I wondered. *Now you're just saying things to make it worse.*

I watched the crowd while listening to him ready the whip, shaking off the excess liquid and letting it uncoil like an evil snake behind me. I made certain my eyes weren't on Penny as I felt more than saw him draw his arm back for the first blow.

A line of burning white fire exploded through my consciousness, wiping my mind clear of every clever thought I might have had. Somehow I had thought perhaps I would be able to clench my teeth and get through the experience without making a sound, but my body took matters into its own hands. A strange yelping left my lips involuntarily, possibly because the whip had struck when my lungs were only half full.

The animal side of my brain was in full panic now, and the sane rational portion of my mind was vanishing quickly. My ears heard the slithering sound of the leather on wood, as he flicked his wrist to return it to the starting position. It took every ounce of will I had to keep from creating a shield then and there.

The second blistering stroke took the air from my lungs. If there was a yell that accompanied it, I couldn't be sure. At that point, I was no longer worried about whether I might make noise anyway. The fragment of my consciousness that was still faintly rational began to compare my current pain to the pain I had experienced during my ordeal with Mal'goroth. It was a bit like comparing apples to oranges, but its final conclusion was that at least I had a well-defined end point for this pain.

Then again, that was then and this is—Unhh!!

With the third lash, I had had enough.

Unwilling to shield myself or otherwise give in, my mind did the only other thing it could, it escaped. Slipping into the half-state that I had learned years before as an archmage, my mind found shelter in the earth beneath me. It didn't abandon my body completely, but my flesh and blood self was now a much smaller part of my awareness.

In fact, the first time I had ever sought mental sanctuary in the stone like that was right before I had fought Celior.

I watched the rest of the lashing almost as an outside observer. My body still jerked, and spasms caused it to twitch after each blow, but I no longer experienced the pain in the same way. It was impersonal, something more of an annoyance than an immediate threat to my well-being.

When it was finally over he put the whip back in its bucket and moved to help unhook the chain from the post. Resuming more direct control over my body, I straightened, and with only a thought I severed the iron chain so that I could lower my arms.

"I thought you were unconscious," the man told me, eyeing the ruined manacles. As an afterthought he added, "You'll have to pay for those."

I had been about to use my magic to pop the clasps themselves open, but I had another thought. "That's fine," I told him. "I'll keep them as a reminder."

Ignoring the crowd, I began walking to Penny. Every movement was painful, and standing, much less walking, was an exercise in misery. I could feel the blood running down my back, but I refused the physician's offer of assistance. Putting my mind partially back in the earth enabled me to reach her without stumbling.

They put my arms over their shoulders, which elicited a fresh surge of pain from my back, and then Walter made us invisible. The three of us made our way home then, and I tried to forget the rest of the day. There was no good to be had in it.

Chapter 54

The months passed quietly at Cameron Castle, and spring had already come again. In all that time I had not returned to Albamarl once. The Queen had sent several letters, but I didn't read them. My rational mind knew my lashing hadn't been her fault, nor her wish, but somehow my heart just couldn't accept it. It wasn't Ariadne I was angry with, it was Lothion itself, and since she represented it, I kept her at a distance instead.

I did let Peter read the letters, to make sure I wasn't missing something earthshakingly important. Once he had told me that they didn't contain any orders or summons, I burned them. I refused to discuss their contents with him afterward as well. I wasn't ready to open my heart yet.

Ordinarily Penny would have been a mitigating influence, but in this matter she was angrier than I could ever be. If it had been up to her we'd have started a civil war. She had always been somewhat protective of me, but now—she had progressed to an entirely new level. I began to avoid any mention of the capital, Ariadne, any of the nobility—the list went on. A single reminder would often trigger an eruption of acid-tongued invective from her.

Immediately after our return, I had used my magic to close the skin over my wounds, but I refrained from healing them. Instead, I let them heal on their own, slowly and imperfectly, which left a crisscross pattern of scars on my back that mirrored the ones in my heart. Penny urged me to erase them, but I refused. "Some things are worth remembering," was my reply.

We hadn't told the children, but the twins had passed eleven years old now, and they were proving to be very perceptive. I'm sure they discovered the truth at some point, but they never said a word to me about it. I told myself we would talk about it someday, but that day never seemed to come.

The fine that Earl Winfield had levied upon me eventually totaled in the hundreds of thousands of gold, one-hundred-sixty-three-thousand and twenty gold, to be precise. Divided up that amounted to something over eight thousand people wiped out. I didn't begrudge them the money at all, although I was fairly certain that many of those who came forward to claim kinship had only the most tenuous of claims.

The sum was enough to bankrupt me and then some. I was forced to take a loan for twenty thousand of it, on unfavorable terms, in order to pay it in full. Rose had suggested I seek a personal loan from the crown, but again, I refused to approach our new queen.

One bright spot was that Cameron Castle, and by extension the town of Washbrook, had received very little actual damage. That was good, since I had no money for repairs. Arundel and Lancaster on the other hand, were in bad shape. The people of the three neighboring areas helped one another with the rebuilding, but financially, I had nothing left to assist them. The most I could do for Walter and the people of Arundel was exempt him from the taxes he owed me that year. That, of course, made it more difficult for me to pay my own taxes, or even pay my retainers and servants.

Peter urged me to ask the Queen for amnesty from my taxes that year, but again—you can imagine my response. The capital needed the money anyway; the fighting there had resulted in quite a bit of damage to the palace and the city.

Instead I produced money my own way. There were no active mines on my lands, but as an archmage, it was easy enough to convince the earth to bring what I wanted to the surface. From its fiery heart, I brought pure iron, shaping it into bar stock even as it emerged. In smaller quantities, I brought silver and some gold as well, molding those into ingots.

It would have been easy enough to turn them directly into coins, but that would have been a crime. Instead I sold the metals directly in a dozen different towns. Initially I got good prices, but within a few trips the market for iron and silver plummeted, so I stopped. I had made enough to pay my debts and remain solvent for another year or two anyway.

I later found out that the Earl of Winfield was heavily invested in several mines, and as a result of my efforts, he lost quite a bit of money that year when the prices dropped. I wished I could claim that I knew before, but it was just a happy coincidence.

Staying isolated became more work when summer arrived, and with it an invitation.

"What's this?" I asked Penny when I saw the ornately decorated envelope.

She grinned at me, "A wedding invitation."

I thought for a moment, knowing that it must surely be someone we were expecting to get married soon. My mind remained scrupulously blank, and my vacant stare communicated the fact to her.

"I know you're brighter than this," said my wife. "I'll give you two guesses."

Rose? That thought brought an inner twinge of pain. *No, that's impossible so soon, maybe ever. Was Elaine seeing someone? Maybe Harold...* Then I remembered that Harold had already gotten married. I felt relief that my memory told me that before I guessed his name. Penny would never have let me live that down.

"I can almost see the steam rising from your ears," joked Penny. "Be careful or you'll get heatstroke."

I stuck my tongue out at her. "Peter!" I said at last.

Her look was one of utter amazement. "No, and that just goes to prove how utterly clueless you are. Peter isn't interested in women."

"Really?" I asked, somewhat surprised.

She sighed, "This could take all day."

"Are you sure about Peter?"

"He's lived with his sister almost the entire time since they joined us. He's never shown the slightest interest in anything other than his job and... I'll stop there, you obviously haven't noticed much about his personal life."

Now she was just being mean. I decided to play even dumber, just to rile her up. "When you say he's only interested in his job—you mean me, don't you!"

She stared at me in disdain. Clearly I couldn't get any stupider.

"I was joking," I admitted.

"Should I laugh?" she replied. "You still haven't made a good guess yet."

"Wait, you said 'he lived with his sister almost the entire time', is Lilly getting married?" I was proud of my deductive reasoning. If Lilly was moving out of their shared rooms it must mean one of them was marrying.

"She is seeing someone," said Penny, "but they aren't past the initial courtship yet."

"I give up then."

"Moira Centyr!" she declared then, almost gloating in her excitement.

"Wait! What?" That truly surprised me. Not only did I not have any idea of a romance brewing in her life, but I wasn't even certain there *should* be one. Technically she wasn't actually a person. She was a magical intelligence, a copy of a long dead person, made immortal by the enchantment I had placed upon her and given flesh and blood by the handiwork of Gareth Gaelyn.

"You never saw that one coming, did you?" added Penny gleefully.

I shook my head, "Not at all, but who...?"

"Gareth."

"What!?" I almost jumped out of my shoes. "That's impossible."

"No..." said Penny slowly, "It's quite possible. In fact, it makes perfect sense."

I was having none of it, "He's rigid, bristly, impersonal, and he drinks too much."

"I don't recall ever seeing him drink much," commented my wife.

"I made that part up."

She peered closely at me, "I'm surprised. I hadn't thought you would be like this. You're actually protective of her, aren't you? She's a grown woman you know."

"She's family," I protested. "I want the best for her."

"Gareth is well suited to her," said Penny. "Plus, he's the only other person around who is over a thousand years old. They have a lot of common history."

"Centuries of shared suffering are hardly a basis for marriage. Most would say they were more likely the *result* of marriage," I shot back wittily.

Her eyes caught fire then, "Is that what you think?"

Maybe, if I don't learn when to avoid stupid jokes. "No, of course not. I meant other people," I said, adding a sly grin that implied I really meant us. At this point she would know I was teasing her.

Penny's face softened, but she put a growl in her reply, "You'll pay for that one later."

"This is turning into a self-fulfilling prophecy," I chuckled.

*
**

Moira and Gareth's wedding was held at the palace in Albamarl. I offered them the use of Cameron Castle, but they chose to accept Ariadne's invitation instead. Naturally, that meant that Penny and I found ourselves in Albamarl for the first time since my lashing.

This isn't about me, I kept reminding myself.

The ceremony was lovely, as was to be expected. One thing surprised me, though. Moira Centyr was fairly brimming with aythar.

Not just a little extra, mind you. No, she was, at my best guess, carrying virtually all the power I had taken from Mal'goroth before he was destroyed. The aythar had been divided up between the three shining gods, but I hadn't gotten around to figuring out what to do with it. I couldn't release them from their immortality until that problem was solved.

It was something I should have taken care of sooner, but I had been too withdrawn to focus on important tasks. Now it appeared that someone had taken the matter out of my hands. The bride had such an immense amount of aythar that she had to keep herself shielded; otherwise the sheer pressure of it might have rendered her guests unconscious.

For some reason, that irritated me a bit.

"You're tensing up," said Penny from beside me.

"Sorry, dear," I told her, making a conscious effort to relax my shoulders. *It had to have been Gareth. I gave him the keys to control the Shining Gods.*

For a moment I had some uncharitable thoughts regarding Moira's new husband. It seemed awfully convenient for him to have placed all that power in his future wife's hands. I pushed my paranoia aside, though. *When did I become so untrusting?*

Trust aside, I couldn't risk anyone having access to that much power, even myself, though until I found an alternative that was my only option. Rather than enjoy the wedding I spent the entire ceremony thinking hard on possible solutions.

Glancing over at my daughter, I saw her talking to the small doll that rode on her shoulder. As Moira Centyr had predicted, she had begun bringing her toys to life over the past few months, animating each of them with distinct personalities. It had been rather unsettling until I got used to it.

Her toys were unfailingly polite and frequently adorable in their mannerisms. She invested each with a small amount of aythar to keep them 'alive', but it would run down in a matter of days if she didn't renew it. Moira Centyr had said they would become more durable with time and practice, or if she put more aythar into them.

They could be very useful and at this point in her life they were mostly harmless. They were nothing like the gods that my ancestor and Moira Centyr had created. So long as I never used *that* enchantment again, there was no fear of another immortal, and eventually, spiteful entity being created.

It was a shame really. Such a being could store unlimited amounts of aythar, was unfailingly loyal and… My mind froze for a moment. "Ha!" I said aloud.

Penny elbowed me in the ribs, "Shhh!"

I hushed, but I began to fidget with my excitement. The idea running through my head was fascinating. It solved a number of problems at once—and it was artistic. I had a feeling none of the necessary people would agree to it, but that was alright. I had a way with people.

The party after the vows were done was breathtaking, but I had no attention to spare for celebrating. I accepted small plates of food and various drinks almost mechanically as my mind fleshed out the details of what might be my greatest achievement.

Gareth will be a problem, I noted mentally. *I'll need him to provide the flesh.*

The enchantments would be difficult as well. I already knew the essential parts, but if my design was to be perfect, I would have to create something new. *Forgetfulness is the death of the mind,* I told myself, thinking of a day long ago, when Marcus and I had been searching his father's library. I knew it would work.

"You seem lost in thought," said a familiar voice beside me.

Looking up, I realized that Ariadne had closed on me while my mind was diverted. If I had been paying attention, I probably would have made certain we never bumped into one another. Now it was too late.

"My apologies, Your Majesty," I responded without too much hesitation. Using my magesight, I located Penny. She had grown tired of my lack of conversation and was now mingling with some of the other guests. "I think I have forgotten the art of small talk."

Her eyes were warm, but behind them I could see a hint of something else. "You should visit the capital more often, there are endless opportunities to reacquaint yourself with it here," she suggested.

That was the last thing I wanted. I had lost all desire for the company of the nobility, and the Queen's presence felt like a burning pain. My scars began to itch.

"I have not been to the capital since…," I paused, unable to finish that sentence. Instead I restarted, "It has been months, Your Majesty."

She reached out toward me as if to touch my arm, but stopped when she saw my involuntary withdrawal. I had stepped back an inch.

"Mordecai, you do realize I never wanted things to happen as they did, don't you?" she said with a sad, almost lonely note in her voice.

"Certainly," I replied, but I put no effort into sounding convincing.

"Yet you haven't answered my letters," she pointed out.

I faced her then, looking into her eyes. "It's difficult, Your Majesty. My mind knows the truth, but my heart, it remembers the shame. Give me time."

"There is no one to hear us," she reminded me. "You don't have to use the honorifics." The space around us was empty, and for a moment I realized, so was she— empty and alone, isolated by power.

Whatever else she was now, Ariadne was Marcus' little sister, the girl who had tried to follow us on our childhood adventures. As Queen, she needed friends more than ever, and yet I had shut her out of my heart.

I stared at my feet. "I'm sorry. I can't help how I am now, but I think it will get easier." It was easier to think now that I no longer had to watch her emotions play across her features. Even then my mind itself turned away, seeking to retreat into the plan it had been working on only moments before.

Blood, that's the key, I realized with sudden inspiration. *Take it now, or else you'll have to come back later.* Using my will alone, I reshaped the inside of my signet ring, creating a sharp, jagged edge.

"The distance between us pains me, Mort. We're still family," she said.

We were first cousins, once removed, and now that her parents were gone, I was the closest family she had, except for one other. I decided to change the subject. "I heard the good news about Roland. Congratulations."

Roland, her younger brother, had turned up only a month past. He had been presumed dead, but his body had never been found. Once his story was told, we found out that he had been away from Lancaster when the attack had happened. Roland had always been an avid outdoorsman, much like his father in that regard. He had returned from a hunt to discover his keep destroyed and had only narrowly escaped being captured by the Shaddoth Krys before he understood his danger.

Alone, he had retreated into the mountains. He had planned to build his own shelter and try to winter there, but by some stroke of good fortune had found a small cottage in the rough foothills. A shepherd, along with his wife and daughter lived there.

They had accepted him into their home, and he had exchanged his labor for a warm bed and food. He had also been smitten by their daughter.

Ariadne grimaced, "I am glad to have him returned, but his situation has made things more difficult."

"You mean his common wife?" I said pointedly. It was a loaded question, since my own wife, Penny, was a commoner too.

She nodded, "For a nobleman it can be managed, but for a royal…"

"I'm sure you'll find a way to deal with it. He seems very happy," I observed. "I would think his reappearance might create bigger problems for you." According to the laws of succession, her younger brother should have been crowned king if he survived. A woman could only ascend to the throne if there were no sons.

"Some have tried to make a problem out of it," she agreed, "but Roland wouldn't cooperate. The first thing he did once he got to Albamarl was to formally abnegate his right to the crown."

"I bet that caused a stir."

Ariadne grinned. "It did indeed, but the troublemakers don't have a leg to stand on now. Roland never wanted the throne. Even the duchy is a burden to him, though I did manage to convince him to resume his place there."

"What would he have done otherwise?" I asked.

She laughed, "He wanted to go back and live out his days as a simple shepherd. Melanie's parents made quite an impression on him."

Melanie, I had probably been told the name, but I had forgotten it. "I can't say that I blame him. I've wished the same a few times," I said wistfully. Without realizing it, I had already begun to relax in my conversation with Ariadne, forgetting for a moment the pain that had kept me segregated from her.

Ariadne peered at me compassionately, "Do you ever wonder what life would have been like if you hadn't discovered your heritage, if you hadn't become a wizard, or a count? You might be there still, hammering away in your father's smithy."

"More so now than ever before," I answered softly.

My words moved her then, and she reached out, seeking to clasp my hands within her own. It was a gesture that was full of warmth and familial closeness. Before she could complete the movement, I opened my hands and caught hers within them, squeezing firmly. She jerked as the sharp metal edge on my ring cut the back of her right hand, drawing a bright red bead of blood.

"Ow! What was that?" she exclaimed, pulling her hands away.

"Damn, I'm sorry," I said immediately, pulling out a handkerchief to daub the blood from her hand. "I caught my ring while working on something the other day, and it left a spur of metal."

I had ruined the moment, and the look in her eyes held a question. Despite our shared history, I saw the seed of distrust there. It was something I had learned to spot in many of the faces of people who still wondered if I could really have regained my full humanity; the doubt, the worry that I might still have something of the monster in me. She blinked, and the fear was hidden again.

"Why don't you fix it?" she asked with some exasperation.

"I've meant to do that, but I keep getting distracted," I confessed.

"I thought you could do something small like that with little more than a moment's thought," she told me.

I could, and it had been just that simple to create the sharp metal point to begin with. "There's an enchantment on the ring," I lied smoothly. "I can't alter it easily without a bit of planning, otherwise I might ruin it."

She accepted my explanation without argument, but I could tell she was suspicious. That was fine, though. She would understand later. I excused myself soon after and made my way over to talk to the newly married Gareth.

"I can't tell you how happy I am for you," I said, shaking his hand.

"Your presence here says enough," he replied congenially. "I understand it must have been difficult for you."

"I have to get over it sooner or later," I said with more confidence than I really felt. "I should thank your wife for choosing to have the wedding here."

He nodded, "I don't doubt that she considered it before she chose; her kind like to scheme."

"Her kind?" I said, unsure if he meant constructs, or humans, or those of the feminine persuasion. Considering both his past and hers, it was open to interpretation.

"Women," he clarified.

I nodded. That was something we could both agree on. Then I brought up the question that had been foremost in my mind, "I've been meaning to ask you about this body." I gestured at myself.

"The same way I created hers," he said without offering any context.

I assumed he meant Moira. "I'm just curious how you did it. Was it wizardry or a product of your talents as an archmage?"

"For normal magic it would be almost impossible. It was the latter, but only a Gaelyn could accomplish it, I think," he replied.

He might be right, but I wasn't convinced yet. "Can you describe the process? Just a rough outline…"

He was happy to oblige. It turned out to be less interesting than I had supposed, and more difficult, as well. Using his ability as an archmage he first expanded his body and then split it into two equal parts, transforming both into duplicates of his original self. From that point, he would withdraw into one, leaving the other fully formed and functional, lacking only a spirit or animus.

The difficulty lay in two areas. One, living organisms are exceedingly complex, which was why most archmages only mastered one fundamental living transformation, the return to their original human form. Transforming into a simple body, like the stone monster I had become in the past was easier physically, but more difficult to return from mentally. Creating a living flesh and blood body, such as Gareth's transformation into the dragon, was far more complex, but it had the advantage of a living brain, which helped to keep the mind intact.

The second problem lay in the duality of what he was accomplishing. He was creating *two* bodies at one time, and simultaneously keeping them both active and alive until someone else could take up residence in one of them. I had experienced a bit of that difficulty, when I brought Walter back from the brink of death after an assassin had stabbed him. The attempt had nearly cost me my own life as I tried to keep both our hearts beating while healing his body.

He had done the same for both Moira and me, which brought me to another question. "You obviously shaped Moira's body into what it is now, rather than a replica of your own. Why didn't you do the same for me?"

He smiled. "A good question, only a Gaelyn archmage could create a living body *and* shape it into that of another person or creature. In your case, I didn't need to bother. As an archmage I knew you could restore yourself to what you had been before."

Listening, I had come to accept that I would need his help. It wouldn't be possible to do what I wanted alone. I would have to persuade him. "Do you still like dragons?"

My change of subject startled him, "What?!"

"You lived as one for over a thousand years. You loved the idea of them before, but are you still drawn to it?" I said, elaborating on my query.

"Yes," he admitted, "though I doubt I will ever attempt something so foolish again."

"I have an idea," I said, easing into my topic, "and I think you will be interested in helping me." I gave him the rough outline, although I glossed over a few parts.

His face remained impassive as I spoke, but at the end he had a clear cut opinion, "You're mad. Not only are you mad, but it's impossible."

"No it isn't."

"They would die immediately. There's no way to keep them alive without an animus," he pointed out.

"I'll have anima for all of them," I insisted.

"Only a Centyr could produce...," he began, but then he stopped, eyes widening, "...oh."

I nodded sagely.

"But you still couldn't do it before they died, the time it would require is excessive," he insisted.

"I have an idea to circumvent that problem as well," I answered.

"Even if you do, have you thought about the moral implications?"

"You mean since my own experiences?" I suggested.

"Yes. It's immoral. I just freed three of your ancestor's tormented creations, yet you want to create more?" He paused and then continued, "My wife would be livid with you, and me by extension."

He was referring to the unmaking of Doron, Karenth, and Millicenth, something he had taken care of in my stead. "Your wife is an immortal construct, yet she seems happy enough," I noted.

"For now," said Gareth, "but she has the means to end her existence someday when it becomes too much of a burden. Will you do the same in this case?"

"No," I said, "I have a different plan." I was less sure about this part, but I felt it could be accomplished in theory. I just had to figure out how to make it happen. I gave him a quick description.

"That is definitely impossible," he declared.

"I can do it," I asserted. "Give me a month and come visit me. Say nothing to Moira, I'll explain it to her myself."

"She isn't going to go along with it," he reiterated.

"She will," I said, "and what's more she won't blame you for any of it."

"If it were anyone else..." said Gareth, looking at me from the corner of his eye.

"You don't have any plans for all the aythar you've got locked up in her do you?" I said, referring to the forty plus Celiors worth of aythar that Moira Centyr was storing.

"No," he admitted. "Frankly it scares the shit out of me, but I haven't thought of a better place yet."

"Then this will work out perfectly," I said, staring at the spot of blood on the handkerchief I held.

Chapter 55

After we returned home I threw myself into my new project with an energy I hadn't felt since I first began working on the World Road. That had been a project that would change the world and reshape the future of Lothion, if not the entire world. This one would be just as grand, and while possibly not as important it would likely be what history would remember me for.

No one gets excited talking about who built a road, even a magical one, but this, this would light a fire in the imagination of generations to come!

If I could figure out how to do the impossible. I knew what I wanted, but the enchantment to accomplish it didn't exist. There were several that did parts of what I needed, but none that came remotely close to the entire thing. Worse, some of the functions were things that had never been done with an enchantment at all.

At first Penny was pleased to see me throw myself into my work, but as days ran into weeks and the weeks ran into a month she began to worry. I rarely showed myself outside of my workshop except to eat and sleep; and I did precious little of those. My only trips beyond Cameron in all that time were short jaunts to our house in Albamarl to raid the Illeniel library of books on runes and mathematics.

What really frustrated her was my refusal to discuss my plans. A year living as an undead monster hadn't cured me of my flaws. I told no one my entire plan, not even Gareth.

My children however, refused to be completely shut out. They were almost as stubborn as their mother and far too clever for their own good. Eventually I let them join me for short periods, partly to satisfy their curiosity and partly so I could question my daughter about her special ability.

"How *exactly* do you mold the personality?" I asked again. Her previous answer had been too vague.

She gave me a look that told me I was too slow to properly understand, but she tried to explain again. "I don't do anything in particular. I just imagine them, as a bard imagines a story, whole and complete. Their traits are just a part of that."

"How long does it take?"

"The first ones, like little Grace, sprang from my dreams, while I was sleeping," she told me. "That's why she's so smart."

Again, she didn't seem to be able to answer my question directly. 'Grace' was the name of her first and favorite animated toy, a cute teddy bear with a red bow. The two of them were almost inseparable, and the toy was uncannily sharp. Talking to it was much like talking to my daughter—except I felt silly talking to a stuffed animal.

"You're saying she's smart because she came from a dream?"

"Not exactly," said Moira. "It's because I took my time, and my conscious mind didn't get in the way. Doing it while awake is harder, because I have to learn how to keep my waking thoughts from interfering with the process. At least that's what my other mother told me."

'Other mother' was the shorthand she used to refer to the other Moira. It helped us to avoid confusion, both with her name and with Penny. "So are you able to make one like her while awake now?"

"Yes," she said, "but I can't be sure how long it will take. Sometimes it's quick and other times it takes hours. The simple ones are always fast, though."

Eventually my questions grew too specific, and I began to share the larger details of what I intended with her, as well as with Matthew. I knew the idea would excite them, I only hoped they could keep quiet about it until it was finished. The last thing I wanted was for word to get out, especially when I wasn't entirely sure I could succeed.

Once I had included them, Moira began working on her portion of my project in earnest and soon she was bringing new 'toys' to talk to me daily. In each case, we would discuss their strengths and weaknesses, along with their quirks. Most of them I rejected, but gradually she began to create more of the intensely complex and intelligent ones, like her original toy, Grace.

After several weeks, her room had become a veritable zoo of talking toys. Luckily she let most of the ones that were too flawed fade out, so while she kept creating new ones, our home was never quite overrun with them.

I suspected there was a limit to how many of them she could sustain at one time without me using the immortality enchantment on them, and of course that was something I would never do. That was how the Shining Gods had been created, and I wanted no part in recreating that mistake.

As it was, Celior was still loose somewhere in the world. He had been freed when the shield around Castle

Cameron had been shattered by Mal'goroth. The feedback had destroyed the God-Stone, and he had wasted no time escaping. I had the keys needed to bind him, but I had to locate him before I could do that.

Another big surprise that came to me while I worked was my son's insight into enchanting. Not being a Centyr like his sister, he couldn't help her with her 'pet' project, so he spent more time watching me struggle to figure out a method to make my potential new enchantment do all the things I required of it.

He had never studied the subject before, and while he would also have access to the knowledge of the loshti someday, he couldn't reach it yet. Even so, he proved to be a natural when it came to understanding the mathematics that underlay the rune structures.

His eyes were always watching me, and though his questions often seemed to stray into areas that seemed off topic, they often led me to a far better knowledge of what I was trying to do than I had possessed previously.

If you want to learn something really well, teach it to someone else, I said to myself.

Matthew's lack of preconceptions proved to be a valuable asset in sorting out how to do the impossible.

"Why do you want it to repeat anyway?" he asked me after I had explained what the portion of the enchantment I was working on was supposed to do.

"I have to have a way for this thing to restart itself at particular times, otherwise..." I let the words trail off. *How do I explain to my son that eternity brings its own particular kind of suffering?* "Let's focus on the *how*," I said instead.

"Can't you link it to a timer?" he asked.

572

I sighed, if only it were that simple. "No, the stasis field will render that meaningless. It would just stop and never begin again."

"You already have it linked to something else that's external," he observed. "That's what this is, right?" He pointed to a different portion of the rune structure I had drawn out. I hadn't told him what that part was for, but his observant eyes had picked it out anyway.

"That specifies the person who will control it," I explained.

"Couldn't you let them use a command, instead of having it restart itself?"

"They won't want to reset it while they're alive," I told him.

"If the person dies won't that create an open fault?" he asked.

He was referring to the fact that, because the enchantment was linked to a person, once they were gone it would create a break in the chain, invalidating the entire thing. It was a basic part of the nature of enchanting, but I hadn't taught it to him yet. Once again, I was amazed at his quick insight. "No," I replied slowly. "That would be a problem, but if you look here, you'll see that when that happens, it shifts this part. That will close the circle again and activate this portion, which allows it to link to a new person."

"Oh," he said. "So can't you have your repeat function tie into that? It sounds like it's something you want to happen at about that same time anyway, right?"

"Well, you can't do that because...," I stopped for a moment, thinking, "...because it would work perfectly. Sonofabitch!"

He grinned at me.

"You've earned your supper today," I told him.

"Does that mean you'll let me see that part over there?" he asked.

The part 'over there' was covered by a heavy piece of parchment to hide it from casual observation. It was the essential part of what I thought of as the 'god-enchantment', the same one I had used to bind Moira Centyr. Eventually he would be able to remember it, since the information was stored in the loshti, like so many other things, but for now I didn't want him to know something so potentially dangerous.

"I'm afraid not," I answered, "but I have something else you can help me with."

His eyes lit up. His enthusiasm was endearing, and I couldn't help but wonder how many more years I would have before working with me was no longer something he would look forward to.

I took him aside and showed him the boxes I had been working on. So far I had completed only one, and I demonstrated its use to him.

"That's neat!" he exclaimed. "What would you use it for, though?"

"Don't worry about that," I said waving my hands. "Do you think you can copy what I've done here?" I showed him the rune design I had sketched out on a long sheet of parchment.

"Sure," he agreed immediately.

"Good," I told him. "I need twenty-two more just like it then."

"Twenty-two?!"

"Practice makes perfect."

He sighed loudly, "Dad, they won't *work* if they aren't perfect."

I laughed, "So you only have to get it perfect twenty-two times. The real question is, how many *practice* tries will it take you to get it right twenty-two times."

His jaw clenched in what might have been determination in an older man. In my young son it was simply adorable. "We'll just have to see won't we?" he replied.

*
**

Gareth Gaelyn came to see me almost exactly a month after our conversation. I had thought he would visit with his new wife, but she was conspicuously absent.

Penny greeted him initially, and after a brief interrogation regarding his first month of married life, I was able to intercede and whisk him away to my workshop. That earned me a frown, since I had been pretty anti-social myself over the past month, and now I was monopolizing our guest.

"Does she know what you're working on?" asked Gareth once we were alone.

I shrugged, "Not really. I'm sure she's picked up some of the details from the children, since they've been helping me with parts of it, but I doubt she knows the heart of it."

"Doubt? She either knows or she doesn't," stated Gareth.

I laughed, "I say 'doubt' because, while I assume she doesn't, she nevertheless surprises me sometimes. It's best not to underestimate her intuition."

"Would she approve?"

"Probably?" I said uncertainly. "She wouldn't be upset by it—I don't think. One never knows with Penny when it comes to magic. Did you discuss my plan with your wife?"

"I know she would not approve," Gareth said confidently. "You claim you can convince her, so I leave that matter to you. She visits here enough that you've surely had the opportunity already."

"I'll broach the topic when I'm ready for her part. Would you like to see what we've done thus far?"

The answer to that question was obvious, and we spent the next hour discussing the enchantment I had been working on. I also showed him the boxes that Matthew and I had been making.

"That's clever," he noted. "That should get around the time problem. I'm surprised I didn't think of that myself after watching you use that enchantment not too long ago."

"Well, this is a much safer, more traditional use," I stated quickly.

The other archmage coughed, "Well, that much is plain to see. The real question is whether this new enchantment of yours will work properly. You still haven't worked out all the wrinkles in it yet, have you?"

"That's true," I admitted, "but I feel close to the solution. A week or two more and I'm confident I'll have it reasoned out. I have a few questions for you, though."

"Ask away," he replied.

"You told me you'd be able to make them living and breathing, but will they be able to grow? Can they reproduce? If my regression structure works, what will the initial state be?" I said, asking all my questions at once.

His face took on a pensive expression for a long minute before he answered, "Yes to the first, an egg to the last, and as far as reproduction goes—I am uncertain."

"Because of the lack of a wellspring?" I suggested.

"Exactly," agreed Gareth. "That question may apply to Moira and me as well."

Since Moira Centyr was an artificial life, a magical sentience housed in a living body, it was unclear whether she could have children. The necessary equipment was there, but since she didn't possess a true wellspring of aythar, a 'soul', it was uncertain whether her union with Gareth could create children who would have them. Without one, any offspring would be stillborn.

"While I wish you the best of luck, I think I'd prefer it if these were unable to breed, to eliminate unanticipated possibilities," I said honestly.

Gareth grunted, "I haven't decided if I could handle children anyway. I'm a little old for that sort of chaos." Gesturing at the empty boxes he added, "When do you want me to start?"

"We should have the last of them ready by next week. How long will it take you to do each one?"

"A full day for the first one maybe, after that it will be quicker, possibly as little as a few hours each," he responded after a moment.

I nodded. "So you'll need at least a week then. You should plan a long visit here with Moira," I told him.

"That wouldn't be wise."

"You really are worried about her opinion aren't you? Frankly, I'm surprised you're willing to participate. When I first brought it up, I anticipated a long lecture before you would agree, but you gave only a token resistance to the idea."

"I still think you're mad. This will probably fail outright, and you'll have a nasty mess to clean up. If it doesn't, then things may just go wrong, which means an even bigger cleanup," he said truthfully.

"Then why go along with me?"

"I can't help it. This idea plays to my most coveted inner dream. If you succeed, it will change the world. The risks are worth it to be a part of that," he explained with a hint of passion in his voice. Gareth rarely got excited, he was famously taciturn, but I could tell that this project had his full attention.

Chapter 56

It was almost three weeks after Gareth left before I was ready. I sent him a message via message box when I was close to done, and then I took up the subject of their visit with Penny.

I hadn't expected any trouble from her quarter, but once again I had underestimated her perceptiveness.

"It would be nice to have them both for a week," she answered when I brought the subject up, but something in her tone begged the question.

"But, what?" I asked. I should have known better.

She gave me a look that spoke volumes; I just wasn't sure what language they were written in. Why couldn't women be simpler?

"But, what?" I repeated, having exhausted my list of clever responses already.

"Nothing," she said in the special tone she used that quite obviously meant the exact opposite.

Unsure what to do, I growled at her instead. It was a special technique I had learned over the years. When in doubt don't try to get 'smart' with them. They just make you suffer more if you try to be rational. Forget the verbosity, and find your inner savage. They'll often take pity and explain themselves if you do.

"If you don't want to tell me, I won't ask," she said, giving me enough information to finally realize what she was getting at.

Early in our marriage I might have played dumb, replying with something like, 'Tell you what?' I had learned that lesson already, though. Instead I took the bull by the horns, "You're referring to my special project?"

She nodded. "I'm sure you've drawn Gareth into whatever it is, as well as embroiling our children in it. I just wish you'd be more open with me."

Given the events of the last year, I knew she deserved better, so I explained my idea in its entirety. I gave her the entire thing, hoping that she wouldn't find something to object to in my scheme. When I had finished I added one caveat, "Please, don't tell Moira."

"Our Moira or Gareth's?"

"Gareth's," I clarified.

"So you want to induct me into your secret and then exclude his wife? Is that really fair?" she asked.

"Gareth is uncertain how to approach her on the topic, so I offered to take her aside and explain," I said.

She frowned, "Why not let me broach the subject?"

"She's going to have some valid objections," I explained, "but I think I can persuade her."

"Alright," she said without further argument.

I couldn't quite believe in her easy acceptance, so I waited quietly for a minute or two.

"Why are you looking at me like that?" she asked eventually.

"You aren't going to try and talk me out of this?" I said narrowing my eyes in suspicion.

"No."

"This could be dangerous," I added.

"Mmm hmm," she murmured, absently polishing some of our dishware. That was a clear sign that she felt the conversation was over, or at the very minimum, it no longer deserved the sort of attention that would slow her progress on her cleaning schedule any further.

"Even if I succeed, there could be far reaching consequences, not just for us, but for future generations," I told her seriously.

"Very true."

At that point I was certain she hadn't really been listening, so I went for the preposterous, "I'm going to sacrifice our children and use their blood to fuel terrible dark magics."

She raised one eyebrow, "Are you *trying* to get me to object?"

"Well, it's what you do," I admitted. "I don't feel comfortable going forward if you don't at least put up a token resistance."

Penny gave me a long sigh, the kind she reserved for special moments of stupidity. Rolling her eyes upward, she spoke in a monotone, "Oh please, Mort, please don't do this. For the sake of our children, don't do this." Switching back to her normal tone she added, "There, is that what you wanted? May I get back to what I was doing?"

"You didn't mean that," I notified her. "Not only that, but you're undermining the foundations of our relationship. You've set me adrift in uncharted waters."

"I'm sure you'll manage somehow," she replied acerbically.

I was agog at the way she dismissed my emotional distress. I let my mouth fall open dramatically to emphasize the feeling, since she clearly wasn't getting it.

She graced me with another sigh. "If I argue with you, will it change anything?" she asked.

"Probably not," I conceded.

"But if I just accept your plan, you'll be riddled by self-doubt and second guess yourself?"

I nodded emphatically.

"Then it's obviously the best thing I can do. If I argue you'll do what you want and never look back, but if I don't, you'll rethink the whole thing. You might even consider deeper consequences, possibly improve your plan or reduce the risks. At the very least, you'll be more prudent and less stupid," she explained.

She had really thought this one through.

"We've been married for years now Mort, and one thing I've *finally* learned, is that if I want you to share your secrets, I need to be more accepting. If that also means you'll think things through more carefully, then it's a win-win," she said.

"Who are you, and what have you done with Penny?" I said incredulously.

She smiled and gave me a quick peck on the cheek, dismissing me. "Go back to your work."

I started to leave, but I stopped for a second, looking back.

"Enjoy second guessing yourself," she added.

I shook my head and left. *I'll show her,* I thought to myself. *I'll recklessly push forward, and to hell with the consequences. I won't rethink a single thing!*

It was empty bravado, though. After I sent the message inviting Gareth and Moira to stay with us, I spent the rest of the afternoon reconsidering my entire plan. Then I began rechecking all the work I had done. Penny really knew how to get under my skin sometimes. Before I was done, I did indeed change a few minor things and decided to add a few extra conditions to make sure my enchantment would continue to work even in the most unlikely situations I could imagine.

Women are evil, and my wife was chief among them.

*
**

Moira and Gareth arrived a few days later. In the past, Moira had been almost a member of the household, she was around so often, but since marrying we had only seen her twice, and only briefly on those occasions.

Penny set them up in the one guest bedroom we kept in our, no longer quite so secret, mountain cottage. We had a nice dinner and drinks afterward, indulging in small talk and letting the children entertain us with their antics.

It wasn't until the next morning after breakfast that I took Moira Centyr aside and asked her if she would join me in my workshop. I chose that time of day since it gave us lots of time. Gareth had taken our older children out on the mountain to give them a lesson on the wildlife that lived in such areas. He had a unique perspective on it, since at one time or another he had actually transformed into many of the animals they could see out there.

The reality though, was that he wanted to be nowhere nearby when I broached the subject of my latest project with his wife.

"Penny mentioned last night that you've been spending an inordinate amount of time in here," noted Moira as I let her in through the main door.

"That's true," I confessed, "but I actually have two reasons for bringing you here."

"I could tell you had a lot on your mind," she answered mildly. "What are those boxes?"

I took her closer, letting her examine the runes. "They should be somewhat familiar to you," I said.

"Stasis boxes, why would you need so many, and why so small?" She looked confused.

"Let me start at the beginning," I said and then I took my time explaining my plan. Her face grew darker as my plan unfolded, but she held her tongue until the end.

"Did you learn nothing?! This is immoral, dangerous, and possibly the very definition of evil! You're just repeating my mistake! You even have his memories, why would you do this?!" Her voice rose with each phrase.

By 'his memories', I knew she was referring to the first Mordecai, the one she had loved a thousand years before, the actual father of my daughter. He had been the one who had originally designed the 'god-enchantment' that they used to create the Shining Gods. "There are some substantial differences here," I began, but she interrupted me.

"Yes!" she broke in, "Differences of scale. What you plan is even larger and more dangerous. Twenty-three! Why would you even consider such a thing?!"

"I've altered the enchantment in numerous ways, to create a system of safeguards, both for them and for us," I explained. "Look here, do you see this part?"

"None of that makes sense," she spat out angrily. "But it hardly matters, think of the suffering! Even if you thought this was safe for the people of this world, think of what you're condemning them to endure. *You* were a victim of this sort of thing for a year; didn't you learn anything from that?"

"It won't be like that," I reassured her. "They will be alive, in every sense of the word. They'll grow and learn, just like..."

Her eyes grew wide. "You're using her aren't you? My daughter—*your* daughter, have you no shame? Do you think she has the slightest inkling what any of this means?"

In her anger, the forty-plus Celiors worth of aythar that Moira Centyr had stored within her began to leak out, creating an almost unbearable pressure. It was becoming an effort simply to breathe while standing in the same room with her.

"And when you say, 'alive', does that mean what I think it does? Have you dragged my own husband into this?!"

I couldn't take much more. Even shielding my mind as strongly as possible, her aythar was crushing my will, and she was still containing most of it. I was no longer immortal as I had been when I faced Mal'goroth, nor did I have the sort of power to protect myself that I had had then. Thankfully, I had alternatives now.

As I had done with Celior long ago, I let my mind slip partly into the earth, gaining some respite from the unbearable power I was standing beside. Once I was able to think clearly, I uttered the words that would reinstate my control over Moira Centyr's enchantment, binding her to my will once more.

"You dare!" she shouted, swelling until she threatened to destroy my small shop.

"Resume your normal size, and reign in your strength, you're making it difficult to breathe," I commanded. "You will do nothing else until I give you leave to act on your own again. Until then you will listen carefully to all that I say."

She shrank back to her normal size, staring at me with fury in her eyes.

"First," I told her, "We need to remove some of that power. It isn't safe to store it in one location like that."

Using short terse commands. I directed her to channel the aythar into the first of my temporary holding 'cells'. In reality, it was the first of my new creations, but the power wouldn't remain there permanently. I had a multitude of plans for how it would be divided up later.

It was a process that would take quite a while, considering how much aythar she had within her, so I used the time to explain the finer points of my plan. I hoped that once she understood the full depth of it, she might rethink her opposition to it.

I talked for over an hour and even went so far as to illustrate my words with visible illusions, so that she could see what I intended. When I had finished her fury was diminished, but she was still unhappy.

"Go ahead and talk," I said, returning her power of speech.

"It is still wrong. You've done much to alleviate the worst of it, but it still isn't right," she said. "Look at me now, bound and helpless. This alone is proof."

"I didn't intend to do that," I said honestly, "but you started leaking aythar when you got angry. I'm not sure if you realize how much power you were putting out a little while ago. It was enough that I feared for the safety of everyone in the house."

"I would never hurt your family. That was unintentional," she stopped, looking down before returning her gaze to me. "Do you think I am unstable now?"

Her question wasn't rhetorical. Her expression told me she truly worried about it. My magical clone, Brexus, had shown every sign of slowly coming apart mentally, and he had barely been a year old. Moira Centyr, or rather the version of her in my home, was over a thousand years old. She had told me before that her creator had had unparalleled talent in making stable personalities, but the recently unmade Shining Gods were proof enough that her skills weren't perfect.

"No more than I am, Moira. You were just angry." I said, hoping to reassure her.

"Yet what you intend to do will only compound the risk that I represent," she insisted.

"I believe it will work this way. They'll remain stable."

"You can't know that," she responded.

I walked closer, until we were almost nose to nose. "Moira, you trusted me enough to give me the care of your daughter. I lived a year as one of them, trapped within a monster that I thought was me, but wasn't. I learned a lot, about both myself and the true nature of the god-enchantment. This will work, and if it doesn't, I have the means to undo it, and so will the generations that follow."

"You're so much like him," she said then, and I knew she was referring to the first Mordecai, the one she had loved so long ago. "He was arrogant and self-confident, and he turned out to be completely wrong."

"I've learned from his mistakes," I told her. "I can remember it. This time will be different."

"It isn't as though I have a choice," she said bitterly.

She had finished transferring all but a small fraction of the power now, though she still held perhaps a half-Celior worth of aythar.

"You can stop now. Keep the power that remains," I commanded.

"Whatever power I have, it doesn't matter. I'm still your slave."

"No," I said then, "I give you your freedom. I only bound you to give you time to calm down. You can do as you wish now."

"You can re-bind me with only a few words," she challenged.

"I won't," I said again, "I just needed a chance to explain. If you insist, I'll drop this project. I leave it in your hands."

"Do you really mean that?" she asked, stepping close to the first stasis box. "You'd let me destroy this one?"

I was sweating now. She still had a half-Celior worth of power in her. There was no way I could prevent her from doing what she wished, short of rebinding her. I was betting she would see my side of it, but I couldn't be sure. "I hope you won't, but I'll respect your wishes."

She tensed for a moment, and then her shoulders sagged. "Fine, do as you will, but I want no part of it."

I didn't need her help for any of it, just her permission, otherwise Gareth would have refused to finish his portion of it. "I just wanted to ensure you would understand."

"No," she added, "That's not what I mean. When I say I want no part in this, I mean I don't want to know."

"What?"

"I've been through this before, and my complicity then still fills me with guilt. I want no part in this. If you insist on going forward, I don't want to know. Take the knowledge from me, leave me innocent," she explained.

Technically, if you agree now, you're still an accomplice, even if you don't remember later, my sarcastic inner voice noted. I decided it wasn't being helpful, so I kept that thought to myself. "I don't think I can create a spell specific enough to clear just that knowledge from your mind."

"You don't have to," she said carefully, "you can order it, remember?"

I understood immediately. The enchantment that bound her controlled her mind just as absolutely as it did her body. Though I had never considered using it in such a way, I knew she was right. "You're sure?" I asked again, to clarify.

"I'll give you the words. You just have to repeat them and make it an order."

After a short discussion I gave her a pen and some parchment to be sure I got the order precisely as she wanted it. When she had finished writing I browsed it quickly before asking, "You really want this last part in there?"

"Yes."

"Very well," I said. "Moira Centyr, by the enchantment that binds you, I command you to forget what you have seen and heard in this room today. You will not think to be suspicious of our time together later, nor will you question me or anyone else on it. When the truth emerges at some point in the future, you will assume that I was the only one involved. You will never suspect Gareth's involvement. If you become angry with me for it at that time, you will forgive me after a few days."

I walked her out into the hall, watching her carefully for she seemed dazed.

"That's odd," she said. "I feel different. What happened to the aythar?" She looked around in confusion.

"I had you channel it into a storage vessel I had prepared," I said, dancing around the truth. "You went too quickly I think. You passed out at the end. Don't you remember?"

"Not really," she replied. "It's possible the rapid loss of aythar could cause memory loss," she added, supplying her own excuse.

"You may be right," I agreed. On the inside though I mourned, for it was as though a part of her had died, even if it was just an hour of her life gone. More than ever, that convinced me that my plan would work. *Memories are at the heart of what we are made of, losing them is the same as dying.*

Chapter 57

"It's Sir Harold Simmons, my lady," announced Rose Thornbear's senior maid.

"Thank you, Angela. I have been expecting him," answered Rose. "Please show him to the sitting room."

Angela pursed her lips disapprovingly. She never liked to see Lady Rose meet with a man alone, even one of Sir Harold's stature, but she knew better than to voice her opinion. "Very well, my lady."

A few minutes later, Sir Harold found her in the sitting room. As its name suggested the room was adorned with a variety of comfortable items of furniture, primarily chairs, though it also boasted a divan and an exquisitely carved table that created a focus for the area. That was where the tea would generally be served.

The lady of the house sat on a rather stiff chair to one side, her back straight except for the natural curve of her spine. Her features and dark hair only served to make the black fabric of her dress more attractive. She rose from her seat to greet Sir Harold, "I see you felt the need to make your case in person." It was less of a greeting than a challenge.

Harold took her proffered hand and bent over it, not quite touching the back of it with his lips. Actually kissing it would have been an affront, given the difference in their relative statures. He held the position for longer than necessary, to show extra reverence to his mentor's widow. "Thank you for seeing me, Lady Hightower," he began, "I felt the need to express myself in person."

As soon as he released her hand she motioned to a chair across the room, indicating he should sit, and then she resumed her own seat. "Please, there's no need to use my formal title. Lady Rose will do," she suggested. She would have preferred Lady Thornbear, but that title still resided more properly with her mother-in-law, Elise. To avoid confusion, she used her first name in less formal settings.

"You do me too much honor, Lady Rose," said Harold. The situation made him uncomfortable. He had been raised on a farm, and courtly etiquette was something that he had learned under Dorian Thornbear's tutelage after being chosen to train for knighthood. Given his background, it was doubtful he would ever be comfortable in such circumstances. Lady Rose had assisted with his education back then, but now she seemed far colder to him.

Rose turned away, looking out the window, "Not too much honor for an old friend of my husband's, Sir Harold."

"You realize why I am here, of course, Lady Rose?" asked Harold tentatively.

She nodded, "Yes I do, and I am afraid that you have wasted your time, Sir Harold."

"Please, just Harold will do, Lady Rose," he responded, "You helped train me, after all."

"You were an excellent student, Harold, but I will not give you the sword," she told him. She was referring to the broken remains of 'Thorn,' the great sword Dorian had once borne.

"The Queen intends to honor him with the founding of a new order of knights, to be named the Order of the Thorn. The name is meant to honor his name, and that sword would be placed in our chapterhouse, as a sort of relic, serving as an example to future generations," said Harold fervently.

"Sir Egan said as much in his letter," said Rose. "There is no need to remind me."

"I don't understand your reluctance, Lady Rose," replied Harold. "Don't you want us to honor him?"

"You choose your words poorly, Harold. It is not 'reluctance'. The appropriate term would be 'refusal,'" she told him. "Do you know the story behind the sword's name?"

"No, Lady Rose," said Harold promptly. "He never shared its reason with me, but we always assumed that it represented the sharper portion of his name."

"Exactly," said Rose with steel in her voice, "you assumed, and incorrectly at that. It was the last part of the sword's name that he used, but the full name was 'Rose's Thorn'. It was a name with special meaning between the two of us. It was not for you or anyone else to revere, it was symbolic of the bond between my husband and me."

"But, Lady Rose…"

"Would you like to put my wedding ring in your chapterhouse, Sir Harold?! Would that be sufficient to please you? For it would be almost the same thing to me. Do you understand now?" she struck out at him with the words, viciously, as if she would share her pain by wounding him.

Harold stood for a moment before falling to his knees, "Forgive me, Lady Rose, in my ignorance I have offended you. It was not my intention to do so. I understand my error now."

She took pity on him then, "Rise Harold, don't cast your eyes downward so. I was too harsh."

He took his feet then, but kept his head bowed, "It was wrong of me to come."

"No," she said, "I have given some thought to your request, and while you may not have Thorn, there is something else you may have." She gestured to the wall, where a long sword was hanging on display.

Harold looked at her questioningly.

"It was his father's sword, Gram Thornbear's. Dorian took it up after his father died. It was the first sword Mordecai enchanted for him. He used it proudly until he switched to the great sword and stopped using a shield," she explained.

"But…," Harold almost stammered, "… shouldn't that go to his son, to Gram?"

"Gram will never bear arms," said Rose with defiant resolve. "It was Dorian's last wish."

Harold stared at her, aghast, unsure what to say.

"Take it and go, Sir Harold," she said then. "I tire easily these days. I will see you at the memorial." Without another word she turned her back and left the room.

Harold stared after her. *His son won't be allowed to train?* Sadly, he took the sword down and made his way out.

*
**

The memorial took place on the one year anniversary of King James Lancaster's death. The King and Queen's funerals had been taken care of not long after the problems created by Tremont and Mal'goroth had been settled. Dorian's had been held in Cameron, and similarly, had been far too brief. The event today was meant to commemorate both the past monarchs and the heroes who had died preserving Lothion.

Traditionally, such an occasion would be handled by one of the heads of the four churches, but that was no longer an option, and rather than allow some other official to handle the event, Ariadne took the initiative. While it was customary for the monarch to make some sort of address during such ceremonies, it was unusual for one to personally oversee the entire thing.

The Queen's speech was heartfelt. She spoke at length about her parents and then began detailing the efforts of all those who died supporting her during Duke Tremont's attempted coup, naming each of them. She then spent an exceptional amount of time on the man she at one point called, 'the greatest hero of Lothion'. She held the attention of the crowd and ended on a high note, announcing the formation of the Order of the Thorn in Dorian's honor.

Several others took the podium after her, including Elise Thornbear, Sir Harold, and Sir Egan, each in turn. Lady Rose was invited, but as Dorian's widow, it wasn't necessarily expected that she would be willing to put herself before the crowd.

I had not been invited to speak. Peter had warned me privately about it already. The prevailing opinion was that having the 'Blood Lord' speak might tarnish the occasion or otherwise taint Dorian Thornbear's memory.

I wish I could say that that didn't bother me, but it did. It burned. Dorian and Marcus had been my two closest friends, and while I had never had the opportunity to speak on Marc's behalf, to be deliberately denied the chance to speak for Dorian...

I had swallowed my pride, though. In one of the pouches at my belt, I held the product of my labors over the past half a year. It was intended to be a gift to the Queen, and today had seemed the best time for it, but now I would have to wait and present it to her in private.

"Can't have me ruining the day," I murmured softly.

Penny picked up my words and squeezed my hand in a gesture of support, her black gloved fingers entwined with my own. I had forgotten how sharp her hearing was. I let my eyes linger on her for a moment, enjoying the sight of her in her rebellious black and red leathers. We had dressed ourselves in the same clothes we had worn for my court case. It was better than disappointing the crowd.

Surprisingly, Rose walked forward when her time came, taking her place behind the podium. Her dress was a widow's black, for she still had a short time before her year's mourning would be over.

"I am here today, to speak on behalf of my father, Duncan Hightower, and my husband, Dorian Thornbear," said Rose solemnly. She gave a short eulogy for the two men who had been so important to her, but as she neared the end her voice choked while she tried to explain what Dorian had meant to her. Ariadne approached her sympathetically, hoping to help her retire from the podium gracefully, but Rose waved her away.

Clearing her throat she raised her head once more. Even the veil she wore couldn't hide her red eyes and tear stained cheeks. "I can't finish, but there is one man here who loved my husband as much as I did," said Rose huskily. Looking to the Queen, she lowered her eyes, "If you will allow it, Your Majesty, I would ask Mordecai Illeniel, the Count di' Cameron to finish for Dorian. I believe he would have wanted that."

A hush fell over the audience and then murmurs broke out, softly, as people wondered how the Queen would respond. Many of their eyes turned to gaze at me, and just as many watched Ariadne, waiting for her reply. I knew how she would answer though, she had been cornered.

With perfect poise, Ariadne took Rose's hand and put one arm around her shoulder. "I'm certain that will be fine, Lady Hightower." Leading Rose gently away, she caught me with her eyes, "Lord Cameron, if you would be so kind." Her voice was just loud enough to reach me.

Glancing at my wife, I moved forward to the podium, thinking to go alone. Penny stayed beside me however, close, almost protectively. Whether it was a gesture of support in the face of so many unfriendly faces, or whether she felt I might actually need physical protection I wasn't certain. She had braided her hair again, including the metal cords and silver end caps, so I knew she wasn't unarmed in the strictest sense.

I didn't really need protecting, but I felt stronger with her nearby. Looking at the assembled noblemen, and the crowd of citizens beyond them, I saw a few friends, and many more who wore openly hostile expressions. It was clear that I was no longer welcome in Albamarl.

"I know that many of you may feel I am unworthy to speak for Dorian Thornbear, but I will speak anyway, for he was my closest friend. I trust you will not hold our association against him, or against James and Genevieve Lancaster, who were also close to me. Others have spoken for them, so I would like to offer you my opinions on Dorian alone."

"Dorian taught me the meaning of loyalty, and the meaning of trust. Many will remember him for his martial prowess, and it is true, he was without peer on the field of battle, but his skill with a sword was the least of Dorian's attributes. He was a man of honor, but it did not define him as much as his willingness to sacrifice for the sake of others. He never shirked his duty, but it was his kindness that marked him as a great man," I paused to let my words sink in.

"But he was not perfect," I continued. "His honesty was so ingrained that it was not only a virtue, but a source of occasional awkwardness. The man was simply incapable of lying, even for something as small as a fib for the sake of social graces. I, and our mutual friend, Marcus Lancaster, spent many a day in our youth trying to correct this 'flaw', but he never had the knack for it."

"In the end, we accepted him as he was, and over time we learned to respect our friend for his inner strength. He walked a hard road, but he never complained. In the end, he did the same as his father did; he gave everything he had to protect his friends and family. He gave until there was nothing left. He gave until he died." My vision had blurred, but my voice stayed strong.

"I cry today for the loss of many, but most of all, I cry for the loss of my friend. I tell myself that we have not truly lost him, for what he gave us is still here, in our hearts. I see his love in the faces of his wife and children, I see his strength and honor in the soldiers and knights whom he trained. I see his kindness in the fact that my own wife and children are still here with me, for they would have died without him." I could no longer see the crowd before me, but my magesight told me that there were few dry faces now.

"I can think of no better description than the words James Lancaster used when he spoke of the loss of his lifelong friend, Gram Thornbear, Dorian's father. When he told of Gram's death, he said that it stood out not as an exception, but instead as a final example of how he lived his entire life. Our late-king was a wise man, and he stood as a role model for both of us, and in this his words still ring true. Dorian, just as his father before him, gave his life in the defense of others, but it wasn't an exceptional moment for him, merely the last moment of an exceptional life. His entire life was spent thus, ready to give everything for those who needed him. My greatest regret is that it was my absence that created the need, the need that required he give everything to save not just his own family, but mine as well."

"But it was not Dorian's regret, for him it was the fulfillment of a life lived for others. That is my only consolation, and the only light by which I may someday be able to forgive myself. For now, I can only begin by offering this gift, to the Queen of Lothion, for the protection of both the crown and the people of the nation that Dorian Thornbear loved." As I finished I reached into the pouch at my waist and drew out a massive egg-shaped stone.

The stone was midnight blue, so deep that it almost appeared black, except under the brightest sunlight. It weighed almost ten pounds and approached the size of a grown man's head. In my magesight, it thrummed with latent power, waiting for the hand of the one who would unlock its potential, for the one I had chosen.

Ariadne looked at me in surprise, and though she hid it well, a small amount of fear. She stepped forward gracefully, and responded without hesitation, "Your gift is unusual, Lord Cameron, but we will receive it with gratitude on behalf of the people of Lothion." She motioned toward one of the footmen, indicating he should come forward to take the stone for her.

I whispered softly, making sure she could hear me, "I know this is a shock, but you have to trust me. Only you can accept this gift. It cannot be handled by any other than yourself."

The Queen moved closer to me and answered in kind, "Are you insane? You can't spring a surprise like this in the middle of an official ceremony. You should have warned me."

"Trust me," I repeated softly. "Put your hand upon the egg, and state your acceptance on behalf of the line of Lancaster." I wanted to say more but there was not enough time with the eyes of the crowd upon us. I had planned to wait, to give her the stone in private, since I hadn't expected to have a chance at a public gifting. Bringing it out at the end of my speech had been a spontaneous impulse. "Marcus would counsel you to accept it," I added.

600

Ariadne blinked and looked straight at me. For a moment the past fell away, and we were kids again. I smiled at her, and blinking she reached out, trusting her big brother's closest friend not to betray her. Placing her hand on the hard surface, she spoke out loudly, "On behalf of the House of Lancaster, I accept your gift."

A sound rang out as her hand touched it, bright and shining, as if a silver bell had been struck. Ariadne stiffened in shock as the power touched her inner source, linking itself to her life. A ghostly image appeared around her in the air, the form of a dragon, but it shrank inward around her and vanished almost as quickly as it appeared. "Carwyn," said Ariadne suddenly, "his name is Carwyn."

"The dragon will hatch in ten days," I told her. "He will serve you for the rest of your life, and when your days are done he will die as well, but not forever. Like the legend of the phoenix, this dragon will return to the egg, awaiting the touch of your successor to be born again as a new being. Care well for him."

Ariadne took the egg with both hands, swaying as she stepped back. Two of her footmen rushed forward to steady her, but I noticed she kept the dragon egg close to her body. The bond had already taken hold, and she was loathe to let anyone else touch it. Her eyes flashed to me, "What's wrong with me? Everything seems different." There was a faint note of panic in her voice.

"Don't worry," I told her, "The bond with Carwyn is affecting your body and senses in a fashion similar to the earth bond that the Knights of Stone possessed. Unlike that bond, however, this one has none of the same drawbacks. You'll get used to it in a few days." I turned away then, an unforgivable breach of etiquette when dealing with royalty, but I wasn't particularly worried about rules these days.

"Wait," she commanded. "I don't know anything about caring for a dragon. I thought they didn't exist, aside from Gareth."

"They do now," I told her. "Carwyn's needs should be small, and you'll know if he lacks anything." I tapped my head to indicate the dragon's ability to speak directly to her mind. I kept walking with Penny close beside me. We went through the nobles and headed into the crowd. The people drew back as we passed, fearful of my nearness.

I suspect the Queen may have considered ordering me back, but she must have thought the better of it. No one attempted to stop our exit, and we proceeded to stroll casually back to our city home.

"That was a rather impromptu way to give such an important gift," observed Penny as we ambled along the street.

I smiled. "I meant to give it to her in private, since they didn't intend to let me speak, but when Rose called for me, I just gave in to impulse."

"You didn't tell her much about it."

"The dragon will tell her what she needs to know. I'll send a letter in a few days. I just couldn't stay any longer. The crowd...," I left my sentence unfinished.

"It still bothers you, doesn't it?" she asked.

I nodded, uncomfortable even discussing it. My back tingled with the memory of my lashing, but it was the shame of it that really made me uncomfortable.

"You've given them more than they deserve," Penny said angrily. "They owe you, not the other way around."

I loved her for that. Penny would stand by me to the end of the world, but I still didn't agree. I knew I was far from blameless. I squeezed her hand but stayed silent rather than argue about it.

We walked a bit farther before she broke the silence again. "You still haven't asked me about my hair ornaments. I'm sure you've noticed them."

They glowed with a powerful enchantment, and this was the second time she had worn them. "I figured you'd tell me when you were ready."

"You could at least *act* curious," she lamented, and then she gripped the metal cap at the end of each braid. Tugging them, they pulled free, drawing the metal cord with them. The metal straightened as it left her hair, and the end caps became handles for two strange rod-like weapons, each slightly longer than two feet in length.

"Those look rather dangerous," I said, noting the shimmering magic that enshrouded each of the metal weapons.

"They are," she agreed as she demonstrated by swinging idly at a lamp post we were passing. Only the tip grazed it, but it cut a shallow gash through the wood with almost effortless ease. "Elaine thought them up so I'd have something inconspicuous to take to your trial, but I have to admit they have one major drawback."

"What's that?"

She pointed at her hair, loose and wavy where the braids had come apart. "There's no sheath, and re-braiding my hair takes a while."

I laughed and leaned over to give her a kiss. The world seemed a much brighter place now that we were alone, and I looked forward to seeing our children once we got back to Cameron.

Epilogue

The years passed quietly, rolling from the future, through the present, and into the past smoothly, without the turbulence that had characterized my life since first learning of my magical ability. I didn't miss it at all. Adventure, at least as I had come to know it, was just a nice way of saying that people were going to die.

Matthew and Moira were thirteen years old now, Conall was nine and Irene seven. Conall and Irene had yet to show any sign of magical ability, but that was to be expected. I wasn't even sure if I could handle it when they did. The twins were already quite a handful, and if they weren't fairly level headed, I don't know how I would have kept them from killing themselves.

Moira was still as sweet as ever, but her moods had begun to swing in sometimes unpredictable patterns. With me it wasn't too bad, but she and Penny seemed to alternate between best friends and antagonistic allies. I say 'antagonistic allies' because I had learned, even if they were fighting, the last thing I (or Matthew) wanted to do, was get involved. They'd turn on either of us like wild tigers if we stepped into their mysterious quarrels.

That being said, my daughter was still fairly easy going, especially compared to other girls her age. It might have been my own optimism, but I saw no sign of her becoming anywhere near as volatile as Elaine had been when she developed into a woman. Her skills as a wizard were developing rapidly. It helped a great deal that she had a father, plus a number of other wizards around to help her learn. Watching her grow, I could only imagine how much easier it would have been for me if I had had the same guidance.

Her skill at enchanting was adequate, but she didn't show too much interest in that area, at least not yet, though her special skills as a descendent of the Centyr line were quite evident. She no longer kept a bevy of intelligent stuffed animals, but she still had two or three that served her as close friends and advisors. They were the complex kind and required some maintenance every few weeks. She could also quickly and spontaneously create lesser ones from nothing but magic alone, with what seemed to be minimal effort. I constantly had to be on my guard, for her tiny allies often followed me about, spying upon my every move. It was a game that my daughter enjoyed, although it sometimes became annoying.

Matthew was as different from her as night from day. His personality was quiet, reflective, and more introverted. His magical strength was stronger than his sister's, and as he matured I began to wonder if he would grow even stronger than me. He possessed a keen interest in enchanting. That was something we had in common, although his mind often went in directions I had never considered. Every day seemed to bring surprises as he began to develop his own ideas. I knew a father's pride watching him and I hoped his inventions would someday change the world.

He and his sister had become somewhat competitive with the advent of their teenage years, especially since she seemed to be developing into an archmage. Her senses were as keen as my own, and she had already begun to hear the voice of the earth.

They remained the best of friends, but neither of them would admit to it in front of their mother or me. I could only hope that their sibling rivalry would subside as they got older, but being an only child myself, I couldn't really understand it.

The Order of the Stone continued, but it was much smaller now. Cyhan had remained in my service, but Harold had accepted the Queen's offer, and now led the new Order of the Thorn. He was still on the rolls of the Order of the Stone, but his full loyalty now lay with the crown. Sir Egan, Sir William, and Sir Thomas joined him, which left Cyhan as the only member to refuse the Queen's invitation.

Cyhan was starting to show his age now, but it didn't seem to bother him much. He took over as the grandmaster of the Order of Stone and continued to train my soldiers and new knights. Whenever I asked him why he had stayed with an 'out of favor' nobleman rather than take service with the Queen, he would just give me a flat stare.

The only response he ever gave me was, "At least now I have a lord who matches my temperament."

I left it alone after that. He was right after all. I still didn't know the secrets of his past, but I guessed that we must have similar scars inside.

None of the knights had the earth-bond these days. Each of them had to give it up eventually, or risk suffering a fate like Dorian's. I politely refused all suggestions that

I should create more of them. The world was at peace now, and I had better alternatives.

Ariadne's bond with her dragon, Carwyn, provided her with much the same effect as the earth-bond, but without the troubling side-effects. Her senses were improved, her body was stronger and faster. Most importantly, she had a dragon companion. The new dragons I had created each possessed nearly a full Celior of aythar. Because of the nature of the enchantment that created them, they had abilities similar to the old 'Shining Gods', but unlike them, they had living, flesh and blood bodies.

After hatching, one of the new dragons would grow rapidly until it reached full size, generally over the course of a couple of years. The enchantment that I designed to anchor their artificial minds was much the same as the old god-enchantment, but it had a lot of additional modifications and contingencies. Each of them would 'bond' with an individual, assuming the right conditions were met. They would live as long as their partner, but would undergo a regressive transformation once that person died. It was meant to be an approximation of death; the body would die and the mind would contract into a new 'egg', returning them to stasis.

At the same time, the dragon's memory would be wiped clean, leaving only the basic information I had initially implanted them with. When they finally found a new 'master' they would have no memory of their former life. It was the best answer I could come up with for the suffering that seemed to necessarily result from an immortal existence.

Some of the dragons I created to bond with normal humans. In each of those cases, I keyed them to their first partner using a drop of blood. From that point on, the only new partners they would accept would be descendants of their first bond-mate. Those that I made to bond with wizards were different, though.

As I had learned from my own experiences, a tightly woven bond, such as that with an Anath'Meridum or even an earth-bond, would interfere with a wizard's abilities. To avoid that problem, the bond forged with a wizard was only a pseudo-bond, allowing the wizard to draw upon their aythar when necessary. It didn't provide the physical enhancements that a full bond would, but it left them with the full use of their natural abilities.

So far I had only given out a few dragon eggs. One to Penny, to replace her earth-bond, one each for Matthew and Moira, one for myself, and one for Gareth Gaelyn. Aside from those, only the Queen had one. The others I kept hidden, against any future need. I had offered one to Cyhan, but he refused.

I planned to give one to each of my two younger children when they were older and perhaps one to Gram someday, though I was uncertain how Rose would react to that. She had continued to steadfastly stick to her resolution that her son would never become a warrior, even though it was readily apparent that the boy desperately wanted to follow in his father's footsteps.

A simple bit of math would reveal that, while nearly twenty-two Celiors of the aythar we had taken from Mal'goroth had gone into the creation of my twenty-three dragons, another twenty five Celiors remained. I used some of that to provide a new stone to power the World Road, and I gave some to Gareth Gaelyn, to create a new shield around Albamarl, similar to the one I had around Castle Cameron.

The rest I hid, separating it into a variety of storage vessels. I split it up to reduce the risk of a major disaster, such as what had happened when Balinthor had been destroyed long ago, but I told no one where or how it was hidden. I had plans to share the information if it were ever necessary, and even if I died suddenly, I knew that Matthew would retain the knowledge by virtue of the loshti, which resided latently inside him, too.

Other than raising my children and my work and projects, life was simple and quite predictable. Until the Kriteck returned and deposited a new burden on me. Lyralliantha had finally grown large enough to bear her first fruit. According to the memories I received from the loshti they usually arrived fully grown, by human standards, but she and Tennick had chosen to create their first child in a slightly more juvenile form.

The girl they brought into Castle Cameron was roughly the same apparent age and size as my twins. She looked almost human, aside from the gently tapering points on her ears, which were mostly hidden by the shimmering silver hair that flowed down and past her shoulders. Like all the Illeniel She'Har, she had icy-blue eyes, and in them I could see far more maturity than a young girl should possess. She'Har children were born with much of the information that humans spent their youth acquiring, things such as language and basic social graces. What they generally lacked was knowledge of the past and experience of the present.

As their first child, Lynarralla would likely be chosen to receive the loshti, becoming the first new lore-warden of the reborn She'Har, but that would be many years in the future. For now, she was expected to learn about the new world that her people would share with humankind.

Tennick and Lyralliantha, having no older 'children' to assist, had chosen me to serve as their firstborn's parent and teacher.

Oh joy.

*
**

We were sitting at the dinner table a few days after Lynarralla's arrival, when the strange girl brought up the subject of Tennick's origin.

"I was given to know that you are my father's great-grandson, many times removed," she began. "Does this mean we are related, even though we are of different species?"

I had been swallowing a large mouthful of roast beef, and I almost choked. *I have no idea in hell how to answer that one,* I thought to myself. "I'm not entirely sure," I admitted. "In the physical sense, I think no, but because of our shared origins, and your presence here now, I think it would be safe to call you family."

"How does my location relate to the question?" she asked.

Penny gave me an amused look but didn't attempt to help, so I continued slowly, "I meant that since your parents chose to send you to us to care for, you are family. Family is about more than blood. Family is more about people caring and supporting one another."

"She'Har do not have 'parents'," said Lynarralla solemnly. "That is why I am here."

It took me a moment to figure out how to continue. "Exactly, so we're sort of like foster parents. Caring for you will bring us all closer together. I believe that's why Tennick sent you here, so that you could learn to understand humans, and perhaps vice-versa."

"I am not sure about your reasoning. I don't think I have any emotional attachment to your family, but I do not have enough experience to judge these things yet," she answered.

She's honest to a fault, I noted, but I had no idea how to respond. Fortunately she didn't wait for me to continue the conversation.

"You bear the loshti. Can you tell me how Tennick became one of the She'Har?"

Everyone at the table stared at me with new interest. I rarely spoke of memories that the loshti gave me. Penny kept her eyes on her food, but I could tell she was listening intently. Matthew and Moira leaned forward with undisguised curiosity, while Conall watched them, unsure what the sudden change of mood meant. Irene continued to rearrange her food in the hope that we would think she had eaten more than she had.

"That's a long story," I said, considering how to answer her question. "To answer it fully, I will need to tell you about his early days, when he was still human."

"I am patient," said Lynarralla.

"Very well," I replied, pushing myself back from the table a bit to make room for my full stomach. "I'll start by telling you about Tyrion…"

Coming Soon:

The Mountains Rise

An exciting new series detailing the events of the first
Illeniel, the creation of the Elentir Mountains, and the fall
of the She'Har.

For more information about the Mageborn series
check out the author's Facebook page:

https://www.facebook.com/MagebornAuthor

You can also find interesting discussions and
information at the Mageborn forums or the Mageborn
Wiki:

http://www.illenielsdoom.com/

http://magebornwiki.com/index.php/Main_Page